# KING'S ROYAL

The Golden Stream
To Remember with Tears
The Bitter Lollipop
The Secret Soldier
The Last Check-point

# John Quigley

# KING'S
# ROYAL

Hamish Hamilton

LONDON

*First published in Great Britain 1975*
*by Hamish Hamilton Ltd*
*90 Great Russell Street London WC1*

*Copyright © 1975 by John Quigley*

*SBN 241 89183 3*

*Printed in Great Britain by*
*Western Printing Services Ltd, Bristol*

# ONE

# FERGUS

# I

Fergus King shivered inside his black, fur-collared coat as he walked towards the horse and carriage waiting for him outside Helensburgh railway station. The train from Glasgow had been cold. The copper warming pan to which first-class passengers were entitled had been missing, a casualty of the holiday rush, according to the harassed guard. 'The company should make me a refund,' Fergus, who liked value for money, had grumbled. If he had been dressed less well, he thought, if he hadn't outgrown the smell of working humanity, he could have left his select icebox and moved in with the people huddled warmly in the overcrowded, wooden-seated third-class compartments.

The gas streetlamps had not yet been lit and the rain, drifting over the small town from the Firth of Clyde, added one more blur of cheerlessness to the darkening Good Friday night. Fergus stopped at the station exit while he picked out his carriage from the many in the street. The horse was crouched uncomfortably inside a sodden grey blanket, head down to the shelter of the big, black-lacquered victoria in front. *It would not need much urging tonight*, he thought. It would be anxious to get back to the stable.

The coachman lifted his hat as Fergus nodded to him. 'Well, McEwan, couldn't you have arranged better weather than this for our first visit of the year?'

'Tomorrow'll be better, sir. The wind is changing.'

McEwan opened the coach door and Fergus climbed into the leathery blackness. When he had arranged himself in a corner he glanced out at the other travellers, hurrying, collars clutched to their throats, towards the lodgings where they would spend this holiday weekend. In all directions the lace, fur, and feathers of the

3

holidaymakers drooped in the relentless downpour. *Where else,* he wondered, *but on the west coast of Scotland could Easter come like this?* The soothsayers had been predicting that this Easter of 1874 would be warm and sunny. Fergus had never believed in their fraudulent nonsense. He was surprised at the *Herald* printing such unscientific mumbo.

He looked again towards the station as McEwan folded the dripping blanket off the horse. The entrance hall was deserted now, shadows shrouding the sacks of potatoes, the scattered mailbags, the two goats tethered to a railing. Robert had definitely not been on the train. Fergus had watched for his elder son in Glasgow and had then spent the journey wondering if he might have jumped into one of the rear compartments as the train moved out. The concern that had been with him all day suddenly deepened as he thought of a girl, perhaps twenty years old and slim almost to thinness. He saw shining black hair and a face dramatically hollowed below the cheekbones, wide-open eyes, and smooth, slightly parted lips, arranged in a permanent expression of mischief or surprise— he could not decide which. He must stop his son seeing this girl. Mary Devine! He snorted the name to himself, swaying slightly with emotion over his silver-headed cane.

So far as Fergus was concerned the name told all that need be known about the girl. She was a Catholic. That she was the daughter of a doctor, that she had herself almost completed her training as a nurse, hardly mattered. Catholicism to Fergus meant slums, sly priests, idol worship, and an involvement in some subtle conspiracy he could not explain but which he believed to be sinister and abominable. He fought down a feeling of panic as he thought of his son becoming involved with anyone of that subtle creed.

He began to comfort himself. All that was needed was a sensible talk. The comfort departed immediately, though, as he thought of his son's infuriating independence. To hell with his independence! He would have to be made to understand. Fergus had intended to state the position clearly and precisely during the train journey. In such an impersonal setting rancour might have been avoided. Now the talking would have to be done at Ardfern, even at the risk of bringing discord into the holiday. He must get it over with tonight, leaving three clear days in the country for the waves to

4

settle. There were still four trains to come from Glasgow tonight. Robert would be on one of them.

He put his cane out and tapped McEwan on the arm. The carriage moved off with a jerk and a jangle, shuddering as it turned a windy corner and joined the procession of coaches heading through the mud for Clyde Street, whips flicking and hooves scattering loose flints. It would be more exposed down there on the sea-front, but that was the route most of the northbound traffic took from the station because the road surface was better. Another stormy blast from the south-west, laden now with salt spray, struck the dark box, heeling it over a little on well-greased springs.

Fergus sat square and stiff with cold in the gloom, his cane between his knees, his high hat almost touching the felt padding of the roof, glad that Rita, his wife, Gwen, his daughter, and James, nine years younger than Robert, had travelled down earlier in the day. Ardfern, his mansion house two miles away at Row, on a wooded and rocky hill overlooking the Gareloch, would by now be comfortably ready to receive him, the servants scolded into a proper state of attention, the windows bright with Rita's fancy lamps, rooms warm and glowing as log fires blazed. He smiled, ruefully, at his selfishness, for the house had probably been freezing when Rita arrived. Mrs. Veitch, his mother-in-law, to whom he had given a permanent living at Ardfern, was a warrior, but casual staff, drawn from the village when required, were slow to get moving after winter's quiet, even with Mrs. Veitch's tongue to urge them on.

For nine years, since he had bought Ardfern, the family had come here for all holidays and most summer weekends. Once or twice Rita had spoken hopefully of France or Italy, telling him which of the neighbours had been there. Fergus had laughed and said the Clyde coast was good enough for him. The air was clean and it was convenient; there was no scenery to beat Scotland's when the sun shone. But there was more to it than that. Under the four mock turrets of his country house, his business thirty miles behind him in Glasgow, Fergus felt safe. From what? At fifty-two he was no farther up the honours ladder than the rung reserved for successful town councillors—in Glasgow they called him *Bailie* —but a proper title would come in time. He had made his ambitions known and now he was doing all those things that a man with his dreams should.

He served on a dozen or so well-chosen committees, contributed with a slight ache but a benign smile to all the necessary funds, and avoided scandal. These days he devoted almost as much thought to the avoidance of scandal as he did to the making of money. He had to tread lightly in case he stepped on his dreams. But an ever-present fear was that someone else might jeopardize them—his son, for one. Robert would have to be tackled with real force, threatened, if need be. A Catholic daughter-in-law could bring only disrepute and ridicule.

He peered seawards. Gourock, on the other side of the Firth, was a faint blot of light. The other carriages seemed to have drawn ahead or fallen behind. All he could see outside was rain dripping around the lanterns of his own coach.

He leaned back in the jogging darkness, imagining his favourite scene: Row on a summer Sunday—any sunny summer Sunday—and he, spade-bearded, top-hatted, silk-coated, leading his family along mossy lanes to the parish church, past the warm tombstones and drowsy yew trees, to the seats they always took—a little behind Sir Charles Laidlaw, chairman of the Clydeside Bank, a little in front of Professor Wallace, whose new techniques in surgery were bringing fashionable renown to the Western Infirmary, just across the aisle from the Irvings, whose fleet of black-and-white merchantmen was now the biggest and fastest sailing out of the Clyde. Fine people! But when Fergus felt insecure and needed comfort he sometimes wondered if even they were totally free of anxieties, impervious to scandal? Was Fergus King the only man on those warm, hymn-singing Sundays with a secret dread? Had Sir Charles always turned away from the doubtful deal, the Irvings never sent a sieve to sea?

Had none of Professor Wallace's patients, who should have lived to laugh, ever been carried dead from the table? Fergus did not know and would never know. He worried on alone about the scandal that might one day ruin what he was working for. Until a week ago it had been as shapeless as smoke from a distant fire, but now ... Mary Devine! The carriage thudded into a water-filled hole, lifting him three inches off the seat and ramming his hat into the roof. Blast the boy, the girl, the weather, the road!

6

Rita King stopped at the foot of the stairs, one hand on the carved mahogany balustrade, as Fergus burst in through the front door in a storm of rain that threw back the Persian rugs and scattered two or three letters from where they were lying on a dark oak chair.

'My dear! Isn't this dreadful? And it's getting worse by the minute.' She came forward quickly, her hands out for his cane and his hat. 'But where's Robert?'

'Dear knows!' Fergus said. His beard was sequined with raindrops. 'You can ask!' He kissed her on the cheek, standing away so that her dress wouldn't get wet. 'He wasn't on the train. I've sent McEwan back to wait for him. It's the horse I'm sorry for.'

She took a folded handkerchief from his top pocket and dried his beard, then put his hat and cane on the stand. 'Are your boots quite dry?' Rita, eight years the younger, had been worrying for almost a quarter of a century now about Fergus getting his feet wet. 'Keep his feet warm and dry and his head cool,' had been part of her mother's advice to her on the successful handling of a husband.

'They're all right, my dear. I didn't walk here, you know.' He lifted one foot from the floor and shook it about loosely as if proving something. 'But I'm cold. Is it Easter—or Christmas?'

She went behind him. 'Let me help you with that wet coat. That girl Helen is never about when she's needed. I must tell mother to get someone else before we come down next time. She broke another plate today.'

He looked alarmed. 'Not another one of the Chelsea?'

'No, but it was a good one. She'll leave us without an ornament if we keep her.'

She went into the cloakroom with his coat, leaving him listening to the batter of rain on the cupola dome and worrying about his collection of china. Some of those pieces were worth twenty pounds each.

When she came back he said, 'What's the time?' then took out his watch, holding it slackly by the thick gold chain as if about to play conkers with it. 'Nearly half past seven.' He shook the watch before putting it away. 'We'll eat without him,' he said decisively.

Rita clasped her hands and looked at him uneasily. 'I hope he comes.'

He avoided her gaze as he crossed the hall and stood with his

7

back to a fire that burned in a basket in a hearth surrounded by a carved stone mantelpiece, his feet apart and his tails hoisted. 'I don't know what you're thinking about. We're all here. Where else would he go?' Suddenly he found the question frightening. He let his coat-tails fall.

'You know how . . . sensitive . . . he is.'

'Insensitive would be more accurate. He doesn't have a proper respect for our position.'

'Maybe we shouldn't have refused to have that girl here. It might have been better to let her come.'

'She isn't suitable for him.'

'I suppose not, dear, but we should have let him bring her anyway. If we had met her and then said she wasn't suitable. . . .'

'I don't have to meet her.' He kicked angrily at the handle of an oak chest. 'They're not putting enough pith into polishing this brass. You'll have to talk to them.'

'Are you sure we're doing the right thing?'

He looked at her uneasily. 'Aren't you?'

'She may be a very nice girl. It doesn't seem fair.'

'My dear, it's an unfair world. It's a world divided into compartments and the people of one compartment are often unhappy if they go into another. Robert and this girl are too young to know that. It's up to us to protect them. And ourselves.' He looked about as if suddenly aware of something unusual. 'It's very quiet. Is everybody else here?'

'Yes. Gwen and James are in the drawing-room with Mother. Tom is—'

'Tom? I didn't think he'd be here yet. I left him with plenty to do.' He put his hands behind his back, looking complainingly at the finely plastered squares of the ceiling. It was bad enough having Hoey in his business without having to meet him socially as well.

Tom Hoey was Gwen's husband. He worked for Fergus, going from one branch of the business to another, checking stocks and sales. 'The Man About Town,' Fergus called him with heavy irony, alluding not only to Hoey's weaknesses but to the use he continually made of the excuse his job gave him for always being in some other place. A waster, of course, although Gwen couldn't see it, resigning a commission at twenty and squandering a twenty-thousand-pound fortune on horses and stupid business deals by

8

twenty-one. A place had been made for him in the business when Gwen had fallen for his polish. Silly girl . . . but she couldn't be allowed to starve . . . Dear knows!

'He's in the library if you want him. He said he was going to look for something.'

'The decanter, I suppose. I can't believe he's taken up reading. Unless there's a racing form in there. No, I don't want him.'

Rita put a hand on his arm. 'Do try to be a little more friendly to Tom. After all, we are on holiday. Gwen says he's behaving very well. Knowing there's a baby on the way seems to have helped.'

Fergus narrowed his eyes as if the naivety of women in love pained him. 'I'm very glad to hear it.'

'Now, promise that you *will* try. We don't entertain them all that often and I'm sure he'll respond.'

'So long as he doesn't start trying to sing, like that last time. He's got no voice. And the song was hardly decent.'

'I'm sure it was more high spirits than anything,' Rita said cheerfully. 'You know what Tom's like.'

*Yes*, Fergus thought, *I do know what he's like. But neither you nor Gwen seem to. You're both still mesmerized by his mess-room manner.*

He felt he could also have made play with the word 'spirits' but the peace of the old place was settling on him. He breathed in the scent of burning birch logs. For him this was the fragrance of a comfortable house where people should be content.

'Silly fool,' he said placidly. 'He's twenty-four. What's he want with high spirits? He'll soon be middle-aged.'

He bent his knees to squint along a satinwood sofa table that stood against a wall under a carved gilt mirror. 'Lovely top on that table,' he said, drugged with the birch smoke. 'Must be over a hundred years old.' He passed a hand over it. 'Smooth, but still woody and good to touch. Not like the modern stuff they turn out now, all glassy with French polish.'

Rita put her arm through his. 'My dear, you really love this house,' she said. 'I hope we're spared to retire to it.'

He was touched to see that tears had come into her eyes, taking them, correctly, as some sort of tribute to himself—to the happiness they'd shared and which she hoped they could go on sharing here when he had passed the business on to Robert.

He put his lips against her hair. It was as fair and shining as when he had first married her. She had carried the years well, not letting herself get fat and untidy the way so many women over forty seemed to go. Maybe it was the late arrival of James that had helped keep her young. On the other hand, a late child often aged a woman, saddling her with work when she should have been able to take things more gently. He didn't know. It was difficult to tell with women. He couldn't understand men who kept running after them. Rita had always been all he wanted. It was amazing that she could still wear these billowy, girlish dresses without looking ridiculous. 'Come along, my dear,' he said. 'That's a beautiful dress you're wearing, but thin. We should be in a warmer room.'

Rita smiled as they walked slowly to the drawing-room. They had been lucky until now. She hoped Robert wasn't going to be a worry.

Behind them, smoke puffed from the fire and rain struck hard at the house, hammering on the cupola and against the curtained windows. Outside, rhododendrons shrank from the wind and conifers tugged on shallow roots until the peaty ground cracked open around them and they leaned over in the darkness, ready to fall.

Tom Hoey raised his glass to Fergus with one hand while stuffing what looked like a small notebook into his pocket with the other. These movements helped disguise the start he'd given when he heard the library door opening. 'I always enjoy your claret,' he said, with the sudden bright smile that had first attracted Gwen. 'Can I tip you out a drop?'

The aplomb to offer a man some of his own drink was one of the qualities in Hoey that Fergus marvelled at and secretly envied. He nodded. 'I think there's time. Mrs. King has just gone to see how they're managing in the kitchen. These part-time servants can't be left alone.' He looked around him. This was the room that held the essential peace of the house. He slowly walked the length of a wall lined with books. At the end he turned. 'Have you been reading?' His glance was innocent.

Hoey looked confused. He pulled at his nose and made a hawing sound, as if deprecating the idea. 'Just looking.' His expression became confidential. 'To tell you the truth, I was keeping away from the womenfolk, really, till you got here.' He made it sound as if Fergus' arrival was a delight for which he had been waiting.

Fergus continued his teasing. It was casual and automatic, and at times he resented that Hoey should inspire this cruelty in him. 'Out of a thousand volumes I'm sure there must be one that would interest you. What about Scott? There's a complete set just over your left shoulder.'

He left Hoey peering uneasily at the books and lifted a bundle of unopened envelopes from a leather-topped drum table. He took them nearer to a lamp. It was a big room, darkly panelled and difficult to light, but there was some talk of them extending the gas pipes from Helensburgh. The sooner the better. He tore the envelopes open—accounts from local tradesmen, tickets for a sale of work held three weeks ago, charity appeals. He put them down and had another look at Hoey, who had lifted down a book and was staring at it as if it embarrassed him. He was tall and strongly built, but there was a lithe refinement there, a grace of some kind, that he knew even Rita had fallen for. It always made Fergus uncomfortably aware of his own country blood.

'Is everything all right with you and Gwen? No problems?' This, he felt, was the kindly approach Rita wanted from him.

'A-one,' Hoey said breezily, emptying his glass and immediately refilling it, turning slightly away as if this would prevent Fergus seeing. 'You know about the son-and-heir, of course?' It was as if they hadn't met for months.

'So you've made up your mind it'll be a boy? I hope you're right. Anyway, I've been meaning to congratulate you. I'll be happy to be a grandfather.'

This would mean an increase in salary for Hoey and the opening of a bankbook for the child which, with luck, might not turn out like its father. His own children had all had assets of one hundred pounds the day they were born. He pointed to Hoey's brimming glass. 'Are you getting all you want to drink?'

Hoey grinned and made the drink last till they went in to dinner. Fergus congratulated Gwen on looking so well, Mrs. Veitch on the splendid way the house was being kept, and ordered James to have his hair cut next day. They were cheerful and talkative until Mrs. Veitch committed an indiscretion. When they had finished the soup she rose from her place. 'These girls are so slow,' she said, and started to collect the empty plates.

Fergus glared first at Rita, then at his mother-in-law. 'Sit down, please, Mrs. Veitch, and let the servants serve.'

Mrs. Veitch stood for perhaps five seconds with rebellion in her grey eyes, then clattered the plates back on the table and sat down with a thud and a contemptuous look at her daughter.

Rita coloured. She was ashamed that she shared Fergus' irritation. These little reminders of a past less grand were only to be smiled at. They hurt no one when they occurred in the privacy of the family. 'We all know you like to do things for yourself, Mother,' she said soothingly, 'but you've had a very busy day. It's time you relaxed.'

Mrs. Veitch gave an amiable snap. 'It's me that *is* relaxed, dear. You and Fergus should follow suit. Have another glass of wine. It might help.'

Fergus did not like the amused light in his son-in-law's eyes. It was as if Hoey felt the stabs he had suffered in the library had been well repaid by this incident. His expression said that something in the Kings had just been exposed—not to him, because he knew all about it already—but to themselves. It was disconcerting to Fergus to think that Hoey had them measured. Snob, he thought, with a clear conscience.

He turned to his son. 'Get grandmother Veitch to make us laugh, James.'

James, who knew this game, turned to his grandmother, who lost her annoyance in the pleasure of watching her favourite grandchild form the familiar question. 'What would the Honourable Rognvald Kennedy have for his tea tonight, Grandmother?'

'Half a banana,' Mrs. Veitch said delightedly, and they all laughed.

The Honourable Rognvald was the ten-year-old son of Lord Glenarden of Row Castle, where, according to Mrs. Veitch, dinner was only served when there were guests, and the family normally made do with a frugal Scottish high tea.

Fergus, feeling he should make amends for having rebuked the old woman, said, 'And what do you think Lady Laidlaw will be giving Sir Charles when he gets in from the bank tonight?' As he said it he began to wonder if he had taken too much wine. It really wasn't wise to encourage Mrs. Veitch to repeat what she heard in her gossips with the servants and other locals, but tonight some unseemly hilarity was perhaps permissible in the interests of restoring the atmosphere.

'Kippers,' Mrs. Veitch said, and led the laughter herself.

In the warmth of this private family humour, with the rain hissing down the hot chimney and the crimson velvet curtains muffling the wind sweeping across the loch, dinner passed pleasantly.

Afterwards, in the drawing-room, Hoey sang while Rita played for him on the piano. He had an untrained voice of attractive strength and huskiness. Even Fergus enjoyed listening to him.

> Could I bring back lost youth again
> And be what I have been,
> I'd court you in a gallant strain,
> My young and fair Florine.

The happy circle they formed was bounded by comforting shadows beyond the lamps. It was a scene Fergus loved and the security it always suggested to him was enhanced tonight by the rain and wind outside.

Robert King arrived at Ardfern shortly before half past nine, aware that he was late, that he had failed to meet his father when he'd said he would and that his father would inevitably be annoyed.

Fergus, who had left Hoey still singing, was in the library studying the catalogues of several auctions due to take place during the following month. When he heard the carriage on the gravel outside his window he started to rise and then thought, *Better let him get something to eat first.* He went back to ticking off possible paintings and furniture but almost immediately there was a knock on the door and his son looked into the room.

Robert King was almost twenty-two. He was taller than his father, but not yet so broad. His black eyebrows were thick beyond his years and they projected incongruously from the smooth skin that often goes with a dark complexion. He had a moustache but was otherwise clean-shaven. His appearance suggested a tight self-control and what his fellow Scots would call a *guid conceit.*

'Hello, Father. Mother told me I'd find you here.' His smile was appraising. 'Are you very busy?'

Already Fergus felt, as he always did when he had anything controversial to discuss with his son, that he was in the presence of a compressed spring.

'Not with anything important. But where have you been until this time? You were supposed to travel on the train I caught.'

'I was delayed.'

Mary Devine had been staring at Fergus from every page of his catalogues and now he could not resist what he felt sure would be an inspired jab. 'Not with a girl, by any chance?'

'Unfortunately not,' Robert said shortly. 'I was working.'

This was not what Fergus had expected. 'I didn't think there was anything that couldn't have waited.'

'This was something of my own.'

Fergus' expression said *Indeed*, but he contented himself with saying, 'Well, anyway, I want to talk with you now you're here.'

Robert sat down on a buttoned velvet chair, put his head back on the antimacassar, and slid his feet towards the brass fender and the fire. 'There's something I'd like to discuss, too, unless,' he said shrewdly, 'you're not in the mood for business?' His father was always in the mood for business. 'Shall you tell me what you have to say first?'

Fergus hesitated, but his curiosity was aroused. 'No. Go on.'

'Business first, Father?'

Fergus ignored the irony. He accepted that his relationship with his son had a flaw in it that could not be accounted for by anything except the boy's perverse nature. It couldn't be anything he had done. They didn't quarrel, they worked well enough together, and yet in Robert's attitude to him there was this air of perpetual challenge. 'Go on,' Fergus said.

'I've mentioned it before, Father, but I don't think you took me very seriously. I think it's time we diversified. Some of our shops are in areas where the houses are bound to be demolished soon. If they're not demolished they'll fall down. Either way the people will move elsewhere. When they go our trade goes. In the next few years the business is bound to shrink. We should be deciding how we're going to face this. I'd like you to let me—'

'Start wholesaling whisky as well as retailing it,' Fergus completed the sentence. 'The answer is still no, Robert.'

'But why?'

'Because I've worked hard for over thirty years to get where I am and I'm not going to let you squander our resources—or your own energy—on a reckless dream. Believe me, there's no future in whisky. Oh, don't think I don't understand that you want to make your mark on the business. But why not try something sensible? Wine-shipping, possibly? That would be a natural extension for us.'

'There are far too many wine-shippers as it is. I want to get into something new where the field's wide open and there isn't a lot of competition. The whisky market is completely undeveloped.'

'Of course it is, and with very good reason. No one wants the stuff. People who drink spirits want French brandy or London gin. No one outside Scotland drinks whisky.'

'It's a good drink. There must be opportunities. We have the money and I'm willing to work till I drop.'

Fergus smiled. 'That, at least, I don't doubt. But energy can be misdirected. I don't want to see you squandering it.'

'I don't intend to.'

'Now, look here, Robert. Whisky's a rough drink for strong, outdoor men, for ghillies, and farmers. Town people could never stand up to it, and they're the people with the money. Damn it, whisky doesn't even look good. You couldn't serve it in a respectable drawing-room. If you put a drop too much water in it it goes as cloudy as an old duckpond.'

Robert had abandoned his lounging attitude. 'That's perfectly true, Father, but I've been experimenting. That's why I missed the train today. I think I've found—'

'Robert, listen to me! Apart from the drawbacks, I'd like to see you get into something respectable.'

Robert stiffened. 'Respectable be damned. As long as it's profitable why should we worry?'

'It's possible to make money and still have people look up to you. That's the position I want to see you in. It's what I'm working for now.' He stopped, fearful of revealing too much of his own yearnings.

Robert grinned. 'If you make enough money, people look up to you wherever it comes from.'

15

'Not in Scotland. Drink's a sin in this country. How often I've had to sit and listen to the minister denouncing it!'

Robert's eyes were bleak. 'And afterwards, I suppose, the same minister would kindly accept your humble donation.'

Fergus ignored the contempt. 'What I'm trying to tell you is that whisky, as well as never being a great seller, will never be respectable. It makes people drunk. Men take it and then beat their wives and starve their children.'

'Good God, Father, hold on till I get you a pulpit. You should be up there with the ministers.' Robert jumped from his seat and walked angrily around the drum table. Then, with a vicious push, set the top revolving so fast that Fergus' catalogues went spinning into the shadows. 'Are you forgetting that on Tuesday you'll be back in Glasgow selling all the drink you can, asking every morning how much business we did the previous day?'

'No, I'm not forgetting. I sell it and I've grown fat on it but, God help me, I'll never praise it.' He walked slowly across the room and lifted the catalogues from the floor.

Robert walked disgustedly to the fire.

'And what did the cream of our Glasgow society grow fat and respectable on? Slavery! Is that more respectable than drink?'

'Slavery's over and done with.'

'It is, and no doubt they'd hate it to be mentioned, but everybody who made his fortune out of the Glasgow sugar trade was depending on the misery of West Indian slaves for cheap labour. There weren't many sugar barons in the Glasgow Emancipation Society.'

'Nobody remembers that now, Robert. The sugar trade's finished. We've had cotton since then. Now it's finished, too. We're on to iron, shipping, and shipbuilding.'

'Oh, yes, and have you heard what the street-corner orators have to say about the ironmasters and the shipowners?'

'I've no time for Socialist agitators.'

'Nor have I, Father, but it's as well to know what we're up against. They'll be after us one day, whether we sell drink or top hats. They're reading the *Communist Manifesto* to each other in the factories now.'

'Rabble!' Fergus said.

Robert watched him. 'I'll agree with that.' He lifted a log and threw it fiercely on the fire, ignoring the sparks showering on the

16

carpet. 'But I can't believe all this anguish has to do just with whisky. There's something else upsetting you. You'd better come out with it.'

Fergus had little heart now for the confrontation that had pre-occupied him for so much of the day. He sighed and sat down. 'Roderick Fraser is lunching with us tomorrow. You can ask him what he thinks about whisky. I know he'd sell that distillery of his if anybody would buy it. He's bringing Fiona.' Normally Fergus thought of Fiona Fraser as 'one of that wild yachting crowd.' Tonight, in his turmoil, he saw her almost as the epitome of what a young lady should be. 'You like Fiona, don't you?'

The question was unexpected and for a moment Robert gloated over a possible answer. *She's not beautiful but her face is attractively healthy*, he thought. *She has lovely, opulent breasts that I enjoy fondling and that she enjoys having me fondle. Miss Fraser loves having me undress her. It can be said that we share a common—a very common—desire.* He wondered what his father's reaction would be if he had spoken his thoughts. Stunned disbelief, probably.

'Fiona's a sport,' he said truthfully.

Fergus looked at him sharply. 'That isn't a word we applied to young ladies when I was your age.'

'Entertaining.'

'I don't know why you can't make friends with—not necessarily Fiona—but someone like her.' He glared into the fire and then, lifting a heavy brass poker, jabbed at a log. 'You seem to be attracted to the wrong kind of company. That girl Devine that you wanted to bring down here. I hope you haven't anything serious in mind there.'

'Why? Is there something wrong with Mary?'

Fergus looked at him appealingly. 'You know very well there is.'

'No, I hadn't noticed, Father. You must tell me exactly what it is.'

'The girl has a different religion from you.'

'What difference does her religion make?'

'I'm surprised you have to ask. It means she's not suitable for you.'

'Suitable for what?'

To mention marriage would be foolish. 'For anything. You

17

couldn't take her anywhere. None of your friends would want to know her.'

'Then to hell with them.'

'If you go on seeing her it can only lead to scandal.'

'You make yourself ill worrying about scandal.'

'In our circle it would be anathema if you married a Catholic.' Fergus recoiled at having used the word, but there was no going back. 'Is that what you're planning to do? If it is, I want to know now. A marriage like that could ruin everything for me, and for your mother. You know what I'm referring to.'

'No, I don't know. You haven't met Mary, but you can condemn her because she's a Catholic. Do you even know any Catholics?'

'I wish them no ill, Robert, but I prefer to keep them at arm's length. They're . . . different . . . from us, socially and in every other way.'

'Mary isn't any different from us socially. Good God! Surely we're not so grand? You started out as the son of a crofter. And what are we now? Alehouses and grogshops. There isn't much high society about us.'

He watched his father's face go still and white and his hands form into tight, hard mallets on the arms of his chair.

Inside Fergus something almost like hatred of this tall dark-eyed young man who was his son, and yet in some ways a stranger, threatened to rise. Desperately he fought it down. He had spoiled Robert. It had been part of his pride, his pretension, to project him as the son of a gentleman. This was his creation and he must now handle it with care and as much sympathy as he could summon. The one thing he could not do just at this moment was look at him, for Robert had struck heartlessly at a very weak spot, the sense of shame he knew Fergus had for the source of his money.

Every day Fergus descended from his town house on the fine height of Park Place into the older parts of Glasgow where the houses were seamy and sagging and reeked of refuse. His money came from the pockets of people poorly dressed and often ragged. Fergus sold them escape when it was food they needed, and although their fecklessness was not his fault he knew respectable people blamed 'the trade'. These respectable people did not approve of the goods Fergus sold, except for use by themselves and those like them. He now owned twenty-two licensed establishments in

Glasgow, including a music hall at the Cross where dancers showed black-stockinged legs and the throaty girl singers were all big-bosomed and dressed to show it. There had been a time when he had surveyed his achievements with pride. Now they gave him a sense of social inadequacy he could only shake off here in this mansion at Row, when he sat chairing his charitable committees or while he delivered sound judgements from the magistrate's bench. He turned to stare down into the fire. 'Goodnight, Robert. We'll—'

'Oh, no, Father, we're not going to leave it like that.'

Fergus' voice was a frustrated snarl. 'I said goodnight. Now get out.' As he turned away he sensed Robert brace himself. For several seconds the battle went on in silence. Suddenly Robert relaxed. 'Goodnight,' he said cheerfully. He went out, closing the door with irritating care.

Half an hour later Fergus was still trying to read his catalogues, but the list of items that had earlier excited him seemed of little interest now. His life would not alter if he did not acquire a Patrick Nasmyth landscape or a painted satinwood Pembroke table, but his son was a possession of a different kind. A log collapsed in the hearth and smoke puffed out at him. He smelled incense and thought of Mary Devine. He rose impatiently from his chair and began to move about the warm, shadowy room, aimlessly lifting books and delicate china figures. Bow was his favourite factory and he had a good collection, all properly authenticated.

A floorboard creaked and tonight the sound alarmed him. He had heard somewhere recently it could be a sign of dry rot. Dry rot, in a sound, well-heated house like this! That damned girl was ruining everything. He crossed the room, opened a glass-fronted cabinet, and poured a very small amount of brandy into a glass. It was late for alcohol, but he would not be haunted by a girl he had never met—and would never meet. In the glowing comfort of the brandy he mused himself into a belief that a solution would be found, that Robert would eventually see Mary Devine's undesirability. There had been other girls.

But when would he cast off this new obsession he had of a business based on the sale of whisky?

Fergus wondered why, after so many smooth years, so many worries were descending on him at once. It was as if this trade he was in, *this cursed trade*, as he thought of it tonight, had some hold over the family. It had killed his father and mother. He, who should have shunned it, had drifted into it. Now here was his son determined to plunge in even more deeply.

Of course, Robert was being far-sighted. The present business would undoubtedly suffer in the next few years. Those crumbling old areas of Glasgow where so much of their money was made were finished. But Fergus had his own thoughts on what should be done—he was far-sighted, too. They would always have a sound licensed business, even after the inevitable losses, but he had been thinking for some time that they might sensibly expand into property. Not those tenements that were going up everywhere for the workers, for already their owners were being reviled as grasping sharks by tenants who appeared to think they should be allowed to live in them for nothing.

What Fergus had in mind was office property. The city was crying out for it, with insurance, investment, and professional firms of every kind mushrooming out of Glasgow's industrial prosperity. Property of that kind would be respectable. The tenants would be other businessmen who would appreciate that the owner must charge a rent. Property was sensible. But whisky! It would bring nothing but trouble.

He crossed gloomily to the window and pulled back the heavy curtains. The rain had turned to sleet. He looked out, startled, at the big flakes swirling past the window, building up already against the windward side of the only tree he could see. He watched, fascinated and frightened as he always was by snow. Even after forty years, despite his translation from that little five-acre croft in Glenrinnes to a rich city life, the memories of one snowy night still lurked beneath the surface of his bearded middle-age—the terror almost as fresh, as if frozen and preserved forever by the snow in which his parents had died.

The Kings, like many of the men in Glenrinnes, had been diligently distilling illicitly for fifty years before Fergus was born. When money was short they paid their rent to the landowner in whisky, and it was from him they received the oats that were their raw materials. Fergus' father had learned the trade from his father, and by the time Fergus was twelve he was able to soak, malt, and mash the grains and man the lookout post keeping watch for the gaugers.

Fergus' father smuggled his whisky to merchants and innkeepers in Dufftown and Aberlour. The contraband spirit he produced was of such a quality that he had regular orders to supply some of the biggest houses in the scattered parish. Fergus could still remember the economics of this illegal home industry, carried out stealthily but with a sense of adventure—no one ever thought of it as a crime. The entire distillery—a mash tun, a warming tub, a lead worm, and a copper still—lying hidden in a heather-covered shanty on the lower slopes of Ben Rinnes, had cost his father only £3. On an outlay of £1 for a quarter of barley the profit had been almost £9. Everyone in the area, from ministers to landowners, protected the distillers by a bond of silence the excisemen found hard to break. Nevertheless, the whisky had to be moved about in secret, usually by night, in small cogies strapped to horses or hidden in carts under legitimate farm produce. Fergus' father and mother died carrying two three-gallon stone jars of whisky to a customer who lived four miles away. Both had been ill, but Archie King had decreed that the order, from one of the most important men in the district, must be met.

Twice in the last two years Archie had been caught by riding officers and fined. Next time he was caught even the local magistrate, who was one of his customers, would have to send him to jail. 'Why don't you take out a licence, Archie, and be free of this worry?' Mrs. King often asked. The answer never varied. 'They've been making whisky in this glen for a hundred years without licences from the English and they'll be making it for another hundred years without them.'

Even more vividly, Fergus remembered his mother's words that wild night as she tied a shawl about her and got ready to accompany his father. They were both thin and weak after a fever.

'No, Archie.' She had sat down suddenly on a stool at the open hearth. 'It's too terrible a night. We can't go.'

'Come on, woman,' Archie King had said coaxingly. 'I've never let the Colonel down yet. He's got guests. Besides, it's only on a night like this that it's safe. You know it's prison for me next time.'

They had gone out into the snow clutching the jars of whisky which, at seven shillings a gallon, were worth exactly two guineas.

After six hours Fergus had gone out to see if he could spot their returning lantern. By that time it had stopped snowing, but a howling wind was drifting the dry snow. The outhouses had disappeared. If there hadn't been an iron post for Fergus to cling to he would have been hurled into the frenzied darkness. The savage north wind tore at his clothes, as if trying to suck him away from the protection of the house. He struggled back inside and huddled down in front of the warm ashes. Three days later, when the thaw came, the bodies of his mother and father were found close together among the rocks where they had tried to find shelter. Fergus had been taken to his father's sister in Glasgow and been brought up by her.

He turned, unnerved, from the scene of driving white and went back determinedly to his catalogues. *The French Fleet at the Broomielaw, by Sam Bough*, he read. He had visited the house where the sale was to be held and had liked the painting. He considered for a moment and then pencilled his price in the margin—twelve guineas.

In the room above the stables McEwan began to undress. It wasn't easy. His limbs ached and the wet garments clung to him. Once he had been unaffected by the constantly changing climate of the Clyde coast, but recently, gnawing pains had started in his arms, legs, and back at even the approach of damp weather. When he wasn't driving the coach McEwan was expected to keep the paths free of weeds and fallen leaves. Over the winter months, with the Kings in Glasgow and the coach laid away, he had been able to take care of himself, fitting his gardening duties to the weather. Tonight's was his worst soaking for a long time. He groaned quietly to himself as he tugged his sopping shirt over his head, almost regretting that he was a bachelor. A wife would have had dry things waiting for him and something hot ready for his supper. As he arranged his clothes in front of the fire he comforted himself by thinking of the less pleasant sides of marriage. Perhaps he was better off as he was. He was adept at counting his blessings. Now he was in a dry nightshirt, even the hours spent in the rain seemed less miserable. 'It could have been worse,' McEwan said aloud, his deep voice filling the small room. 'There were still two trains to come. Mr. Robert might have been on the last.' He quite often spoke as if there was someone else to hear.

The room smelled of the stable below, but he was too accustomed to this to notice. The furniture was old but comfortable and the woodwork had been recently painted. There was even a water-colour of a local scene above the rough stone lintel. It was the mistress who had given him whatever refinements he had. When the Kings had taken over Ardfern, and McEwan with it, the room above the stable had been bare and depressing. The table had been a former workbench, gouged and splintered. There had been a rough stool, but no chairs, and the windows had been uncurtained. With his new comforts, McEwan had become house-proud, sweeping and dusting regularly. He kept his few private papers, along with his one or two articles of clothing, in an old chest of drawers also passed on to him by Rita.

There was a pot on the table with some cold porridge in it. Normally, McEwan would have eaten it as it was. Tonight he felt the need of hot food. He scooped some water from an enamel pail with a mug and emptied it into the pot. Some wood he had put on the fire crackled. Below, the horse moved on the cobbled floor. For McEwan, these were the sounds of home, helping him forget the sleet outside and the aching of his body. He held the iron pot over the fire and stirred the contents with a spurtle. When the porridge was ready he spooned it direct from the pot. It was the first food he had eaten since noon.

# 2

Next morning, by one of those sudden twists which never surprise the people who live in the west of Scotland, the weather had become springlike again. The snow had gone from all but the highest ground and the sun was shining as Gwen came out of the front door, dressed for gardening. She stood looking back admiringly at the house, a sturdy girl of twenty-four with even white teeth, strong features, and a cheerful expression. The walls were of random blue whin, locally quarried, with faded, pinkish-red sandstone facings. Here and there against the old stone the last yellow spurts of winter-flowering jasmine still showed and at the side of the dining-room window a great framework of quince was opening tight clusters of dark pink flowers. Gwen went over and examined the plant. She was glad she had pruned it hard down to the spurs at the back end of the previous year. The thing, as she'd told her father, who was no gardener, was to remove all the new growth so that when the flowers came they wouldn't be hidden behind leaf or disfigured by spindly shoots. She had been right. The blossom was more prominent and plentiful than she had ever seen it. Astonishingly, a bee droned among the waxlike blooms.

These signs of stirring nature reminded Gwen of the new life inside her own body. 'Don't do anything too strenuous out there,' Hoey had called from the lonely position at the breakfast table to which his habit of late rising condemned him.

Gwen was happy that after nearly three years of marriage she was at last going to have a child. She longed for motherhood, hoping that, as well as bringing fulfilment for her, the baby would have a steadying effect on Tom. But steady Tom from what shakiness? It was a question she never allowed to remain with her for long.

Recently, there had been rumours half-heard, glances half-understood. Determinedly, Gwen banished the disturbing ripples from her mind, concentrating on the undeniable fact that Tom had been more considerate through just knowing there was a baby on the way. She smiled slightly as she pictured him alone at the long, three-pillar table with his liver, bacon, and kidney. He was a baby himself, really, quick to sulk, always having to be petted, not grown up at all in some ways, even after his stint with the Greys. Apart from the horses, he had done things with his money a child would have known to be dangerously risky. Maybe it was for this quality of immaturity that she loved him. She was sure it was. It was the need in her to fuss over and protect that made her a good wife and would, she hoped, make her a good mother. Sometimes, since she'd become pregnant, she had lain awake in the darkness, worried and fearful that she might turn out to be inadequate or unworthy. *Please God*, she prayed on these restless nights, *let me be a good mother to my baby*. Once, Hoey had wakened and she had confided her fears to him. 'Nonsense, old girl,' he had muttered sleepily, turning it as usual into a joke. 'You'll be a marvellous mother. But if you need any tips, just come to me.'

She crunched over the gravel to the woodland grass behind the house and started to nip the dead heads from the wide spread of daffodils. *With any luck it might be quite hot later in the day*, she thought. The sky had that promising look about it. It was delicately figured, like some rare wood, with feathery waves and twists of high, transparent cloud. From somewhere nearby came the bleat of lambs. A fat cock pheasant that had staked out a claim for itself in the wood last summer rose at her approach and clattered up through the trees with clucks of protest. Had she remembered it was there, she would have gone to the kitchen and brought it some oatmeal.

*Father*, she thought, *chose his country retreat well*. It was almost as good as the Highlands for peace and grandeur and yet it was only thirty miles from Glasgow. It was far enough into that short inlet of the Firth known as the Gareloch for the shipyards of Port Glasgow and Gourock on the south bank of the Clyde to be out of sight. Westward stretched the low peninsula of Rosneath with its gentle green hills and ducal castle. Northward, towering above the Highland clachan of Arrochar there was a range of high mountains best known for a curiously formed peak called the Cobbler. Behind the house, over the moors and through the wilds of Glen Fruin, an easy day's tramp there and back, was Loch Lomond.

This was a ramble Gwen enjoyed and sometimes bullied Hoey into making with her, but Fergus considered Loch Lomond spoiled these days. It had come down in the world, he said. It was too trippery and commercialized now they'd started running buses there from Glasgow, changing horses at Dalmuir. Gwen smiled at the thought of her father's snobbery. There was no good pretending. That's what it was. He was waiting and hoping and, for all she knew, praying for his title. But she loved him, too. For all his laying down of the law he wasn't half as hard, for example, as Robert, who to all appearances was much more easy-going.

She heard her father call. He was sitting on a bench on the other side of the burn that splashed through the seven-acre grounds, tumbling over rocks and, at one point, rumbling down in a miniature waterfall.

She waved and went down the path to the bridge. He folded his *Glasgow Herald*.

'Anything in the news, Father?'

'More trouble in Ireland, if that's news. They should turn the troops loose on them. Home Rule!' He snorted, trying not to let this reminder of the Emerald Isle bring Mary Devine back into his head. It was too sweet a morning for bitterness—and all the lovelier for its unexpectedness. He ran the back of his hand down the underside of his beard, lazily fluffing it out to the sunshine.

He pointed down the path to where a cloud of insects rose and fell, each keeping an exact distance between itself and the others. 'I hope that's not the midges starting already.'

'No. McEwan calls them "Merry Dancers". They don't bite.'

'That's a blessing. Isn't your mother ready to come out yet?'

Gwen lifted the newspaper from the seat and looked idly down the front page advertisements. 'No. She's desperate to get everything back to her liking.'

'I think Grandmother does very well.'

'Of course she does, but you know how Mother loves her flower arrangements. I told her I'd pick some daffodils and get her any greenery that's about. It's a pity there are no beech leaves yet.'

Fergus turned his face more fully to the sun. 'And after she's done the flowers she'll have to get all the ornaments exactly positioned again. If any of them have been moved an inch since we were here last year she'll know. I shouldn't be surprised if I sit here the whole morning waiting for her. Dear knows!'

They all made fun of Rita's artistry but without it neither Ardfern nor the Park Place house would have been as near perfection. Fergus had an eye for good furniture, paintings, and valuable porcelain, but he was ready to admit he wouldn't have been very good at arranging them.

'You know Fiona Fraser, don't you?'

'Yes.'

'She's coming with her father for lunch.'

'Then I'd better keep Tom out of sight.'

Fergus frowned but didn't ask what she meant. The young had a strange sense of humour nowadays. There wasn't as much propriety as there used to be.

The Merry Dancers moved about them in a hypnotic swarm and a bee—sated from the quince—moved heavily by. Fergus stretched his legs, closed his eyes, and wondered where Rita was in the house and whether he would in the end have to take his stroll without her. She was looking pale. She should spend more time outside when they were on holiday, especially in this precious sunshine.

'I saw a roe deer this morning,' he said. 'It ran off up the hill and into the trees when I came across the bridge.'

'They're gorgeous,' Gwen said. She pointed to one of the *Herald*'s classified advertisements. 'Why don't we get some of these new hybrid rhododendrons for the garden, Father? They're so much more colourful than the wild ones.'

Fergus, who resisted changing anything, said, 'Pretty, no doubt, but I don't know that they'd stand up to our hard winters. It's difficult to tell.' He shook his head as if it was a problem that had long concerned him.

'They come from the Himalayas.'

He felt drowsy. Ridiculous when he was only a few hours out of bed. Still, the Gareloch was known to be relaxing. Some people just couldn't stand up to it.

'Some parts of the Himalayas are more temperate than Scotland, my dear.'

She laughed. There was a surer way of getting hybrid

27

rhododendrons than arguing their botanical suitability. 'Lord Glenarden has them up at the castle,' she said. 'Of course, they are expensive. It's not everyone who can afford them.'

Fergus rallied a little and looked at her suspiciously. 'How do you know Glenarden has them?'

'The head gardener told me. I took a stroll that way yesterday. They do very well according to him.'

'Our grounds are pretty much the same as Glenarden's I suppose,' Fergus said complacently, squinting into the sun. 'Not as big, of course.' He took the newspaper from her. 'Essex they've to come from, is it? Well, maybe we could try one or two. I'll let you make out a list.'

Gwen turned on the bench to face him. 'Father.' She stopped. She was smiling but the quality of her voice made him look at her keenly.

'Yes, my dear?'

'What was wrong between you and Tom last night?'

His mind went back but it was all so indefinable that he could not have explained if he had chosen to.

'Wrong?'

'Yes. At dinner. You were both acting a little strangely after you came out of the library.'

He laughed. 'There was nothing wrong. You must have been imagining things.'

'You've never understood Tom,' she said.

'What's he been saying?'

'He never says anything. But I've got eyes.'

'Then they're deceiving you.' Despite himself he was exasperated. 'Really, my dear, the way you and your mother go on about Tom and me, anyone would think I was at his throat.'

'It's so obvious you're never at ease together. I don't know how you manage at the office.'

Sometimes Fergus didn't know either, but he wasn't going to admit it. No good could come of it. It was Gwen's life. He wouldn't complicate it for her.

He patted her hand. 'Sometimes in business problems arise,' he said lightly. 'Perhaps we get a bit short-tempered with each other, but it doesn't mean anything. It's not the sort of thing a woman would understand.'

But Gwen was not to be put off. 'It makes me unhappy that you don't like Tom,' she said.

'That's not true, my dear,' Fergus said with a mixture of stubbornness and concern. 'And this is no time for you to be talking about unhappiness. You should be thinking of your baby.'

He saw she was watching him, wondering how much comfort she could draw from his words. He must give her all the help he could.

'Don't worry about Tom and me. He's coming along very well in the business.' He smiled, almost, in his anxiety, believing it himself. 'Perhaps I am a bit of a taskmaster at times, but I'm just as hard on Robert. In the future I'll try to be more considerate though. I want you to believe that, Gwen dear. Do you promise?'

He coaxed a smile from her and she nodded, only half convinced.

They sat in silence. After a while his eyes closed and when they opened he saw the Merry Dancers waltz in formation across the path and take up new positions above the forsythia. He had forgotten Hoey.

'That grass is still wet from last night,' he called to Gwen, back among the daffodils. 'Mind you don't get your feet wet.' Then, just as his eyes closed again, he laughed at himself. *I'm getting as bad as Rita*, he thought.

When he wakened, Gwen had gone. He rose and followed the winding path, stopping at every gap in the trees to admire the view of smooth sea and snow-touched hills, except once when he hurried past an open prospect with eyes carefully turned to the primroses on the banking at his feet. A quarter of a mile away, on the same hillside above the loch, there was a house, turreted like his own but, to his eye, with a brooding, downcast air, the blinds often drawn and the tall trees sadly waving. He never looked at this house if he could avoid it. It had been the country home of a successful Glasgow architect called Smith. Less than twenty years ago the man's daughter, Madeleine, had been accused of poisoning her lover. The charge of murder against the girl had been found Not Proven, although Fergus, who clearly remembered the trial, had no doubt of her guilt. The shocking pain of that trial for the girl's family was something Fergus could feel almost as if it had happened to him, and the house now was an unwelcome reminder to him that scandal, black and unbelievable, could strike at the tranquillity of the best-ordered family.

The shore road was turning a dusty yellow as it dried out. Despite the sunshine, Mrs. Veitch was heavily wrapped in black and semi-veiled, her hands muffed in front of her and a tall bonnet hiding all but one or two of her tight grey curls.

She saw, by the chimney smoke rising above the trees, that most of the big houses had been reopened. Easter was usually the time when the affluent Glasgow merchants reappeared. Elaborate iron gates that had been closed for months stood open, shutters were thrown back, and the road was cheerful with the rumble and clop of carriages and the chatter of servant girls carrying baskets to the village store. To these, and to one or two nursemaids pushing prams or walking young children, Mrs. Veitch gave restrained greetings. They curtsied and then, possibly commenting to each other on her hat or her formidable reputation, giggled as they skipped quickly out of hearing.

James bobbed about behind Mrs. Veitch, lifting stones from the road and skimming them out over the loch. He had been entrusted to his grandmother by Rita for the purpose of having his hair cut, as Fergus ordered.

Kerr's Hairdressing Salon was a wooden hut with its creosoted back to the sea, halfway between the store and Row pier. Its shabby proprietor, Tam Kerr, who stood at the door puffing at a black stump of pipe, was capable, according to a faded notice in his dusty window, of giving a *Comprehensive Service*, which included such specialties as *Tong Curling, Shampooing and Singeing*, all up to not just *National* but *International Standards*—and at *Keen City Prices*. But for a slightly larger sum, as announced in a separate notice, he could turn from merely cutting, shaping, and otherwise pampering existing hair to actually making hair flourish where none now grew. This miracle was performed by means of *Expert Massage, Scalp Manipulation, and Root Tonic*—all applied, apparently, from Tam's own deft fingertips.

As Mrs. Veitch and James stopped in front of him, the barber hurriedly stuffed his pipe into a pocket of his stained white coat beside a large collection of combs and scissors. He led them into the hut, which was decorated with illustrations of prize-winning hair-styles from Paris and Rome which Tam of Row was presumably ready to duplicate.

James noticed that the barber himself needed a haircut at the back and sides and some of his own scalp manipulation and root tonic on the bare and shining patch on top of his head.

Tam, who also needed a shave, ran a rasping hand around his chin. 'This way, Mrs. Veitch, madam,' he said, trying to guide her to the chair with an elaborate wave of a comb from which many teeth were missing.

Mrs. Veitch looked at him scornfully. 'Don't be a dolt, Tam Kerr,' she said. 'You've never had me in that chair and never will. It's the boy that's here to have his hair cut and, if you don't do it well, you'll be hearing from Mr. King.'

With this encouragement, Tam settled James into the chair. With the aid of a pair of grating scissors, the comb with missing teeth, tense whistling, sudden sprints from one side of the chair to the other, and the added stimulus of Mrs. Veitch's watchful stare, he did his Boy's Trim. At the end he clicked his scissors. 'What about a nice shampoo for the wee man, then? Weans half price.'

'No, thank you,' said Mrs. Veitch. 'We've got plenty of good soap and hot water at home without paying for it.'

'A singe, then, to tidy up the ends?'

'Och, hold your tongue,' Mrs. Veitch said pleasantly. 'You're being paid to tidy up the ends without any nonsense with lighted tapers.'

She paid him and then, holding James by the hand, glided out of the hut and across to the store where she bought the boy a toffee apple.

'I don't know that I don't prefer you with your hair longer,' she said, inspecting him as his mouth yawned in an effort to crack the hard, amber coating. 'But your father's word goes.'

*Fergus' word has always gone far too readily*, she thought. Rita had married well. No one could deny that. Not even an aggrieved mother-in-law. There was nothing Rita wanted she could not have. Nevertheless, there were times when she should have—not argued or resisted—but agreed less readily to some things. Just at that moment Mrs. Veitch was not able to think of an example. It was simply that, even in a man's world, Fergus was deferred to far too much. That silly business of the soup plates the previous night was just an example of how he imagined himself the law on everything. It still rankled. Heavens, the servants wouldn't be encouraged to start a revolution just because a member of the family undertook

31

some menial task. The trouble was that Fergus was still unsure of himself, rich bailie though he was.

Her heart softened a little as she thought that her son-in-law had come a long way with little more to start with than a few pounds borrowed from his aunt to buy his first shop, and even three-quarters of a lifetime wasn't long enough for everything to come naturally to a man. It took generations. That's what breeding was all about. And yet, now she had warmed this much in Fergus' favour, she had to admit there had been some sense in his rebuke. She really shouldn't have been lifting the soup plates when the whole family was installed there, in state, so to speak. It was true the servants wouldn't have revolted, but they would have felt some resentment. They were snobs, too, after all. It would lower their dignity to work for people who didn't know the established way of things. Servants expected employers to know *their* place—and to keep to it. One could not have a smoothly running, well-ordered world if everybody did not keep to their place. To this extent Fergus had been right. Anyway, she wasn't perfect herself. Hadn't there been moments she had felt something was being done that would lower her socially? What about the time when she had felt that Fergus, the young shopkeeper, wasn't good enough for the daughter of a solicitor? This bout of honest self-examination lasted Mrs. Veitch most of the way home. She felt better for it. Between that and the warm air and all the hired coaches going past laden with gaily dressed holidaymakers from Helensburgh, she felt it was turning out to be a very enjoyable Easter.

On the loch, paddle steamers thrashed the smooth water to ragged white. The regular service steamers were, as usual, racing each other for the passengers and freight waiting at the piers farther up the loch—Clynder, Shandon, Mambeg, and Garelochhead—while those on day cruises looked less excited.

A sea-gull shuffled along the pebble beach as if its feet were sore.

'Is your toffee apple good, James?'

'The apple's green, Grandmother, and the toffee's cheugh.'

'Cheugh!' Mrs. Veitch stopped. 'Cheugh! Your father would not be pleased, James, to hear you use a word like that, good Scots though it is. That's not what he's paying for.' She paused to consider. 'Still, I suppose they get all sorts at the high school these days.'

She ran a hand through the brown waves of her grandson's hair and then, unable to resist it, bent down, her black skirts trailing in the yellow dust, and hugged him.

The Frasers arrived in a new white carriage at half past twelve. It was a colour few people considered practical for use on roads which, if they weren't wet and muddy, were dry and dusty, and Roderick Fraser had been embarrassed by the stares and turned heads accompanying them on the drive from their house on the hill above Helensburgh. The colour had been chosen by Fiona, to whom, since the death of his wife, Fraser left all matters of taste, knowing he had none himself.

He'd protested weakly when she'd made her choice known. 'Isn't it too flamboyant?'

'Striking, Father, and unusual, but certainly not flamboyant,' Fiona had told him. 'White can never be faulted. It's always in perfect taste.'

The Kings came out of the house and gathered round to exclaim in careful tones. It was left to Robert to walk around the gleaming coachwork, only slightly dimmed during the short journey.

'Bravo, Mr. Fraser,' he said. 'Very courageous.'

Fraser, wondering exactly how to interpret this, pointed accusingly to Fiona. 'I've just got to do as I'm bid,' he said. He was still puffing a little with the effort of having manoeuvred his huge weight out of the carriage.

Fiona was looking exceptionally pretty, Robert thought, her wonderful breasts stretching her bodice in a way that made his hands itch not just with hope but with memories. In every way she was built like a statue, and yet so entirely in proportion that the whole effect was of something made to give heroic pleasure. Or *perhaps*, he thought, *that was only because I've already experienced the pleasure*. Perhaps in Fiona's physical exuberance other people saw only excessive size. There might even be some—poor souls—who would be turned away by such quantity.

Suddenly, he had the uneasy feeling that Fergus was trying to watch both him and Fiona at the same time. Was he too obvious? Had he been indiscreet in referring to her as a sport? He must be careful not to appear too familiar. Enthusiasts like Fiona could be trouble. Meantime, no signs, no evidence—nothing that could later be remembered to his disadvantage. When they went into the drawing-room for sherry he left the familiarities to Hoey, who obliged by standing too close to Fiona and ogling her.

'By Jove,' Hoey said with a nudge as Robert refilled his glass. 'No wonder you go sailing so often. I wouldn't mind a bit of tacking and luffing with that lady.' He used the opportunity of someone jostling past to put an ostentatiously protective arm around Fiona's shoulder and was so taken with the experience he did not see Gwen turn quickly away.

During lunch Fraser told them of the new men from Glasgow—shipbuilders, shipowners, warehousemen, and industrialists—who were building houses near his on Helensburgh Hill to get away from the crowded city. It was to be an area, he said, of great style. The Colquhouns of Luss, who owned the land, were reserving the right to reject the plans for any house they felt might detract from the district. All would be positioned, with staff cottages and coach-houses, in several acres of ground, with wide views of the Firth. The streets would be grass-fringed and planted with avenues of flowering cherry and silver birch. Fergus expressed his approval of the Colquhouns' concern for amenity, the ladies nodded as if thinking of other things, and under the table Robert gently pressed his knee against Fiona's leg.

'We owe a lot to these landed families,' Fergus said, 'although it's the modern fashion to deride them.'

'We owe the Clearances to them, anyway,' Robert said. He still had an unfriendly feeling for his father from the night before. 'If you prefer sheep to people and empty glens to farming townships then there's a lot to be said for the gentry.'

'Well, that was a long time ago,' Fraser said diplomatically. 'But nevertheless a disgraceful episode in our history.'

'They were the people who sponsored anything artistic that we ever had in Scotland,' Fergus said, ignoring Robert. 'They employed our architects and supported our painters. They introduced, from England, France, and Holland, every stick of decent furniture we have in Scotland.'

'Well, their day is done,' Robert said. 'Scotland's future lies with its shipbuilders, its engineers, and its coalowners.'

'More's the pity,' Fergus said, resentful that he had to agree.

After lunch Hoey left for a drive with Gwen, Rita, James, and Mrs. Veitch.

'Why don't you take Fiona walking?' Fergus suggested to Robert. 'Mr. Fraser and I have some business to discuss.'

A butterfly with yellow, tan, and orange wings led them down the drive, flitting from bluebell to wild white anemone. 'You've been quiet today, Robert,' Fiona said. 'Apart from trying to annoy your father.'

He put a hand on her arm. 'I was thinking.'

'What about?'

'How we were ever going to get away from that crowd.' He turned to make sure they were out of sight of the house and then quickly kissed her. She responded in a way that made him feel this could be one of the best Holy Saturdays ever. This, he had learned from Mary Devine, was the Catholic name for it. He was surprised again, as he had been for months, that the tender love he had for Mary allowed him to contemplate a passionate and dangerous afternoon with Fiona. This was not how it was supposed to be. Was there something wrong in him? Something shallow and unprincipled? He knew from several meetings with Fiona in recent months that afterwards he would feel no remorse—that his love for Mary would survive apparently unblemished. Was it true the only sin was in being found out?

They crossed the road at the gates and sat on the grass looking out over the pebble beach to the loch. The passing steamers created a wash and it was so hot now that almost as soon as the water ran back down the beach the pebbles were dry again.

'I'm surprised,' Fiona said, 'that Miss Devine isn't here for the weekend.' She pronounced it *de Veen*, as if Mary was French.

Robert flushed. 'How do you know about Mary?'

'Someone at the yacht club mentioned her. Why, is it a secret?'

'Of course not.'

'Who is she? Why don't any of us ever meet her?'

'I don't want to talk about Miss Devine.'

'Oh, dear. Then we must talk of something else.'

'If you don't mind,' he said, feeling foolish.

'I know. Tell me the name of that bird perched out there on the buoy with its wings spread like a German eagle.'

'It's a cormorant.'

'Why is it doing that?'

'It's illustrating one of nature's mistakes,' Robert said stiffly, wondering if the afternoon might, after all, turn out less scandalously than he had planned. 'It lives by diving for fish but it's feathers aren't very oily. It has to keep drying them by spreading its wings. On windy days cormorants have a terrible time. The minute they perch with their wings spread the wind blows them back into the water. But they have to keep trying. If they get themselves too wet they become waterlogged and sink.'

'Why, that's fascinating, Robert. I didn't know you were an ornithologist.'

He took out his watch and decided she had teased him long enough. 'Fascinating,' he said. 'But not very exciting.' He put his hand decisively on her thigh.

'Don't be silly, Robert! Anyone might see.' She lifted his hand and held it between her own. 'I can feel your pulse racing. Are you fevered?'

'Let's go back to the house.'

She laughed. 'But we've just left the house.'

'Everyone's out except your father and my father and they'll be in the library talking till teatime.'

'Are you sure no one will see?' The excitement in her eyes was almost as naked as his.

They went to his room by separate ways. 'We mustn't be too long,' he said as he helped her remove her dress. 'What a nuisance clothes are when time is short. At moments like this I sometimes have visions of a race of women dressed in thin, short, easily removable tunics.'

'You'll be disappointed if you expect fashion to follow your erotic fancies.'

As she stepped out of a petticoat, he eased her back on to the bed. 'There's no time for any more,' he said.

She turned her face away. 'Tell me about Miss Devine.'

'Damn you! No!'

'Do you love her?'

'Yes.'

'Do you love me?'

'Certainly not. Nor do you love me. We want each other—but

36

if we were never to see each other again we wouldn't be heart-broken.'

'You're horrible.'

'I'm honest.'

'Don't you feel you're betraying Miss Devine by being here with me?'

'I don't. So you needn't think you're scoring off her.'

'Pig. Strong pig.' She pulled him down on her. 'Even though you don't love me, Robert, you do respect me, don't you?'

'Of course I do.' Suddenly he put his hand over her mouth. 'For God's sake, Fiona, don't make so much noise.'

She shuddered under him. 'God, I hate you, Robert King.'

They left the house separately, met behind it, and walked together to the front just as Hoey brought his coach up the drive at a trot, the gravel spinning from the wheels on to the lawn.

'Just in time,' Fiona whispered, smiling easily as they walked to meet the carriage.

'What a wonderful afternoon we've had,' Rita said gaily as Robert helped her down. 'Look at the lovely primroses and violets we picked. The lanes are full of them.'

'Violets don't last,' Mrs. Veitch said. 'I told you that. They're better left where they grow. That young lady wears clothes that are far too tight for modesty,' she added into Rita's ear.

'Perhaps she has outgrown them,' Rita said in her kindly way. 'She doesn't have a mother to guide her now.' She put an arm around Fiona. 'Did I tell you this morning how charming you're looking, my dear? And you've caught the sun. Your cheeks have such a lovely colour. Did Robert take you walking?'

Robert, fussing unnecessarily over his grandmother, was interested to see that Fiona blushed.

They had tea in the conservatory, where a star-shaped magnolia and camellias with white flowers floated over them in a milky cloud. The windows were open and, outside, the Merry Dancers performed mysterious quadrilles, while bees and butterflies worked on in the knowledge that such days were rare in early spring. Fergus sagged comfortably, his limbs slack, his face tilted a little to catch a breeze that perhaps only he perceived.

The sandwiches were thin, the scones dainty and still warm, the cream and the jam thick on the golden sponges. Rita and Gwen wavered, giggling, over the cream cakes because, they said, they had been putting on weight. Eventually they decided they might risk one because they were on holiday but when they returned to Glasgow they would have to be doubly strict with themselves. Fiona and Mrs. Veitch had two of everything.

Hoey, pale as if the drive had tired him, drinking tea but refusing food, had drawn back into one of his watchful silences as if still on guard with his regiment in a dangerous place. Even Fiona, her curves insistent whenever she reached for cake or teacup, seemed to have lost her power to move him.

'I think Rita and I will be meeting Her Majesty the Queen later in the summer,' Fergus said casually as he and Fraser lit cigars.

'You didn't tell me that, dear.' Rita's start of surprise made the others laugh.

Fergus blew some smoke to hide his pleasure at the stir he had caused. 'I didn't know myself until yesterday,' he said, as if the matter had slipped his mind until now. He had in fact been waiting for the moment of maximum effect. His plan to produce his surprise at lunchtime had been ruined by Robert's attack on the landed gentry.

'Well, dear, do go on. Don't keep us all in such suspense.'

'Her Majesty is stopping off in Glasgow on her way to Balmoral. The royal train will be accommodated in a special siding during her stay. She will open some new laboratories at the University Department of Science in the morning and has agreed to be entertained to luncheon in the City Chambers by the Lord Provost before continuing her journey.'

Rita turned to her mother and then to the two girls. 'But what will I wear? I haven't anything grand enough.'

'I'm sure Mr. King will get you something absolutely splendid,' Fiona said. 'I wish it was me. It would be a marvellous excuse for getting Daddy to open the cashbox.'

'I can't imagine. . . .' Rita said. 'The shops are always so dull. We're so badly catered for in Glasgow.'

'Oh, no, Mrs. King. Not any longer. Several lovely shops have opened recently in Buchanan Street. People say Glasgow's almost as good as London for clothes these days.'

Mrs. Veitch patted her curls as if to check that they were intact. 'I'm sure the Queen will not be worrying about what you're wearing, Rita,' she said. 'If she's anything like me, she'll be more interested in what they're giving her to eat. I've heard she has a very delicate digestion and is best pleased with simple fare. Like myself,' she added with satisfaction.

'Grandmother's right,' Gwen confirmed. 'I've read that good wholesome Scottish dishes are the Queen's favourites. That's why she is so fond of Balmoral.'

'I thought John Brown was the big attraction up there,' Robert said.

There was a stunned silence. Hoey managed one loud haw of amusement before Fergus' glare riveted him.

It was Fergus who spoke first, looking as embarrassed as he was angry. 'How dare you bring that scandalous gossip into this house! Kindly remember where you are.'

Robert had gone red. 'I'm afraid I did forget myself, Father, but it was really only said jokingly.'

'This is not the yacht club. Nor'—with a glance at Hoey—'an Army mess.'

'I agree, Father—I'm really most sorry.'

Relief rose in Fergus as he realized that in this field at least he still enjoyed an easy authority. Additionally, he felt that here was an opportunity of humbling Robert—for John Brown, for Mary Devine, for the generations of unnamed landed aristocrats he had slighted during the meat course.

'If that's the sort of defamatory humour current in the company you keep, then I strongly advise you to change your friends. It was particularly tasteless in front of your mother, your grandmother, your sister, and a well-brought-up young ladyfriend of the family, as well as being a disgusting slur on the good name of a fine Queen. You should be ashamed of yourself. You can't apologize to Her Majesty, but I want you to apologize to the ladies.'

Fergus put his cigar firmly in his mouth and waited.

Robert's teeth were clenched as he turned to the women. 'Please forgive me, ladies. Father is absolutely right. My remark was despicable.'

Rita had been listening as if she didn't follow what was happening, looking from Fergus to Robert in mystification as abasement followed rebuke. Now she said, 'What has Robert done? I don't understand. Who is John Brown?'

Fergus, pretending not to hear, turned and said something inconsequential to Fraser, while Mrs. Veitch leaned forward and began whispering into Rita's ear. Fiona and Hoey smiled knowingly as a look of engrossed enlightenment spread on Rita's face.

'Arise, Sir Fergus,' Gwen whispered to Robert.

'Come and have a word with Fraser,' Fergus commanded a still subdued Robert when at last the plates had been almost emptied and Gwen had gone off into the gardens with the remaining scones to look for the fat cock pheasant.

Fraser wedged his bulk into a library chair. He had an amiable, hairy face, and although his tailor in Bath Street supplied the finest broadcloth, Fraser soon reduced everything he wore to bags and wrinkles. He had the look of a farmer and would have been pleased to be told so. Lochbank Distillery, on the shores of Loch Lomond, had been built by his farmer grandfather to use the barley that he grew and very often could not sell. The farm had long been gone, but Fraser still considered whisky distilling to be farmer's work, a small industry of the land for thoughtful and unhurried men.

'Your father tells me you've some funny ideas about whisky, Robert.'

Robert made a face in Fergus' direction. 'I think in this case my ideas are sound enough, sir. It's Father's attitude to them that's funny.'

Fraser laughed. He tried to turn a little in the chair but failed. He had one at home and another in his office specially made to accommodate his girth.

'You've got a fighter here, Fergus,' he said. 'I like that.'

Fergus began teasing out his beard. 'So long as he does his fighting elsewhere, Roderick. I'm getting too old for strife. Too old. I don't know. . . .'

He wandered off down the room as if to leave them alone, alighting, as if he had never seen it before, on a Bow plate with lacework rim.

'Your father might be right, you know,' Fraser said. 'Whisky's been with us for a long time without arousing much excitement anywhere but in Scotland, and even then mainly in the country districts.'

'No one has ever put it forward properly, Mr. Fraser.'

'Properly, my boy? Surely there's only one way to sell whisky—

the way we've always sold it? Men like your father buy it in casks, then sell it to their customers by the glass or in jars for them to carry away.'

'That's right. We treat it in exactly the same way as we treat the oil we burn in our lamps or the grease the groom smears on the axles of our carriages.'

'I wouldn't exactly say that.'

'Perhaps not exactly, but we should be more imaginative. We should make whisky *look* more attractive. After all, it's not made in a Glasgow factory. It comes out of Highland glens and down the sides of high mountains.'

Fergus had left the Bow plate and, having completely circled the room by way of Chelsea, Longton Hall, and Coalbrookdale, now irascibly rejoined them. 'Do you know what he's talking about, Fraser?'

Fraser made a calming motion and turned back to Robert. 'To tell you the truth, young man, I don't, but I'm looking forward to having you explain.'

After so much disinterest from his father Robert did not know now how best to present his case.

'Well, Mr. Fraser,' he said hesitantly, 'I think basically the way to sell whisky is to present it as something of quality—even something precious. To lift it right out of the gutter where it more or less is now.'

Fraser looked sceptical. 'With the duty up now to ten shillings a gallon it's precious, all right,' he said.

'But it doesn't look precious. Instead of it swilling around in ugly stone jars, it should be in something smaller and less crude—like a glass bottle.'

'And if you drop the damned bottle that's the end of your precious whisky,' Fergus said, edging restlessly away again in the direction of one of his best Lowestoft pieces. He was irritated not so much now by Robert, as by the fact that he had lost his bearings in the room. Rita had been in while he was in the garden and moved all the ornaments around.

'There's that,' Fraser said, 'but maybe even more important, glass would show up the impurities, this cloudiness that's the curse of whisky. I'm a distiller, but I have to admit that whisky doesn't look as enticing as brandy. As long as we have it in a stone jar nobody sees what it looks like till they get it home and pour it out.' He smiled. 'By then they don't care so much. They just want their dram. In glass they'd be forewarned. I can't think that would be a good thing.'

Robert had been listening with a fixed smile, as if welcoming the objection but anxious to interrupt. 'I know the cloudiness in malt whisky is a terrible drawback, but I think I might be able to do something about that. Maybe quite soon. But meantime I've thought of a way round it. I've been to a glassworks and they've agreed to make coloured bottles for me.'

'Coloured bottles!' Fraser looked at him wonderingly, as if astounded at the simplicity of this idea.

'They'd never made coloured whisky bottles before, but when I suggested it to them they said it wouldn't be difficult.'

Fergus opened a window and stuck his head out as if trying to escape. 'What colours?' he said as his head came in again.

'Green or amber.' He looked from one to the other. 'Well, what do you think?'

'Ingenious!' Fraser said generously. 'But I'd like to know more about your ideas for removing the cloudiness rather than hiding it. *That* could be the most important thing that's ever happened to whisky.'

Robert hesitated. 'I'm too unsure yet,' he said. 'I don't want to talk too soon and look silly later.'

Fergus' expression suggested that he doubted Robert's ever being unsure of himself. 'Disguise it as much as you like,' he said. 'It's still whisky. Rough, heavy, and liable to leave you with a very sore head next day.' He went over to the cabinet and lifted a decanter. 'The sun has just gone down,' he said. 'Shall we have a civilized drink?'

Robert was pleased at Roderick Fraser's interest, but it had been so keen that he had suddenly felt he should perhaps keep his ideas to himself. This was why he had expressed doubt about his experiments. In fact, he had no doubt. He was certain he had discovered not only the way to give malt whisky a golden gleam, but also how to give it a palatable and consistent taste. Why should he reveal this to another businessman? This was the sort of discovery on which a good business—an empire—might be built. His enthusiasm, so recently damped by Fergus, soared extravagantly. All he had to do was get his father's backing. Somehow he would talk the stubborn old devil around. He raised his glass and drank to his own success. When he had gone, Fraser said to Fergus: 'The enthusiasm of a young man is a grand thing to see.'

Fergus made a face but Fraser pressed the point.

'Yes, King, you're a lucky man to have sons to carry on your business. God knows who'll get mine.'

Fergus nodded sympathetically. 'You're the third generation, too. Mind you, sons can be a worry. Don't think they can't. They're not as biddable as girls.' He frowned and shook his head.

'In what way,' Fraser asked with a shrewd smile, 'is Robert refusing to be bidden?'

'Oh . . . there's a girl. . . .'

'That seems a reasonable enough occupation.'

Fergus' heart almost opened to his friend but the disgrace—even the threat of disgrace—was more than he could face. He turned away. 'Let's hope so,' he said with evasive self-pity. 'Let's hope so.'


In their bedroom that night Hoey said, 'I'm enjoying the holiday.'

Gwen smiled. 'So am I, Tom.'

He was slightly bemused by the dinner wine and the brandy that had followed. 'The way it started I thought it was going to be disastrous.' He was thinking of his encounter with Fergus in the library.

'Disastrous?'

He quickly rectified the slip. 'That sudden blizzard last night. But today was like summer.'

'Father says the signs are it will be the same tomorrow.'

'Good.' He laughed as he loosened his tie. 'Old Robert's a dark horse.'

'Why? What's he been saying to you?'

'He hasn't been saying anything. But that Fraser girl. Fiona. I didn't know he had anyone like that in the background.'

'The Frasers are old friends. We've all known Fiona since we were children.'

As he drifted into the dressing-room she sat down at the mirror suddenly remembering the look on his face as he watched Fiona.

43

It had hurt her and it had brought back subsiding fears about another woman. As she brushed her hair and listened to him singing quietly to himself as he undressed she tried to laugh at herself. It must be true about pregnant women being seized by silly fancies.

She watched in the glass as he came behind her and put his lips against her cheek. 'Come to bed, darling,' he said. 'It's been a long day and you are beautiful enough.'

In a room farther along the corridor Fergus sat on the edge of the bed and watched Rita putting her jewellery away.

'Are my reservations about Tom very obvious?'

She turned. 'What on earth makes you ask that?'

'Despite all my efforts last night Gwen seemed to notice something. She spoke to me about it today.'

'I hope you didn't admit anything. She'd be terribly hurt. I thought you both behaved quite well.'

'I put as good a gloss on it as I could.' He shook his head. 'She must shut her eyes to an awful lot.'

'There's a very likeable side to Tom, Fergus dear. To think there isn't would surely be a slur on Gwen's judgement and commonsense.'

Fergus laughed shortly. 'Women in love have no judgement or commonsense,' he said. 'But, of course, Tom can put on the charm. Nevertheless, under it all he's too much the man-about-town for me.'

Rita stirred thoughtfully at the jewellery in the satin-lined box. 'I do know what you mean, dear, but I can't help wondering sometimes if we don't expect too much from our children—and from their chosen ones. Must they always live their lives exactly as we have—accept our values without question?'

Fergus looked at her. 'If they did, it would be a better and a happier world.'

'I happen to agree, Fergus, but they must come to it in their own time and through their own experiences.'

'And perhaps through their own tragedies,' he said with sudden fervour. 'That's what I want to save them from. Robert troubles me because he is involved in a relationship that could bring unhappiness on himself and on us. I get angry with Tom because I know his behaviour could make Gwen unhappy.'

She sighed. 'You've never forgiven him for that business with Mrs. Baxter.'

His eyes widened. 'Have you?'

'We never knew if there was anything to forgive.'

Fergus snorted. 'At the very least his lack of discretion was unpardonable.'

She nodded. 'I can't deny his being seen with her so often certainly gave rise to talk. But ill-informed talk, possibly.'

'By God,' Fergus marvelled, 'how you women stand by him. When a married man's seen dining on numerous occasions with the wife of a friend who just happens to be absent on the Queen's service it would be a damned miracle if tongues did not wag.'

'I'm not trying to defend his indiscretion,' Rita said soothingly, 'but he did serve with Captain Baxter. They were at school together. It's perfectly possible that Tom—misguidedly—thought he was doing a good deed.' When she saw Fergus' expression she added quickly, 'But I must admit it was a relief when Mrs. Baxter left to join her husband in England.'

He turned away as if swallowing a biting retort and said, 'I wonder if Gwen knew.'

'She must have heard rumours. There are always people who take a delight in dropping them.'

'And that's what he should have realized. Even if his behaviour was guiltless it was cruelly thoughtless.'

'Anyway, it's not for us to harbour it against him,' Rita said emphatically. 'He is Gwen's husband and despite all his failings and all your disapproval she is still very much in love with him.'

Fergus took off his coat and loosened his collar. 'I know, Rita. I saw that very clearly today. For Gwen's sake I must put a better face on things.'

# 3

The holiday was over and the Kings were back in Glasgow.

Robert wakened with a sense of exhilaration. He would see Mary today for the first time for a week.

He crossed to the window, deeply pelmeted and heavily draped in plum velvet. He pulled open the curtains and looped the corded tiebacks over the shining brass catches. It was a calm morning, the river a broad band of pewter running between meadows on whose edges the tall superstructure of shipyards added a stately beauty comparable, in this light and in the romantic state of his mind, to a forest before the leaves come out on the trees.

He breathed deeply. Up here, above the burgeoning city, the air was clean. The house was in a terrace on one of Glasgow's residential hills. Beneath the smooth grey frontage of each house was a basement quarters for numerous servants; outside, a high carriage step; and inside, prosperous people—complacent fathers, proud mothers, musical daughters, and pampered sons.

There were no houses opposite to spoil the view. Across the street grass fell away in a gentle, well-tended slope on which, here and there, cherry trees wept delicate pink tears over white narcissus and the first deep red of early tulips.

Over there, perhaps two miles away, in Carlton Place on the river's south bank, Mary lived. Robert strained his eyes in that direction as if he might see her, but all he saw was a grey spread of slated rooftops and a multitude of spires, the nearest belonging to Park Church and Trinity College. From here, no one would have taken it for a Godless city. He went to a bedside table and looked at his watch. Seven fifteen. Perhaps Mary would also be standing at a window looking out at the river, but separated from it only

46

by the width of the street and a grassy bank. It annoyed him that he could not picture her surroundings. He had never been in her house. Once he had driven past, quickly, on a January morning before the white river mist had properly cleared, but the terraced frontage had told him nothing.

Like his father, like all men of his background and upbringing, Robert had an ear for Irish names and from the instant of hearing Mary's he had known her religion. Despite this, he couldn't resist the charm of her delicate dark beauty and gentle manner. There had been no question of his approaching her as he'd approached Fiona—or any of Fiona's predecessors. For Mary he had avoided the rakish act which was part of his usual way with women. He knew, instinctively, that with her, brashness would have an effect opposite to the one he desired.

She, who had been brought up on the reverse side of religious intolerance, had been shy and wary and for all these reasons their relationship had developed slowly, but with a tenderness new and surprising to him. It was marred only by the knowledge they both had of the invisible but terrible barrier lying between them.

In a strange way it initially heightened their sense of intimacy because it lent a sense of adventure to their meetings. Neither made any attempt to introduce the other to friends or parents. They met secretly, in tearooms, parks, and libraries, isolated from society, and because of this thrown all the more together. They had only each other and were so enthralled with the sound and careful, gentle touch of each other that they began to feel they would never again need other people. After three months it seemed incredible to Robert that their religions could really be a barrier. He must surely have been exaggerating? How could two people who loved each other so much, who found each other so delightful in every way—how could these two, he asked himself, possibly be ill-suited by a ridiculous accident of birth?

Then, about six weeks earlier, there had been an incident which had re-emphasized to him that Mary did belong to a group with practices and beliefs alien to his own. It occurred during a brief meeting with her in St. Enoch Square, as she walked towards Great Clyde Street and the Suspension Bridge across the river to Carlton Place. He had steered her to a shop window, past the array of bowler-hatted, pipe-smoking cabbies who waited in the square for hire. By the light of the gas flare she saw delicate porcelain dishes lying on a bed of golden silk. Each dish contained chocolates, of different shapes and variously decorated.

'They're all handmade,' Robert had said. 'They're the best chocolates in Glasgow.' He had put his hand on the door handle. 'Let's go inside. It's a real old-fashioned place. It must date back to the year dot.'

'No, don't tempt me,' Mary had said. 'I'm trying to keep off sweets for Lent.'

He had not understood and she had explained that Lent was a period of forty days between Ash Wednesday and Easter Eve in which Catholics tried to practise some act of self-denial or penitence in remembrance of Christ's fast in the wilderness.

Robert, who'd forgotten that Jesus ever went into the desert, had experienced an uneasy interest. They'd always avoided talking of religion. It was too frightening a subject. Now, the idea of a religion so comprehensive it could concern even a dish of chocolates in a shop window filled him with reluctant fascination. 'Do you mean to tell me Catholics have to give up eating sweets from now till Easter?'

Her small, hollowed face had gone serious in the way he always found strangely touching. 'No, they don't have to. Some of them choose to. And it needn't be chocolates. It can be anything that involves a bit of effort. Some men try not to smoke. A woman might try to stop taking sugar in her tea. Other people go to Mass every morning. I couldn't do that. I don't like getting up early. So I've picked something reasonably easy, like not eating sweets or cream cake.'

'And if you can keep this up for forty days do you get some sort of . . . commendation?'

She laughed. 'I suppose you could call it that. We don't get presented with medals, of course, but we believe that we gain grace.'

'And what the dickens is grace?'

'You could think of it as a kind of spiritual food. Catholics believe that without it the soul dies.' Her smile seemed tinged with sadness. 'Those of us who take our religion seriously are on an endless quest for it—from the cradle to the grave.'

He had hesitated and then asked what he had always wanted to know. 'And do you believe, Mary? Deeply, I mean?'

48

She had pushed her hands more deeply into her muff in a move-ment that seemed to him somehow to suggest vulnerability, or even—perhaps more fancifully—to symbolize a desire to escape. But escape from what? Her religion or his questions?

'I don't know, Robert. I sometimes have doubts. But this is where grace comes in. It helps you to overcome doubt.' She had turned to him. 'I suppose it all sounds very silly to you?' She had sounded so forlorn that he had been filled with a great surge of tenderness for her.

'No, Mary, no, I assure you it doesn't sound silly at all,' he'd said, imploring her to believe him.

The Suspension Bridge had been lined that night with drunken beggars, asleep over their upturned hats, and ragged, barefoot children holding out tin mugs for pennies, the more professional leaning on crutches or tapping along with white sticks. It was after he'd walked her to the other side and watched her cross the gaslit street to her house that he had decided to ask his mother and father if she might spend Easter with the family at Row. It had come back to him that his father knew about Mary. Glasgow, vast and still growing though it might be, was still in many respects a village.

Now, Lent was over, Easter was past, the beggars would be changing into their summer clothes, and still Mary had not met his family. The memory of his quarrel with his father six nights ago at Ardfern was still bitter to Robert, but at least this afternoon he would see her again.

The office and store for the family business, where the books and the accounts were kept, and from where supplies of beer, wines, and spirits were distributed, was in Washington Street in a stone-built, single-story fortress of a building. This dreary street, with slum tenement buildings along one side ran between Argyle Street and the north bank of the Clyde. The area was so squalid and law-less that the warehouse windows had iron bars and the huge wooden doors were immensely thick. The street was cobbled and during business hours it rang and rumbled with sound, as carts carrying goods from the docks passed up it into the city.

Robert arrived at half past eight, but the office clerks had already been at work for a half hour and the warehousemen for an hour. He went through the office premises and into the warehouse to have his usual morning conference with the foreman, then settled at his desk with the letters that had come in with the six-thirty post.

Fergus would not arrive for another half hour. Hoey, whose work of supervising the branches kept him out late at night, wasn't expected at least until noon, although occasionally he had to turn out earlier to audition performers for the music hall. It was part of his work to engage the various acts.

Today, the delivery that interested Robert most was a small, open-sided crate inside which sat a stone jar of about a gallon capacity. The letters were mainly from suppliers announcing price changes, making appointments for their travellers, or heralding new lines, and after glancing through these Robert took off his coat and then, in shirtsleeves, lifted the crate into a small room entered by a door from his own office. This was the sample room, where small quantities of wine or whisky drawn from various casks were kept in bottles, each labelled with a number and a date. There was a sink with running water.

Robert prised open the slats and lifted out the jar. It was labelled GRAIN WHISKY and had been sent to him from a distillery in Edinburgh. This spirit was produced cheaply by a comparatively new process from unmalted cereals in a super-efficient still. It differed so completely in taste from traditional malt whisky that operators of the conventional pot stills objected to it being called whisky, claiming, correctly, that it had none of the accepted characteristics.

Robert turned to a shelf marked GLEN WHISKIES and lifted from it a bottle labelled with the word MACALLAN. This was regarded in the trade as one of the best Glenlivets. It was distilled on Speyside near the village of Craigellachie and it had become known in the Lowlands because it was a favourite of the Highland herdsmen who drove their cattle on the long trek from Morayshire through the mountains to the markets of the south.

From a cupboard he took two glass measures and poured equal quantities of Macallan into each. To one he added some grain whisky from the stone jar. The contents of both measures were pale in colour, but clear. From the tap he ran a little water into each measure, reducing the whiskies to normal drinking strength.

The neat Macallan immediately turned cloudy, but the contents of the other measure remained clear. Robert smiled with satisfaction as he held this second glass to the light. It looked good enough to be poured from a fine crystal decanter in any drawing room.

He had now, over several months, carried out this experiment on more than a dozen makes of malt whisky. In each case the result had been exactly the same. For months, whenever he was sure Fergus would be out of the office, he had worked obsessively in this small room. Sometimes he had been so engrossed that he had come back at night and laboured on in the empty building heedless of cold or exhaustion. Apart from attacking the problem of cloudiness, it had occurred to him to try blending various malt whiskies together before adding his percentage of grain. This had led to one of his most exciting results. He had found that while each individual make of whisky was inclined to vary greatly in taste and quality from one distillation to the next, or at least over a period of months —a blend of several malts showed greater consistency. In a blend of malts the pronounced characteristics of each merged into a completely new taste, which could seemingly be reproduced time after time. The implication thrilled him. And how simple! It was, after all, what they did to ensure consistency in port, sherry, and even tea. And perhaps most important of all, this blending of several malt whiskies with grain whisky produced a taste far more subtle and acceptable than that of any of the individual whiskies used, all of which had far too pronounced a flavour for his palate.

But as he washed and dried the glass measures, his satisfaction began to subside. This morning's experiment had been an indulgence, or at best a substitute for action. There had been no need for it. He had firmly established his process. What he had to do now was develop it. How this could be done without Fergus' co-operation he did not know. He went gloomily back to his room, put his coat on, and sat at his desk with his mind in a restless fever. He had a few hundred pounds of his own money. He could resign from the family firm and try to start his own business—but he would need premises, staff, stock in trade. He did a calculation he had done many times before and came to the usual despondent conclusion: The money he had was inadequate. And then, there was Mary. If there was no Mary he might, in desperation, risk striking out on his own, even without adequate capital. But Mary was there. If he gave up the security of his position with his father, how could he hope to provide a home for her except at some distant time? He put his head down on his desk in an anguish of frustration.

If only he could forget this dream he had of pioneering a brand of whisky that could be bought by name, in small quantities, anywhere in Britain. Probably his father was right. Probably it was an impossibility. Why, in any case, should he have such an ambition? What would it profit him? He was the son of a rich man in a soundly based business. One day—in ten or twelve years, when he was still in his early thirties—the business would be his or, at any rate, he would be at the head of it. What more did he want? In hundreds of big Glasgow houses, in all the good Glasgow clubs, even among the 'wild yachting crowd' on the Gareloch, there were sons standing contentedly by waiting for their inheritance, and in the meantime enjoying themselves.

Why couldn't he do the same? Robert groaned into the red leather desktop, knowing it was beyond him either to abandon his dream or explain it. And to be in love at such a time, with such a girl, was perhaps the greatest agony of all.

A half mile away, nearer to the city centre, Hoey also nursed his head, but for baser reasons. The previous night he had been to a party given by some of the music hall performers in their lodgings in the Cowcaddens.

Hoey could be lured to these theatrical festivities by the smile on a pretty face or by his interpretation of a glance which he often discovered, hours later, to have had an entirely different meaning to the one he had hopefully attached to it. So it had been last night.

Now, midmorning sunlight slanted along the short grey stretch of India Street, warming the old stone. Pigeons perched patiently on warm windowsills waiting for maids to throw out crusts, and in the gutters sparrows pecked at oats spilled from the nosebag of a passing horse.

Curtains or blinds had been drawn against the sun, and Gwen, after instructing the maids to begin the spring cleaning of the drawing-room, had gone out to the small back garden.

Hoey was unable to eat more than a mouthful or two of breakfast, but he was still sitting at the table drinking tea when Gwen came in through the French window, pink-faced and breathless from lifting and bending.

52

'What a lovely morning,' she said. 'The rosebushes are shooting strongly and if we have another day or two of sunshine the wall-flower will be out.'

'It does look nice out,' Hoey agreed with as much enthusiasm as his fragile condition would allow. 'I've been watching you pottering about. You love that little patch.'

It had been barren and depressing when they came to the house and between them they had made it beautiful, Hoey doing the digging and Gwen deciding what they would grow.

'For a time you loved it, too.'

There was a speculative quality in the words that made Hoey look at her quickly and then away again. When he saw her working out there alone he always felt guilty for his neglect.

'I didn't have much time last year, Gwen,' he said defensively. 'But this time it's going to be different. I want to make a little terrace of paving stone by the cherry tree. It would give us a place to sit.'

Her pregnancy was now obvious despite the loose gowns she had started to wear. Momentarily, Hoey mourned the passing of her slim waist. 'Don't let the sunshine lure you into overdoing things,' he said.

Gwen removed some withered blooms from a bowl of daffodils. 'Dr. Drummond has told me to take whatever fresh air and exercise I can. He approves of me gardening.'

She had been trying to ignore the greyness of his face and the rejected food. They saddened her. Now, as she saw him smother a spasm of nausea, she could not resist a comment.

'You've eaten very little breakfast, Tom.'

'I enjoyed the pot of tea,' he said evasively, beginning to rise from the table.

'Tom?'

'Yes, my sweet?'

'Where were you last night?'

'Oh, just sorting out some little problems,' he said lightly, turning away to lift a piece of toast as if he had suddenly found his appetite.

'One day recently,' Gwen said, 'I asked Father about your hours, Tom, thinking I might persuade him to be less of a taskmaster. He said you don't have to be out so late.'

Her eyes were troubled and her movements, at the bowl of daffodils, nervous.

Hoey stiffened and his voice came angrily. 'You had no business discussing me with your father, Gwen. What will he think?'

'The way I said it, he won't think anything.' Already she was beginning to regret the vague and indefinable unease that had made her broach this uncomfortable topic.

'He'll think you don't trust me.' Hoey's brief anger had declined into sulkiness.

'I do trust you, Tom,' she said simply. But, inexplicably, she was remembering again the look on his face as he watched Fiona Fraser.

He took her hands, fighting the sickness, and the throbbing.

'Are you sure, Gwen? It's not so very long ago since you were questioning me about David Baxter's wife.'

She took one of her hands from his and half-turned again to the daffodils. 'That's all over, Tom. Let's not talk about it.'

'You'd been listening to gossip,' Hoey persisted. 'But in the end you apologized to me. Now you have that same look again. Well'—he pinched her cheek playfully. 'Out with it. We may as well clear the air.'

She shook her head in a way that suggested bewilderment and apology. 'I don't know what it is, Tom. It's begun to worry me when you're out till the middle of the night. It's irrational, I suppose, and probably has to do with the baby coming.'

She had moved closer to him in her desire for comfort and reassurance. Hoey put his arms around her and gently pressed her head against his chest.

'Honestly, Gwen, my darling, there is nothing for you to worry about.' His conscience was miraculously clear. 'I know I'm sometimes late when I shouldn't be. But I work hard. You know that. Sometimes when I'm finished, like last night, I go to the club and get involved in a card game. I drink too much and end up next morning feeling rotten. I'm my own worst enemy. But Gwen, you know I love you. I'll try not to worry you again. I promise.'

Her spirit lightened as the sincerity came through to her: not just from the words and the way he spoke them but from the unmistakable honesty of his embrace. She hardly knew whether or not to believe his explanation. It scarcely seemed to matter now. What he had been doing suddenly seemed less important than the fact that in his strange, irresponsible way he loved her and she needed him. Silently, in her heart, she accepted once again what had come as a shock in the early months of their marriage—that there was something unreachable in him. There were times when she sensed he knew it himself. Inside him there was a barrier beyond which no one—not even Hoey—had ever passed.

A half hour later he left the house and began a slow walk through the city, carefully avoiding jostling pedestrians and stepping from pavement kerbs as if they were two feet high. His destination was a chemist's shop in Buchanan Street.

Hoey had taken too much alcohol far too often to have any faith left in the simpler cures. He had tried, on many painful mornings he now preferred to forget, a well-known and completely ineffective remedy concocted of raw egg and sherry. He'd allowed club porters and mess stewards to mix him nauseating draughts which, when swallowed, had only heightened his misery. For the kind of sore heads from which he sometimes suffered even a barber massaging his scalp with bay rum could produce only fleeting alleviation.

The only certain cures Hoey knew were dispensed by Wilson, the chemist at the top of Buchanan Street. Wilson had two of these cures and he had administered them discreetly to two generations of grateful Glasgow businessmen. His No. 1 was a dose of thinly disguised laudanum, and his No. 2, for more serious cases, a larger dose of even more thinly disguised ether.

The street was busy with shoppers and the horse-drawn traffic that seemed these days to be outpacing even the city's considerable expansion and prosperity. 'The streets soon won't be wide enough to take all these carriages,' Fergus often said if he had been held up for a minute of two on his drive to the office. 'I don't know who owns them all or how half of them pay for them!'

In the crush Hoey hoped to enter Wilson's unseen. He stared intently for a few moments into a nearby window, then glanced quickly up and down the street before turning into the entrance. As he did so, the door opened and an elderly member of his club came out with eyes peacefully glazed. Hoey fumbled his hat off, made his embarrassed hawing sound, and tried to mumble a few words of greeting, but to his relief the old man floated by without seeing him.

Wilson led him by the arm into the back shop with gentle sounds of consolation, took his hat, and indicated the chair.

'I think it'll have to be your No. 2, Mr. Wilson,' Hoey said. He always had to resist an inclination to address the old man as 'Doctor'.

Wilson looked at him shrewdly and nodded. 'Very well, Mr. Hoey, I think we can manage that. It's a wee while since you've had the No. 2, so it'll do you no harm. It leaves the system twice as fast as any of your spirits.' He opened a locked cupboard and took out three ominous-looking bottles.

'Make it strong,' Hoey croaked.

When the liquid came he gulped it back in two quick mouthfuls. *God knows what Wilson puts in it to ease it down*, he thought, *but it goes over like milk*. Relief spread rapidly through him and he became so comfortable that he could have sat on. But Wilson, having dusted Hoey's hat with a pad of velour he kept for the purpose, was now holding it out to him. He always liked to get his patients back out into the fresh air as quickly as possible.

Hoey handed the chemist a florin.

Wilson looked at it and smiled encouragingly. 'It was the No. 2, Mr. Hoey.'

Hoey went through three pockets before he found another shilling.

From Buchanan Street he sauntered in a pleasant haze to West Nile Street, his head no longer aching and his stomach cosily settled. There he went into a shop with a very narrow, bow-windowed front and a gilt-lettered sign above the door. GREEN— ANTIQUARIAN BOOKS.

The owner, who was perched on the top rung of a ladder, recognized him. 'Good morning, sir.' He came down carefully, balancing an armful of books. 'Was the list helpful?'

Hoey nodded. 'I had two of the titles you wrote down. Funny thing. I'd never even noticed them before. I don't suppose my father knew they were of any value, either. Never mentioned them once.'

'People don't realize,' Green said. 'It's such a specialized pursuit. Which titles did you find? Do you have them with you?' He ran an eager eye over Hoey, who pulled two books from inside his coat and read the titles: *Webb's Coloured Illustrations of Stained Glass in Mediaeval Scottish Churches* and *Life and Letters of Professor Long of St. Andrew's*.

'Excellent, sir! Excellent! Two very rare and valuable volumes. My customer will be pleased. I've had orders for both those books for over six months. You hadn't any of the others on the list?'

Hoey shook his head. 'Those were the only two.' He stopped in surprise as the man leaned towards him.

The antiquarian bookseller was sniffing. 'Have you been having a tooth out, sir? There's a . . . sort of dental smell. . . .'

Hoey made his neck go stiff. 'Spot of bother with a thing on my neck,' he said. 'Just had it lanced.' He pulled out a notebook. It was the one he had been writing on the night Fergus surprised him in the library at Ardfern.

'I noted down one or two other titles I have,' he said. 'Just ones that look interesting, of course. And only on two or three shelves. Haven't had much time recently. There's hundreds more there.'

He held the notebook out. The bookseller looked at it. 'I don't think I could make you an offer for any of those, sir.' He hesitated. 'As I said last time you were here, the easiest thing would be for me to call on you some day—by appointment, of course—and go through the library in your presence.'

'That wouldn't be all that convenient just at the moment,' Hoey said smoothly. 'Staying at the club mostly these days. Next time I'm passing, though, I'll come in with another list.'

'One or two orders have been placed with me since you were last here, sir. I'll jot the titles down for you. You never know. You might just have them. In the meantime'—he pulled open a drawer—'I think I told you four guineas for one of those titles and two for the other. Shall we say six pounds ten?'

Hoey took the money and left with another list of books he might be able to steal from Fergus next time he was at Ardfern. It wasn't so much the money, he tried to tell himself. It was more the idea of paying the old devil back. For what? Hoey did not know.

He stopped to watch a Clydesdale horse striving to pull a heavily laden cart up the treacherous cobbles towards a carrier's yard at the top of the long hill. Sparks flew as the horse slipped and almost fell. *It's a hell of a world*, Hoey thought with a flash of sympathy. 'Look here, less of that!' he shouted, stepping forward threateningly, as he saw the carter raise his whip above the straining horse.

The carter turned a gnarled face in surprise. 'Whit's up wi' you?' he shouted.

'There's no need for the whip. He's doing his best.'

'Whit do you know aboot it?'

'Anyone can see the horse is tired.'

'It's aw right for you, but ah've goat to get this kert up the hill.'

The cart was now stationary. Hoey went forward and rubbed the horse's head. There was foam at its mouth. 'It's exhausted,' he said.

'He's feenished when he gets to the top o' the hill,' the carter said more quietly. He had come off the cart and was standing beside Hoey, looking at him curiously. No one had ever taken an interest in his horse before. 'Dae ye like hoarses?' he asked.

'I don't like seeing them ill-treated.'

The carter looked shocked. 'Ill-treated? Ah'm no' ill-treating him, mister. Ah've goat to get him up that hill back to the yaird.'

'I suppose you have, but if you let him rest for ten minutes you won't have to use that damned whip.' He looked at the man. 'What's your name?'

The carter looked at him suspiciously. 'Wullie Dickson.'

'Do you take a drink, Willie?'

'Ah take a refreshment,' the carter admitted guardedly.

'Then here's a half-crown,' Hoey said. 'Spend some of it in that pub across the road. Your horse will be ready for the hill when you come out.'

'Thanks, mister.' The carter's face showed his mystification as he crossed the street.

Hoey was surprised to see that one or two people had gathered. He gave them a nod, ran a comforting hand under the horse's chin, and then, thankful to be once more clear-headed, once more in funds, walked off. When he reached St. Vincent Street he looked at his watch and decided he would have time to step round to his bookmaker before having luncheon and a half-bottle of something at White's Chop House in Gordon Street.

Mary Devine clung to the ribbons of her bonnet as she came down the long carriageway of the Western Infirmary. The wind, risen in the early afternoon, tugged at her skirts and rattled noisily through the brittle leaves of the sooty laurel bushes lining the drive. Black clouds swept across the new university buildings on Gilmorehill and dipped menacingly over the hospital grounds, but so far there had been no rain.

Mary hardly noticed the threat of rain and she found the wind invigorating. It was carrying her towards Robert. *Everything now seems to have some association with Robert,* she thought happily, *however foolishly or tortuously the connection has to be made.* There was a bend in the drive just ahead. No need for her to manufacture significance for that spot. That was where he had stopped his carriage the day she'd met him.

He'd been visiting a patient in her ward and she had told him how his friend was and had then found him a chair. His smile had been attractive and she'd particularly noticed that he had the new clean-shaven look that was becoming fashionable with young men. He had still been in the ward when she went off duty. It had been raining heavily as she went down the drive and she had envied the visitors going home in their carriages. Then, just as she reached the bend, one of the carriages had stopped beside her. Robert had looked out, lifted his hat, and asked if he could assist her. If she hadn't met him in the ward, if it hadn't been so wet, if he hadn't looked so handsome in his velvet-collared coat, if she hadn't so much wanted to accept, she would have refused his offer because that would have been the proper thing to do.

It sometimes worried her that she could so easily ignore the conventions when it suited her. He had driven her to Sauchiehall Street and had jumped out to help her down outside Miss Frame's tea shop. This was where she often went when she was off duty. It was warm and quiet and she could sit in one of the alcoves with her books for a couple of hours for the price of a pot of tea and a pancake.

Four days later, as she came out of the hospital gates, Robert's carriage again stopped beside her. 'I thought it was you, Miss Devine,' he said. 'How lucky I happened to be passing. Can I take you into town?'

This time she hadn't had the rain as an excuse and she knew he must have been deliberately waiting for her, but she accepted anyway. When they stopped outside Miss Frame's, he said, 'I often come here myself, you know.'

'Yes, I believe there's a smoke room for gentlemen,' she said pointedly.

'Oh, not the smoke room. The other bit . . . where you must go. Perhaps we'll meet there some time.'

Her heart had jumped at this thinly disguised proposition. 'Perhaps, Mr. King.' Ten days went by before she was able to make another visit to Miss Frame's. Her working hours that week were slightly different and she had amazed herself by loitering about the hospital for almost an hour afterwards so that she would arrive at the tea room at the time known to Robert. She was disappointed, then resentful of her own stupidity when he wasn't there. It was ten days since she had seen him. He would have forgotten her by now. Anyway, what did she know about him except that he was handsome and obviously rich and that she couldn't get him out of her head?

That afternoon she had found it impossible to concentrate on her books, but in the next two weeks she resumed her studious routine. She thought less of Robert and when she did he was sensibly in perspective as someone met briefly and almost completely unknown. Then one afternoon she looked up from her book and he was there, standing inside the bead curtain at the top of the stairs, hat in hand, looking out of place in his finely cut clothes in this setting of faded tablecloths and worn linoleum. Her heart had risen chokingly and she had brazenly held up her hand to attract his attention.

He had crossed eagerly to her table. It was as if they had known each other for years. 'I'd given up hope,' he said. 'I thought I'd frightened you away. Today I was passing and decided to try one last time.'

She had been filled with happiness. 'There was a week or two when I was on a different duty,' she said. 'I couldn't come. Won't you sit down?'

He had thrown off his coat. 'By Jove,' he said, 'those London buns look good. I didn't know you could get them in Glasgow.' She had looked studiously in front of her. 'But I thought, Mr. King, you came here quite often?' There was silence for several seconds and then they both laughed. 'I had to make some excuse,' Robert said. 'Here, let me order a fresh pot of tea.'

That had been almost five months ago but it was still among

Miss Frame's currant slabs and potato scones that they most liked to meet. It was here they had fallen in love.

Now the first drops of rain came as Mary boarded the tramcar. By the time she disembarked outside Miss Frame's an early twilight had fallen and the loose surface of Sauchiehall Street had turned to clinging mud and pools of dirty water.

The old waitress who served their table watched as Robert rose to help Mary with her wet coat. It wasn't a fashionable place and was patronized mainly by older people. You didn't get many young lovers here. *A nice pair*, the old waitress always thought, so happy with each other and so bright except in those odd moments when, turning, she saw shadows of anxiety. Sometimes she worried about them as she trailed home after a day of twelve hours on her feet. She went off to bring their pot of tea.

Mary lifted a wedge of sponge thickly filled with cream. 'It's all right, Lent's over now,' she said as she saw him watching. 'Did you enjoy yourself at Row? It's been an endless week. I've missed you.'

A picture of Fiona came to him and he was astonished that he could sit here with Mary and feel no guilt over his behaviour with the other girl.

'The weather was wonderful,' he said. 'There was only one thing lacking.'

'What was that?'

'You.'

'Thank you,' she said brightly. 'I studied all Saturday and Sunday. But on Monday Father and Mother came and took me for a drive.'

He lowered his voice. 'I did want you to spend Easter with us, Mary. I want you to know that. I asked my parents if you could come. They refused.'

She tried to smile. 'You couldn't expect your mother to be bothered with a guest. Especially someone she'd never met. It wouldn't have been a holiday for her.'

'That wasn't the reason. It hadn't anything to do with that.'

She looked around the room as if for some diversion.

'It doesn't matter, Robert dear. Really it doesn't. I didn't expect to be invited. So long as you enjoyed yourself.'

He went relentlessly on, propelled despite himself. 'Their reason for not having you was a disgraceful one. It's something we've never spoken about, but we must speak about it now.' Her eyes were black with alarm. His hands went to hers across the table. They did not clasp hands because the place was too public. Indeed, as their talk had become more intimately serious they had become aware of the softly watchful eyes of the old waitress and the four women shoppers at a table only three or four feet away, the floor around them cluttered with brown paper parcels. So only the tips of their fingers touched among the cheap white crockery and the spilled sugar, as if by accident. Outside, a newsboy called out hoarsely and the sound of horses' hooves and carriage wheels rose to the wet window behind them. 'They wouldn't have you because you're a Catholic. It hadn't anything to do with there being no accommodation—it's a big house. Or with any inconvenience. We have plenty of servants. If you'd been the same as us, if you'd been a Protestant, there wouldn't have been any difficulty.'

The unexpectedness of this bitter confession left them both speechless. Her face had gone white. His expression was pleading. He was confused and regretful at having so recklessly introduced this dangerous topic, but there was no retreating now.

'I'm sorry, Mary, I had to tell you. I knew it would hurt you and I don't know what good it's done, but I couldn't keep it back. I had to speak or I would have felt that in some way I sympathized with them, that I was on their side.'

'What are we going to do?' Her voice was little more than a frightened whisper, but the trust implied by the simple question opened up vistas of responsibility he had never dared face before.

He said, 'What is a "mixed marriage"?'

They had never discussed marriage, but the question didn't seem to surprise her.

'It's when a Catholic and someone who isn't a Catholic get married in the Catholic Church.'

'I've only heard about it vaguely. But the one who isn't a Catholic doesn't have to change?'

'No. They both keep their own religions, but there are conditions. Hard conditions, Robert. The non-Catholic has to promise that any children they have will be brought up as Catholics.'

He nodded. 'That's what I'd heard. It doesn't seem very fair. What if the children don't want to be Catholics?'

For the first time, she looked surprised. 'Young children do what

62

their parents tell them. If, when they grow up, they don't want to be Catholics then no one can stop them going some other way.'

'But other than that it's simple and straightforward?'

'Well, not really. The Church does its best to discourage the marriage. It doesn't like mixed marriages and only permits them as a last resort. The ceremony isn't even performed in the open church. It takes place in the vestry, or the sacristy—a side room—under what I think they refer to as "conditions of secrecy and shame". It has to be a small, quiet wedding with no show. Usually the couple are dressed in everyday clothes and there's only a handful of guests. It's not very nice.'

Spots of colour stained the skin of her cheekbones, accentuating the hollows below. He was reminded of a waif he'd seen earlier in the day, sitting in a doorway minding a basket of flowers. 'Why do they go to these lengths to make it unpleasant?'

'Because they say it hardly ever lasts.'

He looked about and then lowered his voice. 'We love each other, Mary. We could make it last. It's the only way. I wouldn't ask you to give up your religion and I could never join your Church. But I could agree to being married in it, as long as I didn't have to believe anything.'

She smiled. 'We're talking like this and you haven't even asked me to marry you yet, Robert.'

He looked at her beseechingly. 'But this whole conversation has been a proposal. You will marry me, Mary . . . if I agree to a cere-mony in your Church?'

The old waitress had been hovering nearby. Now, as they looked at each other in silence, she pounced on the empty milk jug. 'All right, my dears? I'll just take this away and fill it.' The women shoppers were getting ready to leave in a loud creaking of chairs and rustling of parcels. Mary glanced at them. 'What a place we've chosen for such a serious conversation. There's no privacy. All these people.'

'It's the only place we have. Aren't you going to answer me?'

'We haven't had time to think, Robert. Of course I want to marry you. But for you it would be such a serious step to take. I don't want to bind you on the strength of a few quick words in a crowded tea room. You must give youself time to think about it properly. What would your people say?'

He turned the question on her. 'Are you worried about your people, Mary? Surely they wouldn't object to me if I was willing to come halfway?'

The old waitress gave them a worried, motherly—almost cautionary—smile as she returned the milk jug. 'There you are, my dears. Such a dreadful evening, now.' People could talk in whispers and try to hide their feelings in various ways, but she could tell when they were happy or when they were anxious. She could see through the grave smiles to the sore hearts. And not just with youngsters like these, who were transparent, but with the older, married regulars, too. She knew the ones who were in love and the ones who were out of love.

'They wouldn't like it, Robert. They would prefer me to marry a Catholic. I know that without asking. They'll be exactly like your parents.' Her eyes filled with tears. 'Why did we ever meet? We've been silly and now it's all so cruel.'

He frowned. 'I wouldn't lose these last months, Mary. I wouldn't change a minute of them. Don't you feel the same way?'

She closed her eyes and he was never to know what lay in them at that moment. He felt cheated even as he listened to the humble sincerity of her answer. 'Yes, Robert. Oh, yes, Robert, I do.'

# 4

It was Robert who suggested it would be sensible for them to find out more about mixed marriages.

'It's not just a matter of us saying that's what we want to do,' Mary warned him. 'In some dioceses the bishops refuse to allow such marriages under any circumstances. Even the ones with a fairly modern outlook are very strict.'

Her parish church was the new Cathedral of St. Andrew on the north bank of the Clyde. This riverside church, which stood almost opposite her home in Carlton Place across the water, had until recently been as humble as any other in Glasgow, built to serve a parish which included the decaying slums lying in the web of vennels and wynds hidden between Stockwell Street and the Saltmarket. But with the Roman Catholic hierarchy newly restored to Scotland for the first time since the Reformation, it had been chosen to house the new archbishop's throne.

'Of course, we won't have to see the archbishop himself,' Mary needlessly assured Robert. 'Any of the priests will do. The one I know best is Father Campbell.'

They chose a Sunday evening when she knew her parents were visiting friends. Robert collected her at a meeting place they had established near the nurses' home at the Western Infirmary. They drove across the city through streets busy with strolling men and women. It was a Glasgow tradition that people should come into town from the outlying parts and windowshop and otherwise see and be seen on fine Sunday evenings. Traders sold sweets, flavoured drinks, and inexpensive gifts and novelties from barrows festooned with ribbons and covered over with tarpaulins.

Father Campbell came to them promptly in a small bare room

off the vestry, where the only furnishings were a polished table with six hard chairs, an oil lamp, and a crucifix on the whitewashed wall above the fireplace. There was the remains of a coal fire, cindery and beyond saving. The priest glanced at it when he came in, then shrugged apologetically. 'This room is rarely used on Sunday evenings,' he said, pulling out a chair and sitting opposite Robert.

Robert noticed that his soutane had been heavily darned in places. His skin was pale where the black beard did not grow, and his way of frequently looking towards the door or window gave the impression he had much to do. He said to Mary: 'So this is your friend? I hadn't realized it was going to be a young man.' As she started to say something he added, 'No doubt that was my own fault. I remember I gave you little chance to explain.' He nodded his head as if towards the church or the world beyond. 'We seem to have scant time for proper consideration these days ... except,' he added hastily, 'when it is formally arranged as now.' He looked from one to the other and smiled. 'So?'

'Robert is not a Catholic, Father. We wanted to get some guidance from you on the marriage laws of the Church.'

Father Campbell looked surprised. 'I see your parents regularly. They have never mentioned to me that you were contemplating marriage.'

'Well ... they don't know yet.'

'Surely you do not mean to marry without consent?'

'Oh, no. Of course not. It's not like that.' She twisted her gloves and looked across the table at Robert, who was staring at the crucifix. 'You see, this is only an enquiry. There is no arrangement for us to be married.'

'But are you engaged to be married?'

'No, Father.'

'But isn't that customary? Isn't this interview a little premature?'

Robert interrupted. 'Perhaps I could speak for us. I think Mary is too nervous to explain properly.'

The priest nodded and clasped his hands in front of him on the table.

'Mary and I have known each other for about six months,' Robert said. 'We are in love, but because we're of different religions we have not yet approached our parents. Neither of us wants to

66

hurt them and when the times comes for us to marry we would each like to keep our own religion.'

Father Campbell's face had gone glum behind the rough black beard. 'I assume you're speaking of what we call a mixed marriage?' His voice was heavy, but whether with disappointment or distaste they couldn't tell.

'Yes.'

'And you realize that there is more to marriage than whether or not the parents approve, important as that is?' The asperity, although faint, was unmistakable.

'We do.'

'In the Catholic Church, Mr. King, marriage is more than a legal contract. It is a sacrament.'

'Mary has tried to explain that to me.'

'Can I ask if our religion attracts you?'

Robert hesitated. 'I'm afraid I know very little about it.'

'But now you want to know?'

He felt that he was being invited to agree. 'I couldn't say that. I don't feel I need to know. I respect Mary's beliefs.'

Father Campbell took a pair of spectacles from his soutane as if getting ready to read something, but having put them on, he sat looking only at the top of the table. When at last he spoke his manner suggested he was concerned to appear reasonable.

'I'm afraid that simply to respect Mary's beliefs will not be sufficient. The Church asks that there be some knowledge. In fact, the bishops have laid down a minimum standard of knowledge. You see, we believe that out of knowledge understanding and tolerance grow. Ignorance can in the end kill the very best intentions and bring the most painful misery. In our position we see it all the time.'

'Are there any books, then, that I might have a look at?'

'It will not be quite as simple as having a look at a few books.' The priest's smile was apologetic. 'Again, we are more demanding. If you truly love Mary and wish to marry her then it should be in her religion. That way would lie the best chance of a happy and successful marriage and one most pleasing to Our Divine Lord.' His voice quickened. 'Before the matter can be considered further I must ask you to take a course of instruction. That is the way all conversions begin.'

All the warnings Robert had ever been given about the Catholic conspiracy, about the wiles of the Scarlet Woman rushed into his mind. Was this the devious cunning in action? There was no sign of it in the priest's face.

'I think it best that I be quite straightforward, Father Campbell. I don't want to become a Catholic. I couldn't accept your beliefs. They are too different from what I've been brought up to believe in.'

'But how can you tell?' The priest seemed to be warming to the debate, as if the challenge of doubt or rejection was a stimulus. 'You've told me you know nothing of the Catholic religion. With more knowledge you might find the doctrine attractive. God may give you the blessed gift of faith. He may want you to be a Catholic. Mary may have been His instrument for bringing you to us.'

Robert looked at Mary across the table, reading the message of troubled sympathy in her eyes. It was damnable that they had to worry about ministers or priests, about whether you stood democratically to pray or knelt humbly. Could God, if he existed, really care about such things?

He smothered his irritation and said diplomatically, 'I'm sure God did send Mary to me, and I thank Him for it. But . . . please don't be offended. . . . I doubt if His purpose in sending her was to bring me here. He brought us together so that we could be together for the rest of our lives.'

'But what about after your lives on this earth are finished? Don't you want to be together in heaven?'

'I'm sure Protestants go to heaven as well.'

Father Campbell looked a little confused. 'Of course, of course,' he said.

While he seemed lost for a few moments in what might have been a closer examination of this proposition, Robert took the opportunity of reminding him, 'It was a mixed marriage we had in mind.'

'A mixed marriage is a last desperate step so far as the Church is concerned, Robert. I could recommend the bishop to permit such a joyless ceremony only if everything else had been tried and failed. Mary should have told you that.' He leaned forward, his face showing his concern. 'Can you really want a ceremony conducted almost in secret, without flowers or music, without smiles or blessing?' He sat back and closed his eyes. All glow had gone from the cinders in the grate and the room was icy. The thin white curtains fluttered slightly against the window.

'There's little left that I can helpfully say, except to tell you that the only step you can take towards marrying Mary within the Church—either regularly or irregularly—is a course of instruction in Catholic doctrine. We have lay people who can do this. You would not require a priest. You wouldn't even have to come to the church. I have someone in mind who would instruct you in the privacy of his own home for an hour or two once a week. At the end you could come to me and give me your decision.'

Robert made up his mind. 'How long does the course last?'

'People can usually come to a decision after two months.'

'Very well. If there is no alternative.'

As they left the room the priest said, 'There's one more thing. Please try to approach this with an open heart, ready to embrace the faith humbly if that is what God wants. You will know in your heart what's right. Do not regard it simply as a device to allow me to recommend the sanctioning of a mixed marriage. Even after the course, if you find you do not want to share Mary's religion, then permission for a mixed marriage is not automatic.'

With this warning he led them out through the vestry into a side aisle. The church flickered mysteriously in the glow from the candle stands near the door. There were still one or two people bent towards the altars in prayer.

Outside, a wind curled along the river and in the quiet street they heard water lapping at the embankment. Resentment had been growing again in Robert and now, as they stood on the church steps, he turned querulously to the priest.

'What's the point, Father, of making it all so difficult and unpleasant?'

The wind tugged at the skirt of Father Campbell's soutane as his eyes followed the lights of a sailing ship passing slowly downriver. 'I do not know if I have an answer that will satisfy you. We believe that what you and Mary contemplate is a danger to your mutual happiness and to her spiritual welfare. Therefore, we try to discourage it.' He stopped speaking and stepped back to look up at the twin towers of the church. The stone was grey and indistinct and the tracery at the top black against the sky. 'My boyhood was spent only two or three hundred yards from here. What the stonemasons erected by day was pulled down by night. Unfriendly people did not want us to have our church. Finally, my father and other Catholic men had to spend their nights standing guard here. We exist only because of constant vigilance.'

When they left he was still standing outside the church, rising, it seemed, from the ground like the stone towers on either side of him.

The next time they met, Robert said, 'Mary, I've found a place where we can have privacy.' He smiled, but his eyes were apprehensive. 'Of course, you may not care to come to it.'

She looked puzzled. 'Why shouldn't I?'

'You may be shocked,' he said, trying to sound softly teasing. 'It's a little place I've rented.'

'Do you mean a house?'

'Well . . . it's a small flat in a tenement. I don't know whether it was a good thing to do or not. What do you think?'

Her laugh was uncertain. 'I don't know either, Robert.'

'It was you who complained that we never had any privacy,' he reminded her. 'Whenever we meet we're always surrounded by people. We always have to talk in whispers.'

'Where is this flat?'

'In Hill Street, up behind Sauchiehall Street.'

To his surprise she said without further hesitation, 'I don't suppose I would dare tell anyone, but I don't see why I shouldn't come to your flat with you. Is it nice?'

'It only has two rooms and the furniture isn't very good, but it's quite respectable.'

'People would think it wrong, but . . . after all, we have known each other for quite a long time and we are planning to marry.'

He could think of no answer to this unexpectedly businesslike assessment except to say, 'Then I'll take you to see it. If you decide it wouldn't be right, you must say so immediately.'

It was the beginning of a new and deeper stage in their relationship. Their initial embarrassment soon disappeared. In their private world, as afternoons lengthened into soft summer twilights, they found their intimacy grew. Mary revealed a more unconventional side which at first surprised and worried him but which he decided was probably inseparable from her work as a nurse.

The contradictions gradually revealed in her nature excited him. She was spiritual enough to stop eating cream cakes during Lent, yet worldly enough to spend evenings alone with him in a setting that would have terrified her parents and perhaps, if it were known, even cause trouble for her at the infirmary.

He discovered she had little false modesty about her body—again, he supposed, because of her work—and she accepted without protest the hand he one night placed gently but nervously on her breast.

As visits to the flat became a regular part of their lives, he began to think that perhaps the apparent inconsistencies lay not so much in her as in him. For all his experience, perhaps he was the puritan, if not by nature, then certainly by upbringing. There was a natural innocence in Mary he did not possess. It was this innocence that made possible the deepening familiarities they experienced together. And yet, to their gentle lovemaking there was an unspoken limit, a boundary beyond which he knew he must not go.

Since taking the flat a new exhilaration had entered them. They had a sense of secret adventure, a sense, almost, of being married. The cloud that remained was the religious one, but now with the added complication that he could not reconcile her beliefs with her behaviour. They had done nothing Robert considered wrong, and yet . . . they were close to the forbidden.

Again he asked her the question that had troubled him before. 'Mary, does your religion really mean a great deal to you?'

'It does, Robert. Why?'

'I just wondered.'

Her gaze was steady. 'You mean, you doubted.'

'Well. . . .'

'Why did you doubt? You don't have to be afraid to tell me. Is it because I come here and behave in a way some people would say was shameless?'

Her directness was disconcerting. 'It's not what one hears about Catholics,' he said defensively.

She laughed nervously. 'Catholics are human.' Her face became serious. 'Perhaps I am shameless, but I love you, Robert, and I trust in your love for me. I don't feel we're doing anything wrong. And I know you wouldn't try to force me. I know I am safe with you.'

Her trust filled him with an enormous tenderness. 'That makes me sound very virtuous,' he said.

'I think you are virtuous,' she said simply. 'I wouldn't love you if I didn't think that.'

He kissed her gently. 'I love you so much, Mary. I wish all our troubles were over.'

He held her so close that he did not see the tears in her eyes.

# 5

Gwen went along to help her mother select the dress she would wear to meet the Queen. Rita walked down from Park Place to Gwen's house in India Street and from there they began a long trek that took them into shops all the way up Sauchiehall Street and down Buchanan Street. They were shown gowns of every material, colour, and price, but by lunchtime they'd found nothing suitable. The fashions were either too fussy or too severe and, if everything else was right, the shade was sure to be unflattering to the colouring of Rita's fair hair and glowing skin.

'It's so depressing,' Rita said wearily as they came out of still another shop. 'I've always found Glasgow hopeless for clothes. I can't think which shops Fiona Fraser had in mind when she said it was as good as London now.'

'Maybe you should have had her with you instead of me,' Gwen said dispiritedly. She was advanced in her pregnancy and after almost three frustrating hours of walking along busy streets or pushing through crowded shops, she was limp.

'Nonsense. I wouldn't have come without you, my dear. If I don't get anything today I'll have to ask your father if we could go through to Edinburgh. The Princes Street shops are said to be excellent and the air there is so bracing. After all, it's not long till the Queen's visit. Sometimes I get quite excited thinking about it. So does your father, although he'd never admit it.'

'Don't worry, Mother, we're sure to find something suitable.' Gwen smiled encouragingly despite her exhaustion. 'It's only one o'clock. We've got the whole afternoon ahead of us.' The prospect dismayed her until she remembered all the uncomplaining hours Rita had spent dress-hunting with her: for her pink first party dress,

73

her turquoise fourteenth-birthday party dress, her red engagement-ball gown, and her ornate, white satin wedding dress. She took her mother's arm but leaned on it more heavily than she had intended.

Rita looked at her with concern. 'How selfish of me, dear. I've been thinking only of myself. You look quite pale. You must be worn out. There's nothing more tiring than trailing about town on a close day. Would you like to sit down?'

Gwen nodded 'We could both probably do with a rest.'

'Then let's go and have something light to eat.'

'That would be lovely,' Gwen said gratefully.

'Lindsay's is ideal for ladies. All the other places near here are full of men puffing at pipes and all they can ever offer you to eat are enormous plates of sheep's head or pigs' trotters. I'm sure we'd both fall asleep after anything heavy like that.'

An hour or so later they came out of Lindsay's. They had eaten more than they intended in the way of cream cake, for which the shop was noted, but they felt rested and better able to face a few more rails of dresses. They began working their way north again towards Sauchiehall Street and were again becoming discouraged when they stopped outside a shop which they knew had a reputation for stocking flashy goods of low quality.

'What cheap rubbish,' Rita said as they looked in at the badly arranged window.

'And there's a clearance sale on, as well,' Gwen said. 'Their stuff will be even shoddier than usual.'

Then, almost at the same moment, they both noticed a dress badly draped over a plaster model in a back corner of the window. A white crack gashed the model's head and the arms stuck out at grotesque angles as if broken, but despite this the dress had a suggestion of suitability. It was of peach-coloured wild silk with a square white bodice and wide sleeves.

'I wonder,' Rita said thoughtfully. The dresses they had seen in other shops had ranged in price from about five to an incredible thirty guineas. This one had a card at the waist which said: *Reduced to 10/-*. 'Oh, for heaven's sake,' Gwen said when she noticed the card. 'It can't possibly be any good at that price. Besides, you could never meet the Queen wearing a dress that cost only ten shillings.' Her hand went out and gripped her mother's arm. 'But

74

let's go in and ask to see it, anyway.' With a guilty look up and down the street they walked quickly into the shop.

The assistant who attended to them looked as if she considered herself demeaned by working with such inferior merchandise. She spoke with the genteel new accent that was spreading among those in Glasgow who considered the local tongue uncouth, and she made a point of telling them that this was her first day in the shop. Her expression suggested she intended to see it would also be her last.

'There's rather an interesting peach-coloured dress at the back of the window,' Rita said.

The saleswoman, eyeing Rita's clothes, said that there was, but added, 'Of course, for the likes of meddom we have a superior range.'

'No, it's the one in the window that we want to see,' Gwen insisted.

'As meddom wishes.' She fetched the dress from the window and helped Rita into it perfunctorily. As soon as it was on, Rita knew this was the dress. Gwen agreed. The saleswoman stood silently by. She gave a small toss of her head when Rita said she would take it.

'What does meddom require the gown for?' she asked in her condescending way, the word 'gown' seeming to stick a little in her throat.

Gwen turned quickly away to hide the smile she felt coming at the look of consternation on Rita's face.

Rita fumbled busily with some buttons, avoiding the saleswoman's gaze. 'It's to meet the Queen,' she said helplessly.

The assistant gave her a withering look. 'Very naice,' she said as she stalked away to get a box. 'Very naice.'

When they left, the woman was in the window throwing a sheet over the disintegrating plaster model to hide its nakedness.

Rita said, 'Don't ever let your father know how little I paid. It would put him off it completely.'

They went laughing up Sauchiehall Street looking for a place where they could have a last cup of tea before going home.

Mary turned the pages of the *Penny Catechism* and selected a question.

' "What is limbo ?" ' she asked quietly across the soda scones and pancakes.

It was mid-afternoon and Miss Frame's was busy. Robert's smile was self-conscious. 'You do keep me at it.'

'I have to. Now. . . . What is limbo ?'

He waited until the old waitress had filled one of the plates with a fresh selection of cream cakes from her creaking trolley. He watched her go trundling away to another table, then said, ' "By limbo I mean a place of rest where the souls of the just who died before Christ were detained." '

Since beginning the course of instruction, Robert had let Mary question him on each week's work, sometimes here, sometimes at the flat in Hill Street. It helped impress the lessons on his mind. Linking them with Mary brought some reality into what he otherwise found dull and insubstantial. There was little of the spiritual in his nature and there had never been a time when he had felt any genuine interest in his own religion. He occasionally went to church because it was the correct thing to do. Never had he consciously applied his religion to his daily life. He had never prayed except along with other people and with his mind on something else. In his whole life he had not once felt himself to be in the presence of God.

His introduction now to Mary's religion was proving unemotional and unrewarding. He read without involvement, remembering enough of it to satisfy Mr. Martin, the schoolteacher who was instructing him. He never questioned anything, disappointing his instructor. Conversion was usually accomplished by argument and debate. It was in the overcoming of doubt that the teacher found satisfaction. Even the more controversial propositions of the faith failed to rouse Robert. When Mr. Martin told him that during Mass ordinary bread and wine was turned into the actual body and blood of Jesus Christ, he made no comment. For Mary he could endure anything.

After a few more questions Mary looked at him. 'Is that enough for today ?'

He pretended interest to please her.

'One more then we'll have another cup of tea.'

'All right. "What are the sins against religion ?" '

' "The chief sins against religion are the worship of false gods or idols and the giving to any creature whatsoever the honour which belongs to God alone." Good God!'

She was startled by this exclamation, clearly not from the *Catechism*. 'What's wrong?'

He was staring past her to the bead curtain screening the entrance. 'It's my mother and my sister,' he said.

Mary's heart thumped as she turned to look at the two women. Both were smartly dressed in grey. The one holding a large brown box was obviously the elder, but she hardly looked old enough to be the other woman's mother. Perhaps it was the younger woman's condition that gave the illusion of a narrow age gap. She was obviously expecting a baby and her face was strained and tired. They seemed to be discussing where to sit. They might pick a table at the other end of the room. If they did, Robert and she might go unobserved. Almost as soon as the thought came, Mary was annoyed with herself. Why should she want to hide? A spark of defiant pride flared in her.

'Hadn't you better wave to them, Robert?'

'I suppose I'd better.' He pushed back his chair and stood.

The introductions, although carried out with smiles and laughing exclamations of surprise, were strained, at least for Mary and Rita. Gwen didn't know about Mary and therefore had a clear conscience, and Robert, after his initial confusion, soon realized he was indifferent to any displeasure his mother might be experiencing. He had to admit she was showing no sign of it.

'How nice to meet you,' Rita said. 'I'm afraid Robert has been very secretive. He has told us hardly anything about you.'

Mary found herself sympathizing with Rita. The awkwardness of the meeting could not be denied. To say something that couldn't be criticized would be almost impossible. She acquitted Robert's mother of hypocrisy. There was a warm maturity—and yet a contradictory youthfulness—about Rita that she felt she could like.

'I'm afraid there's very little to tell,' she said.

'You're a nurse, aren't you?'

'Yes. I've almost finished my training.' She nodded to a satchel of books on the floor beside her. 'I sometimes come here to study in the afternoons when I'm on early duty.'

'Isn't it terribly hard work? With very long hours? You look so fragile.'

77

The social inconsequences began to come more easily to Rita, helped by Mary's appearance. She looked no different from any of the other girls they knew—but then, it would be silly to think she would. Her manner was excellent and her speaking voice attractive. She looked respectable and sounded sensible, not the sort of girl Robert would be likely to get into any trouble with. *That at least is a comfort,* Rita thought, *for as a rule nurses are just a little bit too worldly.* She took another close look to see if her favourable judgement had been hasty. She could find no reason to alter it. *But there must,* she decided, *be a streak of determination in the slender frame.* It was reasonable to assume the girl's parents would not have given in lightly when she first told them she wanted to be a nurse. *Especially,* Rita thought, *when the father was a doctor and would therefore know very well the world of hard work and strict discipline the girl would be entering.*

Suddenly, Rita felt a rush of compassion for her headstrong son and this young, vulnerable girl. She knew already that they were in love. They couldn't hide it. But how terrible their predicament! For them the obscure hatreds of Scottish history, the passions of centuries, had become a personal problem. Their lives would become an arena for the ancient battles people were still fighting. Rita couldn't have spoken logically for one minute of the forces that were at work, but she knew with certainty they could hurt and even destroy. She was startled out of her reverie by the laughter of the other three. Gwen had been telling Mary about the dress.

'The nurses' home is quite near the university,' Mary said. 'The Queen's route passes our window. If I see you, I'll wave.'

Robert sat mostly in silence, marvelling at what words can hide.

One morning a week or so later Robert was alone at the breakfast table staring at the front page of the *Glasgow Herald*. Halfway down the page, wedged unobtrusively between display advertisements for a Grand Revival of *Rob Roy* at the Gaiety Theatre and a special offer of two-ply Scotch carpets at 1s. 11d. per yard by Arnott & Co. of Jamaica Street, were four or five lines of print.

Modest as the print was, the message made Robert ill. Anxiously he read the advertisement again. It was headed by the words OLD CORRIE and said: '*We are pleased to invite discriminating members of the public to try our fine old whisky, sold by the gallon at 18s. or in bottles at*

78

*40s. per dozen. Our* Old Corrie *is distinguished by its mellow flavour, so subtle compared to the strong* gout *characteristic of other whiskies.'*

Angrily, Robert threw the newspaper to the floor. Here was someone usurping his ideas! Here was a whisky with a brand name, sold in bottles and allegedly of a milder flavour than usual. This was exactly what he'd been urging on his father. And now he'd been overtaken because of the old fool's preoccupation with respectability and his failure to recognize a good business idea when it was given him.

He put his head back and groaned loudly at the ceiling. He thought of all the bleary, tiring hours he had spent experimenting in the cold sample room at Washington Street. All wasted. He might as well have been drinking and singing with his less ambitious friends. *The hopes he had built!*

The sun was warm through the window, and in the distance, on the other side of the river, he could see green hills. It was one of the most pleasant and certainly one of the most extensive views to be had in Glasgow. As he looked towards the soothing hills, his thoughts calmed. The world was a very big place and this was a very small advertisement. Most *Herald* readers wouldn't even notice it. The name of the proprietors of Old Corrie was unknown to him. It must be a small firm. Judging by the lack of boldness with which they'd launched their new whisky, it seemed reasonable to assume they didn't have a great deal of money to spare—or that they had a limited faith in their product.

He lifted the *Herald* again and noted the name and address of the advertiser: *James Ross & Co., Provision Merchants, Candleriggs.* He left his breakfast unfinished and instead of going to his office he drove to Candleriggs, near Glasgow Cross, and occupied mainly by dealers in fruit, vegetables, and dairy produce. The street, when he arrived, was jammed with delivery carts and littered with cabbage leaves. It smelled of smoked ham.

He left his carriage in Trongate and began to walk. As well as rotting vegetation, there were dangerous hoops of wire, discarded from the large, empty egg crates that seemed to lie everywhere, to be avoided. After picking a way through the debris he found the premises of Ross & Co. It was a narrow, shabby-fronted grocer's shop almost hidden behind boxes of fruit and sacks of potatoes stacked outside the adjoining warehouse. Robert stared. He could

79

not link this dilapidated place with the stylish advertisement in the *Herald*. He moved closer. The window displayed mainly tea, sugar, and items of grocery, but what held his attention was a group of bottles arranged on a stand and labelled with the small stickers chemists put on medicine bottles.

They were of clear glass and he was pleased to see that the whisky had the usual murky blur. He went into the shop and was further cheered by the faded paintwork, the badly packed shelves, and the sawdust on the floor. There were no other customers. A tall, thin man in his late twenties, in shirt-sleeves and white apron, fetched the bottle of Old Corrie he ordered. Suddenly, with the whisky standing there on the counter in front of him, Robert's curiosity would not let him wait until he reached Washington Street. He told the man he felt unwell and asked if he could drink a measure of the whisky in the shop.

The man hesitated. 'It's against the terms of my licence, but if you're not well . . .' He lifted the bottle. 'You'd better come ben the back shop.' He produced a tumbler and began pouring a torrent of Old Corrie into it.

Robert hastily stopped him. 'I think that will do,' he said. 'Could I have some water, please?'

The man smiled as he turned on a tap. 'For some there's enough water in it already.' It was an old Scottish joke.

Robert almost sighed with relief when he saw the whisky go duller as the water went in. 'My name is King,' he said as he raised the glass. 'Are you the proprietor?'

'Yes. Peter Ross.'

'Then here's the best of health, Mr. Ross.'

The clouding effect of the water on the whisky had made Robert almost certain Old Corrie was just another malt. His first sip of the whisky confirmed it. Mr. Ross's subtle *goût* had been achieved simply by selecting one of the lighter malts, possible a Lowland, like Roderick Fraser's Lochbank. It certainly did not have the pungency of the average Highland or Glenlivet. But neither did it have the character. It was a puny drink—even a raw one. It was in no way comparable to the blend of whiskies he had perfected. His whisky—for which as yet he had no name—was mildly flavoured, but the subtlety didn't come from thinness. His blend of seven or eight first-class malts, combined with grain, still had character and body. It had a rounded taste that made Old Corrie seem incomplete. There was no threat here.

'I saw your advertisement in the *Herald*,' he said, taking another sip of whisky.

'Oh, that.' Ross looked embarrassed. 'It made it sound very grand. The words weren't mine. They wrote it for me in the *Herald* office.' He laughed. 'They had to tell me what *gout* means.'

*His face*, Robert thought, *is bright and intelligent but his voice and manner are those of what he appears to be—a not very prosperous shop-keeper.*

'Do you find that your whisky is popular?'

Ross smiled again in his quick shy way. 'I couldn't say that.' He nodded towards the half-empty shelves. 'It's mainly groceries I sell. The shop's very run-down. My father owned it, but he was ill for a long time before he died. I worked in the shipping depart-ment of a warehouse further up the street.'

Robert looked at him sympathetically, no longer assessing a rival. 'Was Old Corrie your father's idea?'

Ross brightened. 'No, it's something I thought of myself. We've always sold whisky, but I feel it could be more popular than it is. The trouble is, advertising's very expensive.' He smiled ruefully. 'I have a feeling that poor Old Corrie won't go very far.' He took a bottle from a shelf and gave it an affectionate polish.

Robert left the shop no longer worried—but beset by a sense of time racing by. Ross might have ended up with the wrong product, but he undoubtedly had the correct instinct about the whisky.

Robert had liked the grocer, but as his carriage jolted slowly along Argyle Street manoeuvring around carts and buses, he was tormented by a vision of other men like Ross pondering the prob-lem of how to make whisky more popular. One could hit on his idea. It might be true, as he had once read, that no man ever works in isolation—that innovations were in the air and several men might become aware of them at the same time.

Until today, time—apart from his own impatience—had not seemed of desperate importance. Now he had the frightening thought that even time might be against him.

Along Garelochside the primroses faded. On the hills above,

bracken seemed to shoot out of the ground overnight, the tough stalks standing tall and feathery over the crowded bluebells.

Fergus followed the orderly patterns of life which his money and the fashion of the time ordained for him. In Glasgow he and Rita heard Madame Lattie sing, watched Mariovska dance, and made visits to the Botanical Gardens. Once or twice, on warm evenings, they changed into casual clothes and boated in the Clyde off Glasgow Green.

On weekends they left the city and joined the pheasant and the roe deer at Ardfern. After each of Hoey's visits thin gaps appeared on the library shelves and the books leaned over to hide the spaces. Fergus didn't notice. As the weeks passed without catastrophe his eyes had dimmed a little with content. From Robert there had been little talk of whisky and no talk at all of Mary Devine. Rita hadn't told him of her meeting with Mary. Gradually, Fergus came to believe that what he had feared might not happen. He was able, as in previous summers, to take pleasure in his roses. Sometimes he even scraped about in the earth himself, as if he might be about to take up gardening. It was Hoey who shattered his content.

The day was dry and fresh and started in a routine way with Fergus walking down from Park Place to Washington Street.

A new office building was going up in St. Vincent Street and the line of unfinished stonework suggested a castle against the morning sky. Fergus was reminded that he intended to investigate this booming new property market. His trouble was lack of time. Although Robert relieved him of day-to-day routine, he was still deeply involved in his business. Then, almost every day, there was a round of committee meetings, either to do with one of his charities or with his duties as a town councillor.

He crossed to the other pavement to avoid being drenched by two scavengers who were hosing the street. This reminded him that he wanted to see the town clerk about sending a watering cart up to Park Place to lay the dust. It hadn't rained for almost a week and the dry streets were becoming troublesome. If there was a breeze the windows had to be kept shut and, even then, the dust found a way through. Rita had complained about it the previous evening. There wasn't much good his being a bailie, she said, if he couldn't pull a string when needed.

He read the day's letters and went through the latest drawings reports from the branches.

'I see sales at the Corkcutters' Arms are down again,' he said. 'What's wrong with that place? Is it the manager?'

Robert shook his head. 'No. McNair's efficient and well liked. We've fallen badly behind. Most of the other places in the area have been renovated. The customers are going where the comfort is.' He turned again to what he had been doing, as if there was no more to be said.

Fergus frowned. Six months ago Robert had warned him about growing competition to the Corkcutters' Arms. He had rejected the idea, but obviously there was something wrong. 'All right, you can spend up to a hundred pounds on it,' he said sharply. 'But I'll expect a return for the money.'

'It might be slow to come,' Robert said. 'It's always easier to stay in front than to regain lost ground.'

Fergus gave a bad-tempered growl. 'Do any of the other places have gaslight yet?'

'I don't think so.'

'Then we must think about it.' He closed the door noisily as he went out.

He took a cab to the Bridge Police Station where he was due to preside over the morning court. The first three cases were remands to the Sheriff and the fourth and last was a regular. 'Good morning, Patrick,' Fergus said. The sight of the man's regretful smile above the heavy, fisherman's jersey always made him feel benign. Even here one could make friends.

'Good morning, your Honour,' Patrick said. 'And I'm sorry.'

Fergus turned to the clerk. 'What is it this time?'

'Breaking and entering,' the clerk said. 'Stealing four eggs and a bottle of milk. It was a dairy. And as usual he was drunk.'

Fergus turned to the shamefaced prisoner. 'Well, how do you plead? Guilty or not guilty?'

It was always the same. Patrick never admitted anything. 'I'm innocent, your Honour. I just happened to be passing and the stuff was lying right there in the street. I could hardly believe it.'

'Neither can I,' said Fergus, 'but we'll hear your story later.'

Two policemen went into the witness box followed by Patrick.

'Guilty,' Fergus said when he heard the evidence. 'Thirty days,' he added when reminded that the prisoner now had seventeen previous convictions for similar offences.

'God bless you and keep you, your Honour,' Patrick said generously before he was led away.

Fergus' next call was to the Music Hall at Glasgow Cross. An extension was being built to the dressing-room area to comply with new bylaws which he, as a town councillor, had been forced to help pass. His vote, on that occasion, had cost him almost six hundred pounds. If he'd voted the other way the regulation would have languished, but he'd preferred to pay for an expensive alteration rather than be accused of using his position to stymie progress because it would cost him money.

The Music Hall was part of Glasgow's low life. It was packed every evening by men having a roistering night on the town. When it was offered to Fergus on the death of the previous proprietor, he had gone to a Saturday night performance and been shocked by the bawdy songs and jokes. There was a stage, but instead of theatre seats, the customers sat at crowded tables where drinks were served. It had seemed to Fergus that every man in the place was drunk. The performers were all women and of a type Fergus immediately associated with immorality. The audience sang with the singers, and every so often the dancers left the stage and went squealing round the tables with their skirts in the air to roars of delight.

Fergus had sworn he would never own such an immoral place, but Robert had eventually persuaded him to buy on the basis that it would have been more immoral to reject the opportunity of such handsome profits. The overheads were low—the performers being third-raters and the waiters working for tips only—whereas the drinks were probably the most expensive in Glasgow. Nevertheless, Fergus had never attended another performance. If business took him to the Music Hall, it was always before it opened.

He knocked impatiently on the door with his stick until the watchman let him in. The place had a stale smell he didn't like. The dressing-rooms were usually deserted at this hour, but as he turned a corner a girl appeared at one of the doors. She was wearing a green wrap and had bright yellow hair. She looked about twenty years old. In one hand she held an unlit, pencil-thin cigar.

'Got a match, love?' She spoke with what Fergus thought was a cockney accent.

He said he didn't carry matches and continued on his way. The girl shouted something after him, but the clatter of his boots on the bare wooden floor drowned the words and he did not ask her to repeat them. He inspected the extension and returned the way he had come. The door where the girl had been standing was still open and he saw she was sitting on a stool facing the corridor.

''ere. Are you the boss?'

'Yes.'

'I *got* a match, see?' she said pugnaciously, blowing smoke at him.

Fergus pointed to a card on the wall. 'Smoking is forbidden in the dressing-rooms,' he said. 'It's dangerous.'

'Rules!' she said, as if they were made only to be broken. 'Come in an' 'ave a puff.'

As she held out her packet of cigars she allowed her wrap to fall open. Fergus backed away slightly.

'Cover yourself up, child,' he snapped. 'Who are you, anyway?'

She smirked and gave the wrap a token pull. 'The the-eatre bills say I'm "Liza the Lambeth Nightingale",' she said, bowing cheekily. 'An' wot abaht this audition?'

*Her hair makes her look more canary than nightingale*, Fergus thought, *and she seems to be dressed more for a medical examination than for singing*. The guilt of owning this place and of employing people like this child closed around him. 'I don't give auditions,' he said. 'If that's what you're here for, put your clothes on.'

She frowned. ''ere, are you Mr. 'oey?'

'No, I'm not Mr. Hoey, but I'm sure he'll be able to judge your voice without you being naked.'

'It's not wot I've 'eard.' She pulled her wrap open. 'My friend said 'e'd want to see me like this. She said Mr. 'oey auditions all the girls like this. You dahn't get booked, otherwise.' She said it uncomplainingly.

Fergus choked back his anger. 'Get dressed,' he said, 'and take a seat at one of the tables. I'll leave word for Mr. Hoey to see you there.'

'Ah, dahn't go spoilin' 'is little pleasure, guvnor. An' spoilin' my chances. I needs the work.'

85

'Get dressed!'

She sighed. 'You're the boss.' She tossed aside her wrap and began reaching for her clothes. As she saw Fergus' expression she winked. ' 'ere, guvnor. You shore you wouldn't like to audition me yehself? I sings somethin' lovely.'

There had been gossip at one time about Hoey and one of the Music Hall performers, Fergus remembered, as he left the building. He'd dismissed it as malicious, but he had clearly been too charitable. Obviously the man was using his position to get what he wanted from these girls. The cheeky, painted face of the Lambeth Nightingale appeared before him. *God help the poor child and others like her,* he thought, *if she's dependent for engagements on satisfying the lusts of Tom Hoey and his kind.*

The incident stayed with him for hours, souring everything he did. It was forgotten only in the excitement produced by a meeting he had in the smoke room of his club early in the evening. The encounter was with Sir James Spence, stock and share broker, chairman of Fergus' political party association and, for the last year, Lord Provost of Glasgow. In the delicate business of working for a title it was never possible to be completely certain where the genuine lines of communication lay. There were men in the clubs of Glasgow who indicated slyly that they could arrange for titles to be conferred and even named the price. Fergus regarded them as rogues and avoided them. He knew it couldn't be accomplished as blatantly as that. The lines of intrigue and power certainly ran through the clubs and the political parties, but the men who in the end made firm and authoritative recommendations to the Prime Minister could never be positively identified. One could only go by what one heard, what one half-heard. Fergus believed Sir James Spence to be one of these men of shadowy influence. And he knew he had Sir James' goodwill. The old man handled his investments and almost invariably one supported the other's proposals at Corporation meetings.

Fergus saw the bent figure stir a little in a cavernous armchair. It beckoned to him. 'I was hoping you might look in, King. Join me in a glass of something.'

'I don't like being mysterious,' Sir James said after ten minutes of stock market talk, 'but I'd like to be sure you'll be in Glasgow and available on the day of the Queen's visit.'

Fergus' heart gave a jump. He was forever hopeful of some sign from Sir James. Was this one? And if so, a sign of what?

'Without a doubt. Mrs. King will see to that. She mentions it every day. We're both looking forward to meeting Her Majesty. It's one of the few rewards we get for public service.'

'There certainly aren't many,' Sir James agreed.

'Exactly. That's why I don't think it's too vain of us to enjoy, with humility, of course, whatever recognition we are offered.' Fergus had spoken precisely. It wasn't often the opportunity came for him to underline so delicately the fact that his ambitions were still alive. For a moment he wondered if he had been too pointed. Discretion was so important, especially with a man as circumspect as Sir James. Nevertheless, the opening had been there, unless his imagination was leading him astray.

'Anyway, you've put my mind at ease.'

This was even more tantalizing. 'Is there some way I can be of assistance, Sir James?'

Sir James' thin white fingers clasped his empty glass and turned it round and round on the table. He bent over it thoughtfully. 'My dear King! I am sounding mysterious, I know. And I didn't mean to. There is something in the wind, of course, but I daren't come out with it yet. You'll know about it in good time, I promise you that.'

Fergus' mind somersaulted. It had to do with the Queen and Sir James wanted to be sure he would be present. Had it to do with his title? Did the Queen want to see him? Suddenly, he realized that he knew nothing of the mechanics of the Honours System. Did the Queen make knights of men she had never seen? Perhaps she liked a discreet meeting first so that she could fit the man to the recommendation. Or—his pulse raced—perhaps she was going to knight him on the spot. He knew that wasn't customary. There was usually a published list followed by a formal investiture at Buckingham Palace. But a spontaneous ceremony was not an impossibility. They had occurred before.

To try to draw Sir James further would have been a mistake. Fergus crushed down his throbbing curiosity and spoke of something else. He was glad when the old man said he would have to leave him to attend a meeting in a room upstairs. Ordinary conversation had temporarily lost all savour. After the enthralling possibility planted in his mind, nothing else seemed worth talking about. He rose before anyone else could join him, collected his coat, and told his coachman to take him to the offices of the *Glasgow Herald*. The public part of the building was closed for the night but the journalists were still there producing the next issue. Fergus asked if he might examine the files. He explained that he was interested in a visit Queen Victoria had made to Glasgow with Prince Albert about the year 1850. An arch had been built on Jamaica Bridge for the occasion, he remembered. The appropriate issue of the newspaper was soon found for him. It was dated August 15, 1849. Fergus read the report of the royal visit with the thrilled satisfaction of the researcher who's found what he's looking for. He had been right. *Here, in this very city, this reigning Queen had conferred an impromptu knighthood.* The Royal Yacht *Fairy* had sailed to Glasgow on August 14 after anchoring overnight off Row, within sight of his own country house! The Lord Provost of Glasgow had gone on board to present a loyal address to the Queen. Her Majesty had called for a sword. One of her entourage, Colonel Gordon, had given her his, and the Lord Provost had been dubbed on the deck of the yacht in view of thousands of his fellow citizens lining the quayside.

The night air of summer lay softly on the city when Fergus came out of the *Herald* offices and stood looking benignly on the passing people. The one glass of wine he had taken with Sir James might have been several, so euphoric did he feel. The ladies wore airy summer dresses and bright hats. Their parasols were of gay colours. Many of the men were in pyjama-stripe trousers and yellow or pink waistcoats. Some even carried their hats. Normally Fergus did not approve of such informality in the Glasgow male, but his spirits were so buoyant tonight that he regarded them with kindly tolerance.

At this time in the evening, when the shops and offices had closed and the crowds had diminished, Glasgow became a different place. *On such a night as this*, Fergus thought, *a man should walk a little in the city where he lived*. He had left papers on his office desk which he would need for an early meeting. The place would be closed now, but he had his own key. He sent his coach home and, stick swinging, set off down Buchanan Street. He enjoyed every step of his walk until he entered Washington Street. On a mellow summer night like this the ragged outcasts had emerged from their warrens and were lying blatantly against grey walls or lurking in close mouths. The high warehouse buildings shut out the sun, creating grey pools of shadow. Later, when darkness came, sailors making their way back to the docks would be waylaid here and robbed or lured into foul closes by women. Even before darkness, in an hour or so when the light had failed, mist and dampness would start creeping up the street from the river. The wretches now lying about with insolence or veiled menace in their eyes would become so rampant in their lawlessness that this street, housing the head-quarters of his business, would be forbidden territory to Fergus. In twenty-five years he had seen the area degenerate. In a vague way, he was looking for new premises, but the sense of urgency engendered by his infrequent night visits usually evaporated next morning when he saw the rich tobacco warehousemen who were his neighbours and read the respected Glasgow names painted on the heavy gates and doors.

He was angry to find that the bar and padlock was not on the office door. He turned large keys in two locks and went in. Because of the barricaded windows it was dark.

As he approached his office door, fumbling along the wall in dusty-smelling blackness, he saw a line of light under another door. When he stopped he heard voices and then a laugh. He knew Robert sometimes worked late—but always alone. Another man would have thought of burglars. The sense of doom Fergus took with him everywhere told him this was trouble of a worse kind. He could not even guess what it was, but he was tempted to turn and leave it hidden. After a few moments of indecision he tiptoed forward and stood listening to the voices. Then, gripping the handle, he threw the door open.

Hoey and the Lambeth Nightingale were sprawled face to face in an armchair. Fergus stared. There was a frantic rustling and rearranging of clothes before Hoey let out a drunken groan of despair and buried his face in the feathers of the Nightingale's hat. There was a bottle of gin and two glasses on the desk, and the girl's hair hung down from under her hat like crepe streamers. The horror of the scene was heightened for Fergus by the hat. That it was still on the girl's head suggested an attitude to depravity so casual that his mind could not grasp it. He thought of his club and of his forthcoming meeting with the Queen. Could anyone with a man like Hoey in the family mix with decent people?

On the river, a ship's siren wailed and the sound contained all of Fergus' sorrow.

'Yer might 'ave knocked, guvnor,' the Nightingale said, recovering her cheeky humour.

Fergus ignored her. For Hoey he felt a furious hatred. 'Look at me, man! Do you hear?' He waved his stick at the girl. 'Get out of that seat till I see him.'

As the girl moved away Hoey straightened enough in the armchair to reach shakily for the gin bottle.

'Never mind that.' Fergus swiped at the bottle with his cane. It fell from Hoey's hand and smashed on the floor.

'Let me have a look at you. Let me see your face.' He could not have explained what he meant by the words, but somehow they seemed to express his loathing. Hoey stared dumbly at the floor.

'He's going to be a father next month,' Fergus said to the girl as if she was an independent witness to Hoey's shame. But the Nightingale was preoccupied with her straggling hair. 'Is there a mirror 'ere?' she asked.

Hoey's mouth opened. 'I must have had too much to drink,' he said.

The Nightingale hooted.

'Get back to your work,' Hoey snarled.

The mention of work seemed to remind her of her position and, with her hair still hanging loose, she left.

'I never forget the business,' Hoey pointed out hopefully. 'I've been foolish, but I haven't been neglecting it.'

'I'm not thinking about business,' Fergus almost sobbed. 'What about Gwen?'

Hoey looked puzzled. 'Gwen? But she doesn't know, does she?'

Fergus raised his stick and brought it down hard on Hoey's arm. Hoey howled and jumped from the chair. 'Get out!' Fergus roared. 'Before I kill you.'

The moment he was alone he felt the room must be cleansed. It reeked of cheap scent and spilled gin. He crunched through broken glass and struggled to open the window. It was jammed. He turned away, remembering that in any case the fortified shutters would be up. Foulness outside, foulness inside.

He slumped miserably into the armchair until, remembering its recent use, he rose from it with a shudder.

# 6

James had begged to be allowed to spend the school holidays with his grandmother at Row. This meant that he lived in the big house only when Fergus and Rita came down from Glasgow. Most of the time he stayed with Mrs. Veitch at her cottage in the grounds. He preferred it to Ardfern, for the low ceilings and leaded windows suggesting adventure and even mystery. His grandmother would have been surprised to know that her cosy cottage harboured pirates and smugglers. As the wind from the Gareloch rattled at the small windows, streaming rain down them until the only view was of water, James could even turn the house into a boat sailing him towards an island of adventure.

This morning he had been pacing out distances around the house for a treasure map he was drawing in blood-coloured ink. As he came thoughfully into the house, Mrs. Veitch's voice rang out. 'James!' She was at the parlour door.

He knew that tone of voice but could not think what he was doing wrong.

'You've forgotten something, James, have you not?' She was looking down significantly at the bristly brown doormat over which he'd walked without even a token skliff of his boots.

He gave an abashed grin and went back to the doormat. 'Sorry, Grandmother.'

'That's better,' she said as he wiped his boots vigorously. 'I'll have you properly house-trained before the summer's over.' Her voice rose. 'All right, James, that will do. There's no need to rub the mat away.'

A maid came out of one of the rooms carrying a pail. She looked harassed and her hands and arms were black. 'That's the fire cleaned and set at last,' she said. 'But the room'll have to be dusted from one end to the other. The ash from that new coal's terrible.'

'And what about stones?' Mrs. Veitch glanced into the pail. 'Remember to keep them, Millie. Don't throw them away.'

Any stones found among the cinders were kept and put in a large, red-clay flowerpot which stood at the back door. Each time the coalman came, Mrs. Veitch personally presented him with the stones accumulated since his last delivery. 'It's coal I'm paying you for, Mr. Todd,' she would tell him as she thrust the flowerpot and its incombustible contents into his black hands. 'I can get all the stones I want in the garden.'

Usually Mrs. Veitch also inspected the set fires before a light was put to them to see that Millie wasn't using too many sticks. 'Tightly rolled paper is almost as good as sticks, and a lot cheaper,' she told all her maids. It was an economy she had been practising since the early days of her marriage, when money had been scarce.

But today her reaction to the neglected doormat and the stones from the fire had been automatic. This morning she was expecting a visitor. The previous day she'd received a letter from Robert saying he was coming to see her. This in itself had been a surprise, but the letter's tone was mystifying. Some of the phrases came back to her now. *A matter most personal and confidential on which I would value your opinion.* Although Mrs. Veitch frequently gave her opinion, she could not remember the last time she had actually been asked for it. The last part of Robert's letter had set her blood tingling. *I would like this visit to be a secret between us. It would be best if James did not see me.*

How to prevent James from seeing his brother had kept Mrs. Veitch awake for more than an hour the previous night. She could have sent him with the maid on some errand to the village store, but this would have kept him out of the house for a half hour at most. Eventually, McEwan, the coachman, had come to mind. He was laid up with rheumatism. She could send the boy to see him with some broth and tell him to keep the man company for an hour. It was the sort of thing Fergus might not approve of, but he would never know. Having made up her mind, the thought of Fergus' possible annoyance didn't prevent Mrs. Veitch from falling into a sound sleep.

Robert had said he would be arriving at one o'clock, wouldn't want lunch, and hoped his visit wouldn't disturb the household routine. At twelve fifteen Millie served Mrs. Veitch and James with soup, followed by mince and doughballs.

'That soup was excellent,' Mrs. Veitch said when they'd finished. 'There's nothing as nourishing as soup. A bowl of it would do poor McEwan the world of good. Goodness knows what he eats, living up there on his own. You could take it to him, James. I'll get Millie to put some in a milk can. Would you like to do that? It would be a good deed.'

The cab Robert had hired after leaving the train at Helensburgh bumped along the shore road to Row.

He lowered the window on its leather strap. Grey waves rippled the Firth and the entrance to the Gareloch, running in white over the weed-strewn rocks. The wind was fresh from the mountains, and already on the nearer slopes there was a suggestion of the purple haze that would spread as the heather opened.

Robert wondered what Fergus would say if someone told him his son was taking a course of instruction designed to lead him into the Catholic Church. He knew now he would not be converted if he took instructions until he was seventy. But at the outset he had been nervous. He'd heard so much of the wiles of the clergy that he'd been on guard lest he be lured into belief despite himself—by what means he could not think, but the spell of religious intolerance was strong and spawned many fantasies.

The course was almost completed and soon he would have to give Father Campbell his decision—have to tell him he hadn't found faith. Then, he and Mary could formally ask for a dispensation for a mixed marriage. At the thought anxiety stabbed him.

His recent discovery of Old Corrie—the thought of all the other Old Corries that might exist—had given everything new significance. His love for Mary was undimmed, but recently, almost to his horror, it had become tinged with a sharper awareness of reality. What sort of life would they have? Mary's parents would be at the least disapproving. His would be distraught and obstructive. Fergus would withhold the money he would normally have made available for the purchase of a suitable house. On his marriage Robert would have received a greatly increased salary and perhaps a share of the business and its profits. His wife would have been

93

welcomed into the family and into his circle of friends. Now, none of this would happen. They would be outcasts, and poor ones at that. Was he being fair to Mary? It was a question that had begun to torture him. He needed support, but where could he get it? Certainly not at home. Among his friends he could not think of one he could confide in. It was in this mood that he had remembered his grandmother. As a child he had been close to her. Often he'd spent holidays with her as James was now. When he'd misbehaved she had shielded him from Fergus' disapproval whenever she could, cleaning muddied clothes and even, on one occasion, disposing of the incriminating pieces when he had broken a valuable ornament. Perhaps now she could look at the problem dispassionately and give advice untarnished by Fergus' wild fear of scandal.

Gulls sped screaming across the water in pursuit of a steamer heading for the piers of the Gareloch. Scraps from the galley were dumped from portholes and usually some among the passengers would throw bread to the snapping beaks. Robert had done it often himself. Such carefree afternoons seemed distant now, perhaps incapable of recapture. The wind caught at the water churned by the steamer's paddle and spread it about in what looked like a cascade of tears.

Mrs. Veitch had a pot of tea and a plate of gingersnaps waiting for him in front of the parlour fire.

'McEwan isn't well and I sent James to visit him with some broth,' she said. 'He'll be gone for an hour, anyway.' It was an invitation to Robert to explain.

As he told her his story, she grimaced in surprise and made various noises which he couldn't interpret, but she did not interrupt. When he reached the part about taking instruction in Catholic doctrine she shook her head in silent disbelief, then rested it on her hand with her eyes shut.

'Robert, Robert,' she said when at last he had finished. 'You have been very unwise. And the poor girl! She sounds a sweet child.'

'I know, Grandmother. I know. But what are we going to do? We're in love. Does anything else really matter? That's what I want to know.'

'Of *course* other things matter, dear. Many things. You mustn't marry this girl. For her sake as much as your own.' The old woman gave her verdict quietly but with utter conviction.

94

Robert stared miserably into the fire. 'Sometimes, recently, that's what I've thought myself.' The confession—with the betrayal of Mary he knew it held—appalled him. 'I make up my mind that I must talk to Mary and then, as soon as I see her again, I can't imagine ever being without her. I can't believe I'm not deeply in love with her.'

'Robert, what matters is whether you're happy or not. Are you happy? Do you think Mary is happy?'

'We're happy and yet, deep down, we're uneasy and even afraid.' He could not bring himself to admit the full depth of his anxiety, but the old woman wasn't deceived.

'Then it hardly matters whether you're in love or not. Love is only worthwhile if it brings happiness. It doesn't always. Often it makes people miserable.'

'But what I keep clinging to is that once Mary and I were married, things might change. Father might accept the fact. We might all come to see this difference in religion in a lesser light.'

Mrs. Veitch shook her head at the idea of Fergus ever accepting such a betrayal. 'What if your differences grew? What if the difference in religion became a wedge between you? There would be plenty of people to keep tapping it deeper, you know—your father, the priests, maybe even some of your friends.'

She tried to get him to take a gingersnap, but he shook his head. 'You used to like dipping them in your tea,' she said, reminiscing. 'I used to have to scold you for that.'

'If only we could stop worrying about other people and think only of ourselves.'

'You'll never be able to do that, Robert. Your mother and father are part of you. And what about your children, when they arrived?' She stopped as if about to try him again with the biscuits. 'Have you been able to decide honestly what you think of Mary's religion?'

'It's all mumbo-jumbo to me,' he said despondently, 'although I'd never say that to Mary. I don't know how she can believe in it. She's an intelligent girl. Of course'—he shook his head as if to indicate that there were some things you could never know—'I don't know that she really does believe it all. What I do know is that she would never desert it.'

'Would you like to see your children indoctrinated with this mumbo-jumbo, as you call it?'

'No.'

'Then what about this promise you say you would have to make —that they would be brought up as Catholics? If you kept it, you'd eventually be unhappy. If you broke it Mary would eventually be unhappy. We're all trapped by our upbringing, Robert. Society is against you and Mary, and that's the truth.'

'Do you think Father would penalize me financially?'

'I'm sure he would. Finance is what your father understands best. Besides, it would be the only revenge he could take.' She made it sound inevitable, even natural. 'You wouldn't be very happy without money. You've always been used to it.'

It was difficult for him to thank her when he left. She had not told him what he had wanted to hear. He had wanted to be told that above all he should follow his heart without consideration of material things.

When he had waved good-bye he slumped bitterly into a corner of the hired cab. After the cosiness of his grandmother's parlour it was shabby and smelled of old pipe-smoke and damp. The upholstery was marked as if the roof leaked. The wind had lessened but the silver grey of the sea had turned a depressing charcoal. Usually, some boat moved, but for the first time Robert could remember the sea was empty. Across the emptiness sea-gulls complained to each other as they waited hungrily for another steamer. He leaned closer to the window as the carriage passed a cove where he had played as a boy. Sea pinks speckled the tough grass and the ribs of a half-buried wreck stuck out of the shingle, the timbers bleached and encrusted with marine life. It had been there since his first visit, but every year another bit broke off and was carried away. Today the carcass seemed more desolate than ever.

In the room above the stable James sat with McEwan.

'I'm worried that your father will be annoyed about the garden,' McEwan said. 'This rheumatism's kept me right out it. I've not been able to do what I should. I darena go out if it's wet or I'll be in bed for a week. The vegetables are being neglected something terrible. And the paths.'

James had been too busy rummaging in a toolbox at the side of the bed to follow McEwan's worries. But he had heard the garden mentioned. 'When are we going to have another bonfire?' James would have grown nothing else.

'As soon as I get out of here,' McEwan assured him. 'But watch you don't cut yourself on those tools. They're awful sharp.'

'Did you have to go to the university, McEwan?'

'Nane the fear.' McEwan smiled. 'Ah just missed it, somehow.'

'I wish I could miss it.'

'It'll do you nought but good.'

'Father says I've to go.'

'Then you'll go,' McEwan said with conviction. 'Nothing surer.'

'But why must I?'

'Oh, I suppose because you've got a position to keep up, Mr. James.' He put out a cautionary hand. 'Ye'll have the fingers off yourself in that box, then what will your father say to me?'

'Didn't you have a position to keep up?'

'Aye. I had a position to keep up as well,' McEwan said thoughtfully, 'but it didn't require a university education.' He looked about contentedly. 'I havena fared too badly. My mother always worried that I wouldn't get on, but she need not have feared. This is a cosy wee place I have. The roof's good. The fire draws well and there's plenty of wood to feed it. I like the smell of the horse underneath and the rustle of the straw. I can soothe her through the floorboards when she gets restless on a wild night. And in her way, she's company for me.'

A groan escaped him as he moved in his hard chair. 'It's been a healthy life, too, till I got this touch of rheumatics. And not what you could say hard, either. When the family's not here I do a bit of gardening. There's nothing wrong with that, Mr. James. It was like that for me before your father bought Ardfern, and he was good enough to continue it that way. Dear knows where I'd be if he hadna kept me on.' He groaned all the way to the window. 'That's why I'm worried about the vegetables and the weeds,' he said, straining to see.

'People who don't have to go to the university are lucky,' James said.

Father Campbell put away his breviary, crossed himself, and rose from where he had been kneeling as Mary came into the Cathedral.

They met at a small table where rosaries, scapulars, and medals commemorating various saints were laid out for sale, each bearing a price ticket so the money could be dropped into a wooden box.

His daily reading of the divine office always filled Father Campbell with a sense of insufficiency, of responsibility carelessly or inadequately carried. The sight of Mary reminded him of one of his worries.

He put a hand on her elbow. 'If you have a moment, child, I'd like to speak to you.'

As he walked down the side aisle with her he was guiltily aware that he had stepped between her and God. She had come to pray, brought, for all he knew, by some urgent need. She was paler than he remembered and looked more delicate. He smiled reassuringly. 'I'm not going to keep you but it will be more private in the vestry.' He opened the door and bent his knee to the altar before following her into the room. Around the walls hung the variety of priestly vestments required by the liturgical calendar.

'I've been worried about you, Mary,' he said. 'And about your father and mother. I'm afraid I must break the promise I made not to tell them of your association with Robert King. It was wrong of me to make such a promise.'

Her look was imploring. 'Please, Father, not yet. Give us a little more time.'

'I feel responsible for you, Mary. And I don't mean only in a spiritual way. It isn't right that a young girl should have the feelings you have for Robert without her mother being aware of it. You could come to harm. You should be meeting this young man only in your father's house, in his father's house, or in the company of your friends. Not alone as you're doing now. It is a sin, Mary, even to place yourself in the way of temptation. And it's improper of me, to say the least, to allow this situation to continue without making your people aware of it.'

For a terrible moment she wondered if he knew about the flat. Had she been seen? His talk of sin filled her with panic. She had told Robert she didn't feel she had committed any wrong. That was what she believed deeply when she was in his arms. But when she was alone her conscience, especially recently, had begun to nag her. Did love really sanctify everything? Or was that only what she wanted to believe? Was it her way of shrouding what was in fact a sin?

She did not know the answer to that but deliberately she embarked on what she knew without doubt to be a sin. 'We've committed no impropriety, Father. I swear to you. Robert is a kind and gentle young man.' At least the last was true.

He wished he could speak to her with more human knowledge. Usually when he gave advice he could speak out of his own weakness. He knew about greed, laziness, and lying. Even lust came to him sometimes. But he had never experienced the love that exists between men and women. Celibacy had imposed its strains, although he had no doubt that in the end it had saved him much turmoil and perhaps even unhappiness. But it had left a great gap in his understanding. He tried to imagine what life would be like if he lost God. He didn't think it would be worth living. Perhaps the void would be as great for Mary if she had to lose Robert. And yet one day soon he knew that he would have to counsel her that it would be best if she did not see Robert again. The reports from Mr. Martin weren't good. *Intelligent but uninterested.* Father Campbell had heard it all before. He did not look forward to what soon must come. Clearly the young man could not in conscience embrace the faith. Therefore, only if Mary refused to give him up, only if she was ready to marry him outside the Church, would he feel justified in recommending that the bishop grant a dispensation for a mixed marriage as the only way of saving her.

From what he knew of this girl she would not do that—he prayed she would not. Therefore, she would lose the man she loved. He felt the same sense of futile sadness that came to him when he sat at bedsides waiting for people to die.

With an effort he recalled her last words. There was an innocence in them that he found touching, almost unbelievable. He had to remind himself that innocence *did* still exist, difficult though it sometimes was to believe when you had spent the time he had in the confessional boxes of this slum parish, listening to the voices of lost innocence.

'Dear child, you are in danger. And because you cannot realize it the danger is greater.'

'I promise you, Father, we are doing no wrong,' she said firmly. 'I have lived partly away from home since beginning to train as a nurse. My parents have full trust in me.'

'I have full trust in you, too, Mary, but we're all weak. In your work as a nurse you must see much of human weakness, but you don't see it as I do. Almost every week someone comes to me with some new tragedy or heartbreak.'

'Please let Robert finish his instructions before you say anything, Father Campbell. If only I could go to my parents and tell them he wants to become a Catholic, everything would be different.'

The vestments behind the priest were red, gold, and green. Each colour stood out clear and sharp, as if the garments were new. Against them he looked shabby, colourless, and shaggy; his soutane threadbare, his black beard unkempt. His expression was sombre.

'And do you think that will be a likely outcome of his instructions? Has he said anything to give you that hope?'

'Not exactly, Father.'

'Do you mean not exactly, or not at all?'

She saw his expression was sympathetic and tried to play on it. 'We go over the *Catechism* together and he tells me what Mr. Martin talks about.'

'Mr. Martin tells me Robert has an excellent memory and a quick mind. I'm sure he could pass any examination we gave him. Unfortunately, that isn't our object. This is not the Civil Service. We don't hold entrance tests. Could you say you've noticed any significant change in Robert?'

She shook her head, unable to carry the pretence further.

'Has he asked you what it feels like to confess your sins or how you feel after taking the body of our Blessed Lord into your mouth at Holy Communion? Sometimes these are signs.'

The more he said, the less hope she felt. 'I don't think he has, Father.'

'All we can do is pray that somewhere a spark is taking hold.'

'I do pray, Father. That's why I came into the church.'

'Then I will keep you no longer, Mary.'

'No. Please.' Although he had not moved she raised her hand to stop him. She knew that if she let him go now he would carry out his intention of telling her parents. He had evaded her plea that Robert be allowed to finish his instructions.

'Robert has only another month or so of instructions to take,' she said desperately. 'We've known each other for eight or nine months. We'll surely come to no harm in a few more weeks.'

Father Campbell sometimes felt he could be talked into anything. He could never uphold the law like some priests. He would lay it down and then allow himself to be swayed. Pity, which he tried to control, was the fatal flaw in his ministry. It led him into weakness when God's will—and perhaps the safety of an immortal soul, perhaps the soul of this poor child—required strength. He said a quick prayer but God did not seem to hear.

'All right, Mary,' he said. 'I am failing in my duty, but I'll do as you ask.'

He opened the door for her. 'God take care of you. I already include you in my prayers, but I will try to say a mass for your safety.'

She felt tears sting her eyes. Her voice faltered. 'Please pray for Robert, too.'

'I already do.'

She walked slowly up the church under the gilt-framed Stations of the Cross, past the empty confessional boxes, their doors standing open and their curtains drawn. The shadows and the warm, well-known waxen smells of the place were comforting. If only this were the world—if there were no outside. An old man sat on one of the benches, huddled in rags and clutching a dirty brown paper parcel. His eyes were closed, but whether he was praying or sleeping only God knew. She went past the Sacred Heart stand where red candles burned. Farther on there was another stand, with a basket containing blue candles beside it. These were for prayers to Our Lady, the Mother of God. Catholic doctrine taught that a prayer to the Virgin Mary could sometimes be as efficacious as one offered direct to God. Our Lady could not answer prayers herself, but she could intercede with her Divine Son to have them answered. Who better to plead with a son than His mother?

Mary had never seen the stand to Our Lady look more desolate. Not a single candle burned on it. She dropped a coin into the box, lifted a blue candle from the basket, and lit it at the Sacred Heart stand. Sheltering the flame with her cupped hand, she returned and inserted the candle into one of the wax-encrusted holders. Then she knelt on the wooden step in front of it and began to pray with a wild, feverish intensity. Robert, in an early show of interest that had soon diminished, had asked her what the point was in burning candles.

She had replied to what she knew he was thinking, explaining that it wasn't a question of praying to candles, as it might seem. The candlelight was a symbol of faith burning bright and the lingering flame a reminder that prayer lives on after the words have stopped. On a more commonplace level, the flame was an aid to concentration.

The wick burned cheerfully above her head. The brass of the stand gleamed now in a homely way with reflected warmth. She looked up and felt comforted at having brought a spot of light into a dark and neglected corner of the church.

She had offered her prayers for her Special Intention, so emblazoned now on her mind with constant repetition that she no longer felt a need to formulate it. Of course, the greatest prayer of all, the one that cut out all self-interest, that could be said only in total humility, had only four words. Four terrible words. To Mary they always sounded more sentence than prayer. *It is a prayer*, she thought, *only for saints or hypocrites*. With a tremendous effort, striving desperately to submit, she said it, addressing herself directly to God: *Thy will be done*.

Even as she said the words, she knew she didn't mean them. It wasn't His will she wanted. It was her own.

Behind her, the ragged old man had slept enough, or completed his prayers. He opened the church door and went away. As the door slowly swung shut a draught from the street blew across the church. The candle Mary had lit went out. She began to cry.

Rita's secret had become too heavy for her. She put down the sampler she was embroidering. It was a decisive movement but after making it she hesitated.

'Fergus, dear,' she began, 'I should have told you sooner, I suppose, but I knew you would worry,' and then she stopped, looking at him uncertainly across the shadows of the room.

He had been trying to make up his mind about a figurine he had found on a junk shop shelf and bought for five shillings. He was almost certain it was an eighteenth-century Chelsea-Derby piece, and if he was right it was worth about twenty pounds. It had the characteristic marks like thumbprints where the base had been supported in the kiln, but he couldn't be sure. He had sat all evening turning it over in his hands, shutting his eyes and fingering it like a blind man, while the late August sun had left the room, then the street, and finally the sky, and a servant had come in and lit the lamps.

At Rita's words his head moved off the antimacassar in alarm. Where another man would have waited calmly, expecting some trivial revelation, Fergus was perennially ready for calamity. His hand disappeared into his beard as if he was easing his collar.

'What's happened now?' His mind raced on, reviewing the whole range of likely misfortunes.

'Well, you remember about a month ago I went with Gwen to look for a dress I could wear when we meet the Queen?'

'Yes.' He began to feel relief. She had paid more for it than was sensible and had been afraid to tell him.

'In the afternoon, on our way home, we were both tired and we went into a little place in Sauchiehall Street to rest and have some tea.'

She had passed his escape route. It *was* something serious after all. 'For heaven's sake, Rita, come to the point.'

'I met Mary Devine,' she said, stung to directness. 'The girl Robert knows. They were having tea together.'

His gesture of anger almost knocked the figurine from the table where he had placed it. He either didn't notice or didn't care. 'So he's still defying me. And I thought the young fool had seen sense.'

'Don't be too upset, dear.'

'I suppose I've been foolishly optimistic. I'd hoped that after months of not hearing that name, I'd never hear it again. He hasn't been seen about with her. I'd have been told. There are people who would enjoy telling me.'

Rita waited for him to remember her part in this. When he did, he looked at her severely. 'You should have let me know at once.'

'Yes, dear, I should have.'

'It's disturbing to think you and Gwen conspired behind my back to shield them.' He fluffed his beard up and blew worriedly into it.

She sank back in the chair and looked at him limply. 'Fergus, there was no question of a conspiracy. Certainly not to shield Robert and the girl from you. If anything, I wanted to shield you from them. After all, what can you do about it except hope that it goes no further?'

She was encouraged by his silence. 'If I may be quite honest, I'm glad I met the girl.'

Fergus twisted his face and waved his hands about in disgust, as if such an attitude was beyond him.

'Well, I am. At least we know now what sort of girl she is. As well as her religion, I was worried that she might also turn out to be a . . . hussy. Young men are so foolish, so easily led astray.'

'How can you be sure she isn't a hussy?' he asked bitterly. 'Are you confident you would know one? They don't all have dyed hair and painted faces, you know.' He seemed contemptuous of her unworldliness, his anger turning it from what was only proper in a respectable woman into a failing.

Rita ignored the scathing tone. She would say now what she had felt for weeks. 'There's nothing wrong with this girl, Fergus. I found myself liking her. If we had met her without knowing her religion, I'm certain we would have been pleased with her.' She leaned forward, her face showing the concern and doubt that had been with her since the day they'd all chatted cheerfully over Miss Frame's stained tablecloth. 'Are you quite sure, dear, that we're reacting to this as we should? Should we be thinking of social conventions or should we be thinking above all of our son's happiness?' She hesitated. 'It was very obvious they were in love. Gwen saw it, too. It was only necessary to see the look in their eyes when—'

He jumped to his feet. 'Oh, for God's sake, Rita, spare me the melodramatic details.' He felt forsaken. The issue had been a clear-cut one of religious unsuitability, and here was Rita complicating it all in the most shameless way by talking of love and happiness. He paced angrily about, kicking a footstool out of his path to let her see what she had done to him. 'I don't give a damn what kind of look they had in their eyes.'

'I was only—'

'It's what's going on in their heads that worries me. What can the boy's intentions be except marriage? To my knowledge he's known this girl for at least six months. If she's as respectable as you say . . . marriage must enter into it.'

'And what happens if . . . if we do have to face that?'

'I'll see he regrets it as much as we do,' Fergus said fiercely.

She clenched her hands. They were a *happy* family. 'Couldn't you speak to him again? In a gentle way. We may have antagonized him last time. After all, he is a man. He probably feels he has the right to suit himself.'

'He is a man. Quite old enough to know that we all have obligations to others. He expects me to be fair and generous with him, and I have been. Very well, he must consider my position. But apart from that, even if I didn't care what he did, it would be tragic if he married a Catholic. It never works. He would be unhappy and so would the unfortunate girl.'

Rita could feel her head beginning to throb. They didn't often have arguments, but she never came out of them unhurt. 'If you aren't going to speak to him, what are you going to do?'

'Nothing,' Fergus said grimly as he sat down and lifted the figurine more roughly than could have been good for it. 'Eventually, if he wants to get married, he'll have to come to me. I'll be ready for him. Don't worry about that. We'll see then how much he loves her.'

Fergus slept badly and rose next morning heavy-eyed and bad-tempered. He complained that the porridge was lumpy and left the breakfast table in half his usual time.

Rita attempted to return to the unhappy topic of the night before, but her efforts to soothe him resulted only in glares and mutterings from behind his newspaper.

'We're worrying about something that may never happen,' she said as she helped him on with his coat and brushed his hat.

He kissed her with an accusing look and went out.

The sky was clear and already the sun had heat in it. The city's spires and chimneys stood solid and seemingly timeless in the soft light, but for once they failed to give Fergus the usual sense of a community well based on solid endeavour.

For a few moments he stood on the front steps feeling the soft touch of late summer on his face. The grassy slope on the other side of the street had been recently cut and he could smell its freshness. In the shade under the cherry trees dew still lay in glittering circles. Away across the slated rooftops the great river slid tranquilly past its green banks and from the dark industrial shapes which depended on it plumes of smoke rose in many colours.

He breathed deeply. Up here on his select hill the air was still clean and enticing. How many more mornings like this before autumn began to spread its chill? He dismissed his carriage and started to walk.

The street was dusty and he made a note to have a watering cart sent up before Rita started complaining again about not being able to open the windows.

As he went past the big grey houses two or three frock-coated neighbours on their way out to waiting carriages greeted him cheerfully. He raised his cane in sombre reply. Sauchiehall Street was busy with people on their way to work, or in from the spreading West End for a morning's shopping. Young men with frothing pails of soapy water and long brushes whistled while they washed shop windows.

On a day like this everything was mellowed. The stone, some of it already darkened by industrial grime, seemed less hard and the buildings less high. Fergus even imagined the traffic noises to be subdued. The shop windows were well stocked and attractively dressed. He found the signs of prosperity pleasing. Slowly his depressed resentment began to lessen.

As he turned into West Nile Street he saw Green, the antiquarian bookseller, sitting in the sunny doorway of his shop reading the *Herald*. They exchanged a few words and then, with a curious chill, Fergus moved closer to the window, peering in at the display.

Green, seeing his attention caught, came to stand beside him. 'I have some very good things just now,' he said with an enticing smile. Fergus, he knew, could usually be snared by the sight of something rare.

'So I see.' Fergus almost hissed the words. His mind had gone panicking back to the library at Ardfern. He was remembering an odd feeling that had come to him there of something being not quite right. It had been annoying, because he had been unable at the time to pinpoint the source of his unease.

'Is there anything special that catches your eye, Mr. King?'

Fergus was beset by a sense of impending pain. 'That's a handsome binding on Webb's book on stained glass.' He felt breathless and hoped his voice did not betray the agitation of his racing mind. 'And it's a long time since I've seen a volume of Long's *Letters*.'

He knew now what had disturbed him in the library. He could

visualize the books leaning over slightly, robbed of their companions. The shelves had been plundered! Suddenly he saw Hoey alone in the library hastily stuffing something into his pocket. A shudder went through him.

'You'll never see such fine specimens again,' Green said proudly. 'I bought them in specially for an old customer. Unfortunately he's been ill for some time. I decided I couldn't keep them forever.'

Fergus came out of his painful reverie. 'I'll have a look at them,' he said gruffly.

'Certainly.' Green took the books out of the window.

On the flyleaf of the Ardfern copy of Long's *Letters* there had been an inscription. Fergus opened the book with dread and stared bitterly at the faded writing. It was unmistakable.

He turned slowly to Green. All he wanted now was confirmation of his conviction that Hoey was the thief.

'I suppose there's no doubt of their authenticity? Did they come from a good source?'

'Both are absolutely genuine, Mr. King.'

Fergus pressed the point. 'The only people I knew to have both of those books were a family called Bryson,' he said. 'I don't want to pry, of course, but it would be interesting if that's where these came from.'

'I'm afraid I don't know the name of the previous owner,' Green said. He spread his hands. 'Some people when they are selling things are reluctant to say who they are. It's a question of pride. I never press them.'

'Of course not.' Fergus managed to smile, as if musing on the mythical Brysons. 'The son would be about twenty-four now. He's taller than average, with dark hair and a thin moustache. He has a slightly military look.'

Green brightened, pleased that here he could help. 'That sounds very like the gentleman who brought those books to me. I've had quite a number of good purchases from him.' He paused, then added hopefully, 'Perhaps knowing the family would add interest to the books for you, Mr. King?'

Now that he knew, Fergus' effort at control began to sag. He felt he could no longer keep the distress from his voice.

'Wrap them up and have them sent down to me at the City Chambers with the account,' he said abruptly. Then, his face anguished, he turned quickly away, bumping blindly into people, leaving Green holding the books and staring after him in surprise.

He glowered his way through the next week, avoiding his office because there he would have been sure to meet either Robert or Hoey.

In his mind, two pictures persisted of Hoey—one of him thieving at Ardfern, the other of him flopped in the office armchair with the Lambeth Nightingale. Fergus carried the burden of Hoey alone and in silence. To tell Gwen of her husband's treachery had been unthinkable. His worry was that she might find out. He was in the same dilemma over the stolen books. Since he couldn't threaten Hoey with exposure he had thought it better not to threaten him at all—there was no sanction he could apply against him that would not also hurt Gwen.

At home he tried to be normal, but his sense of betrayal at discovering Rita weakening towards Mary Devine still lingered. The Chelsea-Derby figurine had been put away on an unimportant shelf, its provenance still in doubt. *If only*, Fergus thought, *all my worries could be shelved as easily.*

Having to exile himself from his own office did not speed the sweetening of his outlook. Corporation officials found he had developed a sudden interest in ordure. Buchanan Street and Argyle Street, if his bad-tempered outbursts were to be taken literally, were practically blocked with dung by midday. In the police court his sentences were harsher. Regulars who waited unconcernedly for the usual thirty days were led off, blinking, to do sixty. He used the time that would normally have been spent at his desk in going around the branches harrying his managers, one or two of them so new that they didn't know who he was when he stepped off the street and began prodding about the beery, sawdust-floored interiors with his cane.

In Goosedubbs one morning he stood among the litter staring at the facade of the Corkcutters' Arms, the first public house he had ever owned. Thirty years ago it had been a humble place. Now it looked repellent. As a young man he had painted this cracked wooden facade himself. He had manhandled innumerable casks of ale across this unpaved footpath from the delivery drays. Every morning he had sprinkled sawdust on the floor from a sack delivered full on Mondays by an old man who wheeled it in a barrow from a local carpenter's shop. When the customers had been despondent he'd cheered them. When they were rowdy, as on Friday and Saturday nights, he'd calmed them. He had been happy as the business prospered. It was difficult to remember that this was all it had been—a narrow, wood-fronted hole between two tenement closes.

The wood was blistered and patchy. Slogans and initials had been scrawled across it in chalk or gouged into it with knives. The small window was covered with wire mesh and to this dust clung thickly. In the last thirty years this area had become one of Glasgow's most notorious slums. The buildings were rotten, the people who lived in them depraved. Nowadays, Fergus would have been afraid to walk the Goosedubbs at night. It was years since he had visited it at all. Now he understood why the drawings had gone down and why Robert, after attempting to warn him, had sunk into uncaring silence.

He pushed one side of the swing doors with his cane and went in. The bar was an oval in the middle of the floor, but smaller than he remembered. Spilled ale had made the counter top patchy. Hardly any varnish remained and in places the wood itself seemed to have been eaten into—probably, he thought bitterly, by the whisky Robert thought he could introduce into Britain's grand country drawing-rooms. There was no cellar, and barrels of beer stood on the floor behind the bar, connected to the fonts and the water-engine pump by hoses. Two or three empty barrels stood out in the public area awaiting collection, and on these two men with beards down to their knees and coats held closed by string sat clutching tumblers.

Other broken-down customers slouched over the counter puffing at pipes, their moleskins ragged and dirty. Despite the dilapidation Fergus felt an effort had been made to make the best of the place. It was as clean as circumstances permitted. The mirrors advertising different makes of beer were flaking, but they seemed to have been recently polished.

McNair, the manager, came to meet him, looking surprised. He was a muscular, bearded man of about forty, with an intelligent face. Fergus was pleased to see that the apron he wore was clean and that his collar was starched and white.

'Good morning, sir.' He nodded to the door of the windowless box that served as an office. 'There isn't much room, but—'

'No.' Fergus shook his head. 'I want to stay out here.' In that stuffy little room he had planned his future. On a bare tabletop, sometimes by the light of a candle, he had covered a lot of paper with scribbled estimates of future profits, calculating if the time had yet come when he might risk expanding his business. In there he had written countless letters asking for particulars of other public houses for sale.

Floorboards creaked and the customers watched as he walked slowly around the bar. 'I'm afraid we've been neglecting this place, McNair. I'm told other pubs in the area have had money spent on them.'

'They have, sir. I've reported the fact more than once to both Mr. Robert and Mr. Hoey. We're suffering for it, as you'll have noticed.' McNair made a face to indicate his opinion of the customers. 'I do my best but I'm afraid we're only getting the dregs. They've little to spend themselves and the sight of them keeps better people out.'

Fergus looked sceptical. 'Where are the better people in this area?'

'At night, sir, few and far between. But there are a lot of clothing and furniture factories around here. During the day there are workmen about with money in their pockets. We could do well out of them.'

Fergus felt the man's enthusiasm was genuine. 'There's someone there waiting to be served,' he said, nodding at a man who had just shuffled in from the door. 'When you've attended to him you can tell me what improvements you think we might make.'

He watched McNair lift a glass as if to serve the man, then put it down again. As the man spoke McNair kept shaking his head until finally the man turned, muttering, and went out. He had to keep his feet on the floor or his disintegrating boots would have fallen off.

'One of the credit brigade,' McNair said as he rejoined Fergus. 'If I gave in to one, I'd have the life pestered out of me.'

Fergus nodded approvingly. 'It's the best way I know of losing both your money and the customer,' he said. 'Now, what would you like to see done here?'

The man hesitated. He had asked so often and achieved nothing that he felt he must be moderate. 'Nothing too expensive, sir. A lick of paint would make a world of difference. And maybe if we had another lamp in that corner it would make the place more cheerful.'

'It'll take a lot more than that.' Fergus pointed his cane at the customers perched on the empty beer barrels. 'If we had a few tables and chairs people would appreciate them. And some linoleum would hide all these broken boards.'

'That's a fact, sir. And this would be at the scruff of the neck of the first man that spat on it.' McNair raised a thick hand.

'Would that bring us level with the other places?'

'It would.'

'What we need is something to put us in front.' He took another speculative walk around the bar, reluctant to commit himself. 'How would you like to see the place lit by gas? Everybody will have it in the end. We might as well be among the first.'

'We'd really be modern with gas, Mr. King.' McNair was exultant. 'We'd be upsides with all the fancy shops in the city.'

'I don't have to tell you there'll be a lot of expense in all this,' Fergus said sombrely as McNair walked him to his carriage. 'I'll be looking to you to see I get a return on my money.'

It was an unjustifiable expense, he told himself moodily as the carriage moved off with a rumble, scattering the filthy children who'd gathered in a curious pack. He had allowed himself to be moved by sentiment. The area had sunk too low to be worth bothering about. Far better to have closed the place or sold it off cheaply and moved McNair to a branch where he would have had more scope.

The twilight mood he was beginning to feel would never leave him was dispersed with dramatic suddenness. As he entered his club at lunchtime the porter said Sir James Spence was waiting for him in the smoke room. The old man's appearance startled Fergus. He was hunched forward in his seat with an empty glass on the table in front of him. His face was grey and drawn and his eyes gave the appearance of being streaked with dull lines.

'Is there something wrong, Sir James? Are you all right?'

'Sit down, King, and don't fuss.' Sir James pointed irritably to a chair. 'I don't want a damned spectacle made of me. Get yourself a drink. I've had mine.'

When the waiter had taken Fergus' order Sir James eased himself back in his chair. 'I told you there was something in the wind. Well, you're the first to know. I'm going into the Western Infirmary tomorrow for surgery.'

Fergus' surprise and sympathy were mixed with a sense of deflation. Was this all the old man had been hinting at the last time they had sat in this room together? He saw suddenly how childish his romantic fancies had been. It was painful to think he could have been so gullible. He stifled his selfish disappointment.

'I had no idea you weren't well, Sir James.' It was difficult to say much more without seeming to pry.

'They tell me it's not too serious, but I must get it attended to. One of those things that come with old age.' His face twisted. 'I'm afraid I've put it off longer than I should. I've been negotiating for months to buy out James Stewart & Henderson. That's why I had to be so mysterious. The contract was signed yesterday. If they'd known I was likely to disappear into hospital, they might have held out longer in the hope of wringing more money out of my softhearted son.' He laughed sardonically. 'I got very good terms.'

'How long will you be laid up?'

'A month at least. Now you know why I am so anxious that you should be available for the Queen's visit. I'll be flat on my back. As senior magistrate you'll have to represent the city. Till I come back you are First Citizen and the Queen is your guest.'

He laughed at Fergus' expression. 'Don't look so frightened, King. There's nothing to worry about. The officials attend to everything. All you have to do is look attentive and respectful. It'll be good experience for you, and Mrs. King will love it. She'll be inundated with invitations to tea parties for the next year. Take my word for that.'

When Fergus gave the exciting news to Rita, all she could think of was her new dress. She had been happy with it when she'd been going to be simply one of many guests. But now, unbelievably, she was to be hostess to the Queen, representing all the women of sprawling Glasgow. She remembered the cracked plaster model at the back of the tawdry shop window.

'You haven't seen me in the dress I bought.' She tried to hide her panic. 'I'll go up and put it on. It won't take a minute.'

He looked at her in surprise. He had been thinking of the speeches he would have to make and wondering what kind of small talk would be suitable for use with a queen. 'Is that all you've got to worry about?'

'It's so important, dear. I mustn't let you down.'

He put an arm around her shoulder and gave her a tender shake. 'You won't Rita. You never have. I'll have to rehearse my speeches on you. You'll have to imagine you're the Queen.'

'Yes, dear, of course. That will be lovely. Meantime, just you sit down over there and think what you're going to say while I go upstairs and change into my new dress. I won't be happy till you've seen it.'

Fergus had been unable to think of any but the most banal remarks for the Queen by the time Rita came back.

'Well?' she said, apprehensively.

He was beginning to feel the same stirrings of panic she had experienced. 'Beautiful,' he said after a brief, unseeing glance at the dress. 'You couldn't have done better.'

'I'm glad you approve, Fergus.' The relief made her almost too humble.

He glanced up, wondering if she was teasing him but her expression was innocent.

'I'd better take it off before anything happens to it.'

As she left the room an icy sensation came into Fergus' stomach. His mind had returned to his last two meetings with Sir James Spence. How could he have been so naive? He had indulged in optimistic fantasies on the strength of a few cryptic words. Supposing—the thought was almost too terrible—supposing his long-term hopes rested on assumptions just as false. He had based everything on hints—or on what he had taken to be hints. *They had been hints*, he told himself fiercely. *Otherwise, there was . . . nothing.*

# 7

After visiting his grandmother, Robert had resolved that there were only two more moves he could make before the decision about Mary had to be taken. That he should decide for both of them seemed only natural. He had taken stock in the only way he knew. He loved Mary and without her his life would not be complete. But if he married her without Fergus' consent his life would be incomplete in another respect. If he was thrown out of the family business he would find the world a very bleak place. He had no special qualifications except his overwhelming urge to build a great business empire. The family concern was the perfect, perhaps the only, base for this. He was still certain that with Fergus' money he could make a golden future in whisky. If he gave everything up for Mary would he be happy? She came from a good home. As the wife of a poor man would she be happy? A sentimental man would have known the answer. He seemed condemned to work out his life by calculation.

The seeming callousness of his attitude sickened him. Yet he could not turn away from the undeniable realism of the view that had gradually been forced on him in his weeks of anxious pondering.

His approach to Fergus was shatteringly direct. 'I would like your permission, Father, to marry Miss Devine.'

Fergus almost gaped at him, then his face went white with suppressed anger. 'I hardly think the office is the place to raise such a matter.'

'I'm sure it's as good as any other. It will perhaps help us to face this in a businesslike way.' His sense of bitterness was enormous.

'Don't be so impertinent. You've been defying me, I know, but

I won't stand for your impudence.' Fergus could hardly believe this was being thrust on him as he sat at his office desk attending to his business. Until recently he could count on his office being a tranquil place, the clerks working quietly at their books, everyone engaged on some task he knew well. Important decisions had been made here, but never loudly, never in haste, and rarely with regret. But, within a month, he had caught his son-in-law fornicating in an armchair with a cockney singer and now here was his own son virtually challenging him. Fergus felt he would explode.

'I have no wish to be impertinent, Father, or to anger you, but I will not be subservient. I am twenty-two. You must treat me as adult.'

Only the presence of employees in the outer office prevented Fergus from roaring. 'My answer to your question,' he snarled, 'is no. Is that adult enough for you?'

'Before you make that quite final I should explain the exact position to you. Mary is a Catholic, as you know, but there would be no question of me taking her religion.'

'By God, I hope not.'

'It is possible that we could both keep our own religions. There is a thing called a mixed marriage.'

'It's still done by one of their priests in one of their churches. I know all about it. And I'm not having it. No grandchild of mine will be brought up a Catholic.'

Robert felt peculiarly calm. 'I suppose all this shouting means you would refuse me your permission to marry Mary under any circumstances?'

Fergus ignored the gibe. 'It does not mean that. If the girl is willing to give up her religion and marry you in our church then I'll accept her.'

It was a solution Robert had not proposed to Mary and one he knew would never even have occurred to her. Fergus saw his hesitation and read it correctly. 'That would be a different matter, wouldn't it?' he sneered. 'It's all right for you to go her way but not for her to go yours.'

'A mixed marriage would be the compromise solution.'

'Yes. With the compromise nearly all on your side.'

'The position then is that you refuse me your permission? What happens if I marry Mary without it?'

'You live to regret it. And live damned thinly at that.' Fergus rose from his desk. He had control of his voice now. 'While you've been defying me, and defying good plain sense, I've been thinking what I might do about it. I can't stop you bringing unhappiness on yourself and on this girl. I can't stop you bringing scandal on me and on your mother. But I can show the world I don't take it lightly. If you marry this girl you'll have to leave the business and fend for yourself. And once out you'll never get back.'

Robert nodded. 'That's what I thought, Father, I just wanted to be quite sure I wasn't making you out to be harder than you actually are.'

His next call was on Roderick Fraser. Lochbank Distillery was a collection of whitewashed buildings at the side of the public road that followed the eastern shore of Loch Lomond. He approached it over the moor from the clachan of Bearsden. It was a bright, still morning and at any other time there would have been a sharp pleasure for him in the blue of distant mountain peaks, a new one seemingly appearing as he rounded each bend of the twisting road. Highland cattle shook long blond hair at him across dry stone dikes or waded around the reedy edges of small brown lochans. At one point, tired of bumping over the flints, he left the carriage and sat on a rock by the roadside smoking his pipe. Grouse whirred out of the bracken behind him and in the grass at his feet wild orchids grew beside buttercups and pink clover. Peat smoke from a cottage up a stony track drifted past him in scented clouds. A dreamlike peace came over him and when his pipe was finished he still sat on. In the silence of these spaces between the mountains dreams receded. Even heartache seemed less intense. He had to force himself to move. There were miles yet to be travelled and then the long journey back to Glasgow. It would take all of the day.

He saw the steam of the distillery above some trees shortly after he passed through the village of Drymen on the Balmaha Road. The sharp tang of whisky evaporating from the storage sheds came to him as he approached the last bend. The distillery buildings were small and huddled close under a boulder-strewn hill. Down this hill splashed the burn that supplied the water Fraser used to make his whisky. The burn had been dammed to build up a head of water so that even during a drought the distillery would not go short. An attempt had been made at some time to beautify this reservoir with a wooden bridge under which lilies floated. The sides of the bridge had been made in rustic fashion with branches of birch trees. Robert crossed it to the building where Fraser had his office. Two old men covered in a fine white dust passed him with sacks of grain on their backs.

Fraser was surprised to see him. He was in the huge, made-to-measure swivel chair that had fascinated Robert since, as a boy, Fergus had brought him here when he came to order whisky. Robert could still remember how the two men haggled over the filling price, with Fraser puffing every time he got up to consult a ledger or call for a clerk.

'My boy! This is unexpected. Throw those papers off that chair.' Fraser struggled a bit against the arms of his own chair but did not rise.

Robert noted that Fraser now puffed even when sitting. He wore a formal black coat with black cotton covers drawn to his elbows to keep his sleeves from glazing. The office had once been part of his grandfather's farm, and the walls were still clad in the original unpainted pine. The shelf above the fireplace was laden with dusty bottles containing sample quantities of Lochbank whisky. A bigger bottle on a side table contained a grass snake pickled in whisky. This was one of Fraser's jokes. 'My grandfather put that snake in there more than fifty years ago,' he would tell curious visitors. 'It hasn't aged a day since. A dram of whisky keeps men in the same marvellous state of preservation.' Then he would offer them a glass, as he did to Robert now.

'I won't, thank you,' Robert said.

'A man with your ambitions should be setting a better example,' Fraser teased him.

Robert smiled. He knew that Fraser himself left the daytime drinking of whisky to others and would not have accompanied him if he had accepted. 'I'd rather talk about it if you can spare me a little time.'

Fraser gave him a look. 'Talk away if that's what you came for.'

The window looked up to a heather-covered hillside. Years ago, while the men talked business, Robert had scrambled happily about up there searching for lucky white heather. He had never found any and now for him, too, it was the gloom of the overcrowded office, the earnest expression, the careful selection of words.

'You seemed interested in my ideas about whisky when we talked at Easter, Mr. Fraser.'

'I'm in the business, so why wouldn't I be?' Fraser said carefully. 'Have you taken them any further?'

Robert began to fill his pipe. 'I've taken them as far as I can without actually going into the business. Everything's come to a standstill, I'm afraid.'

'That's a pity. Whenever I thought back to that day I always imagined you pushing ahead. I envied you your youth and energy.' He paused. 'It can't be lack of enthusiasm, surely?'

'No. It's lack of money. You saw how sceptical Father was. He hasn't changed. I'm having to look elsewhere for support.'

Fraser rose from his chair with a lot of noise and moved ponderously to the fire. There was little left in the hearth but white ash, but he lifted two lumps of peat and dropped them on the embers. It was an evasive move and Robert sensed it. The rest of the groundwork he had prepared during his drive seemed suddenly pointless. He began to regret ever thinking of approaching Fraser.

'Do you think you could be interested, Mr. Fraser?' It was a lame ending, but he could not now remember the better words he had drafted in his mind. All he wanted was to get it over with.

Fraser dropped back into his chair. 'You mean interested in going into business with you, Robert?'

'Yes.'

Fraser made a friendly sound which nevertheless clearly indicated regret. 'My boy, I'm flattered you should even think of an old josser like me, but running this place is a twenty-four-hour-a-day job. Distilling's a nonstop process and the only time we ease up a little is when we run low on water in July and August. Then we whitewash and paint and do a hundred other jobs that have been neglected while we've been making whisky.'

'Oh, I wouldn't expect you to give much time, Mr. Fraser.' *Not any time at all*, he thought. That was the last thing he'd want. If he ever got this business going, he didn't want anyone interfering. It all stood out in his mind as if it actually existed.

Fraser laughed. 'All you want is my money?'

'Well, I wouldn't like to—'

'I like to call a spade a spade. But whatever we call it, I'm afraid I'm not going to be able to help you, Robert. I'm nearly three times your age. I'm set in my ways, like your father, only more so. I've no ambitions left, except for this business to run on smoothly until I don't need it anymore.' He frowned. 'Unfortunately, that's not what's happening at the moment. There's a glut of whisky. We've all been overproducing. People are using up their stocks instead of coming to us for New Make fillings.' He waved a flabby hand towards the window and the stillhouse beyond. 'We're down to half production over there.' He pointed in another direction. 'Last year, to keep up production, I was buying my own whisky and storing it, hoping that buyers would come along for it later. They didn't come. Now I have an awful lot of capital lying evaporating in those sheds. This is no time for me to get mixed up in a new venture.'

The dusty old men passed the window bent under their sacks of grain. They moved like robots to the accompanying rumble of an empty cask being rolled across the cobbled courtyard. From a greater distance came the rhythmic tapping of a cooper's hammer on the iron hoops of a cask. These were the sights and the sounds of whisky.

'I'm sorry,' Robert said.

'Yes, well so am I, but don't look so downcast. It's not the end of the world.'

*But the end of something else*, Robert thought, bitterly. As he pictured Mary his heart filled with a terrible regret.

'Did your father know you were coming here?'

'No.'

'He mightn't like it. Better not tell him. I won't say a word.'

'Thank you.' He rose to go.

There was a silence during which Fraser's laboured breathing was very noticeable. 'Fiona was saying she never sees you at the yacht club now.'

'Easter was the last time I was there. How is Fiona?'

'Blooming,' Fraser said, 'but she doesn't go to the yacht club very often either.' A proud smile puckered the folds of his cheerful face. 'You know, Fiona's turning out to be a great help to me. In the business, I mean.' His smile saddened a little. 'Sometimes I feel my age. She's been able to take a little of the weight off my shoulders.'

At the door, a breath of peat smoke trailed past them, drifting through the birch trees towards the smooth water of the loch. Even in his unhappiness it stirred Robert. It was, he felt, one of nature's great perfumes, containing in its sweet and flowery tang the very essence of romantic Scotland.

He looked around the cosy group of whitewashed buildings, marvelling, as he had often done, that the miracle of whisky production could take place amid such beauty—the loch sparkling across the stony road and the heather encroaching from the hills in a purple haze. Disconcertingly, he found himself almost envying Fraser the unambitious life spent contentedly on these shores.

'This is a beautiful place to work,' he said.

Fraser smiled. 'That's what Fiona always tells me.' He shook his head musingly and seemed to become lost in thoughts of his daughter. 'A young girl needs a mother. I have to leave her too much on her own, and when I am with her she just twists me round her little finger.'

'I'm glad Fiona's well,' Robert said. 'Please give her my best regards.' If he couldn't be successful, at least he could be mannerly.

Mist was rising from the moorland lochans long before he reached the outskirts of Glasgow. He was tired and heavy-hearted. The mountains behind him had gone black and forbidding and the gloaming was heavy with damp. Bats swooped above the rough road. As the lights of the city appeared ahead of him he made the bitter decision he had known must come. There was no doubt now in his mind. Mary and he would bring each other only unhappiness and poverty. Love would not prevail over what they would have to face. The conventions of the system were unbreakable. The priest had said so. His grandmother had said so. His father not only predicted misery and ruin but threatened to bring them about. Only a few hours ago there had still been hope. If Fraser had been willing to finance a venture into whisky they could still have married with a reasonable chance of happiness. Fergus would have disowned him, but he would have been financially independent. After a while he would have been able to buy for Mary the grand house that she deserved. They would have made new friends. Now he knew what he supposed he should have always known—that he was totally beholden to his father not only for his long-term future but even for his daily survival. There was no one left to whom he could go for either money or advice.

All night he lay awake dreading what he must tell Mary, but knowing more firmly than ever, when morning came, that it must be done. He deliberately chose Miss Frame's for their last meeting, fearing his resolve would waver and break in the intimacy of the flat. They had been too happy there. The old waitress fussed about as if knowing from their faces that she would never see them again.

As he spoke haltingly Mary sat bent forward over the untidy table, bemused and unprotesting, her small features sharpened into an expression of worn fragility.

'I think I knew in my heart it would have to end something like this,' she said at last. She put up her hand and gently touched his eyes, not caring who saw. 'And now it's almost as if I'm seeing you properly for the first time, Robert. Do you know that your eyelashes curl, like a girl's?'

'That's bad,' he said wretchedly.

'No. It's lovely.'

Something sour and choking filled his throat when he rose from the table, unable to say good-bye. As he went down the stairs and out into Sauchiehall Street iron began to enter his heart. The system had won, but from this day on he would use the system ruthlessly. And he would start with his father. He knew now what he was living for.

In the second week of August Gwen and Hoey were among the guests at a dinner party in Park Place. It depressed Fergus that while he looked across the drawing-room feeling embarrassed and uncertain, Hoey stood there appearing not only confident but relaxed. The dark eyes seemed to measure him, discard him, then move on in search of something more interesting. He braced himself for their first meeting in weeks. It would have to be got over with. He felt Gwen was watching, and Rita.

Only Hoey was aware of the tremor in his hand as he lifted his glass to his mouth. He waited for the comfort to spread. His resentment and fear of Fergus mounted as he watched him cross the room. The face seemed dour and threatening, the jawline suggesting clenched teeth and the hardness of the chin discernible even through the beard. Hoey took another nervous gulp of whisky and forced himself to move forward a little to meet his father-in-law.

Fergus, searching anxiously for some neutral remark, felt his mouth opening. His voice came awkwardly. 'Ah, you have a drink.'

Hoey almost dropped it. The voice seemed harsher than ever and in the recesses of his guilt the words rang out as a challenge. They all had drinks. Why mention his? Wasn't he supposed to have a drink?

They faced each other uneasily until Hoey, pulling at his nose, said loudly: 'Things are looking bad in Kabul.'

Fergus was startled. 'Where?'

'Kabul. The natives have been rioting for a week.'

'Oh, yes. Very bad.'

'We're not hitting them hard enough.'

'They say they're all over six feet tall,' Fergus ventured.

'The bigger the man, the better the target.' Hoey rambled nervously on. 'Teddy Dryden, my old adjutant, thinks the Greys might be sent out there. The Greys would soon settle their nonsense.'

Fergus found himself floundering at Hoey's unexpected choice of subject. He was content to leave foreign policy to Lord Beaconsfield, especially as it affected Afghans.

'I can't say I've been worrying much about what they're doing out there,' he said.

*Ignorant old devil*, Hoey thought, his confidence beginning to rise as the alcohol found his bloodstream. He reached for another passing glass and half emptied it in a single smooth movement of a long arm.

*Damned drouth*, Fergus thought, a suspicion aroused by Hoey's interest in Kabul now confirmed. At table, the coasters slid too often in Hoey's direction. As the meal progressed his speech became less clear and his eyes more liquid. A red flush appeared on his cheekbones. The other guests were middle-aged and staid. Despite this, Hoey began to have a party. He ate heartily, informing Rita several times that the quality of the food was superb. Once or twice he found himself on the point of making some remark to the matronly lady on his left which would almost certainly have caused her to faint. Tonight, perhaps because of what he had been reading about the riots in Afghanistan, Hoey's martial blood was up. His thoughts kept turning to his old regiment. Around him, while the others drank moderately, he began to imagine the boisterous atmosphere of the mess. As his elation heightened his perception deadened.

He had placed himself as far from Fergus as he could manage, Rita suffering the upset of her seating in silence. Perhaps because of the distance that separated them, Hoey began to imagine Fergus was warming to him. His smile seemed friendlier and his eyes appeared to search him out as if to include him in the conversation. Hoey, who by now was filled with a benign glow, felt that if Fergus had made the first conciliatory move it was up to him to respond. Whenever possible, therefore, he sent Fergus understanding glances or slightly slack grins of friendship. Rita, who had known all was not well when Hoey had started rearranging her seating plan, found she couldn't eat for the anxiety she now felt at his rapidly deteriorating condition. She dared not look at Fergus who, by his long silences, she knew to be equally aware Hoey was drunk. Gwen, she saw, had gone pale and, when she could, she sent expressions of sympathy to her across the table. Perhaps none of the others would notice. Rita prayed and trembled and tried to be a good hostess.

When the ladies withdrew, the men lit cigars and rearranged themselves at the table. Hoey choked and coughed a lot before getting his cigar to go properly. Robert moved closer to Fergus. 'Hoey's drunk,' he said.

Fergus glared at him. 'Do you want everyone to know?'

'Do you imagine they don't?'

Fergus chewed at his beard. 'The man's conduct is quite insupportable.' His voice was a worried groan.

Robert slid the brandy to a shadowy stretch of the table. 'Better keep that out of his sight.' But the clatter of a chair and a lurch behind signalled Hoey on his way to claim it. When he returned to his seat his glass was full. The skin of his face had tightened and taken on a patchy appearance; the darker blotches were red muddied almost to purple. He swirled his brandy, spilling some of it on his shirt, then addressed the men nearest him.

'Things are looking bad in Kabul.'

Fergus cringed but the subject turned out to be less esoteric than he had imagined. Maxton, a shoe manufacturer, said, 'There's only one thing the black man understands, and that's a good thrashing.' Maxton, it seemed, had lived in the Transvaal for a year or two as a young man. Someone else had been in Lucknow during the Mutiny and he upheld Maxton's view. Fergus was impressed and a little humbled by their knowledge of foreign affairs, but as Hoey, with tears in his eyes, began to tell them how he sometimes pined for the brotherhood of his regiment he decided something must be done quickly.

'I must get him out of here,' he said to Robert. 'See that Gwen doesn't follow.' He left the room and found a maid. 'Tell Mr. Hoey I have some urgent business to discuss with him in the library,' he said.

In Hoey's state, the word 'business' had only one application—the family business. Old man King needed his help about something. He left the table, breathing deeply, straightening his back and shoulders, and bulging his chest. He felt filled with strength and power. His head was amazingly clear and his movements a joy. His tread felt light and catlike and the balance of his body youthful and athletic. He stood in the hall for a pleasurable moment sensing his physical well-being and the magnificent scope of his mind. These were the qualities Daddy King relied on.

He made a barking sound that caused a passing maid to quicken her step towards the kitchen. Well, for once he was going to put his foot down. He was going to speak up for himself. He worked damnable hours. A man's work should allow him to spend the evenings with his wife. They had given him a job rich with temptation and once or twice he had fallen. Well, Gwen had been a brick. She hadn't held it against him and it was up to him to see it didn't happen again. Daddy King would have to come up with something that would keep him out of temptation's way. Mustn't hurt Gwen again. Especially with the baby coming. Yes, Gwen had been a brick. In the future he must be a source of pride and comfort to her—and it was up to old man King to assist him. He should be a partner in the damned business—not a bloody lackey. He had strayed a bit, recently, no use denying it, but all he needed was something to live up to, a spot of responsibility. Yes, a partnership would straighten him out, and it would please Gwen no end. It suddenly seemed highly likely to Hoey that it was about a partnership that Fergus wanted to see him. Sensing the beautifully jewelled movement of his body, he lurched along the corridor, opened the library door, and went in.

The smile disappeared from his face as he saw Fergus' angry crouch. The room was shadowy, but even through his drunkenness he was overwhelmed by an impression of two glaring eyes and a mouth snapped tightly shut.

He stopped just inside the door, the hearty greeting he'd been formulating stuck in his throat. His vision of a warm talk about his future began to crumble.

'Shut that door behind you.'

The anger in Fergus' voice was such that Hoey swung unquestioningly around and closed the door, mumbling, 'Sorry.'

'I should think you would be sorry.' Fergus' voice was as threatening as his air of enraged contempt. 'How *dare* you get into this drunken state in front of my guests. You are a disgraceful wretch.'

Drunk? Wretch? Hoey's head jerked about in disappointment and surprise as the full realization reached him that this was clearly not the prelude to a partnership.

'I'm not drunk, Papa,' he said, trying not to sway. 'Just a little tired. I think I must have been working too hard lately.' He groaned a little as he sagged carefully into a chair.

Fergus reared away, gritting his teeth against the roar of words that threatened to break loose. 'I am not your papa—thank God. And stay on your feet while I'm speaking to you.'

Hoey levered himself out of the chair, still baffled and apparently trying to stand to attention. He tried to focus on Fergus but the flicker of the firelight increased the trouble he was having with his eyes. He swayed gently. His voice was puzzled. 'Have I done something wrong?'

In his anger Fergus had disarranged his beard and the ends stuck out like ferocious prongs. 'You never do anything right,' he said with menacing sarcasm, 'but we will discuss that tomorrow. Just now I want you to leave this house quietly, before you embarrass us further. I'll say you've been taken ill. Robert will see Gwen home.'

A sense of outrage rose suddenly in Hoey. Who did this domineering old swine think he was? 'Who the hell do you think you're ordering about?' he demanded. He had tried to straighten, but his head hung a little to one side.

'I'll go when I'm ready. I'm not a bloody nobody.'

The rage that rose in Fergus at this defiance swept away all thought of the dinner party along the corridor. All he could think of was the black catalogue of Hoey's sins.

'You are lower than a nobody,' he snarled. 'You're an unprincipled lecher and a common thief.'

The last word cut through Hoey's befuddlement, filling him with a sense of danger. He fought to collect himself. 'My God,' he muttered. It was meant, as he struggled to dispel the deadening woolliness in his head, to sound like a warning—to indicate to Fergus that a man could only stand so much and that he had better beware of his tongue.

'Don't bother to deny it. I know you stole those books from the library at Ardfern. I've been to see Green. He'll identify you if need be.'

The shock of exposure sharpened Hoey's awareness. He could see Fergus' certainty. In the face of it, attack rather than denial seemed the better reaction.

'Damn your bloody books,' he said. 'If you paid me a half-decent salary I wouldn't have needed to sell them.' The defence appealed to him. He elaborated on it. 'I wasn't stealing. I was only making up my wages.'

Perhaps because it referred to money Fergus treated the charge seriously. 'I've treated you better than you ever deserved,' he said. 'I even bought the house you live in. Don't forget that.'

It was one of the things Hoey could never forget. The house in India Street had been a wedding present from Fergus but, with his gloomy view of Hoey's character, he had put it in Gwen's name. Hoey had been insulted and it was one of the earliest grudges he had listed against Fergus. Whenever he sang to Gwen his song about 'the way your father treats me' the ownership of the house formed a prominent part of the refrain.

'If you paid me properly I'd buy another place rather than live in that house,' he said bitterly.

Fergus shook his head. 'You are already overcompensated for the little you do. If it wasn't for Gwen I wouldn't put up with you for two minutes.'

'What is it exactly that you have against me?' Hoey looked genuinely puzzled—his infidelities and thefts forgotten.

'You're a waster. You spend too much time between your bookmaker and White's Chop House when you're supposed to be working. And you have no respect for your wife.'

'You've always twisted everything,' Hoey said disgustedly. 'You've never liked me.'

Fergus nodded. 'I never have and I never will, but I'm willing to give you some free advice. If you gave up the gambling and the dissipation, you wouldn't have to stoop to thieving. You would be able to live on your income.'

Hoey had moved away and his snarl came out of deep shadow. 'It's a pittance. And I'm not the only man you've turned into a thief. They all steal from you down in the bottling store. It's the only way the poor devils can live.' All his resentment of Fergus was boiling through the alcohol. His contorted face came out of the shadows as he thrust himself forward for emphasis. 'You're a mean old bastard, King,' he shouted.

No one had spoken to Fergus like this for twenty years. The last man had been a drunk in the Corkcutters' Arms and he had ended up smashed against a wall on the other side of the Goosedubbs.

A chair fell as he lunged for Hoey, his hands stretched out for his throat. The police judge, the chairman of charitable committees, the candidate for high honour had all disappeared in an onrush of fury. But Hoey, white-faced and steady now, was quicker. He got a desk between them and watched Fergus shudder to a blind halt, fighting for control.

'You're a sham, Mr. High-and-Mighty King,' he bellowed. 'You have the money now but under it all you're still a damned crofter. And you'll never be anything else. I'm sick of you, your precious business, and all the other Kings. You've got them all tied to your bootlaces. But you'll never get chains round me. I resign.'

Suddenly Fergus felt sick. 'You're dismissed,' he gasped. He turned away, bowed and breathless, his heart thumping. 'Now get out. Get out.'

Behind him, Hoey moved. There was a moment or two of silence and then something crashed on to the hearth at Fergus' feet. He recoiled and then stared paralysed at the fragments of green and yellow enamel lying in the firelight.

Hoey, his eyes wild, watched one of Fergus' hands go out hesitantly as if to touch the splintered remains of what had been a Chinese *jardinière* made in Canton a century and a half earlier. Then he turned and rushed out into the wet night without collecting either his coat, his hat, or Gwen.

Gwen spent the night in another room, but when they met in the morning she did not reproach Hoey. He was grey and bilious. His hands trembled and he couldn't eat. He shook his head regretfully.

'I don't know what happened to me, Gwen. I went up there determined to be on my best behaviour, but from the moment I saw your father everything began to go wrong.'

'But why? That's what I can't understand.'

He was silent, unable to explain about the stolen books or his increased fear of Fergus since his disastrous night with the Lambeth Nightingale.

From Gwen, pale after a night without sleep, love still flowed.

'Perhaps I've been wrong in trying to bring you together. I keep hoping you'll . . . well, get to like each other more. I'm sorry, Tom. You look so ill.'

Hoey put a hand to his eyes and groaned. 'I know it was another chance for me to ingratiate myself with your father. I knew that's what you had in mind. And I let you down. I let you down again, Gwen. That's the worst of it.'

He was obsessed with the almost mystic sway that Fergus had over him.

'He has always brought out the worst in me. I don't know what it is. The minute I saw him last night everything I'd ever done to displease him came rushing back at me and I knew he wouldn't have forgotten a jot of it. It's not that I blame him, but, oh, my God, what an effect he has on me.'

It was the truth, he felt, even if only a very diluted version of it.

She lifted the pot and poured tea into his cup. 'Try to take that.'

He lifted the cup but, his face wrinkling, put it down without drinking.

'Will you try a piece of toast?'

He nodded dejectedly.

She reached for the rack. 'If I don't put butter on it you'll have more chance of keeping it down.'

He took one small bite and then pushed the toast away.

She pushed her chair back decisively. 'Tom, you're going back to bed. You can't go to business feeling like that.'

He looked at her in surprise. 'But ... you don't know? I'd forgotten.'

'Know what?'

'I'm finished with your father's business, Gwen. Last night I resigned from it.'

Her eyes filled with concern. 'This is even worse than I thought, Tom. I didn't know that had happened.' Her face brightened. 'But Father won't hold you to it. You said it in the heat of the moment.'

Hoey made an almost neighing noise, his sickness lifting a little at the thought of all the wounding blows he had landed on Fergus.

'He won't have to hold me to it, Gwen. I'm going to hold myself to it. Getting away from your father might be just what I need.'

'But what will you do?'

'Don't make it sound as if I'm completely useless,' he said with some of his old flippancy. 'What I'd really like to do is get back into the Greys.'

She looked at him in disbelief. 'I've never heard you say a good word for your regiment. Why should you want to go back to it now?'

'I met Teddy Dryden in the club the other day. We spent an hour going over old times.' Hoey's voice was almost wistful. 'He's the adjutant now. Still as straight as a rod and not a sign of a paunch. Two or three times since I've wondered if the old discipline isn't what I need. I make a damned fool of myself sometimes.'

There was an enthusiasm in his voice that Gwen realized had been missing for a long time.

'Would they give you your commission back?'

'No.' He shook his head sorrowfully. 'I asked Teddy in a round-about way. They have a full complement of officers. And a list of young fellows waiting.'

She hid her relief. 'I suppose,' she said hesitantly, 'I suppose there's no use me asking you—not for a while, anyway—if you would reconsider your resignation?'

'No use at all.'

'Not even if I spoke to Father first?'

He looked up angrily. 'Don't dare do that, Gwen.'

All morning he sat at the dining table staring through the net curtaining at the slated roof of the tenement across the street. In silence he nursed his thoughts and the after-effects of his drinking. He hardly even considered the possibility of taking his aching head and sick stomach to old Wilson's for a dose of ether or laudanum. This morning, suffering the pain seemed more important than evading it. For Hoey, it was a new concept in purification.

At midday he took some soup and soon after Gwen left the room he dropped into a restless sleep, still sitting on a hard chair at the table. When he wakened he was stiff and cold but his head was clear.

Gwen met him in the hall looking for the hat and coat he had left behind in his flight from Park Place.

'Anything will do,' he said, taking a tweed cape from a peg.

'Where are you going?'

'To look for a job.'

'At this time in the afternoon?'

He kissed her cheek. 'The sooner I get something, the sooner your father will realize I'm not dependent on him.'

'But what kind of job?'

'Anything,' he said. 'I'm not all that particular.'

The job Hoey took sent shockwaves through the family.

Gwen told Rita and Fergus about it when having tea with them one afternoon at Park Place. Her voice was elaborately casual but her lips were tight with strain as she waited for their reaction.

'A theatre manager!' Fergus tried hard not to appear as staggered as he felt.

Gwen, who had been dismayed when Hoey told her, was torn between sympathy for Fergus' obvious disapproval and loyalty to her husband. Her vulnerability annoyed her. What she wanted at this late stage of her pregnancy was to be fussed over and comforted. She did not want to squabble. She felt delicate and nervous but something perverse made her accept the challenge in Fergus' exclamation.

'Assistant theatre manager,' she corrected him with deliberately irritating precision.

Rita, sensing the precarious balance of Gwen's emotions, tried to show only interest. 'Which theatre, my dear?'

Gwen held her head up. 'The Scotia in Stockwell Street.'

The Scotia was hardly a hundred yards from the Corkcutters' Arms in the Goosedubbs. As Fergus contemplated its unsavoury reputation, his control snapped.

'That's not a theatre,' he said. 'It's a music hall, and a damned rowdy one at that. I'm told it takes the whole of Sunday to clear up the old fruit and rotten eggs thrown by the Saturday night drunks.'

Gwen, who had been seated by the fire, rose awkwardly and stood over him with her eyes flaring. 'It can't be any worse than that terrible music hall you own,' she said, ignoring the hand that Rita, her eyes wide with concern, held out as if to support her. Her voice rose. 'Are you forgetting that? Tom has taken the kind of job you suited him for, Father. Once he was a soldier. You have turned him into an assistant theatre manager.'

Inside, Fergus reeled. Gwen had never shown such wild disrespect. His eye caught Rita anxiously signalling to him. Her expression was pleading. He turned again to Gwen. Her appearance alarmed him. She was white-faced and breathless. The burden of her baby looked enormous. He fought desperately to stomach the injustice of her attack.

'Please sit down, my dear, and calm yourself,' he said in a choking voice. 'Tom did not work in the music hall. He was our travelling manager and it was a very small part of his job to supervise it. I cannot pretend I was sorry when he left my employment. It was a matter of mutual relief, I think. But I'd been hoping he would find something better than this.'

His failure to be more than half-heartedly conciliatory stabbed him.

'What's so wrong with being an assistant theatre manager?' Gwen asked with unabated anger.

'There's nothing wrong with it if you're a nobody,' he said impatiently. 'But can't he understand we have a position to keep up? If he has no pride himself, he should remember that other people have.'

Rita had been sunk in an unhappy contemplation of the wreckage of what should have been a pleasant afternoon. She had spent her married life working for domestic harmony, calming Fergus' irrascibility, laughing at his foibles, suffering his faults in the knowledge that he was never thoughtless or harsh for long. When everything collapsed, as now, she felt it as a personal reproach.

'Do you feel yourself it's quite a good job, Gwen?' Her intervention was subdued and concerned but there was an intensity in it —the intensity of her determination to restore the peace. If she could not do that she was failing them both.

Gwen detected the note of reason but couldn't attune to it. 'No, Mother,' she said defiantly. 'It's really, as Father no doubt knows, quite a minor post without much responsibility. However, Tom thinks it may have prospects.'

*Prospects of what?* Fergus wondered bitterly.

'He could still have been in the business,' he said. The words suggested resentment, regret, and various other emotions.

'Well, between you, Father, you ruined that.' Gwen had taken her seat again. Her voice was more moderate but in her agitation she was making a lot of noise with her cup and saucer. 'I don't know which of you was the more to blame, but I don't think either of you behaved in a very grown-up way.'

'And neither of you are acting now in a very grown-up way.'

The unusual asperity in Rita's voice made them both turn to her, but before either could speak she said, 'I am ringing for Molly to take these tea things away. I don't want her to hear raised voices.'

By the time the maid had removed the tea tray Gwen and Fergus had sunk into a regretful but stubborn silence. It was left to Rita to dispose of the matter in something like amity.

'It is not for us to interfere in Tom's new job,' she said. 'Despite what has been said here in haste I am sure that your father, like me, wishes Tom every success in it.'

Gwen gave her a grateful smile. 'Thank you, Mother. I think the change will be good for Tom. I think he's always wanted to prove he could make his own way.'

Fergus, still preoccupied with the consequences to his own standing of what he saw as Hoey's slide to the gutter, stirred. 'As long as you're both happy,' he made himself say.

He kept his final comment until after Gwen had gone. 'Assistant theatre manager!' Despite Rita's expression of protest he muttered bitterly on. 'A glorified doorman is what that means—standing in the damned foyer for the whole of Glasgow to see as the crowds go in.'

# 8

It was Her Majesty Queen Victoria's first official visit to the City of Glasgow for fifteen years. The last had been October 14, 1859, when she had turned on the Loch Katrine water scheme. While her subjects slept, the royal train arrived at a siding on the south bank of the River Clyde after travelling through the night from London.

For a week the city had been grey and damp, with factory smoke collecting darkly under drizzling cloud. As if for the occasion, the morning of September 2 broke bright and fresh, all oppression gone. The river still had a brown and swollen look but the swans at Broomielaw circled the moored boats alertly, their appetites sharpened on the keener air. For a while mist trailed around tall, damp trees and at the tops of church spires, but by nine the autumn sun was riding over the city in a yellow sky. Bunting strung across many streets became less listless as it dried in the warming air. Under its bright colours crowds gathered, clutching flags made at home from coloured cloth or, in the case of the very poor, from plain brown wrapping paper. Women in their best dresses held carefully scrubbed children in check by feeding them titbits of bread spread with butter and sprinkled with sugar.

The Queen was not due to start her drive to the university until ten o'clock and the police were still allowing ordinary traffic on the route. People made gay by sunshine and flags practised their cheering on lawyers' clerks on their way to Bath Street offices in public buses and on ham and egg importers travelling to Candleriggs warehouses in private carriages. Behind this horse-drawn traffic, squads of scavengers moved with brushes, shovels, and carts so that the royal progress would be through streets undefiled. Mounted policemen went along the route ringing handbells and warning the people to guard against thieves and to take care their children didn't stray.

Fergus and Rita were dressed and almost ready when Glasgow Corporation's official landau, drawn by four grey horses, arrived half an hour early in Park Place, after driving across the city from the town stables in Bell Street. An official of the Royal Household had come to Glasgow from Buckingham Palace two days earlier to approve the arrangements. He brought the news that Her Majesty did not wish a formal speech when Fergus arrived in welcome at the royal train. She had decided, however, that she would drive with him in the open municipal coach and not, as had been expected, alone in a separate carriage. This delighted Fergus. He'd been nervous of delivering a public speech of welcome while merely deputizing for the Lord Provost, but he enjoyed the idea of so many of his fellow citizens seeing him sitting with the Queen.

Ermine flopped heavily around him as he examined his appearance in the bedroom mirror.

'I'll be glad to get out of these,' he said, crossing to the window and looking down at the waiting coach. 'It looks as if it will become really hot later.'

Rita, who would only come into the proceedings officially when the Queen arrived at the City Chambers after the ceremony, acknowledged Fergus' remark absentmindedly. 'Think how glad you'll be of them if it turns cold, dear. September can sometimes be treacherous, and the carriage will be open. I hope the Queen is well wrapped up.'

'I don't think monarchs are ever "wrapped up", dear,' Fergus reproved her mildly. He turned again to the mirror, smiling to himself at Rita's homely concern for the Queen. Despite the nervous way she was fidgeting with her dress she would no doubt get on with the Queen much better than he would. He thought that 'get on' was probably another phrase that shouldn't be used in connection with royalty. Anyway, Rita would manage to be her natural self.

'Well, I just hope she's warm enough,' Rita was saying. 'After she leaves we can come home to a nice warm fire, but she'll have another four or five hours in the royal train and then a long carriage drive before she reaches Balmoral.'

There was a knock at the door and Mrs. Veitch came in. James, the school holidays over, was back again with his parents. His grandmother had brought him home two or three days earlier. She had stayed on at Park Place to see the Queen, and, more important, to see her daughter dressed to meet the Queen.

'Your taste has always been perfect, my dear,' she said with a sideways glance at Fergus. She liked to remind him whenever possible that he had been lucky in his choice of a wife. 'The white feathers in your hat throw up the delicate peach shade beautifully.' She touched the dress. 'I hope you'll be warm enough. September can sometimes be treacherous, you know.'

Fergus and Rita looked at each other and smiled. 'Like mother, like daughter,' Fergus said, to Mrs. Veitch's mystification.

'And doesn't Fergus look grand, Mother?'

'Fit for the House of Lords,' Mrs. Veitch said generously.

Fergus beamed at her, then at his watch. 'We leave in ten minutes,' he said. 'I'll go down and check my programme.'

'You've checked it twice already, this morning, dear.'

'No matter.'

He turned to Mrs. Veitch. 'Is James ready?'

'He was ready when I came up. When you go down just make sure he isn't up to any mischief. I don't want us to be late.'

'I ordered the coach to come round half an hour after Rita and I leave. The university is only ten minutes' drive away. You'll be there long before the Queen. It'll take her at least an hour to come from the south bank.'

'You're sure James and I will have a good view, Fergus?'

'Of course you will. The coachman has his instructions. I've arranged with the police that you can drive into the university courtyard and draw up beside the eastern arch. The Queen will drive through the arch very slowly. You'll see her as if you were in the coach next to her without any of the discomfort of being jostled by the crowds.' He hesitated. 'I'll be right beside Her Majesty, of course,' he said self-consciously. 'Please make sure James doesn't do anything in the excitement that he shouldn't do.'

'What were you thinking of, Fergus?'

'Well, he mustn't shout out to me. That would never do.'

Rita looked shocked. 'I'm sure James would never dream of it,' she said. 'I hope we've brought him up better than that.'

When Fergus had gone she clasped her hands. 'All this talk is beginning to make me nervous.'

'Just be yourself, dear, like you always are,' Mrs. Veitch said, 'and don't worry about any of them.'

'Yes. I've read that Her Majesty has a way of putting people at their ease.'

Mrs. Veitch looked towards the door as if to make sure Fergus was not about to come back. 'If you feel yourself getting flustered in front of her,' she said in a solemn whisper, 'just remember John Brown. She's only human.'

Rita's surprise turned slowly to horror but before she could think of a suitable reprimand she heard Fergus calling.

'Rita, will you come down, please, and have a look at James before we go? There's something funny about the way he's got his jacket buttoned.'

On the north bank of the river Father Campbell was kneeling to another sovereign. The oil light in its red glass container flickered above him as he leaned, head bowed, on the rail of the Sacred Heart altar. He was examining his conscience. For two days he had been worrying about Robert and Mary. Mr. Martin had reported that Robert had not appeared for instructions for two weeks. No excuse had been sent and Father Campbell had not seen Mary to ask if she knew the reason. He had come to his own conclusion. Robert could be ill, of course, but Father Campbell didn't think so. There had been too many signs. There would be no conversion. There would be no marriage. Two young people who should never have met would part—perhaps they already had. The emotional price would be known only to them. All Father Campbell need strictly concern himself with was that a Catholic soul had been plucked from danger, the authority of the Church had been upheld, and the peace of mind of two sets of parents had been preserved. This was a great deal but, disconcertingly, he had found himself beginning to wonder if it was enough. In the scales of heaven would these three considerations outweigh the pain of parting for Mary and Robert? If not, who was at fault? Was there anything, he kept asking himself, that he could have done to secure a happier outcome? He could not see that he had failed either in good sense or in humanity. And yet, his conscience troubled him. The frightening thought had even come to him that the steering of one soul towards God might be task enough for any man. To take on oneself the guiding of so many other souls—a churchload, a parishful—might be an enormous presumption. And yet to think like that was to commit something very like the sin of Despair. It left out the fact of God's Divine intervention. It meant he was doubting the validity of his own Holy Orders, for it wasn't his guidance that had come between Robert and Mary. It was the guidance of the Church, and therefore of God.

As he tormented himself he became aware that a strange sound had entered the shadowy church, travelling, it seemed, on the long, widening angles of September sunlight that cut down between the pillars of stone. He raised his head and listened. It was the sound of cheering. He was puzzled until he remembered this was the day of the Queen's visit. Father Campbell unfailingly remembered the most obscure feast days but worldly occasions left little mark on him. The saints required special prayers and certain colours of vestments. These things had to be thought about in advance. There had been no similar preparations at the Cathedral to remind him the Queen was coming, for although the priests all included her in their morning prayers, they hadn't put out any flags.

He left the altar and walked to the street. A ship's rigging rose and fell above the sheds of Custom's House Quay. Along the cobbled wall, cargo lay in bales and crates. Lorries that had made deliveries or were there to collect goods stood unattended, the horses contentedly delving into nosebags. Barrows and hand-carts had also been abandoned. The people who would normally have been working on the quay had all moved eastward along the street. They were gathered now on or about Victoria Bridge in a tight, cheering mass, their flags darting colourfully in the sunshine. Father Campbell felt drawn by the excitement.

From the Cathedral steps to the bridge was less than two hundred yards. He started to walk. As he arrived at the back of the crowd the cheering grew more urgent. He strained to see, seeking a gap in the wall of bodies. A man standing with two or three others on a cart held out a hand and said, 'Step ye up, Father.' Father Campbell hardly hesitated. Clutching the skirts of his soutane, he grasped the man's hand and allowed himself to be hoisted on to the cart. He was in time to see four grey horses, an opulent carriage, and the round, familiar face. The man beside the Queen hardly caught his attention.

In the Corkcutters' Arms McNair waited until he heard the vague murmur of the crowd in Saltmarket grow into steady cheering. Then, as Fergus had instructed, he drew pints of best ale and placed them free in front of the surprised customers.

Having decided to spend money on the shop, Fergus had immediately engaged a firm of decorators. The preparatory work of washing, scraping, and burning had started the day before and already the smell of neglect and decay had been replaced by a more hopeful scent. Even the customers looked less decrepit.

'Mr. King hoped you would all drink to the Queen's health,' McNair said.

'The Queen's health,' they said hoarsely, glancing about them in an embarrassed way as they quickly lifted the pint mugs and drained them.

The cheering in the Saltmarket grew louder. McNair poured himself a mouthful of beer. 'The Queen,' he said, raising his tumbler. 'God bless her.'

Fergus, who sat stiffly to the Queen's right, managed a quick glance into Goosedubbs as the coach went slowly north towards Glasgow Cross. He saw some ladders and trestles outside the Corkcutters' Arms and then the crumbling masonry of the vile street was hidden behind hundreds of raised flags and streamers.

The palace official had advised him that during the drive and the official ceremony he would not be required to speak to the Queen unless spoken to. She had commented on their good luck with the weather as he escorted her to the municipal coach from the draped and freshly painted railway platform. Thereafter she had been silent except, as they crossed the river, to ask if the people fed the swans. She was smaller and thinner than Fergus had imagined from illustrations he had seen and, from his one direct look at her, she seemed to be dressed entirely in black.

As the crowds cheered, the Queen bowed. Fergus' heart swelled with pleasure. Some of this tumult was for him. At least for today he was First Citizen of this great noisy city, packed with a half-million people, some of them perhaps poor but all of them friendly. He had to will himself not to acknowledge the cheering. That had been another lesson from the palace official. The Queen alone will display pleasure, Fergus had been told. Stung to sarcasm he had enquired if he would be permitted a pleasant expression, perhaps even an occasional smile, since they were, after all, his fellow citizens who would be lining the royal route. The inscrutable official had said that smiling would be in order.

As he sat just two feet away from the Queen, Fergus wondered if she knew that officials preceded her, telling people how to behave. The thought, he felt, was a shade rebellious and he immediately replaced it with a more loyal reflection. If such precautions weren't taken, this ageing lady would be at the mercy of every civic buffoon into whose company her duty threw her.

Rita was in a carriage some way behind. Fergus wondered if she was enjoying the drive. At least she would be in a position to relax and enjoy the sight of so many happy and excited faces. Even the old grey tenements were looking less worn in the mellow sunshine. At Glasgow Cross the crowd thickened. It would be a profitable morning for the tobacconist on the north-west corner who also sold teas. Thousands of office and factory workers had been permitted to leave their posts to cheer the Queen. Side by side with these clean, well-doing citizens were hundreds of others who had swarmed in verminous rags from the Briggate, Goosedubbs, Fiddler's Close and the reeking vennels of Saltmarket. These were some of the spots that a signatory to a recent Parliamentary Report on Housing had been referring to when he wrote: 'I have seen human degradation in some of the worst places ... but I did not believe, until I had visited the wynds of Glasgow, that so large an amount of filth, crime, misery, and disease existed in one spot in any civilized country.'

Not long after Fergus had come to Glasgow three thousand people had died of cholera in these wynds in a single year. Now he tried not to see those who'd survived. They were a blot on this loyal turnout. They were there not to honour the Queen, but to see what they could beg or steal from the good-natured crowd. The Tolbooth clock showed almost half past ten. *Already*, Fergus thought, *the timetable is fifteen minutes behind in the first half mile or so of the drive*. Policemen had to link hands and force the crowd back before the procession could turn west into Trongate.

Fergus, warm in his ermine, was in a pleasant dream and he was startled when he realized the Queen was trying to attract his attention.

'Lord Provost.'

Her voice was frail and faint to inaudibility against the waves of sound enveloping the carriage.

Fergus leaned anxiously forward. He did not feel it necessary to remind her he was not the Lord Provost. 'Your Majesty?'

'I always find the people of Glasgow very friendly to me. I am very grateful.'

Fergus was touched. There was a sad humility in the Queen's words. 'Your Majesty, it is our pleasure,' he said.

A little later she nodded upwards to some windows one floor above the street. Their lower half had been painted over and on this dark background had been inscribed in gilt lettering the name of a leading gold and silversmith.

'I know that name. That is the firm that supplied all of the domestic silver for Balmoral.'

Fergus, who'd been made a little lightheaded by the waves of public goodwill, felt he might risk a little humour. 'If it is from Glasgow it will give Your Majesty long service.'

'I hope so, Lord Provost. It was very expensive.'

Fergus did not dare look to see if she was smiling.

The ceremony at the university was over in a half hour. The new laboratories at the department of chemistry had been in use for over a month, and despite all activity having been halted for the official opening, the long, tiled rooms still smelled of gas and rubber tubing. The benches were stained and acid had been spilled on the floor. Fergus, who was suspicious of what went on in these technical departments, wondered what the expensive new laboratories would look like after a year of this sort of use. He was a man for the humanities himself. Mad professors conducting experiments over bunsen burners amid all these copper coils and graduated glass tubes only worried him. He thought it possible from the expression on Her Majesty's face that she didn't have much sympathy for such places, either. She was probably wishing she'd completed her journey and was settled at remote Balmoral on the banks of the Dee. Fergus had once spent a few days driving round Deeside. Byron had preceded him and written of 'the steep frowning glories of dark Loch-na-Gar'—the mountain towering behind the royal castle. Fergus remembered there was a distillery on its slopes and that the Queen had visited it with Prince Albert. Even this implied patronage had done little for the sales of whisky. He would have liked to enquire if the Queen permitted whisky at Balmoral. It was said she would not allow pipes to be smoked indoors.

The return drive to the City Chambers, where the Queen was to be entertained at a municipal luncheon, was completed in warm sunshine. The earlier freshness had gone and Fergus felt bent under his ermine. There was a stoical quality in this old lady that he found himself admiring. She, too, must be tired and, most probably, bored. But she did not show it. She still acknowledged the cheering people with small bows.

Elected representatives and paid Corporation officials who were to be presented waited at the top of the marble staircase with their wives. But before them all came Rita. Fergus felt tears of pride rising to his eyes. She looked so slim and youthful in the peach dress as she curtsied neatly. Behind her, the waiting wives of the other magistrates looked dull. Most of them were fat. And shapeless. Fergus' love for Rita was unbounded as she came to stand beside him only a step or two from the Queen. He found her hand and pressed it and did not care who saw.

Her Majesty left Queen Street Station for Balmoral shortly after four o'clock without having dubbed Fergus. He was unsurprised. It had been a ridiculous notion and after the success and excitement of the day he was in a mood that allowed him to look back on that moment of naivety with amusement. At any rate, she now knew what he looked like. That could only be to his advantage, since his bearing and behaviour throughout the day had, he felt, been admirable. He had been solicitous without fussing, restrained in his speech without being tongue-tied, and in the formal words of welcome that he had finally spoken at the City Chambers he had been brief. He was certain Her Majesty would not look back and think of him as boring, pompous, forward, or snivelling.

Would she perhaps mention him in the daily journal she was known to keep? A sentence there would be like a passport to immortality.

He sent Rita home alone because he had business at his office. After he had attended to it an immediate return to Park Place seemed tame after such an exhilarating day. He decided to walk to his club. On the way he bought an *Evening Citizen*. It carried an early report of the royal visit. His own name was mentioned several times and there was a description of Rita's dress. A beggar who approached him out of a lane was surprised to have a florin ring in his enamelled mug.

Fergus joined a group in the club smoke room and when the waiter had brought him a drink he startled them into silence by holding up his glass and saying loudly, 'The Queen! Long may she reign over us.'

Gilchrist, a coal exporter, nodded to a copy of the *Citizen* lying on a table and said, 'I see we had a King as well as a Queen today.'

Fergus joined in the laughter. He offered his cigars round, a move no one present had ever seen him make before. 'A fine lady,' he said in measured tones. 'A very fine lady.'

They nodded and waited for him to go on. He looked round them and took his time.

'I'm proud to tell you, gentlemen, that Her Majesty thinks Glasgow a fine city. She was very favourably impressed by some of our new buildings.'

There were murmurs of approval but some looked disappointed that Her Majesty had not been more revealing.

Currie, who sent iron waterpipes all over the world, said invitingly, 'What we all want to know is something we won't read in the *Herald* tomorrow.'

'No doubt.' Fergus, whose tolerant smile suggested there was much he could have told them, accepted another drink. 'But I think we all know the rules. What Her Majesty says on these occasions is not for repeating. It's perfectly understandable. If she said she enjoyed somebody's smoked salmon, and it came out, the blighter could have it up on the hoardings.'

They were sympathetic to his difficulty.

'On her last official visit she had the Prince Consort by her side,' an old man remembered. He waggled his beard. 'All that red on the map . . . it's too much for a woman on her own.'

'They say she grieves for him still,' Fergus said, 'and I for one don't doubt it, despite the scurrilous jests one hears from time to time.' His face darkened with anger at the thought and he would have been mortified to know some of them had been set to music and could be heard that week at his own Music Hall. 'My abiding impression today was of a lonely woman in a world of men.'

Fergus' sentiments were only slightly heightened by the drink. It had been an emotional day. In all his years as a councillor and magistrate he had never felt more a man of affairs. Today he felt he was living close to history. He hoped that in his eagerness to bask a little in the regard of these important clubmen he hadn't debased something genuine. He was glad to hear Gilchrist change the subject.

'I bumped into young Gordon Spence today. Sir James, it seems, is coming along famously.'

'That reminds me,' Fergus said. 'I meant to ask the secretary if there was any way, as a club, that we could send Sir James our united good wishes.'

Everyone present thought it an excellent suggestion.

Gwen had insisted on making her own arrangements to see the Queen. Because her health varied from day to day she declined to accompany James and Mrs. Veitch to their grandstand spot in the courtyard, feeling she might easily end up spoiling their enjoyment. In her present condition she would not normally have considered joining in the day's events, but the part being played by her mother and father made it imperative that she at least catch a glimpse of them. How would she ever be able to tell her child of the great day when its grandparents had entertained the Queen if she sat at home and let the occasion pass her by?

An old schoolfriend lived nearby in a Bath Street tenement. Gwen arranged to look down on the royal party from her friend's parlour. Her view was imperfect, since the window was three floors above the street, but at least she was not jostled. She remained comfortably in a chair with a cup of tea beside her until the carriages came over the hill at Douglas Street. Fergus and Rita, knowing where she was, looked up as they passed but did not dare respond to her delighted waving.

After lunch Gwen rested and in the early evening her maid called a cab for her. She enjoyed the short drive to Park Place. The streets were busier than usual for the hour and the holiday atmosphere of the morning had not entirely gone. As she crossed part of the route the Queen had taken she saw bunting still enlivening some of the grey buildings. Discarded flags lay in the gutters. The sky had clouded since morning and there were sea-gulls on the house-tops of Park Circus, a sign, Gwen had always been told, of stormy weather to come. Suddenly a flurry of brown leaves rustled across the street in front of her cab. All at once it was an evening on the wrong side of summer. Gwen shivered. Winter babies, the old tale said, were more intelligent than those born in the heat of summer. In that case, her autumn baby would be somewhere in the middle. The best place to be, Gwen thought contentedly, as the cab trundled the last few yards through the secure middle-class district and stopped outside her middle-brained father's solid house.

'You should be warm at home,' Rita scolded her. 'It's going to be a very unpleasant night. It's suddenly gone dark over the river.'

'It didn't look so threatening when I asked Mary to call a cab for me,' Gwen said. But she was glad of the sherry Rita rang for and of the cheerful fire. 'I had a lovely sleep after lunch and I felt I couldn't let the day go without telling you how elegant you looked this morning. Besides, I want to hear all about the Queen.'

Rita looked at her fondly. 'You couldn't have seen much more than the top of my hat from that window.'

'No. It was surprising. I had an excellent view as the carriages came down the hill. Margery had binoculars. We took turns. You were the most beautiful woman there and father quite the grandest man. He looked so pleased with himself! But I was disappointed in the Queen. She looked drab. Why must she always wear black?'

'Well, she's in mourning, dear.'

'But the Prince has been dead for years.'

'It does seem rather a long time. She must have loved him so. And we mustn't criticize. It must be very lonely for her.' Rita looked around the big room in which she had so successfully combined homeliness with elegance. 'I wouldn't like her life.'

'What was she like?'

Rita considered. 'Remote, I think. Or maybe I just mean regal. It's so difficult to judge, really. You couldn't expect her to be ordinary. That would never do. Certainly she was charming. And gracious.'

'But is she human, Mother? That's what I want to know.'

'Naturally she's human. You shouldn't speak like that of the Queen.'

'But what did she talk about?'

'Well, most of the time she didn't talk about anything, in the way

144

you mean. She made remarks or commented, but in such a way that it was only necessary to smile in agreement. She seemed more at ease with the men. She's obviously a serious-minded woman. I know she asked your father a lot of questions about the Glasgow iron works and the Clyde shipyards. It was only towards the end that she spoke to me in what you would call a human way.' Rita made a face to show she still did not approve of the term. 'Perhaps it was the wine. She did take a little. She told me she had enjoyed luncheon and ended up by giving me a recipe.'

Gwen looked delighted. 'A recipe! How wonderful! Why didn't you say so before? What for?'

'For one of the Balmoral specialities. Game soup. I wrote it down the moment I came home and next time you and Tom come to dinner I'll have cook make it for us. If it's the right time of year, that is. It requires grouse and pheasant as well as venison. And there's wine in it, too.'

'You're making me hungry, Mother.'

'Well, I can't offer you game soup tonight, my dear, but you can have whatever cook has for us. I can't remember what it is. I was too excited this morning to pay much attention. And then I'm sending you straight home. I hope your father isn't too late.'

'Where is he now?' Gwen's expression suggested men were always somewhere they shouldn't be.

'He was going to the office and after that, if I'm any judge of the mood he was in, he'll go to his club before honouring us with his presence. I don't think he's come quite down to earth yet. He'll want to play milord in front of his friends for just a little while.' She lifted her embroidery and selected a coloured thread. Then, looking at Gwen, 'I'm glad to see the sherry has put some blood into your cheeks. You look more yourself now.'

'Mother, once the baby comes—' Gwen hesitated.

'Yes, dear?'

'Once the baby comes, do you think it would be wrong of me to try to influence Tom about his job? Against it, I mean?'

Rita's brow wrinkled. 'In what way, dear?'

'He's always so late getting home. His hours are every bit as bad as they were when he worked for Father. It hasn't mattered so much until now, but with a baby . . . well, if Tom could be at home in the evenings I would feel we were more like other families.'

'Of course.' Rita nodded sympathetically. 'I quite understand how you feel.' For many years of her own marriage, even after the children came, she had spent almost every evening alone. Fergus, intent on building his business, had worked from nine in the morning until almost midnight, six days a week, with only a short break at home in the afternoons. Rita knew what loneliness was, but she hesitated over what advice she should give. 'You must think well. You are really the only one who can judge if Tom would resent you trying to direct him towards some other . . . some other career.'

'That's what I can't decide. He seems to like his work at the theatre.'

Rita looked at her carefully. 'If you think you could, dear, then I think you should. It's really a matter for you and Tom, but since you have raised the subject I don't think the theatre is the best sort of place for him.'

An almost apprehensive look came on to Gwen's face. 'I don't know what you mean, Mother.'

Rita's voice had become brisk and businesslike. 'We both know what Tom is like. There's no use pretending. I frequently annoy your father by taking Tom's side, so I feel I can speak plainly. In the theatre there's an atmosphere of . . . well, the people are not quite respectable. In a nutshell, if the job Tom had with your father put too much temptation his way then this one I would think might put an even greater strain on him.'

'But it's purely administration Tom's concerned with,' Gwen protested.

'I realize that,' Rita said firmly. 'Nevertheless I am giving you my opinion.'

They both turned, startled, as rain struck loudly at the window. The leaves of potted plants arranged on a table at the window shivered in a sudden draught. Parts of the room had retreated into shadow and the warm security Gwen always associated with her mother had shrunk to a semi-circle of red carpet and glowing brass in front of the fire.

'I knew it would draw to rain,' Rita said as she leaned over and rang for a maid to pull the curtains and light the lamps.

After they'd dined, Fergus, mellower than Rita had seen him for

146

years, seemed determined to keep Gwen with them, perhaps to make up for the unpleasantness of their last meeting.

'Another fifteen minutes won't make any difference,' he said when Rita admonished him.

'When I've finished my cigar we'll get Anderson round with the carriage. Can you put up with us for a little longer, my dear? When the baby comes we won't see so much of you. For a time your hands will be full.'

'Of course, Father. It's been a lovely evening. I'm pleased to see you looking so happy.' She gave Rita an amused look that seemed to ask—*Is this the same man?*

Fergus waved his cigar. 'Wasn't your mother a credit to us today? A credit to the whole of Glasgow?'

'She looked wonderful—far too young to be a grandmother. Almost a grandmother,' she corrected herself.

'There you are,' Fergus said blandly. 'When people ask what use is money, there's part of the answer. It's handy for paying the dress bills.'

Rita laughed. 'Shall I tell him then, Gwen?'

Gwen pretended to look thoughtful. 'Oh, I think you might risk it, Mother. He seems in just the right mood.'

Ordinarily, Fergus would have been alarmed. Tonight his sense of well-being was too great to be so easily dispersed. 'Come along,' he said. 'Out with it. What have you two been keeping from me?'

'It's about my dress, dear. The one I wore today.'

'What about your dress? Everyone seemed to admire it.'

'I didn't tell you how much it cost.'

Fergus looked at her tolerantly. 'Did I even ask? I knew you'd pay far too much for it. But with the Queen as your excuse, why shouldn't you? Anyway, haven't I just been saying that's what money's for?'

'But Fergus, it only cost ten shillings.'

'It cost what?'

'Ten shillings. Gwen and I got it at a clearance sale. It was the only thing in the whole of Glasgow suitable for the occasion. But I was afraid to tell you.'

Fergus' smile was enormous. 'Well, I'll be damned.' He choked a little on his cigar. 'Dear knows! Ten shillings. I've never heard anything like it. What a nerve, my dear!' He shook his cigar at her.

'I'm glad you didn't tell me sooner. I wouldn't have been happy about it. Not happy at all. I'd have been certain Her Majesty was giving you funny looks.'

Robert arrived in Park Place not long after Gwen had been seen off into the gaslit rain. He stood under a lamp staring sombrely at the green-painted door with the ornate brass knocker outside which his father, mother, and sister had said happy farewells only a few minutes before. He was not completely sober, and hadn't been since the day he and Mary had parted. With the assistance of alcohol he had resisted the urge—at times almost compelling—to wait for her outside the infirmary and tell her he couldn't bear to be without her. But sense kept coming through. Nothing had changed. Their parting had not been a one-sided decision, though he had supplied the initiative. Their relationship had been a doomed one and they both knew it.

Side by side with his continuing longing for Mary there existed in him a fierce determination that Fergus should suffer. While the alcohol had deadened one passion it had inflamed the other. Earlier in the day he had stood sullen-faced in the cheering crowd and watched his father drive past with the Queen. It had seemed to him that Fergus was bloated with undeserved pleasure. They were members of the same Bath Street club and he had entered it that evening to find his father still the centre of attention. He had turned grimly away. A long, brooding walk through drenched streets and the black, tree-lined avenues of the park had eventually brought him home.

After seeing Gwen off Fergus had gone to his study—not, as he told Rita, to work, but to review once more the high points of the day. Robert found him there. The books and the watercolours of old Glasgow—their warmth and brightness thrown up by the flames of the fire—always made it one of the friendliest rooms he knew. Fergus looked comfortable in a jacket of maroon velvet. He was sitting in a faded-blue hide chair. Robert looked at him with a warped sense of elation. He would soon destroy this smug comfort. Nothing would stop him now, not even the realization that he was about to do Mary a terrible wrong. All that mattered was that Fergus would pay.

'There was something I omitted to mention when we discussed

148

Miss Devine recently,' he said in the insolent tone he had rehearsed in the rain.

Fergus felt his scalp go cold. 'Oh?'

'Yes. She's going to have a baby.'

Fergus half rose in his chair.

'Do you understand me? Miss Devine is going to have a child. I am the father.'

Fergus tried to speak, but as in nightmares his throat had solidified. If he had been told he had only a few hours to live he could not have been more bewildered.

'You will soon be a grandfather twice over.'

'What are you saying?' Words dropped at last from Fergus' lips, limp and inadequate.

'I'm sorry I forgot to mention it before. The thing is, what are we going to do? You've told me I mustn't marry her.'

She was no longer the Mary he loved, but had lost. She had become, in his hatred, only a device for tormenting his father.

Fergus' wits began to return. 'You disgraceful, irresponsible scoundrel!'

'I think I should point out, Father, that you're about to start shouting. The servants might hear. I don't particularly care whether they do or not. That's entirely up to you.'

'You must be drunk to take such an attitude.'

'I've been drinking, but I'm not drunk.'

'Then talk to me properly. Are you certain this woman is having a baby?'

'It's hardly the sort of thing a girl would make up.'

'You think not? You don't know how scheming some of these little trollops can be. They'd say anything to get a wedding ring from a man of substance.'

'I didn't know you were so experienced in these matters, Father. I hope this isn't going to have an adverse effect on your title. They won't hold my sins against you, will they!'

'That's just what they will do. You've destroyed me.' Fergus' eyes were heavy with tears of self-pity.

Robert noted them with a mad pleasure. 'Not already, surely? You're the only one who knows, so far.'

Fergus caught at the straw. 'Then you must send her away. You wouldn't want to marry a girl like that. I told you before there would be no happiness in it for you. There would be even less now.'

'And why should I send her away? To save you and your precious title?'

'If you don't care about me, think of your mother. You'll break her heart.'

'What about Miss Devine's heart?'

'Trollops don't have hearts.'

'I got her into this trouble. I can't abandon her.'

'How do you know she didn't lure you into this deliberately? She could have got someone else to put her into trouble to snare you. You might not be the father at all. Send her away.' His voice was imploring. 'I'll see that neither of them starve.'

'It's going to cost you a lot more than that, Father.'

'I don't care. Three hundred a year, say. She could live well on that.'

Robert looked at him with contempt. It had been easier than he imagined. 'For reasons that don't concern you I'm willing to send Miss Devine away, but I will maintain her. For you there's another penalty. I knew this is how you would look at it and to save time I have the price fully worked out. Here it is. Listen carefully. You will put up the money for a new whisky company. Fifty-one per cent of the shares will be in my name. I will be chairman and managing director and you will not interfere.'

Fergus looked at him in astonishment. 'How can you use this girl's tragedy to drive such a bargain? Do you think only in terms of money?'

'They are the only terms you understand, Father. You are a businessman. You know perfectly well you can buy or sell anything. In this instance, you keep your respectability and I get what I want.'

'I don't see it like that at all. I'm thinking of all of us. Our good name. I've worked hard—'

'You snivelling old hypocrite.'

'Robert, my boy!'

Robert leaned across the desk, his face distorted. 'I can't say whether you'll ever get your damned title or not but you'll end up with more than you bloody well deserve. With forty-nine per cent of the shares and me working my heart out you'll be richer than you ever dreamed possible. And I hope it makes you as miserable as I am.'

'My boy! My boy!'

The broken cry dinned in Robert's ears as he slammed the study door, leaving Fergus huddled and shrunken now in the faded blue chair.

Tonight the house was alien and hateful to him. It spoke to him too loudly of his father's dominance. The hot air in the hall rose as if to stifle him. He strode to the door and almost ran along Park Place. In Sauchiehall Street he stopped a cab, then sat in it, not knowing where to tell the driver to take him. Suddenly the quiet, moonlit freshness of the Gareloch beckoned. He looked at his watch. There would still be a train to Helensburgh. His grandmother would put him up as she had done when he was a child. It was an absurd, semi-drunken idea, but the train was on its way before he realized it.

He was sober by the time he came out of the station at Helensburgh, his footsteps echoing dejectedly across the deserted paving. He turned towards the cab rank and cursed when he saw it was empty.

He stood stamping his feet, which had grown cold in the train, wondering whether to wait or walk. After a few minutes he started to shiver, but there was little comfort in the thought of tackling the long tramp along the exposed shore road to Ardfern. By the time he got there his grandmother would be asleep.

The stupidity of the journey sank further into him as the cold wind swirled and rattled around the station entrance and a tired porter pushed the big wooden doors shut.

A couple of hundred yards away a lantern swayed outside the Clyde Hotel. A room there for the night would be the sensible thing. He hesitated at the corner as another thought came to him. He stopped, undecided, and then on an impulse, his blood already coursing faster, he turned into Sinclair Street and began walking towards Roderick Fraser's house on the hill. Fraser, he knew from past adventures, spent several nights of the week in a cottage at the distillery to save him the journey back to Helensburgh. If this was one of his nights away from home, Fiona would be alone.

At the thought, he began to walk faster, the sudden fancy that had not been with him three minutes ago had already grown into a thudding desire.

Ten minutes later he went quietly past the darkened lodge. The long, single-story house looked settled for the night. Now that he was here he hesitated, torn between a bewildered self-loathing and and urge that kept him moving slowly over the grass, keeping to the shadows of the trees and shrubs. In his imagination he saw both Mary and Fiona. What he was seeking would be a heartless betrayal of one and a callous misuse of the other. But on he went, birds rising crying to the stars in fright as he hurried across the big windswept garden.

One of the windows of Fiona's bedroom was pulled down from the top but he couldn't tell whether the room was in darkness or heavily curtained. There was a rosebed underneath. He stood on the damp earth and tapped carefully on the glass. He kept on tapping at intervals until a light went on in the room and the curtains which he could now see to be slightly drawn were pulled a little apart.

He began to move to where he thought she would best see him but the curtains were immediately closed again. As he stood wondering what to do next he heard the front door opening.

At the sight of her his conscience retreated. She held a lamp and by its light he saw that over her nightdress she wore a loose gown of silk or satin. Her lustrous brown hair had been brushed out for the night and it hung glossily over her shoulders, drawn together only at the nape of her neck by a ribbon.

'You're a plucky one, Fiona,' he said admiringly.

'I could see exactly who it was,' she said calmly. 'Otherwise I would have screamed and rung the bell to waken the servants.'

'You're not angry?'

She hardly hesitated. 'No.'

His gratitude rose as she pulled the door open for him. *This*, he thought, as he stepped into the hall, *is one of her attractions*. She didn't always have to be putting on a show and she wasn't forever having to be coaxed.

It was a big house and the servants' rooms were in a wing at the back but they walked to her bedroom in silence.

She locked the door and turned up the lamp. There was no pretence that he was unwelcome. 'This is a surprise,' she said.

'Your father's at Lochbank, I hope?'

'Yes. So you can stop whispering. The door's a heavy one and the servants are a long way away.'

He kissed her. Her lips were slightly slippery. 'I hope I didn't waken you?' He tasted glycerine.

She gave him a lazy smile. 'I'm sure you don't care whether you wakened me or not. Actually I had just put the lamp out.' She loosened her gown. 'If you don't mind I'm going to get back into bed. The room's cold now the fire's gone down.'

As she half turned to throw the gown on a chair the sweeping lines of her breasts and thighs were moulded to the shiny smoothness of her nightdress.

'My God, Fiona, I'd forgotten how beautiful you are,' he gasped as he pressed her down on the bed. 'Hell,' he said, abruptly letting go of her again. 'Clothes. What a nuisance they are.'

She laughed at his frustrated excitement. 'Do you realize you always say something like that, Robert? You should really go about with just a coat on, in perpetual readiness.'

She looked on tolerantly as he threw his clothes off, his fingers distracted and clumsy. 'You disappear for months,' she said, 'then turn up quivering with passion but not so much as a "Please" or a "May I?" It's really very presumptuous of you.'

'Please, please,' he said in mock humility as he knelt by the bed and pressed his face into her silken warmth. 'I've been thinking of this for the last hour.'

'Then come in beside me. You look silly out there.'

Her arms went around him as he joined her in the bed.

'What would Miss de Veen say if she knew?'

The instant she said it he began to go limp, all the hot desperation draining away. His sense of shock was transferred immediately to her. She tightened her arms about him in surprise and regret. Long seconds passed before she said, 'I'm afraid that was very silly of me, Robert. I'm sorry. I didn't expect such a violent reaction.'

He groaned and rolled on to his back. 'Why did you have to say that?'

'I only meant to tease you. I didn't realize this would happen. You're a funny boy, Robert. Don't you want me at all now?'

He lay miserably against her, empty of alcohol and of lust. *Empty*, he thought, *of everything*. 'At this moment, no,' he said.

'I'm sorry,' she said again, trying to cradle him like a baby. 'Can you stay for a while? Where are you going to spend the night?'

'I'll go down to the Clyde Hotel. They'll be empty at this time of year.'

'Then I've got time to make up to you,' she said. 'It's not yet eleven o'clock.'

'You can try,' he said with a bitter laugh.

Gwen, home in India Street, sat by the fire waiting for Hoey's return. It was five past eleven and after the excitements of the day she was tired, but determinedly she opened her book. It was *Alfred Leslie*, by Frederick Arnold, a romantic novel of student life in Glasgow's Old College. As usual, she would sit up. She didn't think it right that after a long day at business Hoey should return to a house already gone to bed. At the beginning, he had arrived home from the theatre between half past eleven and midnight, but for the last two nights he'd been later. It had been the early hours before she heard him moving about in the bedroom. 'Little problems,' was all he would say in his flippant way when she asked what had kept him so late.

Both nights she had lain awake, wondering, long after he had fallen asleep. But wondering about what? She could not have said. Now, after Rita's talk of the theatre's temptations, her uneasiness had returned.

She knew now she would never be happy so long as Hoey worked in the theatre. Rita had been right. It wasn't suitable for him.

The wind roared in the chimney and rain hit the window. The curtains trembled. The maid had built up the fire before going to bed. Now, despite the draughts, the room was warm. Gwen felt her baby move, a faint, fluttering signal from someone she felt she already knew. She longed for the day when she could respond, when she could fondle the warm living reality. 'Go to sleep, my lovely baby,' she said softly.

She read a few pages of *Alfred Leslie*, then put the book down. Her body had begun to ache and she had to rise from her chair and walk about the room, both hands pressed to the small of her back. As she bent over a chair to ease the throbbing pain in her back she heard a faint but unmistakable sound in the hall. The brass flap of the letter box had been opened, then allowed to snap back on the hinge. In its place, at the correct time, it was a welcome sound—associated with invitations to tea and news from friends. At this hour, it made her apprehensive. She opened the sitting-room door and looked into the hall. On the carpet behind the front door an envelope lay. She lifted it and went quickly into a room with windows looking on to the street. She heard footsteps and when she drew the curtain she saw a youth, coatless despite the rain, walking away. There was always someone ready to deliver a message in Glasgow for a sixpence.

She hurried back to the sitting-room and examined the envelope under a lamp. It was addressed to her and she recognized Hoey's writing. No matter how late he was going to be in getting home he never sent messages. Her heart beat uneasily as she opened the envelope and began to read:

DEAR GWEN,
This will be a shock to you but there is no way in which I can lessen it. I am going away. I could blame it all on the way your father treats me, but there is more than that. I have met someone else. By the time you read this note I will be on the night train to London. Forget me and make a life without me. Give all your love to our baby.

TOM

Gwen read the note through again in a daze of disbelief. Her heart and her breathing seemed to have stopped. The normal sounds of the room—the tick of the clock and the faint roar of the fire—were suspended. She began to shake.

She felt blindly for the note but it had fluttered away somewhere. *He couldn't mean it*, she told herself. Not with the baby coming. She tried to think if there'd been any sign. There had been nothing. He'd been no less loving. There *couldn't* be anyone else. It was a cruel hoax. And yet, the handwriting was his. Her anguish had momentarily purged her of physical pain. She knocked aside a heavy chair and crawled frantically about the floor searching for the note. She found it under a cabinet. Holding it to the fire as she crouched on the floor, she read it again. The night train to London had been the one on which they had left for their honeymoon. At this moment it was an unbearable memory.

Behind her, the clock chimed. She turned to it. It was eleven fifteen. Several seconds passed before its significance penetrated her turmoil. He couldn't be on his way to London yet. The train, she remembered, didn't leave until eleven fifty. If she could get to him, perhaps he would not go. She would plead with him to stay. As she struggled painfully to her feet she thanked God for the accident or misunderstanding that had brought the messenger with the note sooner than Hoey had intended. It was a sign! She clung to the idea for comfort. Bridge Station was on the south side of the river and India Street on the north. It wasn't impossible to get there in thirty-five minutes, but in the dark, tired, and carrying her child, it would take every second. Desperately she flung open the front door and ran out into the rain.

She had reached the bottom of India Street before she realized she hadn't brought a coat. For a moment she hesitated, but it would take time to turn back.

In her mind there was a picture of a train at a platform, the driver and fireman already in the locomotive cab and steam swirling around the wheels. Soon her dress was sodden. It dragged at her legs and made every step difficult, but heedlessly she forced herself on against the wind. Rain streamed into her eyes, blinding her. The weight of her child dragged at her sides and sent red, stinging pains shooting down the insides of her legs. Her chances of finding an empty cab at this time on such a night were almost nil, but at every distant rumble she paused, hoping God had sent her the means of reaching Tom in time. Each time her hopes collapsed as a dust cart, a delivery lorry returning to its quarters for the night, or a private carriage passed, usually going in the opposite direction or cutting across her route. Hysteria had dissolved all the inhibitions so carefully and expensively bred in her, and two or three times she called out for help as private carriages drew abreast. But the drivers and occupants either looked at her disapprovingly or kept their eyes averted. She realized with an added jog of distress that by now, with her soaking clothes clinging to her, her hair loosened and straggling, she would be taken for a drunken beggar or a street woman.

Her progress was erratic. She ran till she was exhausted, then walked weakly on until she had the strength to run again. Her breath tore at her lungs. Dread of the damage she might be doing to her child racked her, but every time she was tempted to stop, the unbearable thought of losing her husband spurred her on. Her father didn't like him. He was weak and foolish. But she loved him and wanted him. He was her Tom.

Miraculously, her mind had already closed out the suggestion of another woman. Tom was weak. Tom was foolish. Was Tom bad? Her mind would not consider it. She must get to him before the train left Glasgow. After that he would be beyond her reach. In London's millions he would be lost to her. As a molten pain suffused her body, she began to see this agonized dash through the city as a mission of mercy. She was on her way to rescue her husband. The exact nature of his peril didn't matter now. It could be fire. It could be the sea. It was immaterial. He was in danger and she must save him.

The lamp-posts were widely spaced and the flares did little more than create small pools of grey in the wet blackness. The windows she passed gave no light. There was no comfort anywhere.

Her occasional glimpses of night-time Glasgow had been either from the security of a carriage or in the company of other people. No prudent woman walked alone in this area after dark if it could be avoided, for even pleasant thoroughfares where respectable people worked during the day became perilous at night. Her fear of these black, unfamiliar streets urged her on. In some of the veiled doorways she heard whispering voices and secretive laughter. Men and women clung to each other in these streaming wet cavities. An occasional dark shape shuffled into sight, sending her veering terrified in some other direction. One lunged at her, mouthing obscenities, but as she turned cowering against a wall, her hands held low to protect her baby, he collapsed in a drunken bundle, the street water swirling around him like a river diverted.

In her fright she took several wrong turnings. Once, the entry ahead of her was so narrow and black that she turned back to find a less frightening route. Several times she tripped and fell, once into muddy water, and another time into a mess of refuse, soggy and stinking. She slithered out of it and soaking, bleeding, and sobbing, shambled on towards the station. Pain drove out even the fear for her child. Her tormented body craved rest. But frantically she drove it on. A vision burned in her consciousness, a tender, sentimental tableau of Hoey with his arms opened to her. Five, ten, perhaps fifteen minutes had passed since she ran from the house. She didn't know. Lights moved in front of her vision, above her, and with a smooth, gliding motion. They were the lights of a ship. She had reached the riverside. She turned eastwards. Glasgow Bridge couldn't be far. Once she crossed it she would almost be there. She screamed as a figure stepped around a wharfside hut and grasped her arm. 'Let me go! Oh, God, let me go!' The grip loosened. It was only as she backed away that she saw the policeman's uniform in the glow from his carbide lantern. He looked disgustedly after the mumbling, muddy mess of a woman, then turned away to continue his patrol among the shadows of the quay. It was more exposed on the dockside. The unimpeded wind buffeted her and, catching the running waves of the river, deluged her in spray.

Through the mistiness that had begun to fill her head Gwen saw Glasgow Bridge. She crossed it, bent under the parapet to escape the full tear and suck of the wind.

At last, when it seemed she must collapse under the weight of pain raging through her, the station lights appeared. The paroxysms in her body had now assumed a rhythm so that even in her state of near-trance she knew when the next would strike. People entering or leaving the station shied away at her unsteady approach. One of her hands had been cut when she fell and she had blood on her face. Blood and mud and smeared strands of hair. No one could have recognized her now as the happy, affluent young wife who less than an hour ago had settled by the fire with a novel. As she swayed across the concourse, colliding with barrows and pieces of luggage, a long strident blast of steam galvanized her. Somehow she knew it was Hoey's train announcing its departure. She stumbled towards the sound. The ticket collector shook his head as she approached and began closing the gate. He waved to the guard leaning from the slowly moving rear coach. With a fierce release of strength Gwen pushed the iron gate open, knocking the astonished ticket collector aside. With her hands outstretched she stumbled after the departing train until, all power suddenly leaving her, she pitched sideways over the edge of the platform on to the railway line.

It was four o'clock next morning before Gwen was identified at the Royal Infirmary by one of her maids. The servants, wakened by the banging of the open front door, had searched the house.

They had found the bedroom of their master and mistress empty and gone to the police.

By four forty-five a policeman had called at Park Place and within another half hour Rita and Fergus were standing, shivering with cold and anxiety, in a corridor outside the ward where Gwen lay.

'She has a fractured arm,' a nurse told them with a reassuring lack of gravity. 'And she had struck her head on the railway line. We can't tell definitely yet, but the damage doesn't seem serious. When she recovered consciousness she was as lucid as could be expected.'

'You will know, of course, that she's having a baby,' Rita said. 'How will this affect it?'

The nurse looked surprised. 'I'm sorry. I should have realized you didn't know. Mrs. Hoey's baby was born in a room at the station. I'm afraid we were unable to save it. It was a puny little thing. A girl.'

Fergus put a hand on Rita's shoulder but whether to give comfort or draw it he could not have said.

Gwen was in a deep, drugged sleep and they were forbidden to make a sound. The nurse stood with them by the bedside in the near darkness. After a minute or two she signalled that they should leave.

'I can hardly believe it,' Rita said as they went along the silent corridors looking for the way out. 'Only a few hours ago we were sitting so happily together. My poor Gwen! Her baby's gone. But we must be thankful she'll be all right. What was she doing in that railway station? And where is Tom?'

'Wherever he is I'm sure somehow that this is all his doing,' Fergus said with grim bewilderment.

But Rita shook her head. 'How on earth can it be?'

A door opened ahead of them and the policeman who brought them the news came into the corridor with another man. He recognized Fergus.

'One moment, Mr. King,' he said. 'Perhaps you could help us. This is Lieutenant Grant.'

Lieutenant Grant had a sympathetic face. His shovel hat made him look like an elderly clergyman. 'Do you happen to know anybody by the name of Tom, sir?' he asked.

'Mrs. Hoey's husband is called Tom. Why? Has something happened to him?' Fergus could not have said what he feared—or hoped—he might hear.

Lieutenant Grant looked embarrassed. 'I don't know, sir, that I should—'

'Oh, come on, man. I'm Mrs. Hoey's father. On top of that I'm a magistrate of this city. I sit on the bench of a police court. What have you to tell us about Mr. Hoey?'

The lieutenant brought out a leather wallet and took from it the note Hoey had sent to Gwen. It was wrinkled now and smudged. 'A railwayman found this on the platform near where Mrs. Hoey fell. If Tom is her husband's name I think this explains everything we wanted to know.'

Fergus' sense of humiliation was enormous as he handed the note back to the policeman.

'What does it say, Fergus?'

Fergus took Rita's arm. 'I'll explain on the way home, my dear.'

The dawn streets were already busy with men on their way to factories and shipyards. Although the wind had slackened it was still raining and the workmen looked drab and ugly in stained overalls. The pockets of their jackets bulged with 'pieces' and tea and sugar tins. Never had Fergus thought Glasgow so grey and broken. This was the city where he'd spent his happiest and most prosperous years and yet in one day it seemed that he had come to hate it. In a few hours his seemingly impregnable family life had been dealt two terrible blows—from within. Had he, in the smoky gloom of this grasping town, missed the importance of life? Had he been grubbing too hard for money when he should have been at home helping Rita look after his family? He didn't know, and it was too late now.

'I think I'll tell Anderson just to let me down at the office,' he said gloomily. 'It's almost seven o'clock.' He would have to work out the financing of the disgraceful agreement he had made with Robert. The sooner he did it the better. And when he had, he would lock his desk and bury himself at Ardfern for a month—if Gwen was all right. The bracken would be fading down there now and soon the Gareloch, like all the craggy inlets of the Clyde, would turn a warm russet above the grey waterline. The steamers that had cruised the Gareloch all summer would be laid up, leaving the piers at Row, Mambeg, and Garelochhead to the service vessels and the gulls. Down there perhaps he could begin to forget that at the age of fifty-two he had been blackmailed by his son into starting a risky new venture in whisky; forget what Hoey had done to Gwen and what Robert had done to Mary Devine. The sight of Gwen lying bruised and bandaged in the hospital bed, robbed of her baby, had made him think of the other girl almost with compassion, but that was something else he would have to forget.

His eye was caught by a line of bunting sagging wet and twisted between two windows. Was it only a day since, decked in ermine, he had driven through these streets with the Queen and then gone on, swollen with pride, to strut about in his club?

He realized Rita had been speaking. 'I'm sorry, my dear,' he said. 'I was miles away.'

'I said you will not go to the office until you come home and let me see you eat breakfast.' Her tone was emphatic.

He took her hand without speaking and held it tight.

# TWO

# ROBERT

# 9

The bottle Robert chose for his whisky was the standard tall quart, round and made of clear glass. He had decided coloured glass was unnecessary. His whisky did not cloud. Why hide its attractive appearance?

When a printer's proof of the label arrived he stuck it on a bottle and took it into Fergus' room.

In recent months a working peace had replaced the bitterness of the previous year. In his attempts, with Rita, to dull Gwen's sorrow, Fergus had found relief from Robert's wounding. Since parting from Mary, Robert had become a recluse. If he couldn't have her, he didn't want anyone. But worse than the ache of losing her was his remorse at having destroyed her reputation, even if only to his father. It haunted him unless he kept himself constantly occupied. The part Fergus had played in creating this unhappiness became blurred so that after almost a year father and son had reached a formal civility again.

Fergus lifted the bottle Robert had placed on his desk. The label was engraved in black and white on warm, tobacco-coloured paper. Fergus took to it immediately, perhaps because it reminded him of a bank draft. Only after peering for a few seconds at the overall effect did he read the two words that stood out in heraldic lettering —KING'S ROYAL. The conjunction of his own name with the word 'royal' was extraordinarily pleasing. He had known it was part of Robert's plan that their whisky should have a distinctive and easily remembered name so that people who liked it could ask for it again. He had enquired, months ago and without much interest, what the name was to be. Robert had said he was still undecided and had asked for suggestions. Fergus' hesitant offerings—Lomond Dew and Old Glen—were the only two he could now remember—had been speedily rejected. He had been slightly offended and had decided to have nothing more to do with what he considered to be a very minor matter. He had, however, been ready to dislike and even deride Robert's choice when it was finally unveiled. Now, he found he liked it very much. *It was tactful, even dutiful, of Robert,* he thought, *to have named the whisky after him.* It was a name he wouldn't be ashamed to mention in his club. He would have been hurt, but perhaps unsurprised, if he had known that Robert had been thinking of himself when he put the words 'King' and 'Royal' together.

'Well, what do you think of it?'

'I like it,' Fergus said. 'I'm pleased to see you've made it dignified.'

This was exactly the effect Robert had been seeking.

'I'm glad that's how it strikes you. Quality and dignity are the images we must project. When people are looking for the best whisky obtainable we want them to think immediately of King's Royal.'

Robert's confidence always made Fergus apprehensive. 'Aren't you running ahead of yourself? We haven't sold a single bottle yet.'

'No, but we will. I'm thinking of the future.'

'Think about it by all means but don't let it run away with you. Fly low and you won't have far to fall.'

Robert, remembering how recent and fragile their armistice was, managed to turn a rebuke into a reasonably cheerful laugh. 'That's the style, Father. We'll take one cautious step at a time, being careful to walk before we leap and remembering not to crow too soon or count our chickens before they're hatched.'

Fergus ignored the sarcasm. 'Another thing. Are all those samples you're giving away absolutely essential?'

'I'm afraid they are. You know what your own attitude is if a traveller comes in here with anything new. You always ask for a free sample.'

'Samples can add up to an awful lot of money. I hope we get a return on it.' Fergus clearly doubted it.

'There's no other way of proceeding. We're trying to interest people in a whisky with a new taste. Naturally, they want to try it.

They won't order otherwise, but there's no need to worry. It will all come back to us in the end.'

Before any more could be said he lifted the bottle and left the room, leaving Fergus staring at the dark-brown paint of the door.


When the traditional crowd of revellers gathered at Glasgow Cross just before midnight on Hogmanay, 1876, to hear the New Year rung in on the Tolbooth bells, the whisky many of them drank was King's Royal. In a year of continuous advertising Robert had made it the best-known whisky in the key towns of Scotland.

At first Fergus was alarmed when he saw how much was being spent. Apart from newspaper space, Robert was giving away hundreds of samples and providing shopkeepers with showcards. His alarm turned to astonishment when he saw the orders the new travellers started to bring in. It seemed almost every public house, hotel, restaurant, or licensed grocer that they called on was willing to place a trial order for King's new blended whisky. Industrial Scotland was booming and people were eager for the new. When the travellers called again, a high percentage of customers placed re-orders. These careful repeats soon settled into regular business. The palatable golden liquid in the attractive bottle was a novelty and there seemed no end to the number of people eager to try it. Robert had engaged two travellers to start with, but less than six months later another two had become necessary.

By the middle of 1877 Fergus was having to admit Robert's vision had been justified. In less than two years King's Royal had become a profitable business.

Additionally, the indications were that the potential was immense. The increase of business had forced him to review his public commitments. Somehow he must carve more time from each day. After weeks of indecision he decided to resign his seat on the town council. Sir James Spence was against it, urging that this was the last position Fergus should relinquish. 'After all, when I step down you stand a very good chance of being Glasgow's next Lord Provost,' he said. 'I would be strongly behind you.' But Fergus, whose faith in Sir James' powers had diminished a little as each new Honours List went by without his name appearing on it, stuck to his decision. His work for the Corporation he felt to be the least rewarding of his activities and when the time came he

167

declined to stand for re-election. When Sir James died only eight months later he had to suffer the sight of a man he disliked becoming Lord Provost and at the same time wonder disconsolately if his chances of a title had gone to the grave with his patron.

His disappointment was lightened by the headlong advance of King's Royal. Already, if only in Scotland, it was finding a welcome in the middle-class drawing-rooms from which he had said it would be barred. There was an appeal, if not to snobbery, then to fashion, in having it available in the original bottle alongside humdrum decanters of claret, brandy, and port. There was cachet to be gained in asking for it in public. It was even appearing on the wine lists at important functions.

Fearing the effect this success was having on Robert, Fergus preached prudence. Paradoxically, now that the business was steadily expanding, he felt caution to be even more necessary than at the outset, when all had been risk and uncertainty. When he could find no new stumbling blocks he used old ones.

He refused to be carried away on the stream of his son's enthusiasm. When Robert said, 'One day soon we'll have to start thinking about England,' Fergus' reaction was automatic. 'Why? We haven't reached anything like saturation in Scotland.'

'No, and we won't neglect Scotland, but London's the real market. Eventually we'll have to tackle it. It's the showplace and shop window of the world. If we can get King's Royal into the big hotels and restaurants it will help us to spread into the rest of the world. Foreign visitors will see it and talk about it when they go home.'

Despite himself, Fergus laughed. 'Robert! Robert! I must remind you that we're just a humble Glasgow company. You're dreaming now in millions.'

Robert nodded. 'And in ten years we'll be *dealing* in millions.'

Later that week he picked his way through the broken eggs and cabbage leaves of Candleriggs. The smell of smoked ham was strong in the sunlit air. The premises of Ross & Co. seemed, in the two years since his last visit, to have become buried deeper than ever behind the overflow of fruit and vegetables from the warehouse next door. The window display differed little except that the stand of Old Corrie had gone.

That hope clearly hadn't flowered, and prosperity generally

seemed to have escaped Peter Ross. Robert reminded him of their earlier meeting. 'How are you finding business?' he asked as he looked about the half-filled shelves.

Ross smoothed his white apron thoughtfully. 'Very poor,' he admitted. 'They're pulling down the houses in this area. My customers are disappearing with them.'

'And Old Corrie?'

Ross gave him a disillusioned smile. 'There are two or three bottles still lying about somewhere. Gathering dust, I'm afraid.' He brightened a little. 'Mind you, I still think it was a good idea . . . if I'd had money.'

Robert put his gloves on the scrubbed counter. 'You sound a little dispirited, Mr. Ross. Have you ever thought of giving up here?'

The cheerfulness that didn't seem too far under the dejection surfaced again. 'Why? Would you like to buy me out?'

'Not exactly. I just wondered.'

'Well, you're not far wrong. I often think of it. Not so much of selling out—I only rent these premises—but of closing down.' He shrugged. 'But I've got to live. I have a family. Jobs are hard to find.' He scratched his head. 'My wife never wanted me to give up my job with the warehouse. She was right, as it's turned out. The shop was too far gone when I came into it, like the area. My father had the best out of it.'

Robert found the man's predicament affecting. It made what he'd come to say easier. 'I have a position that might interest you,' he said.

Ross eyed him warily. 'What kind of position?'

'One that should be to your taste. You would be working with whisky. I want a reliable man to take charge of blending whiskies for me. Since blending's an entirely new operation invented by me, no one knows anything about it. I can't get a man with previous experience. Then I remembered you and your Old Corrie.'

A slow, questioning expression had been forming on Ross' thin face. 'Wait a minute,' he said. 'You must be Mr. King of this new King's Royal whisky. Am I right?'

'Right first time,' Robert said. 'Does my offer appeal to you? We can discuss money later, but you can take it I'll be fair.'

Ross hoisted himself on to the counter and sat with his legs dangling.

'There would be no harm in me talking it over with my wife tonight. I could write to you tomorrow.' He looked around him almost apologetically. 'You can understand that, despite times being bad, it will be a thought to close my father's business, even though I've been considering it. But if I have to take a job, nothing would interest me more than whisky.'

'That's what I thought. You won't find it dull. I'm continually experimenting.' He smiled. 'You must have done a little of that yourself.'

Ross' eyes were bright with enthusiasm. 'If I'd been a cleverer man I might have thought of your blended whisky instead of my poor Old Corrie,' he said.

Robert nodded. 'You might easily have done.'

Ross laughed. 'But even if I had thought of it, damn the good it would have done me. I wouldn't have had the capital to push it.'

He jumped down from the counter and impulsively held out his hand.

'I don't think I really have to talk it over with my wife, Mr. King. I've wasted too much time in this shop already. There's no future for me here. I'd like to work for you. In a new business there should be opportunities.'

Robert took the outstretched hand and shook it warmly. 'I think I can promise you opportunity, interest, and perhaps occasionally some fun,' he said. 'King's Royal is not only a new business. To me it's an adventure and I want men to work for me who see it that way.'

On a Sunday morning in August Robert looked from his bedroom window at Ardfern into drenching drizzle. After lunch he and James put on boots and leggings, collected sticks, and set out for a tramp in Glen Fruin. Moisture hung from the trees in silvery globules and clung like dew to spiders' webs in the hedges. It was very still and their boots went through the wet grass with a pleasant swishing sound as they climbed the hill behind Ardfern. Rotting tree trunks, toppled in bygone storms, lay here and there, covered with moss and lichen. They crossed a burn where racing, peat-coloured water whipped itself white against grey boulders. As they went through a thicket of misshapen trees a roe deer appeared momentarily in front of them and then bounded away in a tracery of spray from disturbed greenery. Gradually the climb became less steep, evening out into a tangle of heather that caught at their boots and tripped them. They climbed two or three drystone dikes and after a gentle descent found themselves in the desolate strath of Glen Fruin. The peaty ground gurgled under them and, if they stood for a few moments, pools of water gathered around their feet. They climbed a tumbling dike and poked about in the ruins of a small stone house. There were several in the glen.

'I suppose a shepherd once lived here,' James said, dislodging a stone and hastening the final collapse.

'Or a crofter.'

'They must have had a long way to go for their shopping.'

'I don't suppose they shopped more than a few times a year. What they didn't grow themselves they'd get from the nearest farm. The land at the east end of the glen is fertile. There are still two or three farms there.'

'Hello!' They both turned, startled, as a tall, white-faced figure in a sodden brown cape came through what had once been the front door of the house. 'You won't get much shelter here. The roof looks as if it's been off these last fifty years.'

'Oh, it's you, Lindsay.' Robert smiled. 'Do you know James, my brother? I'm glad we're not the only two who need our heads examined.'

'I wait for a day like this before coming up here,' Lindsay said. 'I think this is how it should be seen. Show me a squelching Scottish glen like this and I wouldn't change it for a South Sea lagoon.'

Colin Lindsay painted and wrote poetry about Scotland's heroic past. His family had a busy brass foundry in Dumbarton, but he had declined to join the business and had become a schoolteacher instead. He taught slum children in Glasgow and believed all Scotland's ills could be cured if only the union with England could be broken.

'It's one of the emptiest places I know,' Robert said.

'It could throb with life one day if we regain control of our own destiny,' Lindsay said, looking over the soggy landscape with the eyes of Ossian. 'Do you know how many young Scots men and women left for the Colonies last year?'

'No.'

'Over thirty thousand. Every year Old Scotia becomes a little emptier. One day, if nothing's done, there will be nothing left but the grandeur. Heavens knows how many more Glen Fruins there are in the making. I feel I help by keeping on my little weekend cottage at Row.'

'Is there a cure?'

James interrupted. 'Yes, Robert, some people say there is.'

'Oh?'

'It's called Socialism. I've been reading about it in some pamphlets one of the boys gave me. I'll let you have them when I'm finished.' James' voice was eager despite Robert's disapproving expression.

'What do you know about Socialism?'

'Very little, Robert, but I hope to read more. It's provocative. The aim is to abolish capitalists and elevate the working classes.'

'Is it, indeed? And if there are no capitalists who's going to provide employment for the working classes?'

'The State will own the means of production, apparently. All men will be equal.'

Robert, wondering if this revolutionary idea would conflict with Lindsay's poetic vision of a revitalized Scotland, said, 'Heaven forbid.'

James looked disappointed. 'Why, Robert? Don't you think Socialism would be a desirable thing? Many people do. Benson—that's the boy who gave me the pamphlets—was at one of those gatherings in Argyle Street. The speaker was a trade unionist. The people cheered him.'

'I've listened to Argyle Street orators,' Robert said. 'It doesn't matter what they're preaching. They're always cheered. On Sunday evenings the people are usually drunk.'

He turned to Lindsay and, wondering if he was being rash, asked, 'And what do you think of this new religion for the masses?'

'I prefer the ancient Celtic myths.' Lindsay sniffed delicately as if scenting the campfires of a bygone culture.

His scepticism pleased Robert. 'It's a pretty picture, I suppose. Socialism, I mean.'

'It should be. They have a monopoly of all the third-rate poets.' Lindsay flapped his cloak. 'I was going as far as the Laggary Burn when I spotted you two. Shall we walk there together? It isn't more than a half mile.'

The Laggary, fed by other, smaller, burns, was brawling loudly in its rocky bed. They sheltered against high boulders and gave themselves up for some minutes to the fascination of moving water and to the forsaken glen, the roofless houses of the people who were gone, the tumbling streams, and the mist that swirled away occasionally to show dark mountain slopes. Robert was beginning to find it depressing, but Lindsay appeared to be dreaming. *What scenes of valour*, Robert wondered, *are being enacted inside Lindsay's head?* He had rejected brass founding for schoolteaching and would doubtless, if it were possible, abandon his pupils for the role of warrior poet at the court of some ancient king.

But Lindsay's thoughts, it turned out, were more contemporary. 'The question of whether Scotland goes Socialist or remains Capitalist seems secondary to me to whether or not she regains her Scottishness. Why should we pay taxes to England? The wealth we produce from our coal, iron, steel, and shipbuilding should stay in Scotland for the benefit of Scotsmen.'

'I like the English,' Robert said irrelevantly and challengingly.

'One day we may be forced to take up guns against them.'

'They'll extinguish you in a week.'

'Liberty or death,' Lindsay said, knowing he would not be there.

Robert, almost as if he could see into Lindsay's mind, said, 'And where will you be when the shooting starts?'

Lindsay smiled gently. 'Probably at home, writing poetry,' he said with rueful honesty. He heaved his long body off the boulder. 'You know, we're all soaked. It might be wiser if we kept moving. Homeward this time.'

When they walked a while in silence, climbing dikes, jumping across burns, stumbling through the entangling heather, Lindsay said breathlessly, 'Well, it's clear I'm an ineffectual dreamer and James is a dangerous revolutionary, but what about you, King? Your sort of chap I can't understand at all. You never seem satisfied. You're hardworking, I'll grant you. In fact, I'm told you never stop. But what is it you're after? Your businesses are never big enough for you. You're always expanding. What is it you want?'

'I want to be a millionaire,' Robert said cheerfully, 'so that I can leave Scotland to the sheep and go and live somewhere sunny and dry.'

Lindsay was not provoked. He laughed good-naturedly. It was

James who took up the challenge. 'Millionaires are immoral,' he said eagerly, as if he had been waiting for a chance to quote again from his pamphlets.

Robert decided to change the subject. 'Do you spend all your weekends down here, Lindsay?'

'Most of them.'

'Next time we're entertaining at Ardfern you must join us.'

They left Lindsay at Row and walked along the darkening shore to Ardfern. As they went up the carriageway Robert said, 'By the way, James, I wouldn't let Father hear you spouting Socialism. I think a few words from one of your pamphlets would send him up in a blue light.'

James looked surprised. 'But Father likes to hear all points of view, Robert. I've heard him say so, many times.'

Robert put his hand out and tousled his brother's hair. 'Yes. Well, if you take my advice, young man, you won't take that too literally.'

# 10

At the start of the new business Robert had taken a warped delight in deliberately excluding Fergus from all decisions. He made arrangements and told Fergus about them afterwards. The pleasure had come in watching Fergus adjust to the realization that, as a minority shareholder, there was nothing very effective he could do about this high-handedness. Gradually, though, the exercise of this petty cruelty had palled. The effort of watching for openings had been disproportionate to the enjoyment. He had also realized that he was depriving himself of his father's experience. Now, in most things, he liked to keep Fergus informed. His method, however, was usually oblique.

'Have you seen Gwen recently?' he asked one morning.

Fergus was surprised at what seemed a sudden change of subject. 'Not for a week or so, but your mother saw her yesterday. Why?'

'I think she's too much on her own. I've been wondering. . . . There's an international food and drinks exhibition going to be held at Alexandra Court in London in the autumn. I think we should take a stand for King's Royal. If we do, it might be good for Gwen to help me run it.'

'You mean, take her to London with you?' Fergus found himself thinking not so much of Gwen as of Hoey. Where he had gone was it wise for Gwen to follow—even after three years, even with all those millions of people? Fergus couldn't follow his sudden, worrying reaction through in any logical way.

'I'd see she was all right. We'd stay at the same hotel. It would only be for a week.'

'But what would she do?'

'The same as me. Be at the stand to answer questions and pass out samples. She might find it cheering.'

The mention of samples brought Fergus back to known territory. 'What's all this going to cost? And what advantage would it be to us?'

'Apart from any samples we might give away, it would cost us approximately one hundred and fifty pounds, but we might gain thousands of pounds' worth of business in return. I think we would also stand a chance of winning a medal or a diploma. They judge the various entries for purity and quality.'

'The judges at these things can never see past cognac or French wines.'

'They'll never have been asked to pass judgement on a whisky like King's Royal.'

'They're very conservative,' Fergus said vaguely. He was thinking about Gwen again. 'I'll have a word with your mother tonight. We'll see what she thinks about Gwen going to London. Don't mention it to her meantime.'

'But do you agree, then, that we should take part in the exhibition?'

'I suppose so. You seem set on it.'

'I think it would pay us and I have no worries about leaving Peter Ross in charge. He's every bit as dedicated as I had hoped.'

Fergus nodded. 'You seem to have made a very shrewd choice in Ross.'

'Then that's settled, but Gwen doesn't have to go. I just thought it would take her out of herself.'

'We'll see how she feels about it.'

After Hoey deserted her, Gwen lived on in the house in India Street for five months. Rita and Fergus had said her old room was waiting for her at Park Place and though she had been glad to go to it for a week or two after leaving the hospital she had never considered it as a permanency. She knew four years of marriage had eased her away from her mother and father. It wasn't that she loved them any the less, but the bonds had inevitably loosened. They would expect her to be the girl who had gone out of the house to be Hoey's bride. Gwen knew she was no longer that, although exactly what changes had taken place in her she would

176

have found it difficult to say. Instinct told her the seeds of dis-harmony were present. Perhaps it was that she hadn't changed enough. Perhaps she was still too much the girl who married Hoey to be completely pleasing to Rita and Fergus. She sometimes felt they were searching for bitterness in her, deeming a little of it to be only proper.

Certainly, the loss of the baby had marked her less than she could have admitted to Rita for fear of being thought hard. She'd been delivered of it when she was unconscious and it was dead by the time she regained awareness. If it had cried she hadn't heard it. She'd never felt its warmth. They had brought it to her bedside wrapped in a sheet. It had rested in the nurse's arms like a doll—small, white, and cold to touch. They had taken the doll away for burial and Gwen had sunk back into her chemical sleep. In a few days she had forgotten what it had looked like. *Hoey she remembered.* This above all, she felt would have been a source of strain if she had gone back to Park Place. Rita and Fergus wanted her to forget Hoey. Gwen loved him still.

In the end, she sold her house and moved into a rented apart-ment in Holland Street. It was noisier than India Street because of its nearness to the shops of Sauchiehall Street but, for the same reason, more cheerful. Park Place was still only a pleasant walk away and Gwen went there for dinner every Sunday, unless Rita and Fergus were at Ardfern.

It was at one of these Sunday dinners, late in August, that Fergus asked her if she would like to go to London with Robert. Rita, at first doubtful of the suggestion, had come to think that perhaps it would do Gwen good. She smiled encouragingly.

Robert was at the table and Gwen turned to him in surprise. 'What's made you think of this, Robert?'

'I just felt it would be a good opportunity for you to get out of the house for a little while.'

'But haven't you always agreed with Father, that a woman's place is in the home?' Her expression was exaggeratedly innocent. 'I didn't think you would want a woman meddling in your busi-ness.'

Robert hadn't expected such a flippant reaction. He knew he was being teased but he was unable to find a lighthearted reply. 'It's entirely up to you, Gwen,' he said stiffly. 'Oddly enough, I hadn't thought of it as business. These exhibitions usually have a festive atmosphere. I thought you might have appreciated the suggestion.'

'Oh, Robert, of course I appreciate it.' Gwen was contrite. 'It was a very sweet thought, but I'm afraid I must decline.'

Rita, as she often did when one of her children was speaking, had been looking at Gwen's lips, her intent expression suggesting she was not merely following what her daughter was saying but that she was actually willing the words into her mouth. Now, she sat back a little, reassured.

'I wouldn't slave-drive you, you know,' Robert said. 'I'm not like Father.'

With deep relief Fergus realized his son was able to joke with him again. Gwen's reaction was also pleasing. He hadn't been completely happy at the thought of her going to London but, like Rita, he had persuaded himself it might be good for her. Certainly he had been determined not to influence her. Now, she had independently arrived at the right decision. He lifted his glass and held it without drinking, savouring the bouquet of the wine and the richness of the moment.

'I'm sure I would have a lovely time,' Gwen said. 'I'm genuinely disappointed that I can't come with you, Robert, but . . . you see . . . I'm going to be fully engaged.' She looked around at them. Her head was held confidently high but there was nervousness in her smile. 'You see, I have a little announcement of my own to make.' She stopped and looked helplessly at her mother.

Fergus tensed in his chair.

Rita's face was bright with encouragement. 'Well, dear?'

'Robert's belief that it would benefit me to get out of the house more is exactly what I feel myself. I've been thinking about it for some time.' Her manner had become slightly defiant again. 'Recently I decided to take steps . . . I have plans . . . for a little enterprise.'

Fergus interrupted with a frown. 'Steps? Plans? You're being very obscure.'

'Then I'll speak clearly, Father. I'm thinking of going into business.'

Robert looked astonished. 'Going into business? You?'

'And why not?'

178

'Because it isn't right. Not right at all. I've never heard of such a thing.' Fergus was aghast.

'What kind of business is it to be, dear?'

'Thank you for asking, Mother. It's always the woman who's practical. I would like to sell antiques.'

'How lovely! Perhaps I could help.' Rita saw Fergus' astounded expression. 'But then ... perhaps not,' she said regretfully. 'After all, I am fully occupied here.'

'I should think you are.' Fergus turned from Rita to Gwen. 'If you're short of money, my child, you should have come to me. I thought the allowance I gave you was quite adequate, but I suppose things become more expensive all the time. We'll go over everything again tomorrow, if you like, and reach a—'

'Father, it's not a question of money. I'm *bored* with doing nothing all day. I want an interest.'

'How can you be bored? You have your sewing. There's the piano. You like reading. What girl has more?'

'It's not enough. That was all right when I was seventeen or eighteen. Like every other girl in Park Place I was keeping myself occupied while I waited.'

Fergus looked worriedly to Rita.

'It's almost three years now since Tom went away. It seems I'm fated to be neither wife nor mother. There's nothing for me to wait for now. I can't go back to pretending that sewing and music are enough. I must do something more positive. I appear to have little inclination to good works. Business seems the only possible outlet for me.'

Fergus had never heard such frankness from a woman. He was certain he should disapprove, but he was experiencing a disconcerting sympathy for Gwen.

'Wouldn't you like to discuss this alone with your mother?' he said gently. 'Perhaps you're unwell. I hardly think it fitting that we should dissect your emotions in front of your brothers.'

Robert finished his wine. 'I can easily leave and take James with me,' he said, 'but I'm anxious to know how Gwen thinks she can manage. What does she know about commerce? Or money? Or buying and selling?'

Gwen was grateful to have the subject switched from her emotions to the practicality of her plans. She refilled Robert's glass.

'It's just a little shop I plan to have,' she said. 'I won't have to be very clever.' She shook her head reassuringly at Fergus. 'I won't even have to be unladylike. I've got it all beautifully worked out in my head. I won't open until ten thirty in the mornings and I'll close at five in the evenings.'

Fergus snorted. 'You'll find it's different when it has to come out of your head and into reality. Dear knows!'

'I've experienced reality before, Father,' Gwen reminded him.

Fergus was momentarily silenced. Rita came to his assistance. 'Let Gwen tell us about it in her own way, dear.'

'Whatever way she tells it,' Fergus grumbled, 'I don't much like the picture of my daughter sitting among a lot of old furniture and haggling with a bunch of rascally dealers.'

Gwen laughed delightedly. 'Old furniture! Father would think nothing of travelling fifty miles if he thought he could get a good bit of antique furniture cheaply, and yet to score a point he's willing to turn it all into a lot of old junk! In any case, I intend to stock only a little furniture. I'm going to concentrate on small pieces of porcelain and silver. You'll be able to pick up quite a lot of things for me, Father. You go to every worthwhile auction held within travelling distance of Glasgow.'

'And where is all this going to take place?'

'I don't know yet. I'm still looking for suitable premises.' She became suddenly serious. 'Really, Father, there's no need to be anxious. Many ladies are opening their own small businesses these days. Things are changing.'

A sigh shook Fergus. 'Not for the better, I fear. Everything's becoming confused.' He closed his eyes and groaned into his beard. 'There's a great hazy blur spreading over the world. People are losing the way. Ladies going into business. Workmen plotting against their employers. Agitators reading the *Communist Manifesto* to audiences of malcontents in the streets on Sabbath evenings. Where will it all end? Can anyone answer me that?'

Robert lifted a decanter of brandy. 'Yes, Father, I can. In the tumbrils. They're after our kind. They want to do away with us and make all men equal. Already they've got income tax up to sixpence in the pound. Next thing we know they'll have it at a shilling. One day they won't let us have anything. That's why I'm working so hard to make you rich before it's too late. You may be the last millionaire.'

He lifted his glass and held it towards Fergus. 'A toast to the last millionaire,' he said, urging Rita and Gwen to lift their glasses.

'The last millionaire!' Gwen said solemnly.

'Stop teasing your father,' Rita chided them.

Fergus raised his own glass in acknowledgment of the fun. 'To the backbone of the country,' he said. 'The British businessman.'

Daylight would last another hour at least but inside the room shadows had already formed. Fergus struck a match and lit the candles. The flames spread a gentle glow over the table, and his red brocade waistcoat was reflected from silver and crystal. Suddenly, he found himself trying to quell an image that had recently begun to haunt him. This wasn't the whole family now. There was a grandchild, the secret burden he had never seen. Had Robert seen the child? They had never mentioned the situation since the night Robert had revealed the dreadful news. Fergus allowed himself to wonder for a moment before banishing the disturbing thought. He was helped by James, who until now had been concentrating on eating. Everyone was surprised when James spoke. They had almost forgotten he was there.

'Perhaps Father would allow *me* to accompany you to London, Robert?'

Robert made a sound that suggested this was certainly a thought, while Fergus looked at Rita as if to ask if there was no end to the problems raised by these children of hers.

'I think you might be just a little too young, yet, James, to be unloosed on the capital. Your mother would worry about you, wouldn't you, dear?'

Rita hesitated, but only for an instant. 'Yes, dear.'

'Oh, but, Father. Mother would have no need to worry. I'll be seventeen in two months.'

'As old as that?' Fergus said in mock wonder. 'Well, we will see. You have the entrance examination to the university to think about, you know. We don't want any mistakes about that.'

# II

Robert heard his name called as, a few mornings later, he walked along the west side of Blythswood Square. It was Fiona Fraser. She was on the side of the street nearest the gardens on to which the houses of the square faced. He crossed to her.

'Fiona! What's a country girl like you doing alone in the city?' She smiled at his surprise.

'Father hasn't been very well and we're spending a few weeks with his sister. Her house is just round the corner in Pitt Street.'

'Nothing serious, I hope?'

'It's serious enough. The doctor says his heart is strained. He's far too heavy, of course, and that doesn't help. He won't take a proper holiday. It was difficult even to persuade him to come to Aunt May's.'

'I am sorry. I'll tell Mother. You must visit us while you're in Glasgow. You've never been to Park Place.'

'No, Robert, please. It's kind of you and I would love to see your mother again but I really must keep Father as quiet as possible. That's the whole idea of getting him away from the distillery.'

'But the carriage would bring him. You needn't stay long. I'm sure Mother will be very disappointed if you can't come.'

'Well, I'm afraid we can't. Father would be sure to start talking business with your father and he would smoke too many cigars.'

Robert gave a sympathetic nod. 'Then you must give him our best wishes.'

It was almost two years since he'd seen her. Fiona was, if anything, more striking. Her hair, which had previously been arranged in fussy ringlets, was now drawn back and caught in a chignon.

The simplicity suited her. The earlier hallmark of clothes tight to immodesty had also given way to fashionableness.

'You've changed, Fiona.'

'Have I?'

'Yes. Your hair's different. And you're thinner.'

Her dark eyes brightened with pleasure. 'You are as observant as ever, Robert. But I don't think the idea of thinness can be aptly applied to me just yet.'

'It becomes you, if I may say so.'

'Of course you may,' she said happily and took his arm. 'Have you time to walk a country girl to the other side of the square?'

'I'm in no rush for a half hour or so. I'll walk with you to wherever you're going.'

'All I'm going to do is have a seat in these gardens. I want to take advantage of the sunshine. It won't be with us much longer. It'll soon be autumn. The gate's on the other side of the square.'

Years ago he had walked along this street with Mary Devine. He looked on that now as on another age. After months of bitterness he had been forced to adjust to a life without her. Other people had unhappy love affairs, other people in love had to part, his emotional pain wasn't unique. So he had told himself and, gradually, the sharpness of his distress dulled until, one night, he realized that the day had passed without him once thinking of Mary. The process of forgetting had continued. He had loved Mary and had been loved by her. He had been enriched by the experience but now, years later, there could be no room for more than a sentimental regret. At this distance he could more than ever see their parting to have been wise.

He began to wonder, as he often had, why he had never seen Mary since the day he left her sitting, on the brink of tears, at the shaky table in Miss Frame's tea shop. For a year he had avoided the places where they might have met, and then . . . it had come to seem less necessary. Certainly, Glasgow was a big place, but in three years their ways might have been expected to cross at least once.

'Here we are.'

He realized with a start that it was Fiona at his side.

A notice at the gate said: PRIVATE GARDENS—RESIDENTS OF

183

BLYTHSWOOD SQUARE ONLY. Fiona, taking her arm from his, pushed the gate open. 'It's all right,' she said. 'I'm a guest of the Ramsays' at No. 7. They're friends of Aunt May's.'

A small white dog crashed noisily out of a shrubbery, surprising an old man who was studying a newspaper through a magnifying glass. Two or three nursemaids walked children on the grass. A pretty little girl in starched petticoats bowled a hoop along the path. Otherwise, the gardens were empty. Fiona led him past some rose-beds to a bench beneath a willow tree.

'This is where I sit,' she said. 'For hours, some days.'

'Do you read?'

She laughed. 'I'm afraid I don't do anything. There are black-birds to listen to and the scent from the roses is beautiful. Someone in one of the houses plays the piano a lot. They must keep their windows open and I just sit with my eyes shut and listen to the music coming over the flowers.'

His expression amused her. 'Does that surprise you?'

'It's not what I would have imagined you doing.'

'Well, you said I had changed.' She looked at him closely. 'And so have you.'

'In what way?'

'You're sterner-looking, I think, Robert. You know—the way men are in photographs, as if they'd arranged their faces so as not to divulge too much to the camera.'

'Are you suggesting I have something to hide?'

'No more than any of us.'

This was a more thoughtful Fiona than he remembered. Could she still be only twenty-two? 'Anything else?'

She shook her head. 'Nothing tangible, except a few unimportant grey hairs.' She held up her hand. 'Listen.' Faintly he heard piano music. It was difficult to tell where in the square the sound originated. It seemed to come first from beyond the dahlias on the west side and then, as the cadence rose, somewhere behind the gladioli on the south became a more likely source.

'What's she playing?' he asked.

'I think it's Beethoven's "Pathetique Sonata." But it's funny you should have decided it's a lady who's playing. I've been visualizing a girl of about twenty in a white dress with long, straight fair hair.'

'Wouldn't it be funny if it was really an ugly old man with a horrible curly grey beard?'

They listened until the music stopped.

'You've become famous since I last saw you, Robert. Father says you're making a wonderful success of this new blended whisky. He boasts to people that he was one of the first to know about it, years before it appeared on the market.'

'I had almost forgotten that. It was down at Ardfern. My father told him about it, thinking he might talk me out of it. Instead of that, your father was enthusiastic!'

She played with a ribbon of her dress. 'It must be satisfying to find your business growing so rapidly.'

'It's very tying. I don't get down to Row as often as I would like. I'll soon have forgotten how to handle a boat. It's years since I've been in the yacht club. Otherwise, we might not be such strangers.'

She shook her head. 'You wouldn't have seen me. Apart from a visit one afternoon with Father, it must be two years since I was last there. Since Father's health declined I've been giving him all the help I can.'

This mention of the Gareloch, the scent of roses, the humming of a bee, made him think of other droning summer hours that he had spent with her in the fields above Row or Helensburgh. He saw a clear blue evening sky through air fresh as mint, heard again the rustle of hill grass against his skin, and felt the eager softness of her all about him. He was startled by the force of the memory, which was accompanied by an almost brutal desire to touch her again. If she had similar memories they didn't show. As he sat in the sway of his sudden lust the nursemaids bounced their babies on the grass and two small boys who shouldn't have been there threw sticks at a tree to dislodge chestnuts. Over the dahlias, or perhaps it was over the gladioli, faint music came again. The intrusion of carnality into a garden still draped with dewy morning cobwebs, and to the music of Beethoven, was so bizarre he almost laughed. The sun rose over the trees and the last shadows left the gardens. Robert began to hum to the renewed piano music. He felt amazingly carefree. Something powerful had been injected into his blood.

'If you won't visit us at Park Place,' he said, 'you must let me take you to the theatre.'

'I'd like that very much.'

'When?'

'When would be suitable to you?'

He was encouraged by her lack of hesitation. 'Tonight?' he asked, marvelling at his urgency. Did it show in his voice? *And why*, he wondered, *am I pretending about the theatre?* There had been no pretending with Fiona in the past. Was his reticence due to the fact that they hadn't met for years or to the subtle change he sensed in her?

'Tonight is the only evening I have free for almost a week,' he said as he felt her hesitating.

'All right. Which theatre have you in mind?'

*I have no theatre in mind, but that*, he thought, with the odd light-heartedness that had risen in him, *will be my surprise for her*.

'Whichever one I can get tickets for. The Royal, probably. I don't suppose you'll mind leaving it to me?'

'Of course not.'

'Good. Then I'll call for you at six thirty, Fiona. What number are you at in Pitt Street?'

Leaves detached themselves from the old trees and drifted list-lessly earthwards past the grey turrets of Ardfern. They fell on the lawns and on the paths, the deep autumnal red of Japanese maple, the brighter red of Virginia creeper, the shiny yellow of oak mixing with the shrivelled brown of birch and the dead golden larch needles.

McEwan watched reproachfully as he made a broom by tying supple birch twigs to the end of an old brush shaft. All yesterday he had swept, gathering the leaves into a dry, crackling heap which he had been able to set on fire without trouble. The fragrant smoke had risen in a high white column before dispersing over the loch. The ash still smouldered, but where McEwan had so painstakingly swept, the leaves again lay thick. It would be like this every morning now. He wondered if his aching arms and legs would take him through another day. The family would be down for certain this weekend. Mrs. Veitch had received a letter. She had alerted the staff. The grounds, at least around the house, would have to be tidy. After this the family would make one, possibly two, more visits and then they would be gone till spring. If the leaves had stayed on the trees for a few more weeks McEwan could have dealt with them at his leisure.

At least things had stopped growing. He was on top of his weeding. Another summer had passed. How he would cope next year he didn't know. He put the thought of next year's vegetables, flowers, and weeds from his mind. His immediate worry was the leaves, beautiful on the trees, elegant in their fall, but a 'bluidy, blastit nuisance' once they hit the ground.

McEwan repeated the phrase with emphasis as he pulled tight the last knot on his broom and advanced stiffly to his work.


Robert called early for Fiona and was shown by a maid into a small sitting-room. He was examining a watercolour, showing anglers from earlier in the century fishing for salmon in the Clyde at Broomielaw, when the door opened and Roderick Fraser came in.

'What a pleasure to see you, my boy!' Fraser's hairy face was as rosy as ever, but there was a slightly furtive look about him. 'You *are* a stranger.' The only obvious sign of illness was the distressed breathing, there for as long as Robert could remember, but now markedly worse.

'Yes,' Robert said. 'It was a bit of luck, really. If Fiona hadn't spotted me this morning we wouldn't have known you were in Glasgow.'

Fraser's face went sombre. 'They're keeping it quiet,' he said. 'They don't want anyone to know.' His humour reasserted itself. 'They're holding me prisoner here. I get out twice a day for five minutes' exercise, like a dog or a jailbird.'

'I suppose those are the doctor's orders,' Robert said sympathetically. 'Fiona told me you haven't been well. The rest should do you good.'

'More likely to send me out of my mind with boredom.'

Fraser, who did not seem at ease despite his obviously genuine pleasure at seeing Robert, crossed suddenly to the door and stood listening. Then he took out a cigar and quickly lit it, his chest heaving with the exertion. 'When Fiona comes,' he gasped, 'take this cigar as if it was yours.' He took another paralysing draw on it and sank into a chair at the side of the fire, apparently exhausted.

Robert looked at him in alarm. The ruddy, healthy look, he could see, meant little. 'Are you all right, Mr. Fraser?'

'I hope so, my boy.'

'I mean . . . the cigar. Is it wise?'

Fraser rallied a little. 'Wise, my boy? Of course it's wise. Any harm a damned cigar might do me is a fleabite compared to the strain of going about longing for one.'

'Possibly.'

'Anyway, a man has to assert his independence.'

Robert felt, sadly, that if Fraser could only smoke in secret it was a sign not of independence but of submission to some superior will—Fiona's, no doubt.

'I hope it's all right for me to take Fiona out for the evening,' he said. 'You won't need her?'

'I'm obliged to you. It means there will only be one jailer for me to contend with. I might even manage to get a dram of whisky inside me if May falls asleep at the fire.'

He looked at his cigar. 'Talking about whisky, I'm glad to see you've made your mark. I knew you would. Your ideas appealed to me from the start, Robert. My only regret is that I was too old and worried to take advantage of your offer to go in with you.' His breathing was easier now. 'You never did tell your father about that, I suppose?'

'No.'

'Just as well.' His eyes wrinkled. 'Mind you, a lot of people would be damned annoyed if they heard me congratulating you.'

'Why should they be?'

Fraser shrugged and made a face. 'We distillers are a conservative crowd,' he said. 'Hidebound, a young fellow like you would say. And you wouldn't be far wrong. That's why whisky wasn't getting anywhere.' He shook his head. 'Anything new always raises opposition. Some of them say it isn't whisky at all you're selling.'

Robert gestured impatiently. He had heard these rumours. 'Of course it's whisky. What else is it?'

Fraser held up a calming hand. 'It isn't me, my boy. I'm too old to care. But some of them are saying it's only whisky if it comes out of a pot still. They say the grain spirit you use for blending is adulterating a traditional product. Their argument is that you can blend if you like, but you shouldn't be allowed to call the result Scotch whisky. They don't like it.'

'Then they can lump it. They're jealous that King's Royal is having such a success. My God, they should be grateful. Blended whisky's opening up a great new future for an industry that was becoming moribund. Of course malt whisky's the real whisky. It always will be. But if by adding a little grain we can sell a hundred or a thousand times as much malt then everyone will benefit.'

Fraser made more soothing noises. 'I just thought you should be warned, my boy. The pot stillers are a rich and powerful group. They would be a deadly enemy to have. I'm sorry to say it, but I think trouble could be coming.' Suddenly he jerked forward in his chair, holding out his cigar. 'Quickly, now, there's a good fellow. I can hear Fiona coming.' He flapped his arms about with alarming energy to waft the smoke to Robert's side of the fire.

He saw them to the door, where they left him on the step, looking restlessly up and down the street.

The uneasiness raised in Robert by Fraser's warning was dispelled by the sight of Fiona. The pale green watered silk dress she wore enhanced the warm texture of her skin and the light that had always been in her eyes was bright. As always it suggested eagerness to him, as if whatever she undertook would be carried out wholeheartedly. The loss of weight that he had noticed was confirmed by the simple elegance of the dress but in a way that made it clear there was still a good deal there, all of it high quality.

As the carriage crossed Bath Street she said, 'Where's your cigar, Robert?'

'Oh, I threw it away,' he said negligently. 'I'd had enough of it.'

'It used to be the pipe you smoked.'

'Actually, it still is, but I enjoy an occasional cigar.'

She began to laugh. 'Did Father really imagine I wouldn't know it was he who had been smoking that cigar?'

'You knew?'

'Of course I knew. I'm not completely silly.'

'I hope you won't make a fuss about it.'

'No. The doctor says an odd one won't do him any harm, but we thought it wiser to tell him he mustn't smoke at all. We worked on the principle that he would smoke four if he was told he could smoke two.'

'You deceitful woman.'

'It's for his own good.' She leaned forward to look from the window. 'I'm not very familiar with Glasgow, but this doesn't seem to be the route to the Royal Theatre. Are you sure your coachman knows the way?'

Now the moment had come to tell her, Robert felt uncomfortably breathless. He wondered if this was how Roderick Fraser felt all the time.

'I haven't had the opportunity to tell you yet, Fiona. We've been talking so much.' He hesitated. 'The truth is, I didn't manage to get tickets.'

'Then where are we going?'

He took her hand. 'Not very far. We're almost there.'

As the coach turned into Hill Street he was filled with an odd feeling of happiness. Part of his youth lived on in this street and in the flat with green-painted windows above the narrow strip of neglected garden. Since Mary Devine, he had brought other girls here, most of them companions of a single night. As the coach stopped it seemed to him only fitting that Fiona should have at last arrived.

'We're here,' he said.

When she didn't move or speak, he said, 'The coachman's very discreet. There's nothing to be nervous about.'

She was looking at him with a mixture of surprise and amusement. 'Am I to assume, Robert, that you expect me to go into one of those houses with you?'

He was still holding her hand and now, in the shadows of the coach, he kissed her cheek. 'I have a flat here. It's very nice. And very respectable.'

'It may be nice but it can hardly be respectable if you use it for what I think you do.'

'I mean it's comfortable and quite well furnished. You'll like it.'

'I'm afraid I'll have to take your word for that. Please tell the coachman to drive on.'

'Don't be coy, Fiona. Perhaps I shouldn't have pretended about the theatre, but what difference does it make?'

'Tell the coachman to drive on.' Her voice was firm.

He sighed. 'Drive on where?'

'Any place where the air will be cool and fresh. I find Glasgow sultry even in September. It's a week since I've seen the sea. Take me some place where there's water to look at. Down by the river.'

'It's dirty and ugly there,' he said sulkily.

'I mean out of town, past the docks and the shipyards. It won't be dark for another hour and a half.' She patted his hand. 'Do as I ask, Robert. It's three years since we last saw each other. You said this morning that I had changed.'

He forced a rueful smile. 'I hadn't thought you had changed quite so drastically.'

'You are remembering a young and very silly girl who no longer exists. Looking after Father's helped me grow up.'

He groaned. 'Oh, all right.' He opened the hatch and gave instructions to the coachman.

They travelled west along Hill Street to avoid the treacherous slopes leading down to Sauchiehall Street. Dumbarton Road was quiet in the setting sun but on the outskirts of the village of Partick people were standing outside the Wheat Sheaf Inn drinking ale, the traditional end to a walk along the banks of the River Kelvin.

Once, when he had been quiet for a while, she said, 'What are you thinking about? That you would have been better with some other girl?'

'Of course not. I was just going over in my mind something your father told me.' He smiled. 'Just a dull business matter.'

At Whiteinch they left the coach and walked across a field to the riverbank. Here, there was little sign of industry. They found a stretch of yellow sand fringed with grass. Robert brought a rug from the coach and they sat on it, hugging their knees.

Despite the collapse of the night he'd planned, despite the alarm bells rung by Fraser, contentment rose in him. For the first time since meeting Fiona that morning Robert felt relaxed. Had he really wanted to revive that dead affair or had he been deluded by memories? Something told him that this new Fiona—though even more attractive than the old—would not be so easily picked up and set down. She would be more demanding. The old reluctance to have strings attached rose in him. Only once had it been re-laxed. . . .

'It's difficult to think there's a city of five hundred thousand people just a mile or so along the road,' he said. 'This is so rural. You can feel the peace.'

She spoke without looking at him. 'You see, you're enjoying yourself, even though this isn't what you had planned.'

'I'm sorry, Fiona. I suppose it was presumptuous of me. You

told me that once before—that night in Helensburgh. Do you remember?' He said it with a slight return of hope, but her answer, though smiling, was firm.

'Vaguely.'

He sank back. 'I hope you're not annoyed?'

'I'm not. But in return I hope you accept that I'm not teasing you. I really have changed. Perhaps I should have made that clear when we met this morning instead of having an evening with you under false pretences.'

'I'm enjoying it,' he smiled. 'There's no pleasure like an innocent one.'

She looked at him with interest. 'I've discovered that, too.'

A flight of ducks flapped V-shaped across the river and a herd of black and white cattle came to the fence of the neighbouring field to look at them.

Fiona lay back on the rug and watched thistledown drift slowly by. The sky was tinged with gold, white, and pink. She looked as lovely as she had in the hills above Ardfern. 'Do all young Glasgow men with money keep secret apartments?'

'Quite a few.'

'How wicked! And they all look so respectable when you see them coming out of their offices or stepping into their carriages.'

'If these things are managed properly, respectability need never be called in question.' His voice was formal and he was turned away from her.

She was silent for a moment, then said, 'I suppose you're thinking I'm the last person who should be referring to others as wicked, even jokingly?'

'Not at all.'

There was another silence. He smelled honeysuckle and, turning, saw it growing over a hedgerow, pale apricot in the gathering dusk.

'I don't suppose you'll believe me, but I was never as wicked with anyone as I was with you, Robert. You were the only one.'

'Fiona, is this a proper subject for discussion?'

She looked at his face, solemn and worried. For a moment her expression was astonished, then she laughed. 'You're absolutely serious, but I can hardly believe it! You terrible old hypocrite!'

He took out his pipe and tobacco pouch. 'May I smoke? It will help keep the midges away.' He hoped he didn't look as prim as he felt. Suddenly he realized there was more of Fergus in him than he knew.

'You may. It will also help to hide your blushes.'

A sailing ship glided silently by, lanterns already lit along the deck and on the tall mast. Soon the wash came rippling smoothly over the sand to them, creating a small breeze. Slowly, night came up the river, and on the opposite bank, houses they had hardly noticed began to show lights.

'Even now it isn't cold,' Fiona said, 'but I suppose we must go.' She rose from the rug and lifted a piece of driftwood from the grass. She walked to the sand and began to scrawl on it. He stood behind and watched the words form. *Fiona Fraser Was Happy Here.*

When she had finished he took the stick without speaking and wrote: *So Was Robert King.*

They stood looking at the writing until the wash of another ship came rolling over the sand. They stepped back but the waves stopped short of the scrawled words.

Robert looked after the ship. 'You don't mind our names being seen together—now that you've changed?'

'Who would see them here?'

'A sailor, perhaps, on his way to China.' He reached out and gently tucked a loose strand of hair back into her chignon.

She laughed. 'He'll have to hurry. The tide's coming in.'

By the time they crossed the field and climbed into the carriage stars had appeared in the sky and the river was reflecting a large white moon.

The storm that Roderick Fraser had predicted broke a week or two later. A letter arrived from the Scottish Pot Still Association asking if it would be convenient for Robert to meet Arthur Morrison, the chairman, to 'discuss an important matter'.

Morrison's Tamnavar was rated one of the best Glenlivets and his family had been distilling it, legally or illegally, for almost a hundred years. He wore a flower and had the squat look Robert always associated with Highland strength. Below thinning silver hair there was the firm face of a man who had spent much of his forty-five years energetically in the open. His visits to Glasgow were infrequent.

'It's about this new mixture you are selling, Mr. King,' he said as they settled in a corner of the hotel lounge where it had been arranged they would talk. 'It worries us,' he added abruptly. 'We don't like it.' He stopped and looked earnestly at Robert from very blue eyes.

Robert, who detested hearing King's Royal described as a mixture, frowned and waited in silence.

'Don't mistake me. I am not talking about the taste. People seem to find that pleasant enough.' His expression suggested there was no accounting for tastes. 'And, of course, in one way we are delighted you're having such a success at an age when you can enjoy the benefits. My entire committee feel exactly the same way. There isn't a jealous man amongst us. It's simply that your drink isn't whisky. We don't particularly want you to stop selling it. We just want you to stop calling it whisky.'

He took out his pipe and began to fill it in a leisurely way.

Robert recognized some of his own tough determination. 'It is unrealistic of the association to ask me to stop calling King's Royal whisky,' he said. 'That's exactly what it is. It's a blend of the best malt whisky with the best grain whisky.'

Morrison's pipe smoke filled the corner with a pleasant perfume. 'Now, you know as well as I do,' he said, 'that there's no such thing as grain whisky. Whisky can only be made from malted barley in a traditional pot still. These new people use imported maize and a still that bears no relation to the pot still. What they produce is a neutral alcohol, a silent spirit. They're chemists producing a chemical in a factory.'

'And you, of course, are alchemists.'

Morrison smiled at the jab. 'If you like. But you can't deny that our tradition goes back to antiquity.'

Robert became serious. 'Of course malt whisky's the traditional whisky of Scotland. It will never be replaced by grain, but it benefits from being blended with it.'

Morrison shook his head. 'You're missing the point. Your King's Royal may well, in the opinion of some people, be more palatable than pure malt—but it is not whisky.'

Robert took a notebook from his pocket. 'Before coming here, Mr. Morrison, I put together some figures. Before we began blending King's Royal we used only about twenty hogsheads of your own Tamnavar each year. Last year we used almost two hundred.'

Morrison gave him a soft look. 'I do know that, and I'm grateful for your business. It makes my personal position very awkward, but I must do my duty. I cannot let personal profit deter me from doing my utmost to see that the interests of the whole pot distilling industry are protected.'

'That was the increase only in our use of your whisky,' Robert persisted. 'We use many others. Because of our blending you distillers are all selling more whisky. And it's not only to our company. Imitators of King's Royal are springing up all over the place. They'll all be using more malt whisky. In fact, it's no exaggeration to say that because of blended whisky the pot distillers have just had their best year in a long time. Is that correct?'

'It is. Everything you've said is correct, young man, but you fail to understand our fears.' Morrison paused and fidgeted with his pipe. 'Can I ask you to let me into a trade secret?'

'If it isn't too big a secret.'

'What is the percentage of malt whisky to silent spirit in your King's Royal?'

'Seventy-five per cent malt, twenty-five per cent grain.'

'A reasonable mixture. And to tell you the truth, if that was the percentage of malt used throughout the blending trade I don't think any of us would be too worried.'

'I won't ever vary it.'

'I believe that, King, but we don't have the same confidence in others. Our fear is that malt whisky may one day almost be cut out if we don't take action now.'

'I can't imagine that ever happening.'

The smooth face was agitated. 'Do you know that one rascal is actually taking ninety per cent of this cheap silent spirit, adding a dash of malt for flavour, and putting out the resultant rubbish as whisky? That's the sort of thing we see as the writing on the wall.'

'We don't do that. We aim at the highest quality possible.'

'That may be, but some of the fly-by-nights who are imitating you care only for quick profit. They're selling the most poisonous brew and calling it whisky. You've shown the way. You could undermine the whole pot distilling industry.'

'You're exaggerating, Mr. Morrison,' Robert said in exasperation. 'I can't deny that some abuses are taking place, but you surely can't compare a quality blend like King's Royal to anything of that low order?'

'Of course not. Nevertheless ... we're still asking you to drop the word whisky from your label.'

Robert sighed and held up his hands in protest. 'You can't turn the clock back, Mr. Morrison.'

'We're appealing for your co-operation.'

'And if I refuse?'

Morrison's expression hardened. The Highland gentleman went out and the threatened businessman stepped in. 'Then you will leave us with no choice but to treat you as the pirates that you are,' he said.

Robert rose quickly. He had control of his features but his voice was angry. 'And that,' he said, 'is the end of this discussion, Mr. Morrison. You can go back to your Highland valley and light the bonfires, or whatever you do to communicate with each other up there. And you can send out the message that the pirates are staying on board ship. We hope for an uneventful voyage—but if it's a fight you want, then I promise that you won't be disappointed.'

# 12

Fergus was outraged at Morrison referring to them as pirates.

'That was a scandalous statement,' he said. His eyes showed his pain.

'Sticks and stones,' Robert said with more breeziness than he felt. 'There's an outcry from someone every time anything new comes along.'

'They won't confine themselves to insults,' Fergus said quickly. 'If you think that, you're deluding yourself.'

'But what can they do?' It was a question he had worried around a score of times since meeting Morrison.

Fergus pulled at his beard. 'I don't know, but I'm not happy. And neither will they be, believe me, till they've smashed us.'

Space, nevertheless, was acquired, at Robert's insistence, for a display of King's Royal at the food and drinks exhibition at the Alexandra Court, named after the reckless Prince of Wales' popular Danish wife.

'The last thing we must not let them do is intimidate us,' he said. 'James and I will leave for London as planned on the first of November.'

'I do hope Robert looks after James,' Rita said as she drove through the park with Fergus after an evening with friends. 'He's really still only a child, and he's never been away from home before. London's such a big place and so far away.'

Fergus gave her a strange look. 'You've only yourself to blame. If it had been left to me he wouldn't be going. They get a lot of fog, too, in London in November. It's the worst possible time of year.' Then, relenting, 'But James is a sensible boy, and we do have Robert's word. We must hope for the best.'

Rita managed to smile. 'I'm sorry to fuss, dear. The week will go by before we know it, I suppose. Fortunately, I have a lot to do.'

Fergus, still brooding on the threatening clouds he saw gathering, took out his pocket diary. 'I won't have too much difficulty putting the time in, either,' he said pointedly. 'I'm going with Gwen tomorrow to look at a shop she's interested in. I don't know. I hope she's not making a mistake with this antique business. Dear knows!'

But Rita's mind, free of business cares, was still on her male children. 'I sometimes worry about Robert, too. I wish I saw him settled. He seems preoccupied with business. Once he had other interests. Do you remember that first sailing boat you bought for him? Now it seems he does little else but work.'

Fergus blew into his beard. His answer was oblique. 'Our expansion has been remarkable, my dear.'

Rita had gathered as much, but not from any direct discussion. Business had always been Fergus' province. She hadn't been expected to show interest. After all, women didn't understand money matters. Gwen, when she announced her plans, had perhaps not realized how heartfelt was Fergus' belief that commerce belonged exclusively to men.

'That must be very pleasing for you and Robert.'

'Of course, of course,' Fergus said vaguely. He hesitated. 'But frankly ... frankly, my dear, I'd be happy to leave well enough alone. It seems that Scotland is not big enough for him. He's talking about sending our whisky to England, the United States of America, South Africa and Australia. I've never heard anything like it.'

'He's your son Fergus—he's young and energetic. And ambitious. These are admirable qualities. But what is he working for? Working's sake? Does he need all the money he's making?'

Fergus looked at her as if there were some things she couldn't be expected to understand. 'A man can get a great deal of satisfaction simply from seeing his business grow, my dear. In the end it can have very little to do with money. Growth and expansion can become ends in themselves.'

Rita shook her head. 'Oh, no, that can never be right. I hope Robert's business doesn't mean everything to him. He's twenty-six now. He should be married.' Her tone was troubled. 'It's family life that's important.'

Fergus' bearing alone of the burden of Robert's supposed fatherhood made this a difficult subject.

'He has time,' he said shortly. 'If he wants to have a business he must work at it.'

Rita, not realizing where she was going, said, 'At his age you were married, Fergus, even though you were working hard at founding your business.'

Fergus leaned forward and stared impatiently out of the window. 'It appears he has no one in view.'

'Exactly, my dear. Even now I often wonder if we did right in interfering when he was so attached to that girl. Do you remember her? Mary Devine. She may have been the only girl for Robert.'

With effort Fergus controlled his anger. Women, it seemed, even at Rita's age, were incurably romantic.

'I'm sure Robert has been amply compensated in other directions,' he said, and was puzzled all the way back to Park Place by her withdrawn expression.

As they stepped from the carriage she suggested they take a stroll. 'Just for a few minutes before we go in. It's a fine night. I feel I need some air.'

She took his arm and they started to walk. Below, the lights of Glasgow spread in a wide semicircle. On the other side of the river the sky suddenly flared red as an ironwork's furnace was tapped. On the river itself lights moved busily as ferries crossed or ships slipped down slowly towards the Firth and the open sea beyond. The sky was cloudless.

'I don't think I've ever seen so many stars,' Rita said.

Fergus pointed to a faint glitter on the grass. 'There will be frost before long.'

The district through which they walked was composed almost entirely of dignified terraces, long, curving, and built of a pleasing light-grey stone. When Fergus first came to Glasgow this had been a wooded hill where rabbits burrowed and people picnicked on sunny days. Slowly the houses had come and Fergus, captivated by the gracious style of living, had resolved that if ever the day dawned when he could afford it he would live here too. His affection for the district had never diminished. His terrace was not the most architecturally distinguished but its situation gave views he never tired of.

When they reached Park Circus people were leaving one of the houses. Carriages lined the pavement and the sound of music came from the open door. The women going to the carriages were wrapped in furs. Inside the house other women in flowing silks and jewels stood chatting under a sparkling chandelier. A rich fragrance compounded of wood fires, cigar smoke, and expensive perfume drifted from the house. The waiting carriages were luxurious and the horses and their harnessing shone. Fergus took comfort from the scene. Suddenly the world seemed a less dangerous place. His fears began to retreat.

Opulence always gave him pleasure and a sense of well-being. He took out a cigar and lit it.

Rita looked surprised. 'I don't think I've ever seen you smoke in the street before, have I?'

'It's a habit I don't have,' Fergus agreed, 'but it suddenly seemed an enjoyable thing to do.'

By the time they'd completed their walk Rita felt less restless. The servants were in bed and she left Fergus at the drawing-room fire, while she went to the kitchen to make a pot of tea. When she returned he was on the edge of his chair staring intently into the glowing coals.

'Here we are,' Rita said as she placed the tea tray on a table between them.

Slowly Fergus turned to her. 'James must not go to London,' he said. 'I have changed my mind.'

The solemnity of his words startled her. 'Why ever not, Fergus? Just because I was a little bit worried is no reason to—'

He interrupted. 'It's not that.'

'Then what? You said he could go. He's set on it.'

Fergus fidgeted with his beard. 'It's too far away.'

She came and stood by his chair. 'I've unsettled you with my silly worries. James will be brokenhearted. He's made a list of all the sights he wants to see.'

Fergus shook his head impatiently. 'Damn it, I know all that.' His voice had the gruff embarrassment in it she knew so well.

'Perhaps I am being silly, my dear,' he said. 'But all day I've had a most peculiar feeling about James. I could never quite rid myself of it. It would go away, then come back. It came to me strongly again when you spoke in the carriage. And then again when I came in here and sat alone. I don't like it at all.' Rita's face clouded with concern. The last thing Fergus could be accused of was over-imaginativeness. 'What exactly do you mean, Fergus, dear?'

'I can't explain, Rita. I just feel that something might happen to James if he goes off to London.'

Rita made up her mind. 'Then he mustn't go,' she said. 'I've never known you to be disturbed like this. It's probably nothing, but we must treat it seriously, anyway. James can go to London some other time. There will be other opportunities. I will tell him so in the morning.'

Now that she had agreed with him Fergus had to struggle with a perverse urge to back down. He mustn't let the fears raised by these rascally pot distillers touch his family life. 'Perhaps it's unfair of me to rob James of this adventure for . . . for nothing.'

'No.' Rita was firm as she lifted the silver pot and prepared to pour the tea. 'Now I would be very worried if James were to go to London with Robert. I wouldn't sleep.'

Fergus drank his tea with a sense of relieved bemusement. The thing was irrational and at first he had tried to shake it off, refusing to admit the sense of foreboding about James even to himself. It wasn't like him. Dear knows! He must be getting old and be-fuddled. Nevertheless, he would sleep better for having brought the matter into the open. It was one worry shed. He looked grate-fully at Rita. The fire had gone low and she was almost in silhouette. She hadn't even tried to talk him out of his 'peculiar feeling'. She had sensed the depth of his unease and entered into his mood as if it had been her own. Rita would have been surprised and pleased if there had been enough light in the room for her to see the warmth in her husband's eyes.

By the time they had finished their tea Rita had come to terms with the odd situation. It was even interesting that after twenty-eight years a husband could show new depths. Anyway, her own purely maternal worries about James going to London could now be set aside. That left only Robert! Well, he obviously loved his business. His life, so far, was not as she would have wished it, but he seemed content enough. And she still had the comfort of having him at home. Many mothers would envy her that. Rita counted her blessings as she went upstairs to bed. She could hear Fergus going from room to room satisfying himself that the fires were safe.

# 13

Fergus' gloomy prophecy of major trouble with the pot distillers began to come true towards the middle of October.

Robert had sent out his usual orders for the following season to the dozen or so distilleries from whom they bought whisky. He read the first reply with surprise. It came from Cragdhu Distillery nears Rothes on Speyside and it said:

'We thank you for your valued order but beg to intimate that owing to production difficulties we will be unable to accommodate you. Our entire production will be required to meet the needs of old established customers. We regret that there will be no Cragdhu New Make available for recent customers such as your goodselves and we apologize for any inconvenience that this may cause you.'

The significance of the refusal escaped him until a letter from Glentoul Distillery came in the midday post. It was more curt.

'Owing to greatly increased demand beyond our capacity,' it said, 'we have been forced to review the names on our filling list and unfortunately we cannot accept your order.'

All afternoon apprehension grew in him. Next morning it turned to alarm when the post brought two more rejections. He concealed the letters from Fergus and spent the next few days in a lonely ferment of growing worry. By Saturday morning it was impossible to escape the crushing conclusion that King's Royal had been made the victim of a vendetta.

All the replies were now in and they contained either blunt refusals, obvious excuses, or vague offers of a possibility of some whisky at an unspecified time in the future.

When Fergus appeared, Robert, pale with anger and strain, put the bundle of rejections on his desk. 'You had better read these,' he said.

After the first two Fergus swore. He went through the rest in speechless dejection and then turned on Robert.

'Blacklisted!' It was an accusation. He scattered the letters over the desk. 'I told you there would be trouble.' He looked up sharply. 'I knew I should never have let you lure me into this. I warned you from the start that we would find no peace or happiness in whisky. There's a curse on it so far as this family is concerned.'

Robert ignored the peculiar mixture of assault and self-pity. 'There are many other distilleries,' he said appeasingly.

'They won't be any different,' Fergus said with sick conviction.

'We don't know that. There's no need for you to act as if it was a catastrophe. We've encountered an unforeseen setback, that's all.'

Fergus squeezed out a morose groan. 'They'll all stick together. You don't know them like I do. They're a secret society. They've always sat up there in the mountains seeing themselves as a race apart.'

'Morrison's behind this and I don't believe he can have them all under his thumb. They may like to think they're magicians, but they're businessmen like the rest of us. They exist to make money. We are offering them money. We're opening up a whole new future for them. Surely they won't all just sit up there in the mist nursing their pride?'

Fergus rallied a little. 'Write to them, anyway,' he said. 'You'll get all the names in this.' He went to a shelf and thrust a directory at Robert. 'There are scores of them, some hardly more than glorified bothy operators, but don't miss a single one. Put Gibson on it as a matter of priority. The sooner we know the worst the better.'

What the worst might be neither of them said. Robert refused to formulate it even to himself.

'We'll see them all damned yet,' he said with shaky bravado.

'I hope they don't see us damned first,' Fergus muttered as he put on his coat and lifted down his hat, automatically running a pad of velour round it. 'How I'm going to concentrate on other people's troubles with this going on I don't know. Dear knows!' He stopped only long enough to check in his diary where his next meeting was being held.

Fergus had not yet been persuaded to install a typing machine and even with Gibson, the office scribe, stung to urgency by Robert's sharpness it took three days for all the letters to be sent out. These were to distilleries with whom King & Co. had never before done business. Many did not even reply. Those who did only confirmed the boycott. In the whole of Scotland, apparently, there was only one distillery willing to sell whisky to the Kings.

The exception was Roderick Fraser's Lochbank, but there was little commercial comfort to be drawn from their old friend's loyalty. 'One puny Lowland,' Robert said ungratefully. 'It has about as much character as the grain whisky they're all condemning.'

'It's something,' Fergus said. 'We might end up very thankful for it.'

They decided that Robert should seek another meeting with Morrison. It was arranged for the following week at the Scottish Pot Still Association's Edinburgh office.

'Remember to be polite to the damned blackmailer,' Fergus warned as Robert left to get the train.

Morrison might have been greeting an old friend. He poured two large glasses of whisky from a crystal decanter and quickly passed a water jug over them.

'I always think even water changes the character,' he said with a smooth, suggestive smile, 'but nowadays dilution seems to be thought refined. That's why I always go through the motions.' He held the water jug higher. 'Of course, you can have some if you like. It's just that I prefer it neat myself.'

'I'll take it your way.' Robert lifted the glass and sniffed at the bouquet. 'Let's see if I can tell which one it is.' *This dangerous man must be humoured.*

He poured a drop of whisky on to one palm, rubbed both hands vigorously together, and then cupped them under his nose.

He looked across the desk with a sudden stab of worry, realizing all at once that if he was wrong he might be adding another coal to the flames.

'I would say it's a drop from your very own still,' he said, hoping he looked and sounded more jovial than he felt. 'The one and only Tamnavar-Glenlivet.' If he was lucky it might help to butter

Morrison. If unlucky, it might increase the antagonism. He relaxed as Morrison laughed.

'Very clever, Mr. King. Right first time. I always keep a bottle of my own stuff here.'

He nodded towards a cupboard. He dropped his voice to an exaggeratedly confidential level. 'To be honest, I can't stand any of the opposition poisons. If I can't get my own I'd rather drink gin.' The man's poised confidence was infuriating.

Robert waited until he had Morrison's eyes. 'It seems you don't much like any opposition at all,' he said levelly, deciding he had grovelled enough.

The change of tone took Morrison by surprise. It was a moment before he leaned back in his chair, smiling slightly. 'I thought that's what your visit would be about,' he said. 'I hear you're having some difficulty with supplies.'

'Let's be more positive. You *know* I haven't been able to buy a single cask of malt whisky in the whole of Scotland for next season.'

'Is that so?' Morrison began to fill his pipe, tucking the long strands of shaggy tobacco into the big bowl with thick fingers, then packing it down with a metal gadget. *The operation could,* Robert thought, *symbolize the rough way King & Co. are being jabbed into a corner.* 'I knew, of course, that we at Tamnavar had unfortunately not been able to accept your order.'

Robert quelled the rising anger at this mockery. He leaned forward and said quietly, 'Is it fair, Mr. Morrison?'

'Is what fair?'

'We know that you're boycotting us. I'm asking you if it's fair to drive a new company to the wall, especially one that's been giving you good business?'

Morrison dropped his fake innocence. 'You were asked to desist, but you chose to fight. We have no wish to drive anyone to the wall. We are protecting our own position. Nothing more than that.' He waggled his pipe at Robert. 'I might ask you if you are being fair. Some of us been distilling whisky for a century and more. We've established a good name for our malt. Now you come along with a nondescript spirit produced in what I can only describe as a factory, use it to adulterate our malt, and then have the audacity to offer the resulting mixture for sale under the name of Scotch whisky.' He paused breathlessly. 'You are shamelessly cashing in on a reputation that has been carefully, even lovingly, built up. If this damned mixing goes far enough the demand for good malt might dwindle away. Is that fair?' His voice had risen dangerously.

'You admitted at our last meeting that the pot distillers were selling more malt than ever,' Robert said. 'The truth is King's Royal has given the distilleries a new lease of life.'

'So far,' Morrison conceded heavily, 'but we have our fears for the future.'

Robert swirled the whisky in his glass. 'We're prepared to bargain with you,' he said.

Morrison raised his eyebrows sceptically. 'I don't think you have anything to bargain with, Mr. King.'

Robert leaned forward. He had one card—a poor one, but he must play it. 'You know we use seventy-five per cent malt to twenty-five per cent grain. We would be willing, if it would help calm your fears, to increase the malt content to eighty per cent.'

'Five per cent increase, Mr. King?' Morrison spread his arms sarcastically. 'It's hardly a staggering concession.'

'Then ten per cent.' He tried to make it sound as if he was producing the last hidden gem and surrendering it to an armed highwayman. 'That would leave us with only fifteen percent grain. The pot distillers could hardly feel threatened by a drop in the ocean like that.'

He had decided on the train that he would agree to any cut in the grain content of King's Royal that would buy the opposition off, binding the company to it in writing, if need be.

But Morrison saw the loophole.

'Forgive my suspicious nature, but we would need a policeman standing over your blending vats. We would have no other way of knowing what the percentage of malt was to grain. No, we are not as simple as that. In any case'—he pursed his lips and shook his head—'so far as we are concerned you can use as much or as little malt in your mixture as you wish. That is not what we are after. The only thing we ask for and the only thing that will satisfy us is the removal of the words Scotch whisky from your label. Without those words your mixture is harmless to us. And you would still have a business.'

*And what a pitiful business it would be*, Robert thought. He said, 'Then you are determined to continue this vicious vendetta?'

Morrison tapped out his pipe and remained silent.

Robert pushed back his chair, his face white. 'You will not crush us. I can promise you that. If the distillers won't supply us direct then we'll buy our whisky on the open market.'

Morrison gave him a look. 'That is a matter for you,' he said. 'And I regret that I cannot wish you luck.'

In the eleven years since its inception the International Exhibition of Food and Drinks had become one of London's most popular winter attractions. Buyers came from all over Europe in search of new 'lines'. Each year new attendance records were created as more and more Londoners realized that here was an interesting and unusual day out, well worth the sixpence entrance fee. The vast hall was a miracle of light and colour after the grim November streets. The warm stuffiness, intoxicating after the damp, outdoor chill, was composed of rare delights ranging from farm kitchen bake-houses and herb gardens to imported fruit and flavouring oils. Smoked ham sizzled in frying pans, sugar was boiled and toffees poured in front of excited children. At certain hours of the evening the crush of people became almost solid, for at these times, an-nounced in advance, sweets, cream cakes, chocolates, fruit drinks, and other delicacies were given away free by the exhibitors.

Robert had been worried that Fergus might want to see per-sonally how their money was being spent. He had felt obliged to invite him to spend a day or two in London, but the invitation had been half-hearted and he had been relieved when it was declined. Although many of the firms exhibiting were famous, the enterprise would undoubtedly have struck Fergus as little better than a fair-ground. The spectacle of his name being flaunted in it, and his son publicly participating, would have been repugnant to him.

As King's Royal had progressed, Robert had discovered a flair for advertising. His more adventurous ideas usually had to be modified to avoid conflict with his father, for Fergus found any form of publicity, other than three or four staid lines in the *Glasgow Herald*, flamboyant and distasteful.

In exploiting the possibilities of a faraway exhibition Robert had felt free of this hindrance. Under his direction the King's Royal stand had been constructed in the form of a Highland distillery, set at the side of an imitation mountain burn, but against a background of genuine heather. It was one of the immediate successes of the exhibition, with people forming an almost permanent queue as they waited to see the mysterious process of manufacture. The highlight of each day at the King's Royal stand was the free distribution, for an hour, of glasses of whisky. These were carried around on silver trays by two young ladies of the Lambeth Nightingale breed—out-of-work dancers recruited from a theatrical agency and dressed in tartan costumes more at home in a variety than an exhibition hall.

No other whisky company had a stand at the exhibition and Robert capitalized on his monopoly. He ran a daily advertisement in all the important London newspapers. It appeared under the heading: RARE EVENT. NEW TO LONDON. The main content was an invitation to *Come and see live Scotsmen actually give away whisky—* FREE. Music hall comedians, who knew that anything Scottish was good for a laugh, propagated the joke, elaborating on it, and in one case even managed to incorporate it in a song. Trade buyers who came to hear more about the commerical side of King's Royal were surprised to find that the man behind the fun was handsome and gentlemanly, sensible and even a little stern, speaking correct English and without kilt, trews, or tammy. Journalists found the contrast between the man and the advertising intriguing and wrote Robert up in their columns as the rich young Scot who liked to do business with a smile.

To everyone he appeared buoyant. For the moment he had successfully banished all thought of the struggle for whisky supplies that lay ahead if King's Royal was to flow in the golden torrent he hoped for.

From Glasgow he'd brought Peter Ross and a clerk to help him man the exhibition stand. With one of them always on duty he was able to go sightseeing for a few hours every day. He visited the Houses of Parliament, the Tower of London, and Westminster Abbey. He walked in St. James' Park, sailed on the Thames, and watched the changing of the guard at Buckingham Palace. He saw Princess Alexandra in her daily carriage ride in Rotten Row. His enjoyment was marred only when he remembered that James could have been sharing the experience. Fergus' reversal had been inexplicable. And it had been hard luck for James.

Revolutionary organizations were everywhere, and Robert was

horrified at the freedom with which they could advertise. Men openly walked the streets with placards proclaiming public meetings to explore the ideas of two international, troublemakers. Marx and Engels. Handbills and bills stuck on boards outside public halls preached unrest: WORKER, LOSE THY CHAINS. THE CLASS WAR. THE MESSAGE OF THE MANIFESTO. LABOUR VERSUS CAPITAL. In Hyde Park, men prophesied rivers of blood in the streets of England while, to Robert's astonishment, policemen stood tolerantly by. Rabble-rousers, Fergus would have said with contempt, but to Robert, the rabble seemed alarmingly interested. Of course, with trade union-ism growing, with co-operative societies springing up everywhere, public unrest was inevitable. The seeds of dissension had been well sown. All this Robert knew, but in Scotland it was still possible to joke about it. It was a shock to see that here, at the heart of the Empire, the revolution had progressed so far that it could now be preached with impunity in front of policemen. He was so angry he almost forgot he was in London to sell whisky. He was grateful James had been kept in Glasgow. The sympathy his brother would have shown for these mob orators would only have increased his exasperation. The newspaper columnists would have been inter-ested to know there was this serious side to the young whisky entrepreneur from Glasgow.

One day when he returned to the exhibition hall there was a note inviting him to contact the caller. He read it with a thrill of excite-ment—Hutt Sons & Buist. This was one of England's oldest wine shippers, with cellars in St. James'. The caller had been Mr. William Hutt, head of the firm. Robert put his hat back on and left immediately for St. James' by cab.

The entrance to the premises of Hutt Sons & Buist was a shop that appeared to have lingered on from an earlier age with little alteration. The walls appeared papered in parchment and were decorated with faded orders for various wines, each signed by an illustrious name, and now all neatly framed. Here and there on the rough floor stood wine casks. Racks filled with dusty bottles took up the rest of the space. There was no counter. The two assistants sat at desks.

Mr. Hutt was not only in, but immediately available, and Robert was taken straight to his office. He was a man possibly in his early forties, taller than Robert, clean-shaven except for a moustache, and with the hesitant look of a country clergyman—the fifth- or sixth-generation look. The grasping businessmen had long since been bred out and the family moved to the shires. If King's Royal continued to prosper, his own grandsons, if he had any, might look something like this, possibly even with an estate in the same part of England. The headquarters of the business would undoubtedly have moved to London by then. It was, after all, the hub of the universe—although, of course, by then the men from Hyde Park might have altered all that.

Robert accepted a glass of wine. Mr. Hutt explained that while visiting his own firm's stand at the exhibition he had been intrigued by the ingenuity of Robert's presentation of King's Royal. He had been even more intrigued by the sample he had tasted—surprised by its lack of similarity to any whisky he had previously encountered.

'I understand this is because you blend traditional malts together and then further blend them with grain spirit.'

'Grain whisky,' Robert corrected him.

Mr. Hutt smiled an apology. 'Forgive me. We Sassenachs aren't very well versed in the whisky mystery.' His manner was precise and businesslike. 'I wondered if your King's Royal was selling yet in England?'

'Not in any systematic way. We started selling it only three years ago and the demand took us by surprise. We felt we should be firmly established in Scotland before expanding into other markets.'

Mr. Hutt seemed to approve. 'I take it that since you have a stand at the exhibition you now feel ready to sell to the English?' He smiled. 'If so, you must be delighted at the stir you've created. I hope it doesn't go to waste.'

Robert winced at this reminder of their vulnerability. He ignored it and took Mr. Hutt's remark at face value.

'I'm afraid a lot of it will. It was unexpected. There are no supplies in the shops or hotels. Our notoriety may have diminished a little by the time we can make deliveries.'

'What a pity! But at least the potential has been demonstrated dramatically. You would be surprised how many of our own customers have asked if we can supply them. What are your plans for distribution?'

'I think I might have to base myself here for a year and establish an organization.'

'That would involve you in opening premises and engaging staff. It would also take time. There's a quicker, and less costly way.'

Robert did not betray the extent of his interest. 'What way is that, Mr. Hutt?'

'If you were able to establish an agency agreement—with a firm such as this, say—you would be spared many worries.'

'Are you making a serious suggestion?'

'Yes, serious . . . but there would be many things to discuss.'

'It's a possibility I hadn't considered. I would have to think.'

'Of course. We would both have to think. First we would have to talk.' Mr. Hutt looked thoughtfully about the panelled room as if remembering other significant talks held here.

'There could be great advantages for both of us. You would acquire the prestige and organization of a firm established for almost one hundred and fifty years. We have customers all over England. We employ six travellers. They would be at your disposal.'

'And Hutt Sons & Buist would have the sole distribution rights in England?'

'Naturally, we would have to have that.'

'It would mean a smaller profit for us,' Robert said. 'A substantial part would have to go to you.'

'Yes.'

'Although I'm the majority shareholder I wouldn't commit the company to anything as important as this without discussing it with my father.'

'Of course, Mr. King. There's no question of me expecting an answer now. If you were agreeable in principle, we could proceed to the details later.'

'I find the idea most attractive,' Robert said, 'and I'm sure my father will agree with me.'

Mr. Hutt rose and stood with his back to the fire, smiling in his hesitant way. 'You realize that with our reputation we have to be very particular about the agencies we undertake. I hope it doesn't sound patronizing, but our interest really is a very great compliment to your whisky—and most sincerely meant, I assure you.'

'I do realize that,' Robert said, 'Hutt Sons & Buist is one of the great names of our trade. We would be proud to have you represent us, so long—'

As he hesitated Mr. Hutt's smile widened. 'I'm sure we won't fall out over the details. Many whisky firms in Scotland have asked us in the past to act as their agents. Whisky is one of the few spirits not on our list and whenever we were approached we went into the matter very carefully. In each case we decided it was not a drink we could happily offer our customers. It was all right during an energetic tramp over a Scottish grouse moor, and I've always enjoyed a malt then myself—we shoot in Glenshee—but it was far too heavy for normal, everyday use. Your blended King's Royal seems to have changed all that. I'm trying to say that I haven't put this proposition to you lightly. You have a whisky we would be happy to sell. As long as you can assure us of consistency, we would have no qualms in offering it wholeheartedly to our customers. On our recommendation it would be taken into half the great houses of England.'

The machinations of the pot distillers suddenly seemed less menacing. Could they destroy a commodity so greatly in demand?

Robert could not hide his rising excitement. 'You really think it's as fine as that, Mr. Hutt?'

'I do, young man. You could waste years of your life peddling it round the hotels and restaurants of London. You would have to spend great sums in advertising before people would ask for it. I'm not saying you wouldn't ultimately do well, but you'll do many times better in a tenth the time through us. Our customers will take it and sample it simply because we suggest it to them. They trust our judgement. They will like it because it's good and then they'll ask for it wherever they go—in the other great private houses, in the best hotels and clubs in London. It is not often I look into the crystal ball, Mr. King, but I prophesy that with our weight behind it your King's Royal could sweep London.'

As Robert sat speechless with elation he had a sudden thought so audacious he almost rejected it lest a display of greed jeopardize this magnificent opportunity. But his gambling instinct lured him on. There might be another prize yet to be won.

'I noticed as I came in from the street,' he said carefully, 'that you are suppliers to the Royal Household.'

'Oh, yes. We've been honoured with the Royal Warrant not only from our present dear Queen but from three Kings before her. It's one of our proudest boasts.'

'Is it likely, do you think, that there would be a demand for King's Royal from the Royal Household?'

Mr. Hutt hardly hesitated. 'Oh, very likely, I should say. Palace officials are among the most conservative of people, but they're aware of all new trends. It's their duty to keep Her Majesty informed. The Queen has a Scottish home. Her interest in Scotland is known to go deep. I feel she wouldn't want to neglect any Scottish development of such obvious worth.'

'Then by appointing you our agents we'd lose all chance of ever holding the Royal Warrant. You would be the suppliers.'

Mr. Hutt looked surprised. 'That's so, but is such a possibility really a consideration at this stage?'

'Not with me, Mr. Hutt, but'—he made an apologetic gesture—'with my father I'm afraid it would be. He is, I'm afraid, a snob. He has so far missed a title. I'm certain he would not want to forgo a Royal Warrant.'

The smiling irony appealed to Mr. Hutt. Surprisingly, he found himself responding to Robert's quiet confidence. Only an exceptional man could talk blithely of receiving a Royal Warrant for a whisky so far known outside Scotland only by reference to it on musical hall stages and in newspaper columns.

'How could your father be placated?' he asked, marvelling a little at his tolerance of this outrageous Scottish gall.

'If our agreement specifically excluded the Royal Household from your agency then we could supply direct,' Robert said. 'I'm sure my father would be happy with such an arrangement.'

Mr. Hutt chuckled. 'Knowing how my own firm's status has been enhanced by these little royal favours I wouldn't want to stand in the way of anyone else receiving them. Besides, the greater the prestige of King's Royal, the easier our job of selling it. Needless to say, if we can put a word in the right quarter . . . mind you, these things take time.'

'Of course.' Robert's face was understanding. 'How long would you think, Mr. Hutt?'

'I couldn't speculate. Two years, perhaps longer.' He felt Robert might benefit from a slight rebuff. Certainly, by any normal judgement, he had earned one. 'And then, of course,' Mr. Hutt said deliberately, 'perhaps never.'

.    .    .

Next morning a panel of judges from six different countries awarded three Gold Medals to King's Royal. It had been competing against Cognac brandies, London and Dutch gins, and German schnapps. The medals were for Purity, Taste, and Bouquet.

To celebrate, Robert ordered the usual hour of free King's Royal to be extended to two. It wasn't quite a Royal Warrant, but meantime the words *International Gold Medal Winner* would look good on the label.

On Sunday evenings contingents of William Booth's new Salvation Army vied in the streets of Glasgow with the propagandists of Mr. Keir Hardie, the leader of organized labour.

James King and Benson, his Socialist friend, had little interest in Booth's evangelists, but they found Hardie's orators exciting. Despite Fergus having warned him to keep clear of Socialist rabble-rousers, James had spent several Sunday afternoons listening to open-air speakers at the corners along Argyle Street. In this street, occupied on weekdays by Capitalist shopkeepers, banners of hope were raised for the poor on Sundays, and a new world was preached from wooden boxes that often collapsed under the speakers.

This Sunday, with the disappointment of his father's last-minute refusal to let him go to London rankling, James was looking forward to diversion. The chief attraction was Keir Hardie himself. The meeting, at the corner of Virginia Street, had been well advertised. Young men like Benson had spent the week chalking advance notices on walls. Now, the crowd—mainly of sympathizers, but with sceptics here and there—was the biggest James had ever seen.

Even on a wintry afternoon that smelled slightly of coming fog, people were anxious to see the young miner whose ideas for the advancement of the workers were considered menacing enough to be denounced in the newspapers, even in Parliament. There was a legend that Hardie lived a fugitive existence, moving his campaigning as the authorities closed in on him.

Benson, whose father was a director of two shipyards and a bank, left James on the perimeter of the crowd while he went off to distribute a bundle of leaflets. Hardie, even on his rickety platform, looked short, but he had the muscular squatness that James imagined as characteristic of miners. He wore a dark grey tweed jacket and a round brown hat. As he spoke he stood quite still with his hands clasped in front of him. He didn't look dangerous to James. Only after he'd been speaking for some minutes did his voice grow louder and his body begin to move with the force of his delivery. Phrases from some of Benson's literature began to reach James: 'The dignity of labour,' 'Poverty amidst plenty,' 'Abolition of privilege.' The quiet passion Hardie radiated gave them new authority.

James, as never before, began to feel a true brother of the shabby men around him. Their hunger was his, and their despair. He hoped no one would notice his good clothes and he thought of his father's fine house with shame. As the crowd cheered, James burrowed happily forward.

After a while, Benson came back. 'The traffic in Argyle Street is almost at a standstill,' he said excitedly. 'The road's blocked with people. This is the best meeting I've ever seen.' He frowned. 'But the bobbies are beginning to gather down there. They don't like Hardie. They're employers' men.'

'Illegitimate agitator,' a man near James shouted as Hardie paused to consult his notes. James was puzzled, for the man looked as poor as any of the rest. Could there be some workers who didn't accept Hardie's message? Some pushing and shouting started around the man. He glared defiantly, then turned and went quietly away.

'We want bread for the hungry, rest for the weary, and hope for the oppressed,' Hardie said.

'This is the greatest message since Christianity,' Benson whispered, his eyes moist.

A commotion started on the Argyle Street side of the crowd. There was shouting, but not loud enough to drown Hardie out.

'The workers must lose not only their economic chains but the even more terrible chains on their minds. It's only the working class that allows itself to be split and thus exploited. Capital is united. We must split it asunder.'

A roar went up and as James turned to say something to Benson he saw the street behind him tightly packed with people. Hardie now had an audience of several thousand—clearly split between passionate supporters and critics.

'There's going to be trouble,' a man behind James said. 'The bobbies have given up trying to clear Argyle Street.'

*Was this*, James wondered, *how the revolution would begin?* He would be sorry to be on the opposite side of the barricades from his father and brother when it did come, but he must follow his conscience.

Above Hardie's voice and the general clamour came the sounds of singing. A score or so of young men marched down Virginia Street with arms linked. The tune was 'Rule Britannia', but the words had been changed, making it a hymn to the sanctity of the existing order.

Benson had gone white. 'It's those rotters from the University Unionist Club,' he said furiously. 'Look at their scarves.' He began scrabbling in the gutter, found a bone, and flung it at the students.

'Capitalist idiots,' he shouted.

Hardie's supporters turned to denounce the students, who withdrew a little, waving scarves and Union Jacks. Hardie stood still on his box till a reasonable peace had been restored.

'Politics,' he said, 'is but a kind of football game between the rich Tories and the rich Liberals, and you working men are the ball they kick between their goalposts.'

When the cries of agreement ended, one of the students shouted, 'Don't listen to this revolutionary. He and his kind will drag the country down and you with it. Does an illiterate baker's boy, an ex-miner, know better than the Prime Minister how our affairs should be run?'

Benson raised his fists and shook them at the student. 'He's not illiterate.' He was incandescent with rage. 'Mr. Hardie taught himself to read and write.'

'Then he's been reading the wrong books,' someone replied. 'His message is evil and he's moved by hatred of his betters.'

At the top of Virginia Street, beyond the taunting students, James saw a group of mounted policemen blocking further entry to the street. A few minutes later a window above the crowd opened and a police lieutenant appeared. He held up his hands for attention. As the crowd went still Hardie looked up in surprise and then, seeing the policeman, stopped speaking.

'You'll have to end this meeting,' the lieutenant said. 'It's causing an obstruction. Argyle Street is impassable to traffic. The public is being inconvenienced.'

'That is unfortunate,' Hardie replied calmly. 'But I am entitled to speak to these people. This is a peaceful meeting.'

'It's an unruly assembly,' the lieutenant said.

'Those Unionist rascals have done this,' Benson said to James. 'Someone's told the bobbies there'd be trouble. I've never seen so many of them before.'

The police lieutenant, his buttons bright against his dark uniform, looked ominous to James. He waited anxiously to see if Hardie would be deflected.

'If unruly elements are seeking to stop free speech it's for the police to deal with them,' Hardie said.

The lieutenant's voice rose. 'You're inciting a breach of the public peace and you'll have to disband your meeting and disperse your followers. Order must be restored.'

Hardie turned away and spoke directly to the crowd, some of whom had started to jeer at the policeman. 'Is it your wish, brothers, that I end this meeting?'

'No!' 'Speak on!' 'To hell with the bobbies!' The shouts came from all sides.

Hardie hesitated for only a moment before turning again to the lieutenant. 'There is our answer,' he said steadily.

'And here is mine!' Leaning further from the window the lieutenant blew two long blasts on a whistle.

Hardie suddenly seemed to realize the ugliness of the situation. He spread his arms out as if in appeal—or perhaps in surrender. The crowd, also sensing the imminence of real trouble, had quietened. James heard Hardie say, 'This was a peaceful gathering—' but the window had no one at it now.

From both fringes of the crowd frightened cries began. James was pushed violently in the back. He turned and saw the mounted policemen charging down the street. The Unionist students scattered, shrinking against the walls on either side. Passing them, the police swept on, only reining in as they neared the crowd. The people nearest them could not run forward for the crush. Nor could they go back without getting under the rearing horses. James saw policemen lean from their horses, batons swinging. He heard thuds and screams and felt the crush around him tighten until, when he was almost suffocating, his ribs ready to crack, the jam of panicking men split open and he was flung to one side. His shoulder hit a wall with sickening force. He cried out in pain. As he began to slide to the ground he felt hands on his arms and Benson's voice in his ear.

'Come on, King! Run! For God's sake, run! The bobbies are out for blood.'

James tried to stagger after his friend. The pain in his shoulder travelled up his neck to his head in blinding waves. He wanted to pitch forward. Only Benson kept him standing. The street seemed suddenly dark. He must get away. Whatever happened, the bobbies mustn't get him. If he was arrested his father's wrath would be terrible. He made a great effort to go where Benson was trying to drag him. A surge of men, desperately trying to avoid the police truncheons, crashed into him. Benson disappeared under a mass of bodies. Almost thankfully, vomit running now from his mouth, James fell. He lay on the footpath, one leg turned under him, the other jutting out into the gutter.

Down the street came another wave of mounted policemen. Three Black Marias followed, their wheels crushing the stones that lay about the broken surface.

With men scattering everywhere, the slim outline of a boy's body flat on the ground in a darkening street made little impression on an excited police driver. Mercifully, James had fainted and didn't feel the weight of the wagon as the heavy iron wheels ground over his outstretched leg.

For Rita and Fergus, days and nights drifted formlessly by as the hopeful surgery went on.

'Please, God,' they prayed a hundred times, 'James is only a boy.'

The doctors said little and promised nothing.

Fergus' sense of responsibility was almost unbearable. 'I stopped him going to London.' Over and over in his head he turned the terrible thought. He poured the story out to anyone who would listen. 'He would have been all right if I hadn't stopped him going to London.'

Day after day he sat hunched at James' bedside deepening the self-torture. 'But for me,' he kept telling himself, 'James would have been safe in London that day.' Each night he had to be led exhausted from the ward and forced to go home. In bed he didn't sleep.

Despite her own grief Rita saw he was on the verge of disintegration. She prayed for strength to comfort him. 'We were both wrong, Fergus,' she said. 'We were sent a message about James and we misread it. But it wasn't our fault we didn't understand. We did what we thought was right.'

Two weeks passed and still the struggle went on. Sixteen days after the accident, with his son's life now in danger, Fergus sagged down at a shaky table in a drab room of the Royal Infirmary and signed a document allowing a surgeon to remove the boy's right leg. Two days later, still with the possibility that James would die, he had to make himself go over with Robert the proposed agency agreement with Hutt Sons & Buist.

For both of them it was a macabre occasion, but the discussion had already been delayed. Mr. Hutt had said he must have a reply for a meeting of his fellow directors. If the two firms were going to do business he wanted the first consignment of King's Royal in London in time for the Christmas trade.

'Certainly there seems a worthwhile opportunity there,' Fergus said leadenly when Robert had finished. 'But. . . .' His voice faded away as he was swept by a huge apathy towards the now almost unreal business of whisky.

Half of Robert's brief, almost ashamed, account of what was proposed had not reached him. Wherever he was or whatever he was doing his mind kept drifting to James. In two weeks the warm cocoon of security had been rent. He saw everything differently now. Despite the tensions that often existed between them he'd always enjoyed his business discussions with Robert, playing them as a stimulating part of his favourite game. Their manner would be formal and important decisions were made with them sitting on either side of a wide table in a room they both thought of as 'the boardroom'. There was as yet no real 'board', but they both foresaw the day when the appointment of other directors would become necessary. Already, small habits had been formed that were gaining the sanctity of tradition. The most pleasant of these rituals was the tasting. A sample from each new blend was placed on 'the boardroom' table and at a prearranged time Fergus and Robert would sit down with Peter Ross to taste it for quality and consistency. These sometimes developed into such mellow sessions that the hour chosen for them was, wisely, the last of the working day.

It all seemed different now. Fergus had not been to his office once since James' accident. He felt that business would never again have savour or meaning.

'Yes, Father? You were going to say?'

He recognized the gentle encouragement in Robert's voice and made an effort.

'I was going to ask what the point was of trying to expand into England with this boycott making things so difficult for us? If the demand turns out as great as you think, how could we meet it?'

'I've given a lot of thought to that,' Robert said. 'At our present rate of expansion we have enough whisky to last a year. Now, I know that's not a long time, especially if we were to start doing well in England, too. But with what Mr. Fraser slips us and what we'll be able to buy on the open market, I feel we can keep going well into next year without a crisis. By that time the pot distillers will have accepted us or their boycott will have started to crumble. It's not going to be easy for Morrison to keep all those distillery owners toeing the line. It will be a worrying time for us but. . . .' He stopped and looked at the bowed, preoccupied figure of his father, wondering if he was even listening. 'Frankly, I'd be far more worried if we were to let this chance pass us by.'

It was an indication of the depth of Fergus' sorrow that he pressed no further.

'All right, Robert,' he said. 'If that's what you want.'

It was a remark so untypical that Robert hesitated, wondering if he was taking advantage of his father's grief. He'd taken advantage of Fergus before and probably would not hesitate to do so again. Now he shied from the thought of extracting a concession unfairly while he was in this state of distracted sorrow.

Recently, he'd wondered if this whisky dream was becoming an obsession, driving him on against all opposition and slowly crushing all normal feeling out of him. Hadn't he even sacrificed Mary to it? Would a man with ordinary decent emotions not have rejected the gross material considerations that had swayed him and simply listened to his heart? Had that been the start of his dehumanization?

Fergus, seeing his uncertainty and sensing the reason for it, said, 'Later . . . in a few weeks, perhaps . . . you can tell me what is happening.'

Robert moved until he was behind Fergus' chair. 'Forget about it all just now, Father,' he said. He stood looking at the sagging line of the broad shoulders, feeling he should place his hand upon it, but unable to reach out. 'I will write to Mr. Hutt tomorrow. It will be the biggest step we've yet taken. It's tragic that it had to come at such a time.'

'Things have to go on, I suppose,' Fergus said automatically. He walked to the study window. A rose that grew against the house still had a flower on it. It was framed by one of the windowpanes, a small, flame-tinted relic of a season passed; delicate, sad, and soon to die. He gazed at it for a long time.

Later, he could hardly look at Rita for the guilt he felt at having discussed business at such an hour. Somehow, this seemed the bitterest day of all. As he sat at the side of James' bed, trying not to see the indentation where there was now no leg to support the bedclothes, he felt the strivings of his life had been entirely pointless.

Another three days of uncertainty followed. On the fourth morning, Rita and Fergus arrived at the infirmary to take up their usual vigil. They walked in silence. Rain drizzled down the windows and the white-tiled corridors slid coldly past.

As they entered the ward they saw the screens had been taken from around James' bed. He was sitting up against a pillow, wearing a fresh gown, his hair carefully brushed. So long had the agony gone on that their hearts refused to lift. Then, incredibly, James made a few slow but definite movements. He was waving to them.

A nurse coming down the ward smiled and said, 'You're going to find him much improved.'

Rita caught at her arm. 'Does this mean he's going to be all right?'

'Yes. The crisis is over. Doctor was very pleased with James today. He . . . Mrs. King . . . you musn't. You mustn't cry. You'll upset the patient.'

But Rita stood in the middle of the ward unable to go further, her hand to her face, tearing sobs of relief shaking her body.

'Leave her to me, nurse,' Fergus said in a breaking voice. 'She'll be all right.' Then, the tears misting his own eyes, he put one arm around Rita and gently steered her up the ward, waving to James with the other.

# THREE

# KING'S ROYAL

# 14

A year passed.

In which James grew slowly in strength and cheerfulness.

In which Rita, her hair now greying, found some acceptance of her sorrow and Fergus regained some of his taste for business.

In which Gwen at last took the lease of a shop in Blythswood Street.

In which Robert spent at least half his time restlessly travelling the country buying whisky wherever he could find it.

Finding whisky to keep up with the demand in England had become one of his besetting headaches. Every week or two consignments of King's Royal were sent to London, but they were never as large as Mr. Hutt would have liked. His complaining letters were a constant goad to Robert, the more so because he knew he'd been unfair to Hutt. He should have honestly revealed that King's Royal was the subject of a boycott before allowing Hutt Sons & Buist to send their travellers on an enthusiastic search for orders through London and the home counties.

Months earlier he had gone to London to explain their difficulty. He had hoped for sympathy, but had received none. Mr. Hutt obviously felt that he had been badly let down. 'This is a fine time to tell me,' he had said angrily.

'But I was absolutely certain the boycott would have crumbled before your distribution started,' Robert lied. He hadn't dared admit that his signing of the agency agreement had been a reckless gamble.

'Well, it hasn't,' Hutt said bitterly,' and from what you tell me there's still little sign of the pot distillers accepting you.'

'We buy up every available cask of whisky,' Robert said. 'If you knew the price per gallon we sometimes pay you would realize how desperately hard we try.'

'I don't doubt you try hard,' Mr. Hutt said, 'but frankly, if I had known your supplies were not assured I would have thought twice before agreeing to sell King's Royal in England.'

Robert read into this a threat that Mr. Hutt might drop King's Royal from his list. He had returned to Glasgow in a panic and for several months had starved his Scottish customers so the demand in England could be met.

It was a nerve-racking and unpleasant way of running a business and Fergus deplored it. But it was only one of their many worries.

The pot distillers' boycott had made the open market the chief source of their supply. Here, the system was to buy through a whisky broker. It was the broker's business to know which merchants held stocks beyond their own needs. Previously, it had been possible this way to buy whisky almost as cheaply as from the distilleries, the merchants being glad to dispose of their surplus. But in six months the demand created by King & Co. resulted in open-market whisky almost doubling in price.

Quickly learning of the company's dilemma, investors rushed to buy whatever open-market whisky was available and then dictated their own price.

'If it goes on like this we'll be ruined,' Fergus prophesied. 'We can't go on absorbing these price rises, and if we pass them on to the customer, a bottle of King's Royal will be more expensive than a bottle of pure malt. One of our great advantages is that we're cheaper.'

Robert refused to consider the possibility of ruin and was furious when Fergus suggested they cut production in half.

'It's your health I'm thinking of as much as anything, Robert,' Fergus protested. 'This treadmill you're on will kill you. You never stop working for a minute. You've no time for any relaxation or hobby. You're not living at all. You're wasting your life.'

'I'm not complaining, Father. I promised Morrison he would never crush us. And he never will. There will always be enough people willing to sell whisky by the back door for us to keep going.'

Even as he spoke, doubts assailed him. Was he really in the grip of an obsession so blinding he could not see when he was beaten? Would a wiser man give in? Surrender could be made to sound so reasonable. After all, the pot distillers were only asking that he take the words Scotch Whisky from his label. By now, the name King's Royal formed a valuable trademark. Certainly, as Morrison had said, they could still have a business. Many people would go on buying King's Royal even if it was no longer described as whisky. But what about his great dream of a worldwide drink? Taken out of the whisky context, King's Royal would be trapped forever in Scotland—forever parochial. A shudder of determination went through Robert at the thought.

Fergus was still preoccupied with his vision of a life thrown away.

'Where are the friends you used to have? You're making the same mistakes I made. When I was a young man I spent far too much time making money. I neglected your mother. I left her alone when we should have been enjoying our best years together. But at least I had an excuse. I was working so that my children would have an easier life. What is your excuse, Robert?'

Robert laughed uneasily. 'I don't make excuses for myself,' he said. It was difficult to tell if he was being wry or bitter. 'I prefer to get on with my work.'

'My God, Robert, I thought I was thrawn but compared to you I'm like India rubber.'

'If it's any comfort to you, Father, I feel perfectly fit. Fit enough to win this fight. And once we've won it we'll be able to devote all our energies to pure business. There will be nothing to stop us then. You asked me what I'm living for. I'm living for the day when we'll have grown big enough to call the tune to the pot distillers.'

Fergus shook his head.

'The fact is, we're only managing to keep one step ahead of them,' he said. 'As you open a new source of supply they track it down and close it. In a way, the harder you work the more you play into their hands. They have you all ways. If we halve our expansion, as I've suggested, that's a victory for them—and, of course, you won't have it. But if we forge on, eventually we cut our own throats by creating a demand we cannot satisfy. You will crack eventually. Meantime, you're enslaved.'

It suddenly occurred to Robert that there would never be a better time for putting forward a thought that had been with him, half ashamedly, for weeks. Even so, he hesitated.

'There's one way I could take things more easily,' he said slowly. 'But you might not agree to it.'

Fergus, despite all the concern that he had expressed was immediately wary. 'What do you have in mind?'

'Why don't we let James travel round the country for a bit buying up whisky for us?' He tried to make it sound like an idea for an unusual holiday.

Fergus looked shocked. 'I've never heard such a heartless suggestion,' he exploded. 'You know perfectly well James is going to go to the university. Apart from that, he wouldn't be up to it.' His voice grew more emphatic. 'And apart from that, he's the sort of boy who could never talk people into selling anything. Dear knows!' He rose from his seat and moved, muttering, about the library.

For weeks it had been Robert's belief that James, as plenipotentiary, wouldn't have to do much talking. In the circumstances of near strangulation they found themselves in, James, he felt, could be one of King & Co.'s best assets. The sight of his pale, almost wistful cheerfulness and his refusal to admit disablement would melt many stones. The thought that this might be coming dangerously near to using James still frightened him a little, but Fergus' opposition spurred him on.

'To me,' he said, 'your determination to send James to university is far more heartless. You must know very well it's the last thing he wants. He has no aptitude for study.'

This was something Fergus had never admitted but couldn't deny. It had been his hope that if James could be manoeuvred as far as the university gates he might, inside them, develop a taste for knowledge. Robert had been impatient of study, and Fergus' dream of having one academic in the family had been pinned on his younger son.

While he was still pondering this, Robert walked to the window. It was late September at Ardfern. A clematis trailed small purple flowers across the glass. He watched a red squirrel run along a sunlit branch and disappear into the woods.

'If there's nothing else, I think I'll have a walk along the shore

228

before the sun goes down,' he said. 'James left to go that way. I don't suppose he'll be difficult to catch up with.'

Although James never complained, and despite what he'd just suggested, Robert still felt a slight bitterness on his behalf. Fate, he felt, had been unforgivably hard on his brother. Fergus caught the feeling beneath the words.

He said, 'How do you think James is taking his accident now?' It was invariably referred to in the family as 'James' accident'.

Robert shrugged. 'On the face of it, very well. But it's difficult to really know. He doesn't say much about it.'

'Have you seen any sign he's ready yet to . . . to do something?'

'None at all.'

'He can't go on forever doing nothing,' Fergus mused. 'It wouldn't be good for him. And yet I don't feel able to talk to him yet about his future. It's only a year, after all . . .'

'It's a problem. That's why I thought it wouldn't do any harm for him to see a bit of Scotland combined with a little undemanding business until something definite was decided. However'—he began to go towards the door—'if you're hell-bent on having him at Gilmorehill—'

'I am hell-bent only on doing what's best for James,' Fergus said indignantly. 'If I thought that he would be unhappy at university I wouldn't insist on it.'

James eased the crutch from under his arm and lowered himself on to the pebbles. He put his back against a rock for support. He had walked no more than three hundred yards from the gates of Ardfern but his shoulders ached. Eventually, the doctors said, his muscles would adjust to the new strain and movement become easier. Meanwhile, this was his limit, especially over rough ground.

He could have taken the easier way of the shore road, but he liked to peer into the rocky pools as he went and sift the shingle through his fingers looking for interesting stones. He had another reason for keeping off the road. On a fine evening like this, even in autumn, people were to be met on it.

James could bear his disability but he couldn't bear the sympathetic or even pitying expressions on the faces of other people. He'd stopped his mother and father enquiring about his health. There was still much he could do and he didn't want to be continually reminded that there were some things now beyond him.

After the initial shock and depression, James had found he had an ability to forget himself. Always alone among the Kings, he had tended to live inside his head. Now, with movement difficult, this capacity was deepening. If he could not go out to things then he would bring them in to him. He noticed things now that had previously gone unseen, especially in nature. Every time he went into the country he found his perception had sharpened. Before there had been trees. Now there were trees either graceful or gnarled—either birch or oak. Before there had been birds. Now there were birds with carmine or yellow feathers. His eyes saw with a clarity that hadn't been in them before.

Several times recently he had found himself inspecting Fergus' paintings, not only with wonder at their beauty but with curiosity. How did the artist set about creating the form and colour? How did he turn dead paint into silk and sunshine? He had looked up some of the names in Fergus' reference books. Alexander Nasmyth, Samuel Palmer, Joseph Mallard William Turner, Charles François Daubigny. The entries they rated were medium-sized, but Fergus prophesied their fame would grow.

James thought now of these painters as he sat at the water's edge watching the setting sun turn the mountain slopes pink. He liked Nasmyth's mountains and Daubigny's sunsets. Waves broke quietly over a ledge of rock and the splash swirled away in golden ripples. James wished he had brought paper and a pencil. Perhaps he could have sketched this beautiful scene. He had been quite good at drawing at school. The hills were remote, still behind their veil of pink light, but even on a day like this there was a restlessness to the sea that fascinated him. Could this movement be put down in paint?

A smell of salt came from the water. As the tide slipped out, long tangles of brown seaweed were left glistening on the rocks. A steamer with a black and yellow funnel passed up the loch with an escort of hungry sea-gulls.

Sometimes, when he smelled salt spray or cut grass, James would have an urge to break loose and run. His body would ready itself and then, with the realization that it was impossible, everything inside him would collapse and he would come near to crying. These were the exceptional times. He could usually find the cheerful side, even turning his disability to advantage.

He'd used it ruthlessly to delay the day when he might have to enter the university. At the same time, he had skilfully managed to leave the question of what might be substituted for study un-answered—even unasked. In King terms, James was an enigma. The family put it down to his accident. James knew this. He knew the question of his future was something Fergus so far felt it unfair to pursue, determined as he was that he should receive all possible latitude. James saw this tenderness and happily abused it.

Behind him, pebbles crunched. He turned and saw Robert coming down from the road.

'I hope you have matches with you,' he said, pulling out a pipe.

Robert threw a box to him. 'How are you managing with that new tobacco I suggested?'

'Much better.' James laughed and the flame of the match flickered over his pipe and went out. 'I don't feel sick nearly so often now.'

'The pipe suits you. With your teeth clenched you look the man of destiny. You remind me of Father.'

'Don't say that.' Another match went out.

They sat laughing at small jokes and puffing at their pipes until Robert said, 'Don't you ever get bored, James?' It was said lightly, but he put a hint of challenge into it.

James threw a handful of pebbles into the loch and watched for the pattern of disturbed water. Shapes, moving shapes, interested him.

'I suppose I do, sometimes,' he said, following the multitude of interlocking ripples. 'When I get bored with Ardfern I go up to Park Place. And when I tire of the city I escape down here again. Doesn't everybody get bored? Except paragons of perpetual motion like you?'

'Of course they do. And so do I, believe me.'

'I'm going to be much more bored soon if Father has his way,' James said moodily. 'When classes start again at the university next month he's hoping I'll be one of the students, all eager eyes and shiny new textbooks.'

'And you still don't want that?'

'Less than ever, Robert.'

'Then we must see it doesn't happen.'

'But the alternative's to go into the business. And that doesn't appeal to me much, either. I don't want to be stuck at a desk in gloomy old Washington Street staring out through a barred window at a grey tenement.'

Robert leaned forward. 'First things first, James. I think I know how you can avoid starting at the university next month and at the same time keep clear of Washington Street.'

James looked interested but sceptical.

'And if you miss the university entry next month you'll have to wait another year—and by then you'll be nineteen, going on for twenty, too old, really, to be starting out as a student.'

James relit his pipe. 'And how do I achieve this miracle? I don't have to lose my other leg, I hope?'

Robert punched him playfully on the shoulder but he felt tears of admiration sting his eyes.

'I'm getting a little tired of all this perpetual motion you mentioned,' he said. 'How would you like to take some of it off my shoulders?'

'You mean, go about trying to buy whisky?'

'Yes. It wouldn't be difficult, you know.'

'Wouldn't it?'

'No.' Robert gave him a shrewd look. 'Of course, it would mean being away from Mother and Father a lot.'

'That wouldn't matter,' James said innocently.

'You could make your own time. Most of your travelling would be in the Highlands. You would go to places like Elgin, Inverness, or Aberdeen by train and then go out to the distilleries or call on the whisky merchants by coach. There are some very nice country inns to stay in. You'd be away from home probably for a week or ten days every month.'

A wave of warm pleasure was rising in James. The idea of leisurely journeys to remote parts of the Highlands appealed to him—he had never been farther north than Perth. He had heard the colours up there among the mountains were forever changing and the scale of things quite different. There would be new sensations to take in. He could take his sketch book along. All this excited him, but the idea that the family might be prepared to let him go off on his own into these strange areas was even more exciting.

Their pity must be diminishing. Perhaps they were beginning to accept at last that, although he had only one leg, he wasn't useless or helpless. Then panic rose in him. Maybe he was helpless. To be disabled while surrounded by family and servants still sometimes raised problems. Would they be crushing if he was alone in an unknown place? Firmly, he beat down his doubts. Here was a chance to escape the threat of being turned into a reluctant student, to be helpful to the business, and at the same time to prove himself!

'Do you think it possible, Robert?' Suddenly his face clouded. 'But I don't know anything about buying whisky.'

'Our need is so great,' Robert said, 'that you don't have to know anything about it. If someone's willing to sell you whisky at prices with which I'll familiarize you, all you do is buy. We'll take all the whisky that's offered to us. It's little more than a matter of putting in a personal appearance.'

'And Father will agree?'

'I've already spoken to him about it. If you would like to give it a trial for six months I'm willing to tackle him again.'

'We'll see him together,' James said. He reached out for his crutch and began struggling to his feet. 'And there's no time like immediately.'

Fergus, harangued and coaxed in turn by his two sons, wavered and fell. Glaring at Robert behind James' back, he said he would agree unless the doctor forbade it. To everyone's surprise the doctor said that seeing a bit of the country would be therapeutic for James.

By the time he was due to leave for three weeks in Inverness, a centre from which he could visit at least a score of independent whisky merchants, Fergus was resigned to the idea, but Robert, his conscience still troubled, had an outbreak of uncharacteristic uncertainty.

'Undertake only the journeys I've outlined,' he said, fussing over the notes he had made for James. 'And do no more than I've asked. If you come back without a single cask of whisky don't be down-hearted. It's happened to me several times.'

As they walked out of the station on a raw October morning after James' train had gone, he said nervously to Fergus, 'I hope he'll be all right.'

Fergus turned to him in surprise. 'It's a bit late to be thinking of that now.'

Rita, who had been barred from the send-off at James' request, had kissed him good-bye in the hall at Park Place and was still weeping in her room.

The loyalty of Roderick Fraser was one of their mainstays. His whisky might be a puny Lowland but Fergus' prophecy that they would be glad of it had turned out to be chillingly accurate. Sometimes Robert fretted at their growing dependence on Lochbank as one of the few remaining sources of whisky at the basic price.

'Fraser will continue to sell us every cask he can,' Fergus assured him.

'I am sure he will,' Robert said, 'but I don't think we should take anything for granted. Now that James is doing some of the travelling, I'll have time for things that have been neglected. I won't be happy until I've managed to get down to see Mr. Fraser and arranged some sort of firm contract.'

Fergus shrugged but Robert was not to be deterred.

'We can't just go on depending on his generosity. For all we know, someone could come along and buy up not only his entire stock of matured whisky but all his production for next season. I want to tell him exactly how many hogsheads we'll need. Then at least we'll know our supply of Lochbank is safe. It will be one less worry.'

On the day of his visit rain smurred across Loch Lomond and dripped from the arthritic old trees on the Balmaha Road. A bedraggled cock pheasant rose protesting at his approach and rattled noisily into a small wood. Water splashed down a rocky hillside in white cascades and some Highland cattle sheltered under the rough arch of a humpbacked bridge. Ahead he saw peat smoke drifting from the whitewashed distillery, and at the next bend the well-loved tang enveloped him. Even with wet clouds hanging low on the hills it was still a homely sight and it gave him the usual sense of pleasure and comfort.

One of his earliest memories was of this fragrant cluster of stone buildings standing serenely on the pebbly shores of the loch, as reassuring in their solid timelessness as the smile on the face of their owner.

He knocked briefly and pushed open the door of Fraser's office almost as if it was his own. To his surprise it was Fiona sitting in the big swivel chair. She smiled at his expression.

'Don't look so disappointed,' she said, pushing away the papers she had been working on.

'Far from it,' he smiled. 'You brighten the old place. But where's your father?'

'He hasn't been well for a week or two. I'm doing what I can to help.'

'I remember you telling me that. Is it his old complaint?'

'Yes. Too much weight and too many cigars. The doctor ordered a month's rest. He's a terrible invalid, but when he knows I'm here looking after things he makes an effort to do as he's told.'

'I had been hoping to see him . . . to talk business.'

'You can talk business with me, Robert,' she said briskly. 'Father says I'm becoming quite good at it.'

He hesitated. 'I'm sure you are. You look very businesslike in that chair. And much prettier than your father.'

She laughed. 'That's a very good start, but you must try to think of me as a man.'

'That won't be easy,' he said with conviction. 'It would require sudden blindness not to mention a complete loss of memory.'

She lowered her eyes. 'I wouldn't like to think you would forget,' she said softly. When she looked up he saw she was smiling almost shyly.

'Can I take my coat off?'

'Of course. Then you must tell me how I can help.'

He looked about for a hook, and then put his coat on a table beside the snake pickled in whisky.

'I wanted to talk about our purchases of Lochbank. Is that something you can deal with?'

'Oh, yes. I've been doing that all morning.'

In the glow from the fire her brown hair looked soft and warm. It was not, he thought, an inducement to business.

'I suppose you know the pot distillers are boycotting us?'

'Father told me. I think it's disgraceful. And so does he.' She hesitated. 'We're members of the association, of course. We must be careful.'

'I realize that and we're grateful to your father for what he's done for us up until now. The point is, we would like to increase our orders of Lochbank for next year.'

She lifted a ledger and turned the pages. 'Father already has you down for double your normal amount.'

'We would like to double that again. And we could take some parcels of older whisky immediately.'

'Suddenly everybody wants to buy our older whisky,' she said. 'It seems to have become an attractive investment.'

He frowned. 'The speculators are trying to move in. They scent easy money. They're buying whatever whisky they can and then, knowing our difficulties, hope to hold us to ransom.'

She lifted some letters. 'These are offers to buy matured whisky from us at considerably more than the usual price.'

He waited.

'They are very tempting offers.'

'But these people aren't in the whisky trade,' he protested. 'They're adventurers.'

Her reply was disconcerting. 'I remember you once saying, Robert, that business was *the* great adventure.'

Behind her, the window gave a view of the cobbled courtyard. Out there it was still as it had always been: the hollow rumble of casks on their way to be filled, the clang of hammers tightening the hoops on shrunken barrels, the dusty old men with their sacks of grain. But inside . . . Roderick Fraser had never talked like this.

She avoided his eyes. 'You must appreciate that this new whisky situation raises a problem for us,' she said.

He pretended not to understand. 'I'm not quite sure I know what you mean, Fiona.'

She pointed to the letters. 'If we ignore these offers we are turning away money.'

'But these are damned fly-by-nights. They have no interest in whisky as such. It's only our difficulty that makes it attractive to them. When things return to normal, you'll never hear from them again.'

Her answer struck deeply into his worries. 'But *will* things ever return to normal, Robert?'

He rose from his chair to hide his agitation. 'My God, I hope so. The pot distillers can't keep up this infamous vendetta forever.'

'According to Father some of the more active ones, like Arthur Morrison, are very determined.'

'Not half as determined as I am,' he said vehemently. 'I'll see them all in hell.'

The room smelled of a delicate perfume instead of the usual cigar smoke. The huge chair diminished her statuesque dimensions. In the soft light she looked elegant and overwhelmingly feminine— too feminine, he thought, for this thinly veiled bargaining.

'Look here, Fiona,' he said angrily. 'We are old customers. I'm not sure what you're trying to say but my father's been buying Lochbank for twenty-five years. That's longer than you've been alive. You're surely not going to sit there and capitalize on our troubles.'

She shifted uncomfortably in her chair.

'I hope I haven't made it sound like that, Robert.' All at once she looked embarrassed and regretful. 'Frankly, what I've found here has been worrying. Father's never been aggressive. The truth is, he hasn't made a great success of this business. It's been going down since his father died. For years he's been too easygoing, possibly because of his failing health, perhaps because he doesn't have a son to carry on after him.' She stopped and twined her fingers nervously together while she looked at the desk.

'I'll tell you as an old family friend that the point has now been reached where we need to gather in all the money we can while it's there.'

A sudden tenderness rose in him. He recalled with wry sympathy the brave words and confident pose with which she had filled the last ten minutes. Both had gone now and it was obvious she knew it. Her vulnerability was immensely appealing.

He sat down and leaned forward. 'Could we try to work something out, then, Fiona, that would help us both?' His anger and disappointment had gone.

She looked at him gratefully and smiled, shamefaced. 'That's what I would like to do, Robert. I'm sorry if I sounded unfriendly.' Her hands went out, indicating not just the untidy room, but all it meant. 'This is new to me. But I do want to help Father all I can.'

'I should have realized we aren't the only people with worries,' he said gently. 'Your father did hint at it once before.'

'It's probably helped ruin his health,' she said.

'You've been frank with me and I'll be completely honest with you, Fiona. If we can't keep on increasing our purchases of whisky we're soon going to be in serious trouble. Instead of stabilizing our sales until this boycott ended I've gone on expanding. Perhaps that was foolish, but I was damned if I'd let the pot distillers stand in our way.'

'I would have felt exactly the same.'

'Now our greatest need is for matured whisky for immediate use. Unfortunately, if we pay the prices the speculators are demanding, it will make King's Royal too expensive.' He looked at her. 'That's why I was so disappointed when you told me these people had been at you. We can't compete, probably, with what they've offered, but we would be happy to pay you more than the normal price.'

He saw her doubt and said quickly.

'Now, I'm not finished yet, Fiona. On top of that, we'll do something the speculators will not do. We'll enter into a binding contract with you to buy a minimum quantity—we can decide the amount later—of New Make Lochbank over the next five years. Does that sound interesting?'

'I can see it would have advantages,' she said slowly.

His voice was eager. 'The important thing for you is that for the next five years, come what may, you would have a guaranteed market for a very large part of your production. No speculator will offer you that. Their interest is only in matured whisky, which can be used immediately, and which they hope we'll be forced to buy.' She'd been scribbling as he spoke. 'You're offering us the double advantage of a good price now for our stocks of matured whisky and an assured outlet for our New Make over a prolonged period.' It wasn't a question. She spoke to clarify his offer in her own mind.

'Basically, the essential point is that we'll always be your customers. These others will soon fade away. Of course, I realize you'll want to talk it over with your father.'

She leaned back in the big chair with a determined expression. 'No, I'm here to stand between Father and this sort of thing. I can make the decision.' She looked at the watch pinned to her dress. 'They'll be bringing in the tea at any moment. I must tell them to set the tray for two.' She rose and left the office, leaving him fidgeting. There was little room in his mind for tea.

When she came back there was a boy with her carrying a tray.

'Put it on the table by the fire, Maxwell,' she said. 'Pull your chair over, Robert, we'll be cosier here than at the desk. Besides, we've finished with business.'

When the boy had gone Robert looked at her anxiously. 'I would like to have a decision today, Fiona.'

She seemed surprised. 'I told you I could make the decision.'

'But you haven't told me what it is.'

'I thought you would have realized.'

'No.'

'Where's your intuition? I agree, of course. Did you think I wouldn't?'

He had never had a business discussion where intuition was required to discover the outcome, and he tried to hide his confusion. 'Well, I didn't know. Nothing would have surprised me.'

She laughed. 'I agree because I think your offer of a contract is good for us and because I prefer you to these anonymous speculators. Besides, I'm sure it's what Father would want.'

They agreed on the details while she buttered the scones and poured tea.

Robert promised to have the contract prepared and sent to her within a few days. When he had put on his coat to leave he said, 'Give my best wishes to your father, Fiona. And tell him not to worry about the distillery. He has nothing to be anxious about. He's right about you being good at business. In fact, you're very good.'

He smiled ruefully.

'This visit has cost me a lot more than I thought it would and, I suspect, more than it would have cost if your father had been in that chair.'

'Is that intended as compliment or complaint?'

'Where's *your* intuition?'

They walked laughing to the door. As he went to give her his hand she said, 'So formal, Robert?' and leaned forward for him to kiss her.

'This is the first time I've ended a business meeting like this,' he said.

'It puts a fond seal on it.'

She stood by the door, waving, until he had crossed the old bridge under which water lilies floated.

·     ·     ·

Next morning Robert called Peter Ross into the sample room. He handed him a glass measure filled with whisky and said, 'What does your bloodhound nose tell you about that, Ross?'

Ross put the measure under his nose and then looked quizzically at Robert without lifting his eyes. Still without speaking, he poured some of the whisky on to his hands, rubbed them together and cupped them under his nose.

'It's a gey thin one, Mr. King,' he said, putting the glass down.

Robert made a face and nodded. 'That's my own feeling. There's a sight too much Lochbank in it.'

It was becoming steadily more difficult for them to go on producing a standardized blend. In the early days there had been a formula and they didn't deviate from it. They had been able to buy precisely the whiskies they needed. Now they were glad to take what they could get.

Since the boycott began, Robert and Ross had become expert in making do. Usually, whatever disparate whiskies they had to work with, they could arrive at the recognizable King's Royal blend. And without tasting a drop. They had found that after tasting two whiskies they lost all sense of difference. 'Nose' was what they relied on. The sense of smell wasn't so easily baffled.

'What it needs,' Ross said, 'is a good ripe Glenlivet—maybe Linkwood or Glen Grant.'

Robert shook his head despondently. 'We haven't any. And no hope of any in the near future.' He went to a shelf and started lifting down sample bottles. When there were about twenty on the ledge by the sink he said, 'Those are the whiskies we have available, and some of them not in very great quantity.'

Ross read the labels. 'There are a lot of new ones here,' he said with interest. 'We've never had Springbank or Scotia before.'

'I didn't particularly want to have them now,' Robert said. 'They're both distilled in Campbeltown. To me they're too oily and smoky.'

Ross took out the corks and sniffed. 'They must use peat instead of barley,' he said, wrinkling his nose.

Robert took off his coat and determinedly rolled up his sleeves. 'Let's see what we can make out of this assortment,' he said.

'I notice most of these whiskies aren't as old as we usually use,' Ross said.

Robert scowled. 'I'm afraid we'll have to be less particular as long as the pot distillers have us under siege. In any case, I've suspected for some time that maturing doesn't make the dramatic difference that's claimed for it. Some whiskies mature much sooner than others. There's no rule.'

'But these younger ones are much paler,' Ross said. 'Even if we get the taste right the blend's going to look sort of peely-wally.'

'I know. They haven't been in the cask long enough to absorb the colour of the sherry from the staves.' Robert shrugged. 'But there's nothing we can do about that. It's always annoyed me that every blend we put out is a different colour from the one before.'

'But never as noticeable as this is going to be,' Ross, the perfectionist, protested.

They worked for the rest of the morning, measuring, discarding, and interchanging the various whiskies. With so many to manipulate, the permutations were almost endless. At last Ross lifted one of Robert's blends and after savouring it said, 'I can't find fault with this one, Mr. King.'

'The fault with it,' Robert said, 'is that it will use far too much good Speyside malt. That's why you like it.'

Ross went thoughtfully back to the ledge by the sink and lifted the samples of Springbank and Scotia. 'We've both been avoiding these,' he said hesitantly. 'But I've been thinking. I wonder if they might just be what we need?'

'In what way?'

'Just a taste of these in our blends would add a lot of character and that would let us cut down on the quality malts until you can buy them freely again.'

Robert considered. 'It's a thought,' he said. 'Let's try it, anyway.'

'There was something else I was thinking about.'

Ross' smile suggested he thought he might be about to make a fool of himself. But he had been emboldened by Robert's ready acceptance of his suggestion for using the heavy Campbeltown whiskies.

Robert had come to respect and encourage Ross' frequent proposals. 'Yes?' he prompted.

'It's about this watery look the blend's going to have with us using these younger whiskies.'

'Yes?' Robert said again.

Ross' expression was embarrassed now. 'It was something I saw the kids doing at home the other day.'

Robert's eyes widened. 'With whisky?'

'No. With toffee balls. Maybe it's silly, but it would be easier if I just showed you what I mean.'

Robert was mystified. 'With toffee balls?'

'I buy them a pennyworth at Maw Meechan's every Saturday.'

Maw Meechan was the owner of a dilapidated sweet shop on the other side of the street. 'She makes them herself.' Ross opened the door and shouted. When a boy came he handed a coin to him. 'Run over to Maw Meechan's and get a half-penny bag of her homemade toffee balls.'

When the boy returned, Ross crushed one of the sweets, put it into a glass measure, and added a little water.

'The kids do this to make a sweet hot drink,' he said. 'It works quicker with hot water, of course.'

Robert waited patiently while Ross stirred. Slowly the water turned from a pale straw colour to a golden amber.

Robert's laugh was puzzled. 'It certainly looks like whisky, Ross, if that's what you're demonstrating. But you're not suggesting, are you, that we put Maw Meechan's toffee balls into King's Royal?'

'Not toffee balls, but whatever that dye is. It must be harmless.'

'And what is the dye?'

'I don't know.'

Robert had a high respect for deceptively simple ideas. His business had been founded on one. 'Run over and ask her what her secret is,' he said.

Five minutes later Ross was back. 'It's nothing but sugar,' he announced. 'It gets slightly burned when she boils it.'

'And that's all?'

'So she says.'

'And would your Maw Meechan be prepared to burn sugar for us without putting in any of the other ingredients?'

'That old beesom would do anything if she got paid for it,' Ross said.

'Then ask her to make us up a trial batch for tomorrow. In the meantime, let's see how we get on using just a touch of these Campbeltown malts.'

Next morning Maw Meechan proudly delivered a pot filled with burnt sugar. It was dark brown and thick as treacle. Ross took it to Robert in the sample room. They added a spot of it to a blend of almost colourless whisky. As they stirred, the spirit took on the rich gold of a malt matured for many years in a sherry cask. Robert tasted a little of it and turned to Ross with an interested look. 'The colour's every bit as good as sherry and the taste is completely unaffected.'

'And it's cheap and it's harmless,' Ross pointed out.

'Would Maw Meechan work for us? I don't mean she should close her shop. We could install proper equipment in a corner of the warehouse and she could come over and burn sugar for us whenever we needed it.' The oddity of the proposal amused him.

'She'll do that, all right.'

'Good. Well, I'm going to be out for most of the week. Arrange it with her and then get on with working out the top dressing on this next blend.'

Ross installed a cauldron in a far recess of the warehouse for Maw Meechan's sticky operation. Even with windows and doors open the aroma spread everywhere.

The first time Fergus smelled it a faraway look came into his eyes: Robert hadn't yet told him of the experiment. 'Someone's making toffee,' Fergus said. He went to the window and looked across at the old tenements. 'That's a smell that brings back memories.' He sighed. 'Near where I lived with old Aunt Peg there was a little shop that used to make toffee balls. They smelled just like that.'

Robert hid a smile. 'There is a certain similarity,' he said. 'I've been meaning to tell you about it.'


As in previous years, the Kings gathered at Ardfern in the last week of October for their final visit of 1878. Only James, now in the last days of his Highland expedition, was missing.

Already the days were cold. There was frost on the ground in the mornings and darkness came early. The rough road winding along the shores of the Gareloch from Row to Rosneath had quietened, as the owners of the big houses went back to Glasgow and their carriages were put away for another winter: the Kings, as usual, would be among the last to go, for Fergus still loved his place in the country. For weeks, fragrant white smoke had been drifting across the loch as McEwan and all the other gardeners burned the sad debris of summer—the wrinkled leaves, the rotting flowers, the shrivelled stems. On the hills above, tall bracken fell lifelessly over and features which had been hidden—rock formations and waterfalls among them—came back into view, old horizons and landscapes restored.

For weeks, Rita and Fergus had been helping Gwen prepare and stock her new shop. The colour scheme she had chosen was a pale Adam green with discreet embellishments in gold.

'I'm delighted with the enterprise Gwen's showing,' Rita said to Fergus at one point. 'I am sure this little venture is going to be good for her. She's very much alone, you know, and is probably low in spirits on many occasions we know nothing of.'

'That's all very well,' Fergus had grumbled, uneasy at being reminded that Gwen was being unconventional, 'but what are people going to think?'

He was worried enough already about what they would think of him sending his crippled son trailing around the Highlands so he could go on making money. He knew how they twisted things. Dear knows!

'If a little business gives Gwen a healthy interest I don't care what people say,' Rita said stoutly. 'I sometimes think, dear, that we have on occasions thought too much of what people think and too little of what was best for our children.'

Fergus hadn't been pleased at hearing this recurring refrain of Rita's and had wandered off to another part of the shop to examine the quality of craftsmanship that was being put into the new wooden display fitments. He had spent several happy days at auctions, buying for Gwen. In furniture, he had advised her to go farther back than Hepplewhite, Sheraton, or Chippendale. 'Queen Anne walnut is the thing to specialize in, my dear. Take my word. It's rare, and it will be expensive, but the people with the greatest discernment are beginning to collect it and you'll make a very nice profit. I want to see you getting a good return on your money.' Gwen had agreed and not long after he had arrived excitedly at her door one night, straight from an estate sale in the Stirlingshire countryside, to tell her he had been lucky enough to buy three pieces of Queen Anne walnut—a lowboy, a bureau, and a chest of drawers. Gwen had been worried when, after much paving of the way, he had disclosed the prices. 'I did tell you that walnut was expensive,' he soothed her. 'One always has to pay for quality.' When they arrived, Gwen was thrilled. 'They're exquisite,' she said. 'Yes,' Fergus said, hiding his relief. 'I knew you would be pleased.' From then on, every time he went into the shop to see how the work was progressing he would lift the dust sheets covering the Queen Anne furniture and spend a few moments admiring its mellow beauty. They were in his mind again that night at Ardfern as they gathered for dinner. Guests were expected but had not yet arrived. A wind risen in the late afternoon rattled the windows and puffed smoke from the fires.

Fergus took Gwen's arm and manoeuvred her slightly apart from the others. 'I've been thinking, my dear,' he said, 'that it would be a fine thing if I were to buy those walnut pieces myself. We could have them either down here or at Park Place.'

When he saw her surprise he said hurriedly, 'It would give you a quick turnover of your money. That's very important in business.'

'But it would leave me without my finest pieces,' Gwen protested. 'Oh, no, Father, I'm not going to let you plunder my shop before the public's had a chance to see it.'

He plucked at his beard. 'I tell you what, then. If any of those three pieces hasn't been sold after the first month, I'll buy it. You might be glad of the money by then.'

She poured him a glass of sherry. 'I'll agree to that, Father, with pleasure. But I must warn you that you won't get a discount. In fact, for you, I might raise the price a little.'

'I wouldn't put it past you, my dear.'

She put her hand on his arm. 'I hope you're not still as disapproving, Father?'

He made blowing noises to give him time to think. 'It's not the way things used to be,' he said. 'Ladies in business? No. Never. Still, things are changing, more's the pity. You know, my dear, I saw an extraordinary thing the other day in F. & F.'s. There was a well-dressed and respectable-looking woman of your mother's age sitting with her daughter drinking tea—and smoking a cigar. I almost fell off my seat. I thought she would be asked to leave, but nothing happened. It seems anything is proper these days.'

Gwen knew this was the nearest she could hope to get to approval. Perhaps Fergus was right. Perhaps it wasn't fitting for a woman to engage in commerce. She might find it distasteful once her shop had opened. It was all wonderfully exciting at the moment, choosing colour schemes and instructing the workmen, moving in the stock and arranging it artfully, but if dealers started coming in and bargaining with her, trying to bully and cheat her, as Fergus predicted they would, that might not be so pleasant. The drawing-room was warm not only from the log fire but from Rita's homely arrangements of lamps and colours, and from the family laughter, but anxiety crept into Gwen's heart. Life had let her down before. She had lost her husband and her baby. At twenty-five she lived alone with the hopes natural to most young married women already years behind her. She was often lonely or bored. Suddenly she found herself hoping desperately that she would find her new business congenial. In moments of emotion her thoughts often turned to Hoey. Since his note had been pushed through her door she hadn't heard from him or of him and she had made no attempt to have him traced.

His mother and father were both dead and he had been an only child. Any relatives he had lived in England and she had met them only at her wedding. If Hoey were dead he couldn't have disappeared more effectively. Gwen was only lifted from her reflections when the first guests came in thankfully from the noisy wind. Ten were expected and in the next fifteen minutes most of them had assembled with the family in the drawing-room, glasses full and jewellery gleaming, the wild night forgotten. Outside, McEwan dragged himself off gratefully, but painfully, to his room over the stables. As usual, when guests were arriving, he had been stationed in the bushes bordering the lamplit driveway with two helpers, their task to rush out as each carriage passed and rake the displaced gravel back into place before the next arrived.

Colin Lindsay, who had been a guest at two or three such gatherings since his meeting with Robert and James in Glen Fruin, was the last to appear. His absentminded preoccupation with times gone or dreams unrealizable always amused Gwen. His lodgings in Glasgow were near her shop and the previous week she had noticed him stop and watch curiously from the other side of the street as deliverymen carried in various pieces of furniture. She had waved to him and he, after a long hesitation, had waved back in his other-worldly way, then turned and hurried down the street.

Tonight he came straight across the room to her.

'Was it you in that shop the other day, Gwen?' It was as if the words had been in his mind for some time and he spoke them without even greeting her. He looked younger without the tweed cloak and rough clothes he usually wore. Formal dress suited the long pale line of his face.

'Yes,' she said. 'It was me. I hope I didn't frighten you?'

He looked at her uncertainly. 'I wasn't sure who it was at the time. It was only later I realized. . . .'

His expression was enquiring.

'I'm going to open a little business there,' she said.

'Really? A business?' Lindsay's surprise was almost laughable.

'I'm going to sell antiques.'

'Very good. I must buy something from you.' The quick recovery did not quite conceal his thoughts.

It interested Gwen that even in a man as unconventional in his views as Lindsay there still lived the belief that commerce was for the male alone.

'Are you interested in antiques, Colin?'

'I'm interested in anything to do with Scotland's great past.'

'Then I'm afraid you may find my stock in trade a little disappointing. Most of it is English.'

Lindsay was disconcerted again until he saw her expression. 'I believe you're teasing me, Gwen,' he said reprovingly. 'It's a habit you Kings seem to have.'

'Surely not?' She made a face. 'It's just that you don't understand us. We're uncomplicated business people who say bluntly what we think. We lack your artistic graces.'

He laughed aloud. 'Now I know you're teasing me!' He gave her a close look. 'But may I say, using my artistic grace, that you're looking lovely tonight?'

She blushed slightly, wondering if he meant it or if he was now teasing her. The absurd complications of such thinking struck her and she inclined her head a little in pleased acceptance.

He took the empty silver cup she held. 'Can I get you a little more punch?'

'Not just at the moment. But'—her expression became apologetic —'I am sorry, Colin. You're being neglected. You've had nothing to drink yet. And the night is very cold.' She stopped a passing maid and told her to bring Lindsay a large measure of punch.

Fergus never stinted the drinks before dinner and his guests invariably went to the table in a relaxed mood. Tonight, two surprises had been planned for them and the first was a success well up to Rita's expectations. It was game soup prepared according to the recipe given to her by the Queen. None among the guests had tasted the dish before, or heard of it. Rita's explanation of how she had come by the recipe was greeted with the mixture of awe and delight she had come to expect on these occasions. It had occurred to her at the first dinner party where she planned to serve game soup that if she revealed the recipe—which she was bound to be asked to do—royal soup, as she thought of it, would soon cease to be a source of distinction. Half the hostesses of Glasgow would be making it, all claiming, or at least hinting, that they had received the recipe personally from the Queen.

So Rita had embroidered her story, claiming the Queen had pledged her to secrecy before revealing ingredients, quantities, and method of preparation. Tonight, when the usual excited requests came from the ladies at the table, she was able gracefully to decline. Who could expect her to break a pledge given to the Queen? Under cover of the cries of understanding or disappointment that followed, Mrs. Veitch unscrupulously diverted a little attention to herself by whispering to the lady on her right that although the Queen might think her soup a secret, she could clearly remember her own grandmother making it on special occasions.

The second surprise of the dinner was a red, plumlike object placed in front of each guest. Rita explained these were a vegetable new to Scotland, although becoming known in the south of England. They were called tomatoes and she invited them to eat them along with the lamb cutlets. No one present had encountered tomatoes before, but they all rose to the occasion boldly. There was only one dissenting voice. 'That was quite a novelty, my dear,' Mrs. Veitch said, 'and probably in England tomatoes will be very popular, but in Scotland I think we prefer our vegetables hot. Besides, I'm not too happy about the seeds. They could be injurious.'

A third surprise came at the end of the meal when Fergus offered the gentlemen King's Royal instead of port or brandy. Robert was astonished that his father should be so indecorous as to misuse the hospitality of his own house to indulge in what might be interpreted as a piece of crude business advertising. A slightly bitter memory came back to him of Fergus' oft-repeated declaration that whisky would never be admitted to any decent drawing-room.

'Really, Father,' he said, 'I don't think we should force our own preference on our guests.' He sent a servant to fetch port and brandy, but by the time it arrived everyone had good-naturedly declared their intention of settling for nothing less than the famous King's Royal.

Fergus, to underline whose writ prevailed at Ardfern, sent laughingly for another bottle, but shortly before eleven o'clock the party came to an abrupt end.

Snow had started to fall—quite suddenly swept down from the north on the howling wind in huge Arctic flakes. In minutes, it seemed, the driveway had disappeared and the hedges lining it had become a solid wall. The carriages went down to the road with the coachmen holding the horses in careful check, the sound of the wheels blanketed, and the lanterns already blotted out in the muffling white.

Fergus waved them off with the old sense of anxiety snow always dredged out of his past. 'It's a blessing none of them has far to go,' he said. 'Another half hour of this and there won't be a wheel turning in the county.'

His foreboding was dispelled by Robert returning good-humouredly to his after-dinner lapse. But he was not to be abashed.

'It's up to us to set the style,' he said expansively. 'King's Royal's the match of a fine brandy and I'm certainly not ashamed of it. If we don't treat it as a drink of importance how can we expect other people to do so?'

Robert went to bed still marvelling at the extent of his father's conversion. God knows what credit the old devil was now going about claiming for the success of King's Royal. He might even be posing as the originator of blended whisky.

Shortly after midnight Rita wakened Fergus.

'There's something happening,' she said. 'I can hear voices and people moving about.'

Fergus sat up in bed, fumbling for the matches that lay beside the lamp. The window was shuddering and the wind thundered through the trees that grew close to the house. They could hear the old branches groaning.

'It's only the storm,' he said. 'Perhaps a window or a door has blown open.'

'No.' Before Rita could say more there was a loud knocking on the door.

Fergus opened it and looked out in alarm at McEwan standing in the corridor with an anxious maid—both of them holding lamps and wearing coats over their nightclothes.

'What is going on?' he demanded.

'It's Mr. James, sir,' McEwan said breathlessly. 'He's stuck in the blizzard on the Black Hill.'

This was the back road winding over the moors from Helensburgh to Loch Lomond.

Fergus stared uncomprehendingly. 'James is in Inverness,' he said. 'He can't be on the Black Hill.'

The door was almost torn from his grasp in a sudden blast. Outside, there was a rending noise and then a crash as a branch was torn from a tree and thrown against the house.

'How do you know this?' Rita's eyes were wide with alarm.

'His cabbie roused me, madam,' McEwan said, his voice hushed. 'He was bringing Mr. James home but they were caught on the hill when the snow came. He says it's terrible up there. The coach was blown off the road and broke an axle. The man undid his horse and rode down here.'

'And he left James alone up there in this?'

'He says it was all he could do. He had to get help. The horse couldn't have taken both of them on a night like this.'

'Then he must take us to where James is, at once,' Fergus said in a sudden panic he couldn't control. 'Wake Robert while I get dressed. Then get dressed yourself and fetch some lanterns.'

'The snow's two feet high, sir, and coming down thick. We maun hurry.'

'Then be off, man.'

Rita threw back the curtains and peered out into the snow as Fergus struggled quickly into his clothes. 'The garden's disappeared,' she said in a trembling voice. 'Fergus, I'm afraid for James.'

Trying to quell his own fears, Fergus put his hands gently on her shoulders. 'Get the servants to light the fire in James' bedroom and warm his bed,' he said comfortingly. 'And don't worry.'

'I can't understand why he was on Loch Lomondside. I've been imagining him warmly in bed in Inverness.'

Fergus shook his head as if it hardly mattered. 'He must have left for home a day early and missed the last train from Glasgow to Helensburgh. There's a later train to Alexandria. I've used it myself at times.'

Rita sank down shivering on the bed with her eyes closed. 'If the snow is like this down here it will be ten times worse on the hill.'

This was the frightening picture that Fergus had. 'James will be safe enough in the coach,' he said gently. 'Once you have told the maids what to do, go back to bed and wait.'

In the almost overturned coach James crouched numbly, shivering back into wakefulness from the second or third brief sleep into which he had fallen since the cabbie disappeared into the snow on the frightened horse.

His nervous loneliness had turned gradually to bleak anxiety as an hour passed and the coach, at first rocking and creaking in the wind, had settled tightly into the rising snow.

His determination to reach home that night he could now see to have been folly. He had arrived in Glasgow weary after the long train journey from Inverness and the wise thing would have been to spend the night there.

But he had had all he wanted of hotels in the previous six days. The novelty of being away from home had soon worn off and although the quantities of whisky that he had been promised had kept him buoyant he had decided to catch the first train home when he reached the end of Robert's list of calls.

The endless jolting over rocky mountain tracks had tired him. His itinerary, easy as Robert had thought it, had revealed to him for the first time the full burden of his disability. It had been a depressing discovery, only partly kept at bay by his excitement at the awesome grandeur of the wild country through which his business took him.

There had been the added burden of dealing with the constant expressions of sorrow that had been heaped on him when he had explained, in reply to concerned enquiries, about his accident.

Now James was afraid. It was black inside the coach. One window was buried in the snow and the other covered by snow.

He was on the floor, stretched out in an awkward position halfway between lying and standing because of the angle at which the coach had fallen.

At first he had moved his arms as much as he could to keep his blood circulating, but after a time the chill had sunk so deeply into him that he could not make the effort. He had read that people froze to death because they fell asleep. His fear grew each time he wakened. Perhaps one time he would not waken and if the cabbie did not soon return with help he would never waken again. At the thought, he struggled out of his icy torpor. He manoeuvred himself stiffly into a position from which he could reach the window strap. He released it and tried to force the window open. It had half frozen and it took all his strength to move it down. Snow fell in on him. He had expected to see the sky, or the driving snow. He saw nothing and although he could hear the wind he could not feel it.

With a sudden stab of terror James realized the coach was buried. He put his hand up to where the glass of the window had been and he felt only cold. Wildly, he seized his crutch and jabbed it at the snow. He sobbed with relief when the crutch broke upwards into open air and the frozen crust that had gathered fell in on him. He saw a faint blur of sky. He dragged himself into a standing position and put his head out. The wind struck him brutally, carrying away his hat. It wasn't snowing now, but the wind was gathering the fallen snow and building it into a drift around the coach. Very soon it would be entombed. James took a firm hold of his crutch and hauled himself out through the window and on to the side of the coach. The wind almost knocked him over, tearing his coat open and making him gasp for breath. Above him, the thin branches of a maddened tree lashed the air like scourges. The drifting snow enshrouded him and he had to turn his head out of the wind to breathe. He had a confused impression of high mounds of snow on the edge of the open moor. There was no shelter he could see. No one would ever reach him through this. If he sat where he was, the snow would cover him over. His limbs were already freezing into rigidity. He manoeuvred his crutch under his arm with frozen fingers and slid down the side of the coach, filled with a terrified urge to get home. The snow reached his knee, but it was soft and he began moving laboriously across the tormented moor. The vicious wind struck at him but he drove himself on.

Countless times he fell, thudding into snow-covered rocks that littered the wilderness around him. When he recoiled from one he would hit another. He tumbled through the soft snow into marshy hollows and icy pools, losing his crutch and then feeling around him, sobbing, until he found it again.

He was more than a thousand feet above sea level and with his clothes now sodden the piercing cold of the terrible wind sank into him with deadly ease. His misery was so extreme that several times, as he stood swaying in the vortex of the swirling gusts, he was tempted to turn and let the wind carry him back to the coach. But where was the coach? Behind him there was only a smear of white, then impenetrable blackness.

These impulses were only momentary, followed directly by a vision of the bright lamps and warm fires of Ardfern, that lay perhaps only a mile away. He knew he must go on. Once as he looked back, he fancied he could hear the hoarse sound of men shouting and thought he saw moving lantern lights. He called out, but no reply came and the lights he thought he saw had gone.

Once he staggered out of the turmoil into a sheltering wall of trees that ran in a narrow belt across the moor. At first he couldn't understand what had happened, or where he was. His drained and battered body could feel the overwhelming relief of the shelter, but his defeated brain needed time to adjust.

The tops of the trees shook clatteringly. He felt he remembered this spot from happy summer walks with Robert or Fergus. New hope rose in him and with it a burst of strength and determination. He moved from one tree to the next, forcing himself on. His exhausted body wanted to stop. It clamoured to make him hear it. It swayed and tottered, sinking into the gripping snow in its desire for rest. Grimly he lashed it on.

The vision of safety at Ardfern still burned in his mind. He lurched agonizingly towards it as if it was just a little way ahead. As he neared the farthest fringe of trees the wind reached out for him again. It sucked him to it, tearing and tugging at his clothes. Again his suffering body fought to halt him where he was. It wrung him, hoping it could force him to cower down among the trees and stay there. Beyond the trees it had started to snow again. Even before he left the last fringe of cover he was enveloped. Dimly he was aware of it, but it hardly seemed to matter. He was going home.

He stumbled on. Now the blizzard raged even more murderously, spinning him until he could not stand. He slithered for a few yards across the demented moor, then sank behind the meagre shelter of a great rock. It seemed hours since he had clambered out of the overturned coach. He felt that if he could just crawl on he would soon find a house. He was convinced he had travelled a long way. As he lay against the rock the screaming wind built the snow against him. He could see the flakes flying, but didn't feel their touch. He began to drift, quite warmly, almost as if he was in a very soft bed.

With an enormous effort he undid his scarf and tied it with solidified fingers to the leather pad of his crutch. Then, with his last strength, he drove the crutch into the snow. He fell back with the scarf flapping wildly above him as snow began to cover him.

That was the point of recollection beyond which James could never go. Blackness had filled his mind but some instinct must have triumphed over the icy cold. The signs were that he had continued to knock the snow off himself, slithering out of its deadly embrace each time it had him almost buried.

Memory reasserted itself at the point where he realized he was cradled in Robert's arms, still under the rock and the snow still falling. 'He's opened his eyes—oh, thank God, he's opened his eyes,' he heard Robert say.

'Can you hear me, James? Try to take some of this.'

He spluttered on the brandy but some of it went down and soon a slight flush of returning warmth began to flow through his frozen body.

Then it was his father bending over him. 'We can use the blankets as a stretcher and carry him down between us,' Fergus said. 'We'll rouse Dr. Ramsay.'

Robert's arms were around him again and his voice strangely pleading in his ear. 'Forgive me, James. Please forgive me.'

'Forgive you for what, Robert?' They were the first faint words James had spoken since they found him.

'Just forgive me.'

'I'm very cold.'

'You'll soon be warm in bed, James. You'll soon be home.'

Bed was all the doctor prescribed. 'There's no frostbite,' he said. 'He's bruised all over, of course, and completely exhausted. When you get him home he'll sleep most of the day. I'll look in on him in the early evening if the roads are clear. Give him all the hot drinks and soup he wants.'

Robert spent most of the day reading by the fire in his brother's bedroom.

Late in the afternoon James sat up.

'You don't even seem to have caught cold,' Robert said.

James smiled. 'For a moment I was going to say it's because I am tough. But that's something I've learned in the last week. I'm not tough—and I'm not nearly as independent as I thought.' He looked at Robert. 'Another thing I discovered is that I don't really care much for business.'

'Well we won't worry about that. Your week as a businessman did one thing for you. It saved you from the university. By the time they're enrolling again next October you'll have the excuse of being too old.'

This cheered James. 'It was worth almost freezing to death for that,' he said. 'By the way, aren't any of you going to ask me about the whisky?'

'I told you before you weren't to worry if you didn't get any.'

James looked indignant. 'Why should you assume my time was entirely wasted? I did get some.'

'Marvellous. Every little helps. How much did you get?'

'Almost five hundred hogsheads.'

Robert gaped. 'Are you joking, James?'

'No, Robert. The exact number is four hundred and seventy-five. Isn't that good?'

'It's absolutely wonderful. I wouldn't have been able to buy that in two months. You must have been pouring on the charm.'

James smiled shyly. 'Well, I did lay it on a bit thick, sometimes,' he said. 'I told them all what lovely views they had and how I envied them the sunsets. And how I had been sketching in their hills. The colours in the Highlands at this time of year are un- believable.'

Robert's eyes widened and then he began to laugh. 'Well, I'm damned,' he said. 'I must remember that. Especially the bit about the sunsets.'

Later that week Fergus received a letter from Fiona Fraser telling him her father had died. As in the previous year, Roderick had gone to his sister May's house to rest. He had seemed to be benefiting from his respite from business, Fiona wrote, and had been looking forward to returning to Helensburgh the following week. On Thursday evening he had collapsed without warning, lapsed into unconsciousness, and died during the night. It had been his wish that he be buried where his people lay, in a small cemetery overlooking Loch Long near the Argyllshire village of Ardentinny. Arrangements had been made for his body to be taken to his house in Helensburgh, and the funeral procession would leave from there for Loch Long at ten o'clock on Monday morning.

The news shocked Fergus. He had known Fraser for a quarter century and though their friendship had never been closer than a half-dozen meetings a year, it had been steady and sincere. Fraser had watched without envy as Fergus' business had grown, rarely complaining that over the same period his own had greatly declined. Fergus remembered how on his first visit to Lochbank Distillery to arrange for supplies of whisky Fraser had waived the usual requirement of two business references. After a half hour's talk the two men had weighed each other and neither had ever had cause to revise his opinion. Fergus held Fiona's note in his hand and searched his memory for some sign he might have missed that his friend was near death. There was nothing. But receiving the news at his holiday house seemed to sharpen the shock.

'What an unhappy thing for Fiona,' Rita said. 'She'll have no one now.'

'At least she'll have no financial worries,' Mrs. Veitch said practically. 'Mr. Fraser will have left her well provided for.'

Fergus exchanged a glance with Robert. 'I hope so,' he said.

'But is there any reason to doubt it, dear?'

'Things hadn't been very buoyant at Fraser's end of the whisky business for a long time,' Fergus said. 'It depends how far the poor chap had been forced to eat into his private resources.'

'Has Fiona any close relatives? Where will the poor girl stay now? She can hardly live on alone in that big house in Helensburgh.'

'I don't know, Mother,' Robert said. 'There's the aunt in Glasgow. Presumably Fiona will stay with her for a while. There's also an uncle in Perth.'

'I wonder if she needs help? Don't forget when you're replying to her, Fergus, to say that she must call on me for any assistance she thinks I might be able to give. I've always liked Fiona.'

Rita stopped and seemed to hesitate.

'Would you like me to tell Agnes to draw the blinds, dear? It's a custom less and less people seem to be observing, these days, leaving it to the immediate family, but I wouldn't like it said that we were lacking in respect for Mr. Fraser.'

Fergus looked at her gratefully but shook his head. 'I was wondering about that, myself, my dear, but I don't think we will. Fraser couldn't get enough sunshine. I don't think he would approve of it being shut out now on his account. It used to worry me anytime I visited him in Helensburgh. The sun would be streaming in, fading the carpets and rotting the curtains, and he never seemed to mind. Some of his furniture—not bad stuff, either —was bleached white.' He shook his head in wonder at the diversity of human priorities. 'I hope the sun shines for him on Monday.'

Perhaps twenty mourners surrounded the coffin while the minister enumerated the various benefits that would flow to Fraser now that he had shed his earthly burdens. The misty drizzle of the previous day had turned to heavy rain and, as the black figures stood bowed in silence, the drops could be heard striking mournfully at the window of the darkened room.

The minister, perhaps mindful of the long journey ahead, was brief. He stood back and left the undertaker in charge. Fraser's brother was put at the head of the coffin on one side. His son, Fraser's nephew, went to the other. As arranged, Fergus, Robert, and two workers from Lochbank Distillery lent their shoulders. For a few seconds they wavered then, the weight equally distributed, they carried the coffin slowly from the room, the other men who had come to mourn shuffling behind. Fiona and three or four black-veiled women remained.

Fraser's gardener, coachman, and other servants stood under a dripping tree in their best clothes as their master's remains were placed in the hearse. The undertaker's horses were black and the horses drawing the carriages of the mourners, though of various colours, had black plumes fitted to their collars.

As the cortege moved off, Robert looked back at the house. At all the main windows, blinds were slowly being lifted as if in farewell. He had a glimpse of Fiona at the window of the room where Fraser had lain. She had a handkerchief to her eyes and the arm of an older woman—possibly Aunt May—was around her shoulder. At his side, Fergus sighed heavily. 'This is going to be a long depressing day. We'll be very lucky if we're home before dark.'

*For a man so considerate,* Fergus reflected, *Fraser picked an awkward place to be buried in.* By road from Helensburgh it was a distance of at least sixty miles to Ardentinny, much of the way twisting around lochs or scaling hazardous mountain tracks. To have gone all the way by road would have meant the funeral would last two days. Two days for a funeral in remote parts of Scotland was not uncommon, but the mourners often ended up drunk, having taken so much whisky to combat the effects of exhaustion and exposure. The corpse could have company, for unsteady mourners often stumbled into the grave on top of the coffin. Fergus was glad the undertaker had advised Fiona of a shorter route to Ardentinny.

As the carriages reached the foot of Helensburgh Hill and turned on to the shore road, Robert leaned forward and lowered the window a little on its leather strap. 'Over the hills to Ardentinny,' he said, quoting the words of a song. 'If we could go that way, like birds, it would be a journey of only five or six miles—not twenty.'

Fergus nodded. 'A loch becomes noticeably less beautiful,' he said, 'when you have to go ten miles up one side to the top, then ten miles down the other, when the place you want to get to is only quarter of a mile away across the water.'

'Especially when it's raining.'

'If you think this is wet, wait until we get out into the middle of Loch Long.'

'Is it an open ferry?'

'If the ferryman's in a good humour he may have rigged up a bit of tarpaulin we can crawl under. Your mother and I crossed once for a picnic, six or seven years ago. It rained on the way back and we were thoroughly soaked. It's treacherous in there between the high mountains. The wind and rain come out of nowhere.'

Robert laughed. 'I think the whole thing's Mr. Fraser's final joke. I don't believe there's a burial ground at Ardentinny. We'll all have to turn round and come back, bringing him with us.'

Fergus frowned a little at such levity. 'Fraser was born there, Robert. His mother and father and some of his brothers and sisters are buried there.' He clutched at his hat as the carriage rocked through a succession of deep holes in the road.

At Garelochhead, a steamer was leaving the pier for its return journey to Gourock. Sea-gulls hovered, screeching for food. Men with sacks draped across their backs to help keep them dry were loading discharged cargo on to carts and barrows. Down the opposite shore of the loch the houses became less frequent.

A ship with sagging sails wallowed, almost becalmed, two or three hundred yards off shore, the water around it so smooth that each drop of rain left a mark. Mist had cut off the tops of the hills, making it look as if they ended abruptly in a straight dark line of green.

There was less flooding on this side of the Gareloch and the horses began to make better time. The procession passed through Kilcreggan and Cove early in the afternoon, with Fergus staring appraisingly from his carriage at the new villas facing the sea. This rural stretch was becoming another weekend haven for Glasgow's rich.

The road became rougher and more twisting. After a few more miles it ended at a small jetty where two boats lay waiting. The ferryman, notified in advance by the undertaker, had called out an auxiliary so the entire funeral party could cross without the necessity of two journeys.

The mourners emerged stiff and cold from the carriages and stood under umbrellas while the coffin was manoeuvred on to the bigger of the two boats and lashed in position. With a full load there was no room for the rough tarpaulin shelter Fergus had said might be available. Although it was calm close to the shore it was obvious that, farther out, there was a current and a wind. 'We're in for a rough time,' Fergus warned. Soon the boats began to heave and gusts of wind made it impossible for the umbrellas to be kept up. For half an hour the mourners crouched in sodden misery, even the most faithful silently cursing Fraser's loyalty to the place of his birth.

When they reached the other side, numb and dejected, Robert was glad he was one of the coffin-bearers. The burial ground, which could be seen from the pebble beach where the boats had grounded,

259

lay behind a low wall several hundred yards up a stony hill track. The exertion would be welcome. His enthusiasm for what he knew would be a blood-pounding trudge turned to concern when he thought of his father. Fergus was pale, shivering, and miserable. For the first time, Robert saw his father as a man well along the road to old age. It was a strangely affecting discovery. The signs he'd never noticed before were there in abundance, accentuated today by cold and wet—the thinning and greying of the hair, the slight loss of height as the bones rounded and contracted, the stiffness as he had stepped from the ferry after the cramped crossing. All his life Robert had seen his father as the same unchanging figure—broad, black-bearded and strong. He couldn't remember him ever being ill enough to stay away from business for more than a day or two.

In business he had always seemed unstoppable, succeeding in everything he tackled, triumphing over every temporary setback. That his father's powers must one day begin to fail was something he had never considered. This sudden, revealing glimpse was disconcerting. It was, Robert supposed, an insight that mightn't have come to him, in the course of their normal city life, for years yet. As tactfully as he could, he suggested that Fergus might like one of the other, younger, mourners to take his share of the burden on the last stage of the journey. Fergus stubbornly refused, but he was obviously exhausted when, after the stiff climb, they lowered Fraser's coffin to the grass beside the open grave.

The minister spoke into the wind and his message of hope and continuing life was swept away from the mourners into the empty hills. The headstone on the Fraser grave was weathered and broken, the lettering badly carved and partly obscured by moss. Robert deciphered names and dates. Not only Fraser's mother and father but also two brothers and two sisters who had died in childhood in a single month. Rain ran down the grey stone, making the wording even more obscure, as Robert strained to read the record of family tragedy:

Mary, died January 6th, 1825, aged four months.
Colin, died January 10th, 1825, aged two years.
Kenneth, died January 23rd, 1825, aged four years.
Alice, died February 4th, 1825, aged five years.

*How*, Robert wondered, *had Fraser survived?*

'Roderick was with his grandmother in Dunoon when the epidemic broke out,' Fraser's brother told them later as they sipped steaming whisky toddies in the local inn while they waited for the traditional funeral meal. 'It was diphtheria. Children that age didn't have a chance. It raged for nearly two months and in the parish of Ardentinny alone twenty-eight children and nine adults perished. I was born three years later.'

The men, their mournful duty accomplished, warmed now by the inn fire, cheered by whisky and the prospect of hot food, gossiped in cheerful groups. But the deaths of all those people seemed strangely near to Robert.

It was still raining when they left the inn and crunched over the pebble beach to the waiting boats. Some of the men were already sniffing and sneezing. The food and whisky had come too late. Fraser had rejoined his people. At what cost to his friends would never be known.


James stopped the cab at the corner of Sauchiehall and Blyths-wood Streets. When the cabbie jumped down to help he motioned him away. 'I can manage on my own,' he said. He lowered himself backwards on to the street and pulled his crutch after him.

When he had paid the fare he hobbled the few yards to Gwen's still unopened shop. The windows were covered in whitewash to screen the activity inside but someone, a workman, he supposed, had rubbed the white away to form a face with pitcher ears and a grinning mouth. James peered through the outline and saw Gwen was alone.

He knocked on the door and when she opened it he said, 'Is the kettle on?'

'It's not,' she said in surprise, 'but I can soon put it on.'

'As long as I'm not keeping you back.' He looked around the jumble of furniture and ornaments. 'You still have a lot to do by the look of it.'

She took his hat and coat. 'Not as much as it might seem. The great thing is, I'm rid of the workmen at last. I've been falling over them for weeks.'

He smiled at her appearance. The sleeves of her dress were rolled up and her hair had come loose. She looked flushed and pretty in her delight in the shop. He moved around inspecting things while she went into a small back room to fill a kettle and put it on a spirit stove.

'You seem to have recovered from your ordeal,' she said when he had settled in a wing chair by the fire. 'You're looking extremely well.'

He had become used to such remarks in recent days and he gave her his usual heroic answer. 'Well, I'm tough, you see. It'll take more than a snowstorm to get rid of me.' He was secretly proud that he had confounded the doctor by surviving the blizzard without even a sneeze.

'Nevertheless,' Gwen said, 'Robert should never have sent you up north, especially in winter. He should have been more thoughtful.'

She stopped and walked quickly into the back room. He heard the rattle of teacups. He knew the reason for her abrupt exit. What she had said was an unthinking reference to the forbidden subject. He smiled to himself. He knew by now it was expecting too much of them never to refer to it. Well, he didn't mind. There were burdens just as sad and heavy, though less obvious, than a lost leg. Sometimes it seemed to James that the Kings, with the exception of his mother, were all disabled.

There was Fergus, crippled by his fear of scandal and by his social frustrations, Robert, with the pot distillers on his back, limping towards his grandiose vision of a whisky empire. And Gwen, 'poor Gwen,' as they all thought of her, striving against her memories to make some kind of useful life for herself. He, of course, was the prize specimen, fighting not only his physical handicap but, a dawning insight told him, the possibly far greater handicap of his aimlessness. Lost in a bout of rueful introspection, he was startled when Gwen said from the back room, 'There's a hint, in fact, more than a hint, of ruthlessness in Robert. I sometimes wonder if we're the same family we used to be.'

Had she read his mind? He looked at her closely when she came back carrying a tray. A beam of sunlight, diffused by the whitewash on the windows, filled the shop, making him disinclined to follow these sober thoughts.

'Robert's all right,' he said, taking out his pipe and tobacco

262

pouch. 'He's inherited just a little too much ambition from Father.'

Was he being fair to Robert? Was his view distorted by his own lack of ambition?'

He gave her a teasing smile. 'You've shown a pretty iron determination yourself, Gwen.'

She laughed. 'I'm afraid Father is still a bit bewildered.'

'I think it's admirable. Probably Father does, too, but it will be a long time before he admits it.'

'He's been very helpful.' She looked around the confusion. 'I'm relying on Mother to help me arrange all these things.'

He drank two cups of tea, then said, 'Well, I'd better go and let you get on with it.'

She was in the process of moving a small table. 'You're my second visitor this morning,' she said breathlessly. 'Colin Lindsay looked in a little earlier.'

'Lindsay? What did he want?'

'He was curious to see what was going on behind the whitewash.'

'Oh, was that all?' James looked at the smeared window with its funny-face. 'Well, I shouldn't think he'll be the only one who is wondering.'

'I suppose not, but he also asked if he could help in any way, with lifting and laying. He saw there was a lot to do.'

'Somehow I don't think he would be very practical.'

Gwen laughed. 'Nor do I, but it was nice of him to offer.'

'He would probably drop anything you gave him to move. His mind's on higher things.'

At the corner James stopped another cab and told the man to take him to the city centre. He had no plan, but on impulse he paid the fare in St. Vincent Street and went to the window of a shop displaying a painting on an easel. The sign above the door said: CRAIBE ANGUS. FINE ART DEALER. He knew Fergus had bought some of his paintings here.

Mr. Angus was out, but when James mentioned his father the assistant invited him to look around. The paintings were almost all by Dutch and French artists. Most of the names were unknown to James but the scenes appealed to him. They were unlike any Scottish paintings he had ever seen. These Continental artists had chosen to paint everyday studies of outdoor life and they seemed more concerned with atmosphere than romantic detail.

He spent a half hour looking at the paintings and talking to the assistant. When he left, he felt that in some wonderful way his eyes had been opened.

# 15

Fergus walked uneasily to a lane behind Jail Square. The cobbled surface was littered with herring barrels and dead fish. He passed kippering sheds and the offices of auctioneers from the nearby market. Everything, including the people who walked about the lane, seemed covered in fish scales. Fergus stopped outside a single-story brick building and read the nameplate: CHARLES CRUICK-SHANK. DEBT COLLECTOR. MAKER OF CONFIDENTIAL ENQUIRIES. He had been brought here by worries about the child he believed had been born to Mary Devine. In the last week his occasional wonderings had become obsessive. He wanted to see the child. Now the urge was in him he wondered why he had not been visited by it sooner. Nothing could be more natural than that a man should wish to see his only grandchild. That the mother and father had sinned, that they had been entirely unsuited, in no way reflected on the child. The child was blameless. It was his flesh and blood. However correctly he had acted in blocking Robert's wish to marry Mary Devine, the result had undoubtedly been a tragedy for the child. Fergus recognized this. Could he now atone?

Money settled on the child anonymously must be helpful and at the same time it would ease his feeling of guilt. But, above all, he must see the child; perhaps even touch it momentarily, as a fond, passing stranger. The problem was to know where to go. Perhaps the girl no longer lived in Glasgow. Fergus' pride would not allow him to ask Robert. He still had his sense of decency even though he had been overtaken by sentimentality.

He took a quick look along the lane before entering the brick building. There was a narrow passage with an enquiry window on one side and on the other a door marked PRIVATE. An old man took his name and a minute or two later he was shown into the private room.

The Maker of Confidential Enquiries was a small, round man of reassuringly ordinary, well-dressed appearance. He endowed his dull, badly furnished room with a respectability for which Fergus was grateful.

'I want to find out the whereabouts of someone,' he said, when he was seated. 'Is that the sort of commission you undertake?'

Mr. Cruickshank seemed doubtful. 'Missing persons are more properly the province of the police. However. . . .'

Fergus felt alarm rise in him at the mention of the police. 'It's not a missing person in that sense,' he said hastily. 'It's someone I . . . someone with whom I've lost touch. There's no trouble. No mystery, or anything like that.'

Mr. Cruickshank nodded. 'Please go on.' He lifted a pen and pulled a pad of paper across his desk. 'I'll just jot down anything that sounds helpful while you speak.' His smile was courtly.

The window was closed but the fishy odours of the lane had penetrated the room. Mr. Cruickshank's work, Fergus suspected, would be mainly the collecting of debts, and the fish market, with its attendant conglomeration of box-makers, carriers, and salesmen, his principal source. He hoped he hadn't been foolish in coming here. The furtive and the melodramatic were anathema to him and the only comfort he could extract from the situation was the fact that his presence in such a place was a tribute to the genuineness of his desire to make restitution for his neglect.

'The person I'm concerned to trace,' he said, 'was a nurse at the Western Infirmary. That was some three or four years ago. Her name is Devine. Mary Devine.'

Mr. Cruickshank asked, 'What age would this lady be?'

'I suppose about twenty-two or twenty-three.'

'I see. A young lady.' Mr. Cruickshank spoke as if here was a significant fact. 'And where did she live, when you last knew her?'

'With her parents, I think. Her father is a medical practitioner.'

'He is a Doctor Devine?'

'Naturally.'

Mr. Cruickshank was unruffled. 'Devine might have been the lady's married name,' he said quietly.

Suddenly Fergus realized that the embarrassment of illegitimacy and unmarried motherhood would all have to come out. He should have prepared himself better for this interview.

'I take it Miss Devine does not now live with her parents?'

'If I knew that I wouldn't be here,' Fergus said unreasonably. 'I'm asking you to find out where she is.'

Mr. Cruickshank was accustomed to clients made gruff by embarrassment. 'The more we can eliminate before we start the greater the saving in time and expense.' He paused. 'So Miss Devine might still be living with her parents?'

'Yes.'

'Apart from me discovering her whereabouts, is there anything else in particular you want to know, Mr. King?'

Fergus was beginning to wish he had given a false name. 'I want to know if she has a child.' The words nearly choked him.

Mr. Cruickshank wrote it down as if he couldn't trust himself to remember even this, but his pen moved a little faster. 'Anything else?'

'I would like to know what her habits are. With regard to the child. For example, if there's a park where she walks it, I would like to know. And the time she walks it, if there's a regular hour.'

'In short, Mr. King, you'd like to know where you could observe the child?'

Fergus was horrified by Cruickshank's understanding expression. Was it possible the man imagined *he* was the child's father? His face grew hot under his beard. He was on the point of making his position clear—or as clear as need be—when he realized it might only deepen any misconceptions Cruickshank might have. The prudent thing was to say as little as possible and get quickly away to the nearest place that didn't smell of fish.

He rose. 'Will there be anything else?'

'You haven't given me your address. For my report.'

'You can report to me through my solicitors,' Fergus said quickly. 'They are Boyd, Paton & Galbraith of Ingram Street. Mark the report private and for my personal attention.'

When he reached the mouth of the lane a woman in a shawl sitting on the shaft of her handcart tried to interest him in kippers at a halfpenny a pair.

Gwen, in pursuance of her belief that business could be gracious as well as profitable, had invited some friends to help her celebrate the opening of her shop.

Colin Lindsay had volunteered to assist, and Gwen, though remembering James' assessment of his practicality, had accepted. She delegated him to pour glasses of sherry and soon the atmosphere became festive.

Fergus stationed himself as close as he could to the Queen Anne furniture, explaining to Rita that he wanted to be on hand with his handkerchief if any sherry should be spilled, especially by that dreamer Lindsay. He saw to it that empty glasses carelessly placed on valuable pieces were quickly removed by Miss Murray, Gwen's young assistant.

Later, Rita, who had been chatting to a group of Gwen's contemporaries and telling them how thrilled she was at her daughter's enterprise, approached him. 'Are you still on duty, my dear?'

Fergus frowned. 'Duty?'

'Yes. You look as if you're on sentry duty. Why don't you relax and enjoy yourself? Everyone else seems to be.'

Fergus' serious expression softened into a shamefaced smile.

'It's all very well people enjoying themselves, but someone has to look after Gwen's interests. You would be surprised if you knew how much money she's spent on stock. If anything gets damaged or broken, it could cost her a great deal.'

'Yes, but I'm sure nothing will be damaged. These are all very nice people.'

Margery Forsyth, from whose Bath Street window Gwen had watched her father and mother in procession with the Queen, took Gwen's arm.

'I've been admiring the way you've arranged everything,' she said. 'It's not like a shop, at all. It's like an exquisite drawing-room.'

It was Rita who had done most of the arranging, but Gwen took the compliment on her behalf. Margery pointed to a shelf. 'What are those beautiful little porcelain jar things?'

Gwen turned to look. 'Chinese snuff bottles. Ones of that quality are quite rare.' She broke off. 'Oh, there's Mother trying to catch my eye. If you'll excuse me, Margery, I must see what she wants. Don't be afraid to take the bottles down if you would like to examine them.'

She crossed the room. 'Yes, Mother?'

'I hope I didn't interrupt you at anything important with Margery, but there's a young lady over there anxious to ask you about the Queen Anne lowboy.'

'Where? Oh, that's Jill Aitkenhead. They've just moved to a house in Buckingham Terrace. She wasn't sure if she would manage to come today.'

'Now remember, Gwen, not a penny less than the price we agreed would be fair.' Fergus' whisper was anxious at the thought of the precious lowboy being sold so quickly.

'You don't imagine Jill would haggle about the price, surely?' Gwen looked shocked at the imputation. 'Really, Father! Her husband inherited a fortune.'

She turned away. 'Can I help you, Jill?'

'I wanted to ask about this little table, Gwen. Can you tell me something about it? I'm afraid I'm terribly ignorant where antiques are concerned but I think this is just what we need for our hall.'

'Well, the date will be about 1710. It's Queen Anne, of course. You don't get walnut with that beautiful grain nowadays.'

'If you don't mind me mentioning it, it is rather expensive. Does that mean it's something special?'

'Oh, yes. Good walnut furniture's very rare now.'

'It seems well made,' Jill said hesitantly.

A young couple seemed also to be attracted to the lowboy. The man opened the drawers and examined the dovetailing. Jill watched him uneasily then quickly made up her mind.

'I'm going to have it, Gwen,' she said. 'I've been looking for months and haven't seen anything as nice.'

*Poor father*, Gwen thought. Of the three pieces this was the one Fergus had admired most. But Fergus, when she told him that the lowboy had been sold, smiled bravely.

'There you are, my dear. Exactly as I said. If you buy pieces of that quality you won't have them lying around for long. You'll never have to put them into dead stock. You'll get a nice quick return on your money.'

Rita watched approvingly. She couldn't remember when she had last seen her daughter look so full of life. For the occasion, Gwen had deliberately selected a completely unbusinesslike dress of blue silk with daffodil yellow trimmings. Although, despite Lindsay's prompting, she had refused sherry, her face was delicately flushed and her eyes sparkled. Gwen, Rita realized, was in her element, carried away by the novelty and success of this start to her little venture. This was how Rita still thought of it. She wouldn't think of it as a business. Fergus was right. Well-brought-up young ladies did not engage in business, therefore Gwen didn't have a business. She had a little venture. Unpleasant considerations like bills, rent, rates, and debt arose in business. Rita did not like to think of her daughter having to deal with such things, therefore she preferred to think of her embarking on a little venture on which no such distasteful realities would ever intrude.

Fergus and Rita left with the last of the guests at half past twelve. Lindsay was corking the sherry and wiping the bottles with a damp cloth. *He was*, Gwen thought, *remarkably helpful*. She turned eagerly to him. 'Was it a success, Colin, do you think?'

He grinned. 'A great success.'

'I knew it would be. And, do you know, I don't feel demeaned or sullied. I'm sure no one was looking down at me or sniggering behind my back. I'm sure even Father will have to admit that.'

Lindsay looked at her, then, sensing the anxious quality of her almost challenging gaiety, put a hand on her shoulder. 'Sit down, Gwen. You must be tired. Those people didn't give you a minute. I'm going to pour you a glass of sherry.'

'I'd like that, Colin.' Suddenly she seemed to sag.

Lindsay watched with concern. 'What are you looking so worried about? You were in such high spirits only a moment ago.'

'Almost every one of those people bought something.'

'They did! You must be very pleased.'

'They didn't have to buy. I hope they didn't feel obliged to.' She caught at Lindsay's arm. 'Oh, Colin, do you think they might have thought they were being blackmailed? Is that what it looked like? I would be mortified if that's what they thought.'

Lindsay smiled gently. 'My dear Gwen. It didn't look like black-mail at all. You mustn't think such a thing. I'm sure no one else had such a thought. They all enjoyed themselves. They were surrounded by beautiful things. They were substantial people. They could afford to buy and they bought.'

Gwen looked only partly convinced. 'I hope you're right. My only thought was to have a pleasant gathering, not to make money.'

Lindsay was too bewildered by the somersault of emotions to do more than stand a little apart and give staunch, if slightly hesitant, sympathy.

'You've been working hard for weeks preparing for today,' he said. 'It's been a strain. You must close the shop for the rest of the day and go home.'

'I can't do that. There was an announcement in the *Glasgow Herald*. People might make a special journey. It would never do if they found the place closed on the first day.'

Lindsay's face brightened. 'You have your Miss Murray. You could leave her in charge. You needn't close.'

Gwen looked as if she might accept this suggestion. Then she shook her head. 'No, Colin. It would be unfair to leave Miss Murray here alone so soon. It would be too great a responsibility. Besides, the sherry's beginning to cheer me. I'm afraid I just gave way to an attack of nerves.'

Lindsay had been fumbling with his hat. 'Then would you allow me to take you to luncheon, Gwen?' he asked shyly. 'It will do you good to get out of here for a little while.'

She looked about. 'I suppose I'm entitled to close the shop for an hour in the middle of the day?'

'It's your shop, Gwen.'

'Is there somewhere near by?'

'There's Stewart's Rotunda in Sauchiehall Street.'

She smiled at him. 'Then that is very kind of you, Colin.'

In the afternoon, a dozen people visited the shop, most of them, as they entered, indicating that they were 'just looking', a phrase Gwen would become very familiar with. Her only sale was of a silver punch ladle with an early Edinburgh mark. She was able, at her leisure, to enter the day's business in a ledger and label various items for delivery. At five she locked the glass door.

'Well, Sadie,' she said to Miss Murray, 'that's the end of our first day. The morning was exciting but I think the afternoon was a truer indication of what we might expect until the business is established.'

'Yes, miss.' Miss Murray skewered her hat to her head with a long pin and examined the result in a Venetian mirror.

'Do you think you'll like your job?'

'Oh, yes miss.' The girl looked around the graceful room, richer than ever now with the fire spreading a warm glow in the fading light. Her expression suggested she was sorry to leave even for the night. 'It's such refined, ladylike work, miss.'

Gwen saw her out and relocked the door. The fire was cheerful and she sat down in front of it. She was in no hurry to go home. It was pleasant to have the place completely to herself at last. She reviewed the day and decided it had been a success. Her earlier fears that she might have taken advantage of her friends were, she could see now, hysterical and without foundation. Luncheon with Colin Lindsay had dispelled the last of her worries. He had made her laugh with his absurd dreams of an independent Scotland. That she succumbed to nerves was understandable. To have envisaged this unconventional breaking out of her sheltered environment, and to have carried her plans through to completion, had taken courage and much nervous energy. A reaction had been inevitable. She was grateful it hadn't come in the presence of her parents. They were worried about her, and even a momentary breakdown would have increased their worry. It must have cost Fergus a great deal, she knew—not just in time, but in the subjugation of his pride and prejudices—to have spent a whole morning lending the dignity of his presence to what he must still feel to be a stain on the family honour. Did he, in his gloomier moments, Gwen wondered, think of her as a black sheep? Was there a female of the species? She smiled. Her mother had been marvellous, too. She felt a small stab of guilt at the thought of her shameless acceptance of compliments more properly due to Rita. The great thing was not to become anxious, to remember her survival didn't depend on this business, that she had entered into it not, principally, to make money, but to provide herself with a means of escape from the boredom of her empty apartment.

As she sat in front of the warm fire, surrounded by the discreet lustre of silver and the unfakeable mellow beauty of old wood, Gwen honestly admitted to herself that it wouldn't be a perfect life, but it would be a life of some purpose and modest fulfilment compared to her barren existence of the last four years. And Colin Lindsay had been so understanding, so supportive when her courage had faltered. . . .

A coal fell from the fire. As she bent to lift it with the tongs she became aware of a tapping sound. It took her a few moments to realize there was someone at the glass door. It was completely dark now in the street and the figure at the door was a bulky blur. Was it Fergus on his way home, unable to resist finding out what else she had sold during the afternoon? She lifted one of the lamps Miss Murray had lit before leaving. When she reached the glass door she began to tremble, unable to turn the key. Tom Hoey stood on the doorstep.

One morning a long manila envelope was delivered to Fergus by special messenger. It was the report he had commissioned from Mr. Charles Cruickshank. A month had passed since Fergus had made his way around the herring barrels to the shabby riverside office of the Maker of Confidential Enquiries. He had expected news long before this. He hadn't been pleased by Mr. Cruickshank's lack of urgency and he frowned as he unfolded the report. It had been sent in the first place, as he instructed, to his solicitors and this subterfuge had probably caused further delay. The report half-filled a foolscap sheet and to Fergus' surprise it had been written on a typing machine. He hadn't expected anything as up-to-date as this from Cruickshank. It was a shock to read the three words that formed the heading: MARY DEVINE, SPINSTER. He looked at them uneasily. Did he have the right to pry like this? He shrugged guilt away. Beneath the heading were the words:
*First Purpose of enquiry, to trace above.*
'In accordance with instructions received, steps were taken to ascertain the present whereabouts of Miss Mary Devine. This has been accomplished. The young lady's parents no longer live in Carlton Place, which was their place of residence when Miss Devine was a nurse at the Western Infirmary. Dr. Devine, the father, died two years ago, and shortly afterwards the mother moved to a house in Edinburgh. The young lady now lives with her mother.' Here there was a subheading: '*Second purpose of enquiry—has Miss Devine a child?* Our enquiry established that there is no child at the Edinburgh address. Questioning of people in the area further established that no child has been seen at the house since the young lady arrived to live with her mother approximately a year ago. The next stage of our enquiry was to ascertain whether or not Miss Devine does in fact have a child or has ever had one. Young ladies of this class who are unfortunate enough to arrive at motherhood without benefit of

wedlock frequently have the offspring adopted or cared for in an orphanage.'

A chill entered Fergus at the thought that his grandchild might be an inmate of some bleak institution.

He went on with his reading. 'Enquiries at the Western Infirmary showed that Miss Devine remained in employment there until the summer of 1875. She did not have a baby while there and she severed her relationship with the infirmary because of a general decline in her health. This occasioned her being sent to Switzerland by her father for treatment in a clinic and she remained in the mountain air of that country for more than a year, returning to Glasgow when her father died.

'It was for the sake of Miss Devine's health that the mother moved to Edinburgh, where the air is said to be less harmful. The girl's health, although apparently recovered, has not allowed her to engage again in such a strenuous occupation as nursing.'

Only when he reached Mr. Cruickshank's concluding words did Fergus fully grasp the message.

'It is clear from our enquiries that Miss Devine does not have a baby and has in fact never had a baby at any time.'

In a sudden fever, Fergus read it all again. His first understanding had been correct. Mr. Cruickshank was confident there was no baby. Robert was not a father. At first, Fergus couldn't work it out. It was Robert himself who had told him Mary Devine was pregnant. Had the baby, then, been born dead, or died at birth, like Gwen's? No. The girl had worked on at the infirmary too long for that to have happened without it being known. She had been nursing until the summer of 1875. The truth staggered him. For three years he had been the victim of a lie. He sat at his desk stunned by the enormity of Robert's duplicity until there was a knock at the door and a clerk looked in.

'Mrs. King is here to see you, sir.'

'Mrs. King?' Fergus wondered if he had misheard. Rita hadn't been in his office since he had taken the place over twenty-five years ago. He would have been as disconcerted if she had suddenly confronted him in the smoke room of his club.

'Yes, sir.'

He looked foolishly at the clerk. 'Is there something wrong?'

The door, around which the clerk had been hesitantly straining, was pushed open. 'I'm sorry to intrude, Fergus,' Rita said as she came agitatedly but resolutely into the room.

As they waited for the clerk to go, Fergus crumpled Cruickshank's report and put it in a trouser pocket. His face had gone pale and his expression was a mixture of anger and baffled dismay. He came anxiously around the desk, staring at her as if he might read the answer in her face.

'Something's happened. Tom is back.'

'What?' Fergus did not immediately understand. His mind was too fragmented by worry piled on shock.

'Tom Hoey. He's come back.'

Fergus had been braced to face any catastrophe. The reality, when he appreciated it, came almost as a relief. He fetched a chair. 'Sit down, Rita, and tell me calmly what's happened.'

'I have told you, my dear. Tom Hoey's come home.'

At any other time it would have been unbearable news, but Fergus, after Mr. Cruickshank's revelation, was almost empty of emotion. He felt his family was cheating and harassing him. 'Don't just go on repeating yourself. Where is he?'

'With Gwen, of course.'

'How do you know this?'

'I've just come from her flat. I called to see her and there he was, in the parlour, reading a newspaper.'

'A racing newspaper, no doubt.'

'I don't think it matters what kind of newspaper it was. I was so startled I thought I was going to faint. He arrived on poor Gwen's doorstep three days ago, apparently. Completely out of the blue. I'm astonished and disappointed she didn't turn him away. She can have little pride.' Rita looked huffily into her muff.

'Do you mean to tell me Gwen's consented to take him back?'

'So it seems. I could hardly question her in front of him. But he's there.'

Fergus took a grip of his beard. 'The scoundrel should be scourged. I've a good mind to go round and do it myself. I can't understand Gwen. He deserted her for another woman, murdered her baby—because that's what it amounted to—I don't know how she can bear to have him under her roof again, even for a second.'

He took the cork from a bottle of KING'S ROYAL and poured

himself a drink. 'Well, he'll never be under *my* roof again. I'll swear to that.' In his excitement the whisky caught at his throat and he doubled up purple-faced and coughing.

By the time he had regained his breath Rita was calmer. 'Forgive me for bursting into your office, Fergus. I couldn't wait to tell you.'

'You did right, my dear.' Suddenly Fergus began to yawn. As one paroxysm ended another began. He felt exhausted. 'I don't know what's come over me,' he said.

'It's a nervous reaction.' Rita put a comforting hand on his shoulder. 'I shouldn't have come. I should have waited till you were at home.'

Fergus shook his head. 'She's a silly girl.'

Already Rita was relenting. 'I suppose we must accept her decision. For her sake. He's her husband and it's her life. That's what she's bound to tell us.'

He stifled another yawn. 'She doesn't need the scoundrel.' He stopped, puzzled by the look in Rita's eyes. 'Well, does she?' She didn't reply. 'After all, she has her shop to think of now,' he persisted.

There was a hint of a tired smile on Rita's face. 'I hope you won't use that argument with Gwen. After all, it isn't so long since you were against her going into business.'

Hoey came away from the sitting-room window overlooking Holland Street. He had been standing at it since Rita left.

'I must say your mother's looking very well,' he said. 'The years have been good to her.'

'I suppose they have.' Gwen turned in her chair to face him. 'She still dresses youthfully, but I'm afraid some grey hairs came when James had his accident. She had weeks of terrible worry. It was only after that I began to see her as . . . well, as getting on.'

'We're all getting on, but I think she still looks remarkably young.' He bent over her. 'And so do you,' he said softly. 'I can't stop admiring you.'

The firelight was warm on her face. She put her hand over his and smiled contentedly. Often in her years alone, sitting by herself in this room, she had wondered how she would readjust if he came back. She imagined a lengthy period of awkwardness—perhaps that they might even, after so long apart, find it impossible to begin again. In moments of bitter self-pity, there had even been doubts that she would want him.

In fact, their reunion had been astonishingly easy. After the first tongue-tied hour by the fire in her shop, Gwen's bewildered shock had been replaced by a surprising calm.

Hoey's plea for forgiveness had been made with a stumbling sincerity she couldn't doubt. She had asked that he give her until the next day to consider, though in her heart she already knew what her answer would be.

He had lingered uncertainly, then said, 'Shouldn't I tell you where I've been and what I've been doing?'

Despite the firm shake of her head he had been anxious to unburden himself. 'It might be better. And then that would be it over with.'

But she hadn't wanted that. 'No. I don't want to know about the past. I've lived it and it's gone. It's the future that's important.'

'Gwen, I must.' His voice had been choking. 'There are two things I must say. I didn't know until very recently that you'd lost the baby and . . . there hasn't been anyone else . . . for a long time. Even if you won't have me, I want you to know that.'

She had remained silent, trembling slightly again. He had gone off to his hotel and next day she had said he could come back. With each hour that had passed she had become more convinced her decision had been the right one. Steadily, her belief in a new life had grown, nurtured not so much by her long dream of the old Hoey, but by the comforting presence of a man who seemed to have undergone a subtle and hopeful change.

The Hoey who had returned to her had the same sudden smile and quick humour, but the disfiguring moodiness that had marred his charm seemed gone. *His eyes now hold less of their old, guarded look and his expression is softer; almost,* Gwen thought, *gently sad.* Physically he was leaner and fitter than she had seen him since the early days of their marriage and, when she mentioned this, some of the missing years came out.

'I got some of my muscle back in good honest work,' he said. 'I won't go into details since you don't want me to, but I've worked on farms and in racing stables.' He seemed proud of the fact.

She learned almost immediately, too, that he had stopped

drinking. 'It was half my trouble,' he said as he cheerfully declined even one glass of claret before their first meal together.

Rita's unexpected visit had been disconcerting, almost an ordeal, but they were both in a relieved mood now it was over.

Hoey's smile was mischievous. 'Would you like to offer a prize for a correct guess as to where your mother will be hurrying now?'

She laughed. 'Home, to wait for Father.'

'Not home! Didn't you see the way she hurried down the stairs? I wouldn't expect her to keep the news to herself for the rest of the day.'

Gwen's eyes widened. 'You mean his office? If she does that he'll collapse.'

They laughed like children.

'Anyway,' Hoey said, 'that's the cat out of the bag. You won't be able to keep me hidden any longer.'

'I haven't kept you hidden,' Gwen protested. 'You didn't want to go out.'

'No.' He sat down on the arm of her chair and took her hand. 'I'm nervous, you know. Can you believe that, Gwen?'

'I can, Tom. It's as well Mother came. I was wondering how we would tell them. Now it's been solved for us.'

'How do you think your father will take the news?'

'It doesn't matter how he takes it,' she said firmly. 'Although I must say I don't think he ever disliked you as much as you imagined.'

Once, she knew, he would have reacted angrily to a statement like that. Now he turned away with a tolerant smile. 'Perhaps you're right,' he said from the window again. He pulled the curtain aside to have a better view of the street. The flat was on the top floor of the tenement and the height seemed to fascinate him.

'I've never lived so far above ground level,' he said. 'Don't you miss having a garden?' He spoke without thinking, forgetful that this was the delicate stuff of memories.

'I did, for a long time,' Gwen said. 'Now I have the shop to occupy me.' She had a sudden memory of the flowering cherry at the foot of the India Street garden and of the terrace he had started to build under it.

Perhaps, later, they could leave the flat and go back to a house with a garden.

'I still can't get over you running a shop,' he said. 'It's the last thing I'd have thought of.'

'That's what everyone says.'

'And yet, you're obviously enjoying it.'

'I love it. And I think I'm going to do very well. It's not a harassing business.'

'It had to be antiques, of course,' he said. 'You wouldn't have been happy selling just anything.'

Her voice was bright. 'Oh, I don't know. There's a thrill in adding up the sales to see how far they exceed the purchases. Profit-making, I've found, is something of a drug. It's stimulating. I think now I understand Father and Robert better. I wouldn't be happy selling ham and eggs, it's true. But I could imagine myself with a flower shop or a picture gallery.'

As she spoke, she was thinking not so much of her own career, as of Hoey's. What would he work at now? He had his two hundred a year, and he had told her he had saved some money, so there was no urgency. But eventually he would have to have work of some kind. So far he hadn't spoken of his intentions and she had felt it too soon to ask.

Hoey's thoughts must have been similar, for shortly afterwards he said: 'Now your mother's broken the spell, I'll have to shake myself and start looking for something useful to do.'

'Have you anything in mind, Tom?'

'Not really.' He smiled almost wistfully. 'It's a sad thing for a man to have to admit to himself that he isn't qualified for anything.'

'Nonsense!'

'No, Gwen, unfortunately it's not nonsense. I'm totally unskilled.'

'Well, it's true you don't have a degree, or anything like that. But you have other qualities.'

He pretended to be expectant. 'Such as?'

'Well, you have initiative, energy, intelligence.'

'And absolutely no references,' he said, 'except as a farm labourer, a stable lad, or a seaman on a coaster plying the Channel ports. And I don't think you would approve of me coming home in muddy moleskins.'

For the first time she asked a hesitant question about the years apart. 'Were all the jobs you did like that?'

279

'Most of them, but for a while I worked as an office clerk and as a salesman for things like pen nibs and paper clips.' He laughed. 'I'm afraid I never scaled any of the commanding heights.' He seemed to be reminded of the Army. 'I'm really just an old soldier, I suppose. Perhaps I should put on a tattered coat and squat on the pavement at a corner in Sauchiehall Street with a tray of cufflinks and bootlaces.'

He saw how uncertain her smile was and added, 'But perhaps not.'

'I suppose,' she said, 'I suppose there's no use thinking of you working for Father again?'

'No use at all, Gwen,' he said lightly but firmly. 'Not ever.'

'Well, we needn't worry too much. My little business is doing well.'

For a moment, Hoey's expression clouded and then, as if ashamed of whatever thought had come to him, he smiled. 'It obviously runs in the family.'

'At least it will help us to live,' she said practically.

She saw him begin to form a protest, but before he could speak she said, 'Why don't you consider joining me in business, Tom? We could run it very well between us. You could go to the sale-rooms. You would soon learn to tell the difference between what's antique and what's simply old.'

Hoey straightened in his chair. 'That's a very generous offer, Gwen. But it wouldn't be right. It's your business. I can imagine you must have had a great deal of prejudice to overcome before you were able to get it established.'

'I would be happy to share it with you, Tom.'

'No. I have learned some self-respect.' It wasn't a rebuff but she saw he wouldn't be persuaded.

Two days later he came into the shop, whistling. 'Good news,' he said, throwing down his hat.

She waited.

'I start tomorrow with Wilson & Co., the shipping and insurance agents, in West Regent Street. I used to know David Wilson, one of the sons. This war we're fighting in Zululand has made them busy.'

'That's wonderful. What will you be doing?'

He shrugged as if it hardly mattered. 'I'm supposed to be David's assistant, but it's really only glorified clerking. It's a start, though, Gwen.'

'Of course it is. I'm very pleased for you.'

They had dinner that night in His Lordship's Larder to celebrate.

# 16

Aunt May was as thin and healthy as her brother Roderick had been stout and ailing. This she attributed to the drinking of a special 'tea', made from the large dark seedpods she bought from a herbalist in Queen Street. The botanical origin of the pods was the herbalist's secret and not a matter that troubled Aunt May. Their efficacy was what counted, and of this she was convinced. She had on many occasions recommended the bitter, straw-coloured infusion to her brother. He had found it nauseating and after two or three half-hearted attempts to acquire a taste for it had sworn that he would touch it no more. Aunt May believed Fraser might still have been alive if only he'd persevered with her tea. Similar gentle efforts she had made to introduce Fiona to her 'little cup', as she liked to call it, had been unsuccessful. She was unhurt by repeated rejection and generously renewed the offer from time to time, firmly believing the good things of the world were meant to be shared.

Since Fraser's death—feeling that with him she had perhaps been lacking in persistence, and with such a sad result—she had not failed at least once a week to give Fiona another chance. 'Are you going to join me in my little cup, today?' Aunt May would ask sweetly—or, with a small hint that time was moving ruthlessly on, 'You know, it's not too late to change your mind about my little cup, my dear.'

Avoiding giving offence to Aunt May was only one of Fiona's worries, and among the more minor. Fraser had kept his affairs in businesslike order and the drawing together of the strings of his estate was proving straightforward enough. This, though satisfactory from one point of view, had soon revealed quite another situation. Fraser had died leaving no liquid assets worth mentioning. His creditors outweighed his debtors and he had a large bank overdraft. In life, Fraser had been solvent, his assets theoretically superior to his liabilities. By juggling the two he had kept his business going while he waited for a return of good times. In death, Fraser's finances crumbled. Creditors who had been content to place their faith in his honour couldn't be expected to have the same patient confidence now that their jolly friend lay under a green hill in Argyll.

That Lochbank had a brighter future due to the contract made with King & Co. was all very well, Fraser's solicitors informed Fiona, but the immediate outlook was of a very small residue, indeed. It would all go to her, but at their most optimistic they couldn't see there being enough to provide her with, perhaps, more than two hundred a year.

The one remaining asset would be Lochbank Distillery, but its future profits, if any, could not be assessed.

On the two hundred, they said, Fiona would be able to live in careful comfort and the capital might in time grow a little. But there would be no splendid house on Helensburgh Hill, no striking white carriage—in fact, no carriage at all.

After a lifetime of only having to ask, Fiona found this new future difficult to visualize. What would two hundred pounds a year buy? She had no idea what rent she might have to pay for a flat. It was a shock when she realized she didn't even know the cost of food.

These depressing thoughts occupied her much of the time as she sat with Aunt May in a room from which all flowers had been excluded, the bright cushions removed, and the pictures turned to face the wall. Aunt May believed in rigorous mourning and had herself stayed indoors, apart from Sunday church, for a full year after the death of her husband twenty years before. She had remained perpetually in widow's weeds and her personal attire had needed no regulation when Fraser died. But on Fiona the effect of mourning was marked. Even her robust glow couldn't triumph over a wardrobe of total black, nor the convention demanding that, for at least six months, she devote herself to grieving. The drab apparel and outlook darkened her mind as well as her appearance. A month after Fraser's death she was finding the strain almost unbearable. Additionally, she regarded it as hypocritical. To rebel against it, however, never occurred to her. Somehow, she must survive until the spring without entertaining or being entertained, without theatres or concerts. Church was permissible, but other outings must be strictly governed by the demands of good health or imperative business. In practice, this had so far meant two visits to the offices of Fraser's solicitors to discuss the sale of the Helensburgh house and sedate daily strolls, morning and afternoon, around the gardens in Blythswood Square.

On days when brief spells of sunshine brightened the square, accentuating the yellow tints of the stone houses, Fiona sometimes lingered for a few minutes on the seat under the willow tree. Even in November the garden was a fresh, attractive place. The trees were bare but the thin branches made pleasant patterns against the sky. The shrubs around the perimeter were mainly evergreens, and the leaves rustled soothingly, softening the harsh city noises that intruded even on this select hilltop.

Today, returning from her morning walk, she rang for tea, and the maid, as usual, brought two pots, one containing Aunt May's special brew. After a few minutes the old lady joined Fiona at the fire. Frost lay in the streets and the slate roof of the house opposite was white. Pigeons huddled for warmth around the smoking chimneys. There was a damp white haze in the air, that opened a little from time to time as if the sun might break through, but each time settling in heavier than ever.

'I doubt there'll be fog later,' Aunt May said comfortably, reaching out her thin hands to the fire. The room was pleasant with the smell of toasted teacakes on which melting butter formed warm yellow pools.

As if to verify Aunt May's prediction, the sad bass note of a foghorn groaned from the river. The window in its frame, the cups on their silver tray, trembled a little as though in response to a grave warning.

Aunt May savoured her 'little cup'. 'I wouldn't be surprised if we have to have the lamps lit soon,' she said. 'It's been such an early winter.'

Fiona, who had a black shawl across her shoulders, drew it about her and bent close to the fire. Aunt May looked concerned. 'Are you getting a draught, my dear? And I had thought the room so cosy. It's always a pleasure to me to be by a warm fire looking out on a winter's day. Perhaps I'm being thoughtless. Will I ring for Maisie to liven the fire?'

Fiona shook her head and smiled reassuringly. 'No, Aunt May, I'm quite all right.' It wasn't possible to tell the old lady she was painfully bored.

'Perhaps on these chill mornings you should forgo your walk.' Aunt May's concern was never easily dispelled. 'You're still suffering from the shock of bereavement. Your resistance will be at a low ebb. You could easily catch a chill.'

'I don't think it's anything like that, Aunt May.'

'I understand, my child. You're melancholy. Your poor father's been gone only a month. Winter has descended on us early and you're finding the company of an old woman tedious. Oh, I can imagine how you feel, my dear. Am I right?'

Fiona smiled. 'Perhaps in everything but the last part. I'm content in your company, Aunt May. And I'm grateful you've taken me in, meantime.'

The old lady was pleased. 'Nevertheless, we must be careful of your health, my child. I've noticed you've lost much of your colour. Possibly that's only to be expected, but I'm uneasy to see you crouch so close to the fire.'

'You mustn't worry about me.' Fiona straightened in her chair and lifted the *Glasgow Herald*, which the maid had brought with the tea tray.

Aunt May lifted her pot of tea. She hesitated. 'I can't persuade you to join me? It would help to strengthen you at this trying time. It's so wonderfully beneficial. Your cup has been used but I can easily ring for another.'

Fiona hadn't been listening. She was staring at the newspaper, her face alive with surprise and pleasure. 'Listen to this, Aunt May!' She leaned towards the old lady and began to read excitedly.

' "A noteworthy distinction has been conferred on the well-known Glasgow whisky firm of King & Co. The company has been awarded a Royal Warrant and will henceforth supply their King's Royal whisky to the Royal Household." That's Robert's whisky they're writing about, Aunt May! Isn't that a wonderful honour for him?'

Fiona had forgotten her emotions were supposed to be in a state of suspended animation.

Aunt May made no direct reply. She had in fact been blinded to Fiona's lapse by a sudden agitation of her own.

'I don't know what's happening to my memory, these days.' Aunt May's voice was also excited. 'I knew there was something I had intended to tell you. Robert King's sister. You know her, of course?'

'Gwen? Oh, yes.'

Aunt May's voice fell. 'My dear, I wouldn't be prepared to swear to this, but I think I saw her yesterday with her husband.'

'Tom Hoey?' Fiona looked disbelieving. 'Oh, no. You must have been mistaken, Aunt May. Tom Hoey's been gone for years. Gwen's just opened her own little business. Robert told me all about it.'

'But I assure you, I am almost positive, my dear. I'm not given to imagining things. I'll admit my eyesight isn't as good as it was and the cab I was in went past very quickly, but I know it was Gwen and there was a gentleman with her. My first reaction was: *There's Mr. and Mrs. Tom Hoey.* Then, almost immediately, I thought I must be mistaken. But, really, I'm sure I wasn't. He was such a distinguished man, Gwen's husband. Well, there was the same dark, military look about this man.' A puzzled expression came on to Aunt May's face. She shook her head. 'I can't think how anything so noteworthy went so completely out of my mind. It was only when you read the paragraph about Robert King that I remembered.' Her voice trailed off as she worried over this baffling lapse.

Fiona's interest had risen. 'I'm sure no one in the family ever expected them to be together again. Gwen herself must have felt they had parted forever. Why else would she have involved herself in opening this little antique gallery? I know her father was very disapproving. I wonder how we could find out?'

Aunt May was struggling with her defective memory, a faculty, apparently, to which herbal tea gave no support. 'Is it three or four years ago, now? He had rather an attractive face, too. But then, you never can go by that. Poor girl. I don't know how she survived.'

Fiona, practically a prisoner, sat wondering how she could discover the truth. Before either of them expected it Maisie was announcing the midday meal. *With such diversions*, Fiona thought, *time will somehow go by.*

So fearful was Fergus that Gwen might bring Hoey to Park Place, that on the Thursday morning of that week he told Rita they were leaving for Ardfern by the noon train. If Hoey and Gwen were indeed together again then eventually he would have to be taken back into the family. But not yet. *No, not yet, by God*, Fergus swore to himself. His sudden decision that they should leave for the Gareloch threw Rita into a panic.

'But the house is closed for the winter,' she protested.

'We have the keys,' Fergus said shortly.

'It will be so cold.'

'We can light fires.'

'I have one or two ladies calling this afternoon.'

'Write them notes of apology and I'll have Anderson deliver them.'

'Then what about James?'

'James is quite independent again. He'll have Robert's company in the evenings. They can both come down on Saturday if they like.'

'Oh, Fergus, this is inconvenient and unnecessary. Gwen won't bring Tom here until we invite him. She'll be as conscious as we are of the delicacy of the situation.'

'That man has the audacity for anything. I'll feel easier out of his reach for a day or two.'

'I wonder what he'll do?'

'He can sweep streets for all I care.' He crossed to the window as if to see what sort of job it would be.

'If he did that you would care,' Rita pointed out. In such a situation Fergus, she knew, would plead with Hoey to take his old job back. But she didn't point that out.

'He did have a few hundred a year of his own,' Fergus remembered.

'And there's Gwen's little business now.'

Fergus looked enraged. 'You're not suggesting, I hope, that Gwen should allow herself to be sponged on?' He shook his head. 'Dear knows! Why couldn't she see she was better off without him? She should have shown him the door.' His anger flared as he saw Rita's expression. 'And don't stand there looking so damned understanding. You were horrified the day you came barging into my office. What's happened since? Nothing I can see. You were always far too ready to excuse him. Just like Gwen.'

'I was not ready to excuse him.' Rita floundered, annoyed that her soft spot for Hoey should be so obvious. 'You know perfectly well, my dear, I've been in agreement with you all along that Gwen was well rid of Tom.' She spread her hands. 'But can't you see? Now he's come back and been accepted by Gwen, we must be helpful where we can.'

'Helpful!' Fergus looked scandalized.

'Yes. It is Gwen's life as well as Tom's. He may have changed. After all, it is almost four years. If she feels they can build a life together again, we mustn't do anything that would wreck her chance of happiness. Life's been empty for her since he went away. She will have been lonelier and more unhappy than we've realized. Why else do you think she opened her shop? It's only now I appreciate that we've been badly lacking in understanding.'

Fergus had refused to be diverted from his flight to Ardfern. 'I'm tired of having to understand people,' he said. 'I'd like them to start trying to understand me for a change.'

Rita thought they—whoever they were—might find that difficult. Sometimes she found it difficult, herself, but she saw Fergus would not be moved. 'Well, I think you're being very unreasonable, dragging us off into the country in the depth of winter. We'll probably catch pneumonia. Have you looked out of the window?'

'There are people who live in the country winter and summer,' Fergus said sarcastically, deliberately turning his back on the view of bleak sky and grey river.

'And how long are we going for? I must leave some word with the servants if we're to have any order in our lives.'

'We'll return to Glasgow on Monday morning.'

'Ardfern will barely be heated by then.'

Fergus crossed to her and put an arm around her shoulder. 'Have I ever dragged you off like this before?'

'Never, dear.'

'Then you have little to complain of.' He kissed her cheek. 'Your mother can move into the big house with us and bring her servant girls with her. We can confine ourselves to one or two rooms. We'll be quite comfortable.'

Rita sighed and her expression softened. 'Perhaps it won't be too bad. But we must take warm clothing.' As she caught sight of a clock she disengaged herself from his arm. 'If we're to catch the noon train I must start Agnes packing.'

Mrs. Veitch was dithery with surprise when the cab they had hired at Helensburgh station stopped outside her cottage and Fergus alighted to tell her that her servants would be required at the big house for a few days.

'I think you might have given a body a day or two's warning,' she complained breathlessly when, not long afterwards, she was transferred with a hastily packed portmanteau to a bedroom on the first floor at Ardfern. A newly lit fire burned smokily in the grate, but the room was very cold. She put a hand under the bedclothes. 'It's like ice in there,' she lamented.

Rita looked at her mother with sympathy. The old lady was noticeably less sharp. She had celebrated her seventy-second birthday that summer. She couldn't be expected to be as adaptable as before, when a descent like this would merely have meant an exhilarating diversion. The parlour from which they had so unceremoniously plucked her had been warmed by a cheerful fire and made cosy by lamps lit early to combat the grey haze that came in from the loch and hung about the trees. It would be hours before Ardfern was comfortable. As if to accentuate their inconsiderate treatment of the old lady, heavy grey smoke puffed from the cold chimney and spread suffocatingly about the room.

Rita ignored the choking pall and said with determined brightness, 'Don't worry about the bed, Mother. Naturally, it's cold. It will have to be turned down. Tell your girl—what's her name—Millie, to keep the fire well built up during the evening. We're well supplied with hot water jars. It's barely half past three. By the time you're ready for bed this room will be as warm and comfortable as your own bedroom in the cottage.'

'I hope so.' Mrs. Veitch gave her daughter a reproving look. 'I wouldn't mind so much if I knew what it was all about.'

Rita busied herself with the bed. 'Your servants are so harassed I suppose we must give them what help we can. Catch an end of this spread, Mother.'

'A body wouldn't mind being put out if they only knew why,' Mrs. Veitch persisted.

Rita tried to make light of it. 'I thought Fergus had explained he just wanted a few days in the country?'

' "A sudden notion," he said.' Mrs. Veitch's smile was wry. 'Fergus has never had a sudden notion in his life. If Fergus King fell in the loch he would count to ten before holding his breath!' The old lady's derisive laughter filled the room.

Rita almost ran to close the door. Her voice and expression were shocked. 'I don't know what's happening to you, Mother. You musn't speak disrespectfully of Fergus. And some of these expressions you pick up are fit only for servants. I suppose that's where you get them.'

This quickening of the scene restored Mrs. Veitch's humour. 'I'm not being disrespectful of Fergus,' she said. 'It's his solidity that makes him the man he is. If he ever does anything rash or hasty he won't be Fergus.' As she started to unpack she added with quiet triumph, 'That's how I know it wasn't any sudden notion that brought him away down here two days from the start of December. In his trade, December's the busiest month of all.'

'Very well, Mother. I had planned to tell you later, when you were comfortably settled downstairs with a glass of sherry, but since you're so insistent I'll explain now. There's no great secret involved.' Her voice was too casual and her mother's face sharpened with interest. By the time Rita had finished her story of Gwen and Hoey Mrs. Veitch had lost all thought of cold or discomfort. She went downstairs in a warm glow of pleasure, keenly looking forward to the promised sherry. Even Fergus' expression of baleful preoccupation as he passed her in a corridor did not spoil the enjoyment she now felt at this unexpected visit.

Fergus was finding that merely to have removed himself physically from proximity to Hoey wasn't enough. He was still burdened with him mentally. Eventually, the Man About Town would have to be faced. If Gwen was going to give him another chance then Fergus would be duty-bound, as Rita had so annoyingly pointed out earlier in the day, to do everything he could to ensure the success of their efforts to re-establish their marriage. This might entail a great deal, but it would never extend to him having Hoey back in the business. The less he had to do with him the easier he would find it to stomach his company when normal family life made it inevitable that they meet.

Additionally, Fergus was still suffering a sense of shock at the result of Mr. Cruickshank's investigation. He had left Glasgow without an opportunity to confront Robert. Which was worse—a son who sired a child out of marriage or one warped enough to falsely claim that he had? Materially, Fergus' star was still rising, but he had an uneasy feeling that another spell of darkness was settling over his family life. Was this the inevitable price of success? Fergus couldn't admit it was. Gwen could have married a waster even though the Kings had been poor. The peculiar coldness that seemed to characterize all Robert's personal relationships would presumably still have been there had Fergus' business never extended to more than a modest tenth of its present prosperity. And James? Would a less-successful father have saved James?

In an effort to divert himself Fergus walked to the stable block and hammered on the wooden door at the foot of the stair that led to McEwan's room.

There was a muffled shout that he took to be McEwan's acknowledgment of the hammering, then silence. Just as he was about to hammer again he heard hesitant sounds on the stair. There was a click as the latch was lifted, then the door creaked open. Fergus was startled by McEwan's appearance. His face was grey and his eyes oddly bright. With a coat pulled on over what looked like nightclothes, he seemed more bent and shrunken than when Fergus had last seen him two months ago.

McEwan was even more startled than Fergus. He made a visible effort to straighten but almost immediately subsided with a faint groan. 'It's yourself, sir.' The exclamation was peculiarly lifeless, followed almost immediately by a gasping intake of breath, as if the effort of speaking had emptied McEwan's lungs.

Fergus frowned with alarm. 'Are you all right?'

'I'm fine, sir. A day or two'll see me right again. It's them rheumatics.'

It looked, to Fergus, a peculiar form for rheumatism to take. 'What are you doing for it?' He was beginning to regret having disturbed McEwan. The man was entitled, during the winter, to work his own hours. He hadn't been warned Fergus was coming. Clearly, the sudden appearance of his employer had upset him. All Fergus had wanted was a chat about something wholesome—drainage, fencing, spring planting, anything—to take his mind off

Hoey and Robert. Now he felt he should have been more considerate. It was after four o'clock and darkness was coming down fast. Even a healthy gardener would have been finished work at this time on a winter's afternoon.

'There's nothing can be done for the rheumatics,' McEwan said. 'I try to keep dry and well happed up, but my mother had them and when they're in the blood, they're in it. There's nothing can be done but thole them.' He paused as if to brace himself, peering across the faded grass to the bare trees and the iron sky beyond. 'Did you want the coach, sir?'

'No.' Fergus was worried. Did he just walk away and occupy himself with something else? None of his servants had ever been sick before. If he hadn't knocked at this damned stable door he wouldn't have known McEwan was ill. 'Were you in bed?'

'Aye.'

The guilty look in McEwan's eyes stabbed Fergus' heart. 'I'm glad you had the good sense,' he said. 'What have you had to eat today?'

'I havena felt much like eating, sir.' McEwan began to shiver so violently that a lock of white hair fell over his brow. 'I fear it'll be a cold, wet night.' Between shivers he sniffed at the damp wind like an apprehensive old dog chained in an exposed place.

Fergus' concern deepened and with it the puzzling sense of responsibility he felt for the man. 'I want you to go back up to bed,' he said. 'I'll send one of Mrs. Veitch's maids with something hot for you to eat. Leave the door so she can get in. Is your fire lit?'

'It's been out this while.'

'Then she'll see to that, too. Let her tidy the place. I'll get Dr. Ramsay to look in on you tonight.'

McEwan withdrew in alarm. 'I'll not be needing a doctor, sir. I'll be as right as rain in a day or two.' The little space at the foot of the stairs where he crouched was suddenly filled with fear—his fear for his job, and for his future.

'Up to bed with you, man, I say.' Fergus went down the darkening path to the house, still seeing the anxiety in McEwan's bright, pain-filled eyes.

It was next morning before the doctor got there. Fergus, coming down from the woods, saw him leave the stable. He called to him. Ramsay, a small, frock-coated man of Fergus' own age, turned. 'Mr. King! I was hoping for a word with you.'

It was dry now, but a cold wind was blustering off the loch and the branches of the big trees around the house rose and fell noisily. Here and there, some rotten wood had already fallen.

'We'll be safer in the house,' Fergus said.

They went into the morning-room and stood, as if by agreement, at the window. The loch was charcoal colour and its surface as rough. A fishing boat with a dirty brown sail plunged into deep troughs as it made for the open firth. For long moments it would wallow as if the crew had lost control and then, with the wind at the right angle again, it would surge ahead until the next onslaught struck it.

Fergus said, 'The worst possible weather for rheumatism, I suppose?'

'Yes, but your gardener has more than rheumatism, I'm afraid, Mr. King. His heart is very weak. Do you know if he's ever had a seizure?'

'Not to my knowledge. Can't he tell you himself?'

'He denies it, but I think he's lying.'

'Why should he lie about a thing like that?'

The doctor shrugged. 'I've learned to accept some of the more puzzling quirks of human behaviour. Some men take illness as a personal insult. Perhaps he's too stubborn to admit such a thing could happen to him.'

'Or too afraid?' Fergus was surprised at his sudden insight.

'Of what?'

'Afraid he'd lose his job if it became known his heart was unsound.'

Ramsay considered. 'Yes, but you'd know that better than I.'

'He needn't worry. He can rest all winter. I won't need him till March or April.'

The doctor turned from the bleak view. 'That's what I wanted to speak to you about. McEwan will never be able to work again.'

Fergus was incredulous. 'Not even after a four- or five-month rest?'

'His outlook is very poor. Strenuous work could bring on a fatal seizure. It's as well the gardening season had come to an end. Has he any relatives?'

'None at all, so far as I know.'

'So it will be Dalreoch Hall for him?'

'Dalreoch Hall?'

'The poorhouse at Dumbarton.'

A choking feeling rose in Fergus' throat. 'Would he get treatment there?'

The doctor looked unenthusiastic. 'They would do what they could for him.' He turned again to the window. 'It wouldn't be for long.'

'His condition's as grave as that?'

'In Dalreoch Hall it would be. Medical attention there is minimal. They depend on charity.'

There was a picture in Fergus' mind of McEwan sitting cheerful and sturdy behind the horses the first time he'd driven the family from Helensburgh to Row. 'He came to us with the house. He's been here longer than we have.'

'They're a problem, these old servants, when they become ill and there's no family for them to go to.'

Fergus was beset by memories. 'I think he said he came here in the summer of 1845. That's over thirty years ago.'

'You can hardly be expected to make yourself responsible for him.'

'No, of course not.' Fergus shook his head as if to clear it of unwelcome thoughts.

'Then will I make arrangements with Dalreoch Hall? You'll want his room as soon as possible. Even in winter I suppose there's work to be done in grounds like these. You'll have no difficulty finding another man.'

Throughout, the doctor's tone had been flat, unemotional. It seemed to Fergus this was a situation the man had encountered many times before—like death, it was regrettable, and like death it had to be accepted.

'You're quite sure the rest will not restore him to health?'

'Certain.'

'Supposing it was possible for him to stay on quietly in that room above the stable, how long would he ... would he—'

'Longer than if he goes to the poorhouse. A year. Perhaps a little longer.' The doctor was looking at Fergus with careful interest.

Fergus walked to the fire, struggling with his reluctance to say what he wanted to say. The cost of keeping McEwan until he died, and of employing another gardener to do his work, would be small—if he lived a year, perhaps fifty pounds. He wouldn't grudge the money. What held his tongue was the thought of what people might think. When servants were finished they went. That was the established order of things. Even servants didn't argue with the inevitability of this. Why should Fergus King defy it? If people heard he was keeping one gardener-coachman in idleness while paying another to do the work they would think he was going soft. Their respect for his good, sound Scottish sense would lessen. Fergus thrust the disturbing thought from his mind.

'I don't want to do anything hastily,' he said. 'In the meantime, McEwan will stay with us.' It seemed important that he should try to justify this unjustifiable decision. 'After all, we weren't due another visit here for at least four months. This is an unexpected few days we're having. If we hadn't come, we wouldn't have known about McEwan's condition and he would have stayed on here, anyway.'

Ramsay lifted his bag. 'If you hadn't come, Mr. King, McEwan would probably have died in that room of his some time over the weekend. There would have been no problem about what to do with him then.'

On Saturday morning the grounds of Ardfern sparkled in sunshine. Heavy frost had fallen overnight, transforming bare trees, tired grass, and drab outhouses with its glistening powder. The air was dry and clear and, seen from indoors, the sky looked summery. Wisps of white trailed across the high blue curve that started in the hills behind the house and sank into the sea somewhere beyond the Rosneath peninsula. Boats moving on the loch might have been freshly painted, so clearly did their colours show under the white winter sun. For a while, thin icicles hung from rocks at the side of the burn and, around the edges of still pools, fragile wafers of ice became transparent, then non-existent as the sun rose above the trees.

Fergus walked all the woodland paths, discovering views hidden in summer. Like a boy, he cracked with his boots ice that had formed in wet hollows, scattering the smooth pieces, and then, unlike a boy, regretting the destruction of something beautiful and transient. His nose and his ears turned red and his misted breath floated away among rhododendron leaves sagging under a thick coating of crystallized dew.

He arrived at the end of his walk tingling and exhilarated. He collected his *Herald* and took it to a small greenhouse near the entrance to the walled garden. It was a good retreat on a cold but sunny day. Here, he could be out of the house, yet remain warm. The slatted benches were empty except for a few pots and plant boxes from which only weeds grew. It was clearly many months since McEwan had worked in here. He didn't mind. At a holiday house all that mattered were tidy paths and lawns. One man couldn't be expected to do more. If you were to go in seriously for flowers and vegetables two or three gardeners would be required. One day, when he retired here, that would of course be necessary. He wondered, vaguely, when his retirement would come. Instead of his business coasting along it had, in his late middle age, started to gallop. It was exciting, no doubt about that. Despite the pot distillers' boycott, new accounts were opened every week. Where would it all end? In his bones he knew now that Robert's dream of a worldwide business was neither extravagant nor ill-founded. The makings were there. One day the boycott would crumble and they would leap forward. Ah, well, he was too old now, he had been prosperous for too long, to allow himself to be carried away by it all. He had learned the limitations of money. The loch glittered at him through gaps in the trees, and the birds, perked up by the outbreak of fair weather, swooped busily about the back door of the house where there was always something thrown out for them. It was like a summer's day in the greenhouse. Fergus began to go limp with comfort. Lazily he opened his newspaper but soon it fell from his hands as he sank into a gentle sleep.

When he wakened, the first thing he remembered was that tomorrow would be less pleasant. Robert had telegraphed that he and James would spend Sunday with them. Some men might have thrown Mr. Cruickshank's report in the fire and done their best to forget it. But Fergus was determined to confront Robert with the evidence of his duplicity. If it meant wrecking the Sabbath, then he would wreck it. *The better the day, the better the deed*, he told himself bitterly, as he rose stiffly from his chair and went to the house to see if Rita could be persuaded to come and sit with him in the sun.

On Sunday afternoon Fergus summoned Robert to the library and asked for a detailed report on all outstanding business. He wanted to know what was going on before he ruptured their relationship with Mr. Cruickshank's report.

'Mr. Hutt seems to be working hard for us,' he said when Robert had finished.

Robert nodded. 'I'm pleased you're as thrilled as I am at the way things have developed for us in England.'

Fergus drew his eyebrows together. Business, so far as he was concerned, was no place for thrills. It was an area for cool, rational thought, unclouded by emotion. However, to say so would be pointless and might even be interpreted by this strange son of his as a damper on his enthusiasm.

He contented himself with saying, 'It was the cheapest way of getting into the English market, though in the long run our profits will be smaller than they would have been if we had started our own organization. However, I suppose we can't have it all ways.'

'I'm pleased you take the bright view.' Robert rose from his seat and walked to the window, leaving Fergus to ponder the cryptic remark.

He opened a drawer and fingered Mr. Cruickshank's report. He hesitated. Was he being wise? His son's betrayal was monstrous but did anything matter more than peace? And yet . . . he would have no peace till they had this thing out.

He pushed the report across his desk. 'Just sit down and have a glance at that.'

The tone of his voice made Robert wary. He lifted the report but remained standing. Just to see Mary's name in print was a shock, but the facts that shook his emotions as he read were not those that had meant so much to Fergus. Mary ill. Gone to Switzerland and now to Edinburgh. So that was why, in all these years, he had never seen her. The nature of her illness was obvious. Its gravity filled him with a concern that should not have been possible after all this time. Perhaps she'd experienced a complete cure. But was there such a thing? His eyes rushed on. She hadn't married.

A peculiar melancholy gripped him—till Fergus' angry voice roused him.

'Well?'

Robert looked at him blankly, seeing another face.

'What do you have to say to that?'

'Nothing.'

'I suggest you think of something.'

'Then I'll say I'm obliged to you.'

Fergus gaped. 'Obliged?'

'I've often wondered what had happened to Mary. I'm sorry to learn her health hasn't been good.'

'I'm not concerned with her health. You told me she was having your child.'

'Yes. I've regretted that more than anything else in my life. It was a terrible thing to say.'

This wasn't what Fergus had expected. He had to recollect himself. 'You admit then you did me a great wrong?'

'You?' Robert looked as if he was emerging from a dream. 'Not you. It was Mary I wronged.'

'By God, it was me you deceived. There never was a child.'

'You deserved to be deceived. Your only thought was for yourself, Father. You didn't care that Mary and I were genuinely in love. You were desperate to have me abandon her, even when you thought she was going to have a child. That wasn't admirable—it was despicable.'

Fergus saw that what he had planned as an onslaught on Robert was being turned into an attack on his own character. The thought enraged him further.

'It's you who're despicable. You blackmailed me—your own father. You cheated me into financing your business.' It infuriated him that he had failed to break Robert's calm. 'You care for nothing but money.'

Robert looked at him coldly. 'Why are you so angry? You'll make yourself ill. You should be grateful.'

'Grateful!' The word almost strangled itself in Fergus' throat.

'Yes. On two counts. Firstly, you should be grateful there is no child.'

Fergus struck his desk. 'You tricked me!' he shouted.

'That is the second count. I tricked you into being a millionaire, for one day you will be one. Not many people would complain of that.'

For several seconds there was a possibility Fergus would attack him physically. He had entered the fight certain right was on his side. How Robert had gained the ascendancy he couldn't say. Violence seemed the only way of re-establishing a bearable balance. Through the blood that pounded blackly in his head he saw Robert put Cruickshank's report on the desk and walk to the door.

'I think we should stop this,' Robert said calmly. 'In another minute you'll have apoplexy.'

He was gone before Fergus could move.

Behind James pebbles crunched. He turned and saw Colin Lindsay coming towards him from the lochside road. He closed his sketchbook. For the first time that afternoon he realized how cold it was. His absorption in what he was doing had kept him unaware of the December chill.

Lindsay's long dark cloak flapped as he waved. 'Hello, young King,' he called.

James remembered that their first meeting had been on a very wet Sunday in Glen Fruin. They had scrambled over dikes and slithered down wooded slopes using the trees as brakes. He would never do that again.

They sat with their backs against the rocks and watched the last of the day go down behind the mountains and the sea turn dark. Somewhere, nearby, wood was being burned and the smoke drifted sweetly over them.

The slight feeling of sadness that had been with James all day began to subside, sliding away, with the last of daylight. He put his pipe in his mouth and struck a match. He watched Lindsay as the flame rose and fell over the tobacco. The Lindsays of the world puzzled him. Their preoccupation with ancient glories seemed unreal to him. James was interested in the immediate, even the fleeting—the pink haze left by the sun on a mountain slope or the dance of light on a lively sea. He remembered Lindsay cheerfully admitting he would be numbered among the deserters if his nationalist dream of a rising against the English oppressors ever came true. He puffed smoke and said, 'Well, Mr. Lindsay, stands Scotland where she did?'

Lindsay's expressive face suggested pain as he lifted a smooth stone and held it between his hands as if drawing something from it.

'Alas! poor country,' he said, ignoring James' raillery. 'Almost afraid to know itself. It cannot be called our mother, but our grave.'

'It's not too bad a place when the rain stops,' James said teasingly.

'Something has died in it,' Lindsay said. 'There's something wrong with a willing slave. Where are our Home Rulers? That's the difference between the Scots and the Irish. The Irish have never really accepted English domination. We could do with men like the Fenians here. It seems Scotsmen would rather emigrate than fight.'

'Thank God for that,' James said, stifling the cruel thought that all this talk about fighting from a gentle coward was a bit too bizarre, even making allowance for the poetic vision.

Perhaps Lindsay had a similar thought, for he went silent. Some ducks floated past and a heron alighted for the night in a stretch of long, reedy grass. At last Lindsay turned to James.

'Robert tells me you've decided not to go to the university but that you haven't started to work yet.'

'Yes.'

Lindsay looked severe. 'Haven't you thought what you might do? Your brain will rust if you don't use it, you know.'

James could accept this friendly brutality, which recognized the fact of his crippling without crying over it.

'I might try to paint,' he said, much to his own surprise.

Lindsay looked surprised. 'I didn't know you had artistic inclinations.'

James lifted a stone and plopped it into the loch. Damp was rising now from the sea in a grey velvet haze. 'Nor did I,' he said with a cheerful laugh. 'Not until recently, anyway. But I think I'm going to have a shot at it.'

He opened his sketchbook and handed it to Lindsay.

'Very good,' said Lindsay, not quite able to hide his pleasure. 'Is this all today's work?'

'All except the page at the beginning.'

'Very good, indeed. I have some books at home which might interest you. And I know some of the Helensburgh artists. Not amateurs like me, but men who sell their work. I'll introduce you to them.'

James looked at him eagerly. 'Will you? I would like that.'

'Good,' Lindsay said again, still with some signs of surprise. 'At least this is a more conventional interest than the last one I remember. I can imagine your father tolerating an artist in the family.'

James laughed. 'You mean my Socialist period. I outgrew that.'

'Of course,' Lindsay said with a smile. 'After all, you're nineteen now. The grey hairs will be showing soon.'

They turned up their collars and sat joking with each other until bats swooped above them and a moonlit mist began to creep over the pebbles from the water.

As they rose to go, Lindsay said, 'Your people are well, I hope?'

'They are,' James said breathlessly as he struggled in the darkness with his crutch. He was pleased and a little amused that Lindsay didn't try to help him. He had trained them all very well.

'I sometimes see Gwen in Glasgow.'

'Have you heard the news? About Gwen, I mean.'

'No.' Lindsay's voice was puzzled and a little anxious.

'Her husband's come back.'

He realized Lindsay had stopped. He turned. 'Have you dropped something?'

Lindsay didn't answer for a moment. 'No,' he said quietly.

'Did you know Tom Hoey?'

'I did meet him once or twice.'

They completed the rest of the walk to the road in total silence. When they reached it Lindsay said, 'That is a surprise.'

James leaned heavily on his crutch, tired by the difficult crossing of the dark beach. 'What is?'

'Tom Hoey's return.'

'It's a good thing, I suppose,' James said manfully. 'I think poor old Gwen was lonely. Anyway, this seems to have perked her up.'

'I hope they'll find happiness together again,' Lindsay said, but his words sounded curiously hollow.

# *17*

Though Fergus, with his talent for self-torment, had imagined Hoey's return to Glasgow would cause almost as much gossip as his departure, few seemed excited by it. A face once seen about town was there again. Who was he? Oh, that's—that's—dash it, you must know the fellow. Hoey's acquaintances had been mainly in the drinking and gambling set where wife-desertion had a limited capacity to sustain interest. Among people who would have cared, he was practically unknown. The gibes, the looks Fergus feared never came. After a week or two he could enter his club without embarrassment or keep a business appointment without dread. He even admitted to himself that Hoey seemed to be showing some sensitivity. Clearly, he was allowing his return to become an accepted fact before attempting to re-establish himself. For this, Fergus was sure they had Gwen to thank. She knew how he felt about Mr. Man About Town. He had told her often enough. Of course, Gwen would eventually want Hoey taken back into the family. How long would she wait? She would soon discover that Rita had weakened. She would use her mother as a lever. There were times when Fergus felt he had been too lenient with them all for far too long—Rita included.

It was Rita, on a visit to Gwen after their return from Ardfern, who was the first to learn Hoey had taken a job. She felt a stab of anxiety until Gwen said it was in a shipping office. She had feared to hear he had returned to the ruinous ambience of the drink or theatre trades. There could be little temptation in a shipping office. Even Fergus would have to admit that.

Seeing her mother's relieved expression and guessing her thoughts, Gwen said, 'Tom's much more settled now, Mother.

He's usually home by six and we spend every evening together, mostly just sitting here by the fire.'

Rita's voice was gently enquiring. 'And are you quite happy to have him back, dear?' Her anxiety for reassurance was touching.

'Yes, Mother.'

'Then that is good enough for me. I'm very happy for you, Gwen. You know Tom best and I'm sure you'll have done the right thing.'

Gwen was emphatic. 'Every day I'm more certain of it than ever.'

Rita took her hand. 'You had never really, in all those years, forgotten him or given him up, had you, Gwen?'

'I don't think I had.'

'I want you to know I understand.' Rita's eyes were bright with the tears Fergus would have denounced as romantic but which in fact sprang from a complex mixture of joy, sadness, concern, and, finally, pride in her daughter's steadfastness.

'You're a loving girl, Gwen,' she said with great feeling. 'I only hope Tom realizes it.' Then, suddenly sensing the delicate balance of Gwen's emotions, she added hastily, 'And I'm sure he does, my dear.'

Fergus was pleasantly surprised when Rita gave him the news.

'Wilson & Co. are sound people,' he said judiciously. 'He could have chosen worse.' Then, with a jolt of apprehension: 'Mind you, they won't stand any nonsense.'

'If Gwen's right, and she seems very sure, I don't think there'll be any nonsense,' Rita said cheerfully.

She saw Fergus was mollified, even impressed, and decided with a burst of valour that she should pursue the advantage.

'I would like to invite Gwen and Tom for dinner one night next week,' she said, then held her breath.

To her profound relief Fergus only hesitated for a moment. 'Well, if you think so, my dear.' But he couldn't resist a note of caution. 'As long as you think there'll be no awkwardness.'

'I am sure there won't,' Rita said boldly, adding a fervent inner prayer that her confidence was not ill-judged.

If she had known it, the suggestion was less distasteful to Fergus than it would have been a week earlier. The embarrassment of the situation had been worrying him. Hoey's return was a fact. If Gwen had accepted him, sooner or later he must be absorbed back into the family. His worry was how it would be managed—and how soon. He had reluctantly come to the conclusion that the sooner the better. The longer it was delayed the more difficult it would become. His fear eventually had been that Rita might be too apprehensive of his reaction to make the suggestion.

'Then I'll leave the arrangements to you,' he said, masking his relief with an energetic tug at his beard.

He put in a nervous week and, when the evening came, he was heavy with doubt. In fact, it went more smoothly than any of them could have hoped. Robert and James were unconcerned, Rita and Gwen bright and talkative. The alarm came when Hoey ended a long silence by saying, 'Things are looking bad in Zululand.'

Fergus' mind went flashing back to the disastrous night four years earlier when Hoey had been worried about Kabul and they had ended up snarling at each other in the library.

But a glance told him that tonight Hoey's concern was genuine, fuelled by nothing stronger than patriotism and military interest.

Later, when they were alone, Rita said with quiet satisfaction: 'I think Gwen was right about Tom.' She stood close to him. 'Thank you, Fergus, for letting me have them.'

He gave her a kiss and a cautious smile.

Personal feelings had once again been subordinated to the good of the company. Business was good but frustrating. Expansion was still having to be held firmly in check, and two or three days after Christmas a letter arrived from Mr. Hutt expressing hope that the supply position would improve in the coming year. It seemed doubtful, but one morning just before New Year Robert reported excitedly to Fergus that two distilleries which had for years refused them whisky had just accepted orders.

'I knew this boycott would eventually begin to crumble,' he said jubilantly. 'I've never stopped writing asking for whisky from all the distilleries we used to buy from. Let's hope this is the first sign of a break.'

'Let's hope so,' Fergus said.

It was a gleam of hope that allowed them to close for the New Year holiday in a mood of cheer.

When business resumed on the third day of January, Fraser's old distillery was advertised for sale in the *Glasgow Herald*.

Robert sent for the particulars and after studying them said, 'I've been waiting for this. I think we should buy it.'

To Fergus, there was something vaguely wrong in them even considering buying a dead friend's property. Since this wasn't a business argument, he tried to find another reason for opposing the purchase.

'Lochbank's hardly a wonderful whisky,' he said moderately.

The years of fighting the pot distillers had considerably modified Robert's contempt for Lochbank.

'It's a good Lowland,' he said. 'Even when this boycott finally ends we'll still use a proportion of it. I think it's good policy that, wherever possible, we own the source of supply.'

'I'd rather see us with a good Glenlivet.'

Robert's smile was brief. 'Naturally. And one day you will. But at the moment there isn't one for sale.'

Apart from confessing that he was too old for all this expansion, that it frightened him sometimes, Fergus didn't know what more he could say.

'There's the added question of prestige,' Robert pointed out. 'It would do us no harm to have our own distillery.'

'Who would be impressed, apart from other members of the trade?'

'I think the ordinary customer notices these things. We'd have it on the label, of course. These things must be projected.'

They had recently altered the label to include the Royal Warrant.

'Would that mean redesigning the redesigned label?' Fergus asked tartly.

Robert ignored this to suggest something he felt would appeal more to Fergus' practical side. 'We'd do far better out of Lochbank, of course, than Fraser ever did.'

'How can you know that?'

'Despite the pot distillers, whisky blenders are springing up all over the place. They all hope to copy our success. If there's Lochbank in the King's Royal blend—and that would be obvious if we owned it—they would all buy it to put in their own blends.'

There was a cunning farsightedness to Robert that Fergus felt he had not possessed even in his prime. He said, 'Do you think anyone else will be after it?'

'I can't think of anyone. It would only pay for people like us, able to use it ourselves.'

'Then the fifteen thousand pounds they're asking seems rather high.'

'Well, we wouldn't pay them that, of course. The price has been set by the solicitors. They're trying to do their best for their client.'

He smiled slightly as he remembered the client was Fiona.

'You don't think there's a question of propriety involved?'

'I don't know if it's a matter of propriety but it's certainly more delicate than it would be if a complete stranger was involved. We're clearly not going to offer an unrealistic price simply because it's Fiona. She wouldn't expect that. On the other hand, we wouldn't want her ever to think we'd bought too cheaply.'

'No, that is my main concern. After all, Fraser and I were friends for twenty-five years.'

'Would it be fair to tell Fiona's solicitors we'll pay more than the highest offer they receive?'

'Would it be ethical for them to divulge offers?'

'If Fiona instructed them to they would have no choice. I could speak to her. It's time I paid my respects.'

A picture of the ancient, whitewashed buildings on the shores of Loch Lomond came to Fergus. He remembered the bent old men plodding along under their sacks of grain. He'd marvelled more than once that Fraser had never even bought them a wheelbarrow.

'Supposing, as you've said, that no one else wants it? There may not *be* any other offers.'

'Then if we offer half of what they're asking I think they'll accept. A distillery's not an easy thing to sell.'

It was a conclusion that didn't make Fergus happy, but, excluding sentiment, he could find no grounds for opposition.

Aunt May was doubtful if Fiona should receive Robert even to discuss an important business matter.

'It's sometimes not so much what happens in this world that's important, my dear,' she pointed out, 'as what people *think* is happening. People might well think that Robert was here for purely social reasons. That would never do so soon after your poor father's passing.'

'But, Aunt May, he wouldn't be here for social reasons,' Fiona protested. 'And, in any case, who'll know he's here at all?'

Aunt May appeared surprised at her simplicity. 'The servants will know if you receive him,' she said, 'and that's the same as everyone knowing.'

'Then what am I to do? You've seen Robert's note. He says it's an important matter. He's a family friend. Have I to refuse? He might be hurt.'

This hint of possible discourtesy was all the excuse Aunt May needed to allow her to relent gracefully. It was decided Robert could call next afternoon.

It was the fifth day of January and as even death couldn't be allowed to interfere with the pagan rites surrounding New Year in Scotland, Aunt May offered Robert the traditional glass of sherry and a piece of cherry bun. She noted with approval that he wore a black tie and his manner was restrained. So often, these days, the young didn't know how to behave.

'Ladies.' Robert raised his glass respectfully. 'At least 1879 can bring you no greater sorrow.'

Aunt May was impressed. Later, Robert unwittingly completed his conquest by accepting when she asked if he'd join her in her 'little cup'. In food and drink he was adventurous, and although he found the herbal tea unpalatable, his good manners prevented him from showing it. Fiona, who had been afraid he might be nauseated, relaxed when she saw that, as usual, he could be relied on. She gave him a small smile of sympathy when he declined a second cup.

At last, Robert felt he might decently explain why he had come. He apologized for intruding business into a period of such sadness and asked Aunt May to remain so she might give Fiona the benefit of her more mature wisdom. His offer to improve on any bid made for Lochbank Distillery was so obviously to Fiona's advantage that, with Aunt May's approval, she readily agreed to instruct her solicitors to divulge the highest tender to King & Co.

Robert found the reversed pictures and the unrelieved black of Fiona and Aunt May depressing. As soon as the business talk was finished he rose to go. Fiona's disappointment was unmistakable. To ask him to prolong his stay—in normal times the natural and courteous thing to do—would now be improper. Her lips moved with the words she couldn't speak. Robert sensed she would have welcomed his staying. Aunt May, still living by the severe conventions of an older generation, was clearly the problem. An intense sympathy for Fiona rose in him. The wayward girl of nineteen had matured into the same bondage as most other girls of her background. Convention had won and Fiona was now bravely accepting the restraint on her high spirits that the hospitality of Aunt May's house demanded. *Six months of this rigorous gloom must*, he thought, *seem a life sentence*. As they stood looking at each other, Aunt May suddenly excused herself, saying her presence was required in the kitchen, but only for a moment. She would be back to bid Robert good-bye. Whether sympathy for her niece had risen in the old woman's heart, or whether her absence was as necessary, as she said, Robert could only guess.

'You've lost your colour, Fiona.' It was the first personal remark he had dared to make.

She took it as a compliment. 'At such a time anything else would be unbecoming. I didn't think I would ever be so good at conforming.'

He smiled at a passing memory.

'But this seclusion is testing me.' She looked down dejectedly at her dress. 'And these black weeds are so oppressive. No wonder I'm pale.'

He touched her hand lightly. This new Fiona inspired a tender interest in him. Over the last year, although their meetings had been infrequent, his attitude to her had changed. Since their chance encounter in Blythswood Square he had been aware there was much more to know about her than he had thought. Her shrewd handling of the situation when he had visited Lochbank in search of increased whisky supplies had confirmed it.

'Now I know why Father felt like a prisoner when I brought him here to rest,' she said. 'He was allowed only a stroll round the gardens twice a day. That's all I manage now.'

'Would it be wrong if I accompanied you sometimes?'

He was pleased to find her sense of humour wasn't too far below the surface. 'Only if we were found out.'

'We did meet there accidentally once before. It could happen again. When do you take your walks?'

She told him and then they heard Aunt May returning.

· · ·

308

Two days passed before he was able to go to Blythswood Square.

Fiona couldn't conceal an eager smile when she saw him. 'I thought you had forgotten,' she said.

'It's only two days,' he reminded her.

'I don't suppose I should tell you, but it has seemed longer.'

He opened the gate and they went into the gardens. The grass was damp and a cold grey veil hung over the trees. Smoke from house fires rose only a little way above the chimneys, then spread out in a dark canopy hiding the sky. Their footsteps on the gravel were muffled and the discordant city noises reached them as if from far away.

'It's a perfect day for conspirators,' Robert said.

'And I feel so innocent. I'm sure I can't be doing anything very wrong.'

'How long can you stay?'

'Twice round.' She laughed. 'If I was any longer Aunt May might come looking.'

'I like her.'

'She's been very kind to me. I'm quite ashamed sometimes when I find myself blaming her for my depression. If she wasn't there I would be in strict mourning, anyway. It's very important to conform.'

'I never thought I would hear you saying anything like that,' he teased her.

'Don't you think it's true?'

He appeared to consider. 'Yes, I do. Usually, to conform is to be happy.'

'And yet. . . .' She hesitated. 'You do not conform.'

He stared ahead at the upper floors of the houses, the pale stone made drab now by the heavy light. 'You're thinking of my apartment and of the night I tried to take you to it.'

'Perhaps.'

'But I conform by keeping it secret.'

'Can you really believe the only sin is in being found out?'

He was amused at the suggestion of primness. 'No. I would like to. It would make life much simpler, but that much self-delusion's beyond me. Besides'—he stopped and looked down at her—'I'm probably not nearly as bad as you imagine. In Glasgow misbehaviour isn't all that easy, even for a bachelor.'

She made a face. 'Oh, I am sorry for you. All that money going to waste. To say nothing of the good looks.'

'I'm still a little ashamed when I think how I drove you up to Hill Street.' He smiled ruefully. 'It was an awful letdown when you wouldn't go in, but I did enjoy our drive to the riverbank. Do you remember the message you wrote on the sand?'

It was a moment or two before she answered. 'It seems so long ago.'

They were silent until Robert said, 'By the way, has anything developed yet about the sale of Lochbank?'

For a moment she looked slightly confused. 'I don't think so. I'm still waiting to hear from the lawyers.'

The gate creaked and two nursemaids wrapped in scarves came in with prams for the last walk of the day.

'That's our second time round,' Robert said.

'Yes.'

'I suppose you haven't thought yet of the future? I mean, about where you'll live?'

'No, but when I come out of mourning I have an invitation from Uncle Malcolm to stay with him for a while at his farm near Perth. You met him at Father's funeral.'

As they turned towards the gate the sound of a ship's siren came up over the hazy rooftops from the river. 'That's a sound that goes very well with a winter afternoon,' Robert said, 'but I preferred the music of the girl pianist. I wonder what happened to her?'

'I suppose she had to close her window. Perhaps we'll hear her again in spring.'

Already, lamps had been lit in some of the houses. A man passed with a flame burning at the end of a long stick. He touched the gas posts as he went, shedding circles of yellow light under the trees. The dusk was chill and damp. Spring seemed very distant.

Towards the end of the following week Fiona wrote asking him to meet her at her lawyer's to discuss the sale of Lochbank.

White, Semple and Fleming occupied what had once been a dwelling house halfway up West Regent Street. He arrived early and was surprised when an old man at the counter told him Fiona was already there.

'She will see you immediately,' the old man added.

They went down a dark corridor on one side of which leather-bound books lay on the floor in untidy bundles. Robert wondered why so many Glasgow lawyers thought it necessary to work from slums. It seemed accepted among them that decrepitude was somehow reassuring.

The old man pushed open a door. Robert went in and then stopped. 'You seem to be making a habit of this, Fiona,' he said. 'I keep finding you sitting behind desks.'

She was wearing glasses. 'Do you find it unnerving?' Her voice was bright, in startling contrast to her mourning.

He put his hat on the stand. 'Only a little.'

She leaned back in her chair, smiling, but not, he felt, entirely at ease. 'Mr. Fleming sat me down here. He had laid out these papers.' She nodded to two or three folders in front of her. 'But if it makes you uneasy, I'll willingly change places with you.'

'Not at all. I told you once before that you look thoroughly at home behind a desk.' He glanced around the drab room. 'Have I arrived too early for Fleming?'

'He'll join us when we want him. It was just that first I wanted to speak to you alone.'

He folded his arms and smiled encouragingly.

She took a letter from one of the folders and pushed it across the desk. 'I agreed to divulge whatever offers were received for Lochbank.'

'Only one?'

'I'm afraid so.'

His expression changed as he read the letter. It was from another firm of solicitors and offered £10,000 for Lochbank on behalf of an undisclosed client. It was more than he'd have expected and almost what he thought the distillery was worth. He made a face. 'This is a very fair sum,' he said.

'That's what Mr. Fleming thought. He was very pleased.'

'Are you going to accept?'

She looked a little confused by his directness but seemed to try to disguise it by leaning across the desk to retrieve the letter. *Fiona the businesswoman*, he thought with amusement, *will have to learn to hide her feelings.* She'd have been better leaving him to talk the thing over with her lawyer.

'You did say, Robert, that you might be prepared to improve on any bid we received.' She removed her glasses and put them away in a leather case. 'But, of course, if you're not interested now . . . Perhaps this sum is more than you would think Lochbank worth?'

He shook his head. 'No. I'm still interested, Fiona. If you're prepared to look on that offer as the best you're likely to get then I am prepared to put another—' He looked enquiringly at her. 'What would you think? Would it be fair if I put another five hundred pounds on top?'

Her face twisted in protest. 'Oh, I wouldn't expect anything like that. I thought if you put another fifty pounds to that offer it would let Mr. Fleming say quite honestly that a better offer had been received and accepted.'

Unselfish gestures in business worried him. 'That's very generous of you, Fiona,' he said slowly, 'but I really think you should talk with your Mr. Fleming before turning away four hundred and fifty pounds.'

'No,' she said decisively. 'I know my own mind.'

He slapped the desk. 'Then it's a deal. We will pay you ten thousand and fifty pounds. Is that the position?'

She suddenly looked very nervous and he was reminded of their previous business discussion at the distillery. 'The only thing is, I don't want you to pay me in money, Robert.'

He stared at her. 'Then what the devil do you want to be paid in, diamonds?'

'I wondered if instead of money I could have shares in King & Co.?'

Now the confusion was his. 'Who on earth put that idea in your head?'

He felt foolish as soon as he had asked, for it was the sort of thing, if the roles had been reversed, he could well have thought of himself.

His surprise was so obvious that she laughed, clearly pleased, for he had been unable to keep a tinge of admiration from his voice.

'No one put it in my head, Robert. I thought of it myself.' Her expression was innocent. 'Why? Isn't it a good idea?'

He was still too disconcerted to be sure of the right answer. His mind was racing. The situation had suddenly become one of hard business. It was the last thing he had expected. He was alarmed and annoyed to find himself so unprepared.

'It had never occurred to me,' he said defensively. 'I naturally thought you would want money.'

She nodded sympathetically. 'Yes, well that's what I thought at first myself, but when I started to consider it I wondered what I'd do with the money.'

'You'd invest it, of course. Fleming could advise you.'

'But what better to invest in than King's Royal?'

'We're a private company,' he said impatiently.

'Yes.' She adjusted the collar of her coat. 'That's what would make it so nice. We would all know each other.'

'But it's a family business, Fiona, don't you understand that?'

'Oh, I do. And I like the reassuring sound of it. Our families have been friends for a long time. I would feel my money was safe.'

Before he could find words, she continued. 'It would also allow me to feel I still had some interest in Lochbank. It would be a wrench to part with it completely. The Frasers have owned it for almost a hundred years.'

He ran a hand through his hair. 'I don't know what my father would think, Fiona.'

'But he must want the distillery, too.'

He looked at her sharply. 'Do you mean if we don't agree you won't sell?'

'I didn't say that, but . . . it's how I would like to do it. I think it would be to our mutual advantage.'

'Wouldn't you be better leaving Fleming to talk to me about this?' he said hopefully. 'He will understand these matters better.'

'I did suggest that to begin with but, to be honest, he didn't think you would agree. That's why I said I would speak to you myself. He would only have been half-hearted,' she added disarmingly. She had never looked so self-possessed or quite so charming.

'There is the possibility, of course,' he said thoughtfully, 'that we could increase our offer.'

'Oh, no, I wouldn't have that,' she said quickly. 'We've agreed a price and I won't go back on my word.'

'You could be putting your money at risk. To some extent the pot distillers are still maintaining their boycott.'

'But owning Lochbank would strengthen your position.'

It was the first business discussion he had ever found it impossible to come to grips with. Each point raised seemed to drift away, leaving only her obvious resolve to acquire a share in King's Royal. He realized she was lifting the folders from the desk and placing them one on top of the other.

'I can see it's your father you're worried about, Robert,' she said. 'The best thing is for you to go and talk it over with him. You can contact Mr. Fleming here or me at Aunt May's.'

Clearly the interview was over. He was halfway to Washington Street before he could smile.

'We've acquired a partner,' he said to Fergus later that afternoon, realizing with wonder that already he was beginning to accept the situation.

Fergus put down his pen and frowned. 'What are you talking about?'

When he explained, Fergus was flabbergasted. 'I've never heard of anything so ridiculous. She's a woman. How can we work with a woman? They have no logic or understanding of business.'

'You wouldn't have said that if you had seen her behind that desk today,' Robert said. 'In any case, she'll have nothing to do with the running of the business and her stake will be very small. All she wants is a good investment, and she's shrewdly picked us as the best available.'

'Couldn't you see her lawyer and get him to talk her out of it? Surely he wouldn't let her hold on to a distillery. The thing's unthinkable. She would never be able to run it herself.'

Robert shook his head. 'I'm beginning to think she's capable of anything.' He stared at the ceiling for a while. 'We need Lochbank to safeguard our supplies,' he said, as if for the first time reducing the situation to its inescapable essentials. 'And the only way to get it is to take Fiona along with it.'

Fergus rose from his desk and walked snorting to the door. 'I'll leave it to you, but how she managed to talk you into this I'll never know.'

'I don't think I'll ever know myself,' Robert said to the closing door.

As the raw haze of another winter settled over Glasgow, bringing the smell of fog, slippery footpaths, and dismal darkness, Gwen thought she could sense a restlessness in Hoey.

He was still unfailingly considerate, good-humoured, and sober but he seemed slightly on edge, as if engaged in some inner battle. As they sat by the fire in the evenings after dinner his talk became less concerned with his job or her business than with events far beyond their daily lives.

Gwen was perplexed and disturbed. Had the constraints of Wilson & Co. become unbearable already? Or worse, had his visits to ships lying in Glasgow or Leith docks reminded him of horizons beyond those of Sauchiehall Street and St. Vincent Place?

The Zulu War was one of his recurring themes and he followed it closely in the *Glasgow Herald*. One morning he threw the newspaper down disgustedly, bitterly cursing Lord Beaconsfield for playing politics with men's lives.

Gwen's response was automatic and absentminded. 'Surely he wouldn't do that, dear?'

'Oh, yes,' Hoey said with a frown. 'He's scared of a row with Gladstone. He's deliberately holding our men back.'

Gwen, for whom the war was a distant disturbance unconnected with their own affairs, tried to look interested. Dark Glasgow was a chill and smoky reality beyond the curtained window. Darkest Africa she could not imagine.

'Of course, Gladstone's no better,' Hoey said. 'It's only votes he's after. It's a dirty business all round. As usual, though, the poor damned troops are having to suffer for the duplicity of the politicians. It's them I'm sorry for.'

That night, fearing that perhaps their trivial domestic talk was beginning to pall on him, Gwen, with uncertain feelings, suggested he should join his old club. But Hoey was uninterested.

He put his arms around her. 'Why should I pay good money to join a gloomy old club full of dreary old men when I can come home to you?' He stepped back, pretending to be taking a closer look at her. 'Unless you want to be rid of me in the evenings, of course?'

She smiled. 'I just thought it might be boring for you stuck here at home with me all the time.'

His expression became serious. 'That's when I'm happiest,' he said simply. Then, with concern: 'But perhaps there's something you would like us to do, Gwen? Perhaps you're right and we are too much at home. I'd imagined you would be glad to relax after a day at business.'

'Oh, but I am, Tom,' she said quickly. 'It's only you I was thinking of.'

He crossed to his lookout post at the window and gazed down on the jogging lights of the traffic. There had been an icy drizzle earlier and the streets were churned and muddy.

'I do miss our old garden sometimes,' he said.

They were able now to make unembarrassed references to certain of the happier episodes of their old life.

'Sometimes I feel these old muscles need stretching.' He touched his toes, then flung his arms out, filling his lungs and putting on a ferocious face.

She laughed. 'One night I'll take you down to the shop and give you all the exercise you want moving the furniture for me.'

'Certainly,' Hoey said, touching his toes again.

She looked at him closely. 'Or would you like us to leave this flat, Tom? We could look for a house with a small back garden, like the one in India Street.'

Hoey seemed to retreat a little. 'Let's not think about that until spring. These damp, foggy days are not the time for moving house. Besides, it's convenient here for your shop.'

'That wouldn't matter,' Gwen said. 'A flat's rather restricting. I used to enjoy being able to walk out through the windows into the fresh air.'

'Let's not think of it until the spring,' Hoey said again.

Two or three mornings later there was a hoarse shouting in the street as a news vendor passed, his message lost in the grinding traffic noises of Sauchiehall Street.

Hoey looked surprised. 'There's nothing much in here to shout about,' he said as he put his *Herald* down.

Gwen poured another cup of tea for him. 'And what does Wilson & Co. hold in store for you today?' she asked lightly.

A shadow passed over Hoey's face, but his voice was cheerful enough. 'What does it ever hold? Freight rates, shipping documents, sailing routes and times.'

Gwen had caught the fleeting look. 'Are you still quite pleased with them?'

Hoey laughed. 'Reasonably. Yes.'

'What are you laughing at?'

'At the clever way you always manage to make it sound as if Wilson & Co. are working for me.'

There was a knock on the door and a maid came excitedly into the room holding a newspaper. 'Terrible news, ma'am.'

'What is it, Sally?'

'Murder, ma'am. Them Zulus are slaughtering our boys.'

Hoey seized the newspaper. It was a special edition. Lord Beaconsfield had announced to a stupefied House of Lords that one thousand five hundred British and native troops had been massacred at Isandhlwana by the impis of King Cetewayo. It had happened on January 22. Today was February 12. The news had arrived in Britain by sea only the previous day.

'They've all been dead for three weeks,' Hoey said, stunned.

'But how could it happen?' Gwen asked, reading over his shoulder. 'How could naked savages armed only with spears massacre a British camp defended by rifles and cannon?'

She stopped. Hoey wasn't reading. He was staring unseeingly at the newspaper, which he had allowed to sag. When she put a hand on his shoulder she was astonished to find he was trembling.

In the streets that morning people gathered in incredulous groups to discuss the unbelievable news. In the basement smoke room where he went to drink his morning coffee Fergus asked the question Gwen had asked.

'How could a horde of black men with spears beat our guns?' No one could tell him.

At lunchtime, Hoey appeared at Gwen's shop. Her eyes widened when she saw him. These days any deviation from the normal could fill her with alarm. On these occasions she became distressingly aware that her long insecurity had left a permanent mark.

He was smiling, but she fancied she could detect something else on his face. 'Is there anything wrong, Tom?'

He shook his head. 'Nothing's wrong, darling.' He threw his hat on a chair. 'I didn't feel much like eating today. I decided a stroll would do me more good. The whole city seems on edge.'

She knew what he was referring to. Her customers that morning had all seemed stunned by the baffling disaster in Africa.

'You could make me a pot of tea,' Hoey said invitingly.

'Of course. I'll tell Sadie. She'll be glad of an excuse to stop polishing the silver.'

She went into the back shop, leaving him prodding about among the ornaments.

When Miss Murray appeared with the tray two news vendors were passing with bundles of newspapers. Their cries were unintelligible. Hoey held out a coin. 'See if you can catch them, Sadie. We had better know the worst.'

But this time the news was more inspiring. There had been another dispatch from Africa and Lord Beaconsfield had made another announcement. While British soldiers and British pride were being slaughtered at Isandhlwana a small British garrison at Rorke's Drift was courageously fighting off another Zulu onslaught, outnumbered twenty to one. On receipt of the news the Queen had immediately awarded Victoria Crosses to eleven officers and men.

Strangely, Hoey wasn't cheered. It was the dead of the other engagement that weighed on him and his shock was the shock of a nation. Lord Beaconsfield, recovering from influenza, had suffered a relapse, the newspapers said. Gladstone, Leader of the Opposition, while mourning the dead of Isandhlwana, had denounced the British presence in Zululand as a brutal attack on a peaceful people. Europe was laughing at Britain's humiliation. The government had ordered a court of enquiry to be held on the spot.

'Even out of the deaths of brave men they can't resist making political capital,' Hoey said in disgust. He finished his tea and left, still in his strange mood.

When Gwen arrived home in the evening he was in the hall putting on his coat.

'I'm just going to the corner to post a letter,' he said.

'Who are you writing to, Tom?'

He looked evasively past her. 'Teddy Dryden,' he said at last. 'He's colonel of the regiment now.'

A vague alarm began to rise in her. 'I didn't know you still kept in touch with him.'

'Gwen!' He took her hands in his. 'I want to go back to the Greys.'

'Tom!' She felt her eyes filling with tears.

He put his arms around her. 'It's what I've wanted to do for a long time, Gwen. I mentioned it once before, years ago, but it wasn't possible then. The news today has made it seem more urgent.'

'But why, Tom? I thought you were happy here.'

He kissed her eyes. 'There's no need to cry, Gwen. I have been happy, yet, recently I find I don't seem to fit properly into anything. Ever since I left the Greys I've made a mess of things.'

'But not now, darling. That's all past.'

'The discipline would be good for me.' His embrace tightened fiercely. 'I feel it's the right thing for me. I don't ever want to let you down again, Gwen.'

'Then couldn't you wait?' Her voice was pleading. 'Until this war is over?'

'Don't you see, Gwen? My only chance is when there *is* a war. They'll need men now.'

'They don't need you,' she sobbed. 'There are plenty of other men.'

'You may be right. They may not need me.' He shook her gently and smiled in a way that seemed designed to mock himself and reassure her. 'I'm an old man now. Almost twenty-eight. They may not take me. All I've done is ask Teddy to consider me.'

But he was right. The war had created a shortage of soldiers. Within two quick weeks he had been accepted, restored to the rank of lieutenant, and ordered to report to regimental headquarters outside Edinburgh on the last day of February.

The Kings took the news in their various ways. Rita was sympathetic, Robert surprised, James saddened, and Fergus, seeing the move as a sign that Hoey was really as unreliable as ever, cruelly amused.

'I don't know what he'll do to the Zulus,' Fergus said, 'but my God, even the thought of him with a gun terrifies me. I know now exactly how the Duke of Wellington felt.'

Rita was annoyed, then alarmed. 'The Zulus? Surely they won't send Tom to fight the Zulus?'

'Well, I'm not the Commander-in-Chief, but I should think there's a fair chance of it. Our men are being sent out there by the thousand. I don't know much about it, but attacking the Zulus seems to have been a major blunder.'

'I do hope you're wrong, Fergus.'

'I don't think you need worry. He must be the oldest lieutenant in the British Army. Even if his regiment's sent out there, they're bound to give him something to do well behind the lines.'

'Please don't say anything about this to Gwen. You may be quite wrong.'

Her manner irritated him.

'Don't look at me so accusingly, Rita. It's not my doing.'

She withdrew a little. 'If only you had been able to fit him into a corner of the business. He can't have been happy with Wilson & Co.'

Fergus stared at her. 'The matter was never raised,' he said in protest. 'We all accepted that he was better off being independent. You felt the same way yourself.'

Rita sighed. 'You're quite right, dear. I am sorry. It was unfair of me. It's just that I'm so sorry for Gwen. I know how she must feel. She's had him back for such a short time. He must have felt that he had been called to go.'

Suddenly Fergus felt slightly ashamed. The only call he had ever felt in his life was the call to business.

# 18

Robert sat at the desk that had been Roderick Fraser's. He pushed aside the bottle containing the pickled snake. It had taken the distillery handyman to open the office window but now, possibly for the first time in fifty years, air fresh from the loch and the hills circulated in the dark room.

It was still Fraser's room. His linen sleeve protectors lay in a drawer beside one or two pipes and a pouch of dried-up tobacco. The specially made chair stood where Robert had pushed it—he hadn't wanted to sit in that.

Through the open window came the sound of a cooper's hammer and the sweet scent of peat smoke. A trailing branch of creeper rattled against the window in the March wind. The sky was blue but on the hills snow still lay in the high gullies, intensely white and remote in the cold sunshine. Some of that snow would end up as King's Royal. When the thaw came it would trickle over the hard rock till it joined the mountain burn from which the distillery drew its water supply. More than ever would be needed this year. He had, it seemed, created a commodity for which there was a limitless demand. Wherever King's Royal went it made friends—and kept them. But most exciting of all was the slow but undoubted collapse of the pot distillers' boycott.

The great names of Speyside were still pursuing Morrison's vendetta with determination, but smaller distillers were showing an increasing willingness to accept orders. The improvement in supplies had cheered Mr. Hutt out of his resentment and spurred him to new efforts. The orders sent from London were phenomenal. Mr. Hutt himself had come north for three days simply to meet Fergus, see the blending process for himself, and visit the King's newly acquired distillery. The purchase of the distillery from Fiona had been quickly completed once the transfer to her of King's Royal shares had been agreed.

Today, Robert's preoccupation was with the planning of increased production. The re-decoration of this room, the removal of three generations of family debris, could wait. All morning he had worked on details which, basically, he found boring—increased grain requirements, the best use of storage space. It was necessary but tiresome. It was work that could well be done by someone else. Unfortunately, there *was* no one else. Throughout the business it was the same. In deference to his father's sense of thrift he delayed engaging new workers till even Fergus couldn't deny the necessity. Consequently, everyone was overworked. Every week the travellers opened new accounts and soon he planned to begin exporting. The United States of America, Australia, New Zealand, South Africa, and Canada were full of people very like the Scots or the English. These, he argued, were natural markets for King's Royal.

Since the first batch had been blended and bottled the number of workers directly employed on that side of the business had increased from nine to thirty-six. In the first year the turnover had been less than £30,000. This year it should be nearly £250,000. Next year it might touch the half-million. The drinking of blended Scotch whisky seemed to be the world's fastest growing habit. For it was no longer just King's Royal. Others had been quick to see the potential. The door Robert had opened had revealed a treasure so rich that no man or company could hope to monopolize it. Previously, in excise warehouses all over Scotland, great quantities of whisky, hopefully distilled, had collected, no one knowing how to sell it. Blending had been the key and now with the distillers' boycott ending a torrent was ready to pour forth from the glens.

A new industry had arrived. Robert could have named from his head at least a dozen whisky blenders who had come into existence in the last two or three years. In a cupboard in his Glasgow office he kept their bottles, his travellers having instructions to buy any new ones they saw. He received each with eagerness, assessing the label, measuring the whisky against his own. He graded them from excellent to undrinkable, recognizing worth without alarm, having happily decided the market was enormous enough to absorb them all. The commercial editors of the newspapers wrote so enthusiastically of whisky's future that speculators who wouldn't have known a distillery from a glue factory had begun to invest in casks of new whisky as they would have in gold or diamonds.

A legend had been born in a seamy Glasgow street. In the newspapers, each distillery was credited with having its secret water supply, each blender his magic formula. Rheumaticky old men who toiled on in the glens as they had always done were elevated to the status of alchemists. Recognizing it as a myth worth its weight in gold, Robert did what he could to encourage it. King's Royal, he claimed now in his advertising, was based on an ancient blend of malts created to celebrate the coming of age of Prince Charles Edward Stuart. No one questioned it.

And to this new industry the adventurous, the imaginative, and the enterprising were being irresistibly drawn. One blender Robert knew was paying penurious gentlemen to go around the hotels and restaurants of West End London asking for his particular brand and refusing to drink any other. The blender himself would arrive after a discreet interval and was usually given an order. Extravagant claims were beginning to be made by some firms regarding the length of time their whisky matured in the cask before being bottled. Inscriptions like *Old, Very Old, Of Great Age, Special Reserve*, began to appear on labels. No one knew their validity except the proprietor. The age of King's Royal varied according to what was available for purchase. Eight years was the age Robert would have liked to maintain, especially for the more pungent Glenlivet whiskies. Lighter malts, such as Lochbank, hardly improved after three years.

Conventions were already forming around the naming of bottled whiskies. Certain words had grown to assume special significance—*Old ... Glen ... Mist ... Dew. ...* Some merchants began to see the value of labels bearing eye-catching illustrations. Claymores, targes, kilts, bearded faces, and hairy knees abounded, usually against a background of heather. Never had a mythology been so quickly or firmly established.

On his best days, Robert could survey it as his personal creation. Today, surrounded by musty reminders of Fraser's unsuccessful tenure, bored by calculations that could have been worked out by a clerk, he was uninspired. He yawned, lit his pipe, rose from his desk, and went out. There was a farmyard cosiness to the cluster of distillery buildings. He passed the warehouse block. Thousands of casks lay in there, the whisky slowly growing old in the dark. The massive doors were double-locked, he with one key, the resident exciseman with the other. He stopped for a while to watch colourless, new-made whisky splashing from a copper pipe into the first of a collection of butts assembled on the bare earth floor of a building adjoining the stillhouse. It was a twenty-four-hour process, yet so simple that the whole distillery could be run with not many more than a dozen men. The continuity of it all, the casks of maturing whisky lingering on for years at their birth place, pleased him.

He left the distillery and crossed the rough road. The wind blowing across Loch Lomond was dry and sharp. It came chilled off the mountains. By the roadside there were some birch trees adorned with the delicate green of buds beginning to open. Beyond these, shingle dotted with boulders ran to the water's edge. He sat on one of the boulders and relit his pipe. Suddenly, his head was full of unwanted questions. He was twenty-eight years old and if his calculations were correct he would be a millionaire by the time he was thirty-five. He was successful. He was rich. Was he happy?

He peered determinedly across the loch, trying to preoccupy himself with what he saw. Here was another stretch of romantic Scotland—empty and, by turns, beautiful or forbidding. Today it was sunny, and high on the mountain slopes he could see sheep grazing. Tomorrow it might be misty and frightening. In an hour the colours could change from blue and purple to grey and black.

The wind curled restlessly across the water, creating rough patches and white waves. A small brown boat with dirty grey sails was running in front of the weather towards the clachan of Balmaha. There was no other traffic afloat. The islands were low and wooded and from a cottage on one of them smoke rose. He tried to remember the names. Inchmurran . . . Inchfad . . . he could go no further.

Another name came to him. He visualized the girl to whom it belonged, in this mood seeing the full, welcoming figure as a refuge. He hoped tomorrow to join Fiona for her afternoon walk. He had come to look forward to their secret meetings. There was a lack in his life that these strolls with her helped to fill. Business, it appeared, was not enough—a woeful discovery. What had it brought him? Little apart from the achievement itself and he had come to realize that material achievement had an end to it. Worse, its ability to satisfy diminished. It must, to retain its savour, be allied to some larger aim. His father seemed to have come near the winning combination. He had his business anxieties, his family worries, but against the span of his life Robert was sure these would seem small. There must be some wear and tear in living. No one could win all the time.

He rose, shivering, from the boulder. It wasn't a day for sitting long. He stood for a few moments looking at the peak of Ben Lomond, sharp and white under the snow. Once he'd climbed to the top with his father. There was a cairn up there and he had placed a stone on it. That simple deed might be his real handprint on time, enduring long after there were no men either to make or drink whisky. It seemed a day for memories and sad speculation. Once he had come here to see Fraser with another girl on his mind. He could think of her now without pain—but sometimes he wondered if her memory would ever completely leave him.

Robert's day at Lochbank convinced him of the urgent need to appoint a manager. Fraser had managed the place himself. No one among the workers was a natural choice to succeed him. All were trustworthy at their particular jobs, but they carried them out mechanically, with no thought of the overall situation. Since Fraser's death the distillery had run itself, but inevitably the administrative work had been neglected. Robert had no intention of becoming involved with this himself. He explained the position to Fergus, then said, 'I thought about it all last night and I think I know the ideal man for the job. If you agree.'

Fergus raised his eyebrows. 'Me?'

'Yes. He works for you. McNair of the Corkcutters' Arms.'

Fergus pushed his chair back. 'That's a novel thought.'

'That place should be closed. You keep it going from sentiment.'

'I suppose I do.' Modernizing the Corkcutters' Arms had been a poor investment. The area had been debased beyond redemption.

'McNair always struck me as deserving something better,' Robert said. 'There's no doubt of his loyalty. He's stayed with us for ten years. He's honest, eager, and intelligent.'

Fergus, still amused at the novelty of Robert's suggestion, said, 'But he knows absolutely nothing about making whisky.'

'A month's training would be all he would need. We do a lot of business with the Mortlach people. I'm sure if I asked them they would take McNair for a month.'

'If you think it would work I'm willing. It's the excuse I need to get me out of the Goosedubbs.'

'The cottage Mr. Fraser lived in when he wasn't at Helensburgh came to us with the distillery. It's big enough for McNair and his family.'

'Then that's settled. Will you make the arrangements?' Fergus was pleased. It gave him a glow to think they could solve a business problem and at the same time lift a decent man out of a lowly job into a new and more prosperous style of life. There were two boys, he remembered. The country life would be better for them than a Glasgow slum, and when the time came they could have jobs in the distillery. It was one of the best days he had known for months.

And yet, when the day came for the key to be turned for the last time in the door of the Corkcutters' Arms Fergus was overcome by sentiment. It was where he had started. For years it hadn't made him a penny, but he couldn't let others close it for him. He must be there himself. A cart was at the door with two men who had paid a few shillings for the mirrors, the gantry, and the counter. He watched them carry the things away, not even asking what use they could make of them.

When they'd gone, the place looked bigger. There was hardly anything left now to occupy the space—two old barrels, some empty bottles, a length of rubber beer piping, a mirror too cracked even for the men with the cart. He opened the door and looked into the cubbyhole office where he had planned his future. Now it would be considered cruelty to sit a man in there for hours on end, even with gaslight. He had written his letters and made his endless calculations by the glow of the candles which he bought in a shop across the street at six for a penny. For three years, when this had been his only shop, he had worked here fourteen hours a day, six days of the week. Nothing had been too much for him. He had scrubbed the floors himself to begin with rather than pay a woman two shillings a week for an hour's work every morning. He had manhandled casks containing sixty gallons of beer and he had been

326

strong and courageous enough to break off a conversation, when need be, throw a customer out, and return to take up his story. *When a man is twenty,* he thought, *and anxious to make his way, nothing is too much for him.* In memory, the grinding work seemed happiness itself. He had done it all cheerfully, or so memory told him. There had been so much to look forward to in that third decade of his life. And now, with so much more accomplished than he had ever set out to do, he was looking back. There was something to be learned from that, but he didn't know what.

As he walked slowly, almost reluctantly, to the door a thought came to him. He put two fingers into a pocket of his brocade waistcoat and brought out a penny. It was dull and a little twisted. The date he knew without looking: 1817.

It had been lying on the floor when he took this shop over. He had kept it for luck. The Corkcutters' Arms, now disreputable and unwanted, was the origin of his wealth—he must leave something. He put away his lucky penny and took some coins from a pocket. They were all silver. He went through his pockets looking for a copper—a shilling or a florin would only be spent. When he found a penny he flicked it into the air and let it fall on the bumpy wooden floor. It landed on its rim and rolled shakily into the shadows. Perhaps the man who found it would be as lucky as he had been. He went out feeling, as never before, that he had been alive for a long time and that, inevitably, the greater part of his life had been lived.

# 19

Gwen was alone in her shop late on a breezy Friday afternoon early in April when Hoey arrived on his first leave. It was the first she had seen of him in uniform and she couldn't admire him enough. Hoey, proud of his regained military dash, obliged by replacing the red pillbox hat he had swept off as he entered and went strutting about, solemnly saluting a portrait of a lady in blue silk and bending his knees in an exaggerated way to make fierce faces into a gilt mirror.

'What do you think of the old man now?' he asked, and before she could answer he began to tell her what Teddy Dryden had been saying.

His red uniform, trimmed and faced with blue, broad at the shoulders and belted at the waist, gave him a straight-backed grace. Gwen, not caring that passing pedestrians might see, put her arms around him.

'You look very handsome,' she said, her sadness at his new status driven out by the pleasure of seeing him.

Hoey did not deny it.

'I'm going to shut the shop immediately,' she said, 'and we'll walk the length of Sauchiehall Street before it gets dark so that everyone can see you.'

It became obvious, in his short visits home in the next month, that Hoey was happier than she had seen him since the early days of their marriage.

In an odd way, she felt surer of him now than at any time since his return. Before, she had always been watching him, as if expecting an outbreak of the old Hoey who had deserted her, and been ashamed of herself for her lack of faith. Now, the watchfulness had

328

gone. His redemption, she was certain, was complete and permanent. Others noticed the change in him. When they were told he had rejoined his regiment, they had said knowingly, 'You can't play a new tune on an old fiddle. He's got the wanderlust again.' Now they could be heard muttering, 'My word, I believe Tom Hoey really *has* changed.'

In April, too, Fiona came out of mourning. She wore a suit of green corduroy and a fluttering boa when Robert met her for their first walk in the gardens after her return to a free and normal life. Already, as if merely by casting off her black clothes, she had regained some of her healthy country glow. He had almost forgotten how attractive she could be. When he complimented her she said, 'Just to be able to wear bright clothes again makes me feel I've taken wine. If it wasn't that it would make a scene I would walk barefoot on the grass.'

The thought appealed to him. 'Do you remember the night we drove to the riverbank? The water was clear and the sand clean. You could walk barefoot there without making a scene.'

She nodded happily. 'If I was there.'

'Why don't I order the carriage for this afternoon?'

Her voice became mischievous. 'I wouldn't want you to neglect the business on my account, Robert. Especially not now that I have a share in it.'

They looked at each other and laughed. Heedless of the nursemaids and the two or three old men sitting along the sunny side of the gardens, he put his arm around her shoulder. 'You don't care how much I neglect the business,' he said. 'Will I order the carriage?'

They took rugs to sit on and towels to dry their feet. Fiona cried out in surprise at the coldness of the water and urged Robert to hurry and join her. For ten minutes they paddled up and down the sandy stretch, holding hands and looking for shells. Then, misjudging the wash of a passing ship, Robert got the legs of his rolled-up trousers wet. They splashed out of the water and sat barefooted on the rug they had spread on the grass fringing the sand. Wood smoke rose from a cottage across a field and a lark sang above them. On the other side of the river, sea-gulls swooped and screamed above a farmer ploughing a field. Far away, farmland rose through woods into high hills. All over that flat agricultural stretch other men would be ploughing. It had been a wet spring and only now was the land drying. Farther up the river, towards Glasgow, they could see the beginnings of a ship cradled in high steel stocks.

'I wonder why we like this spot so much?' Fiona said.

When he didn't answer she said, 'I suppose it's because it seems to have a bit of everything. Across there, a simple farmer. Up there, men in greasy overalls. And if we sit long enough we're bound to see another ship passing down to the sea.'

'It does seem to have taken on a special significance for us,' Robert agreed. 'We've only been here twice, but I feel I've known the place all my life.'

'It's sad that I may never see it again.'

He looked at her in surprise. 'Why ever not? It's only an afternoon's outing from the centre of Glasgow.'

'I think I told you Uncle Malcolm had invited me to stay with him at his farm near Perth. . . .'

'I remember.'

'I'll have to go soon. I can't expect Aunt May to put up with me much longer. She insists, of course, that I'm welcome, but I feel it's becoming a bit of an imposition. She's looked after me now for more than six months.'

'And how long will you stay in Perth?'

'All summer, I suppose.'

He dug his heels into the sand. When she went, his life would be emptier. He had grown to depend on her company and to need the solace of her abounding femininity. 'I'll miss you,' he said, an odd tremor shivering through his sense. Suddenly the world around him seemed to stop moving. He was still aware of the ploughman, the sea-gulls, and the river, but as if they were painted on canvas. Inside him things quickened. His heart and his mind gained speed. Something momentous was working in him.

'And I'll always be grateful for your company these last months, Robert.' She was smiling with a fondness that contradicted the rather cold formality of her words.

He sat up very straight on the rug, as if bracing himself, forgetful of his bare feet and his wet trousers. 'Will you marry me, Fiona?' The intended words sounded clearly in his head, but in a panic he stifled them. Was it what he really wanted? He couldn't be sure.

Damn it, he couldn't be sure! He sank back on the rug feeling as if he had run a mile.

Hoey and his regiment sailed from London on the Royal Mail Steamer *Pretoria* along with the 91st Highlanders and the 1st Dragoon Guards. The people who had said he would never be a soldier again shook their heads wonderingly and said, 'Imagine old Hoey off to Africa.' All the family, with the exception of Fergus, saw him off with his men from Bridge Station. When the train had gone Gwen broke down and had to be helped from the platform between Robert and Fiona. In recent weeks she had taken a morbid interest in the news, seeking balm for her private fears. But what she read about the Zulu War was depressing and worrying. The court of enquiry into the massacre at Isandhlwana had revealed nothing and had been dismissed by Gladstone as 'a solemn mockery.' Disasters to the British in Zululand had become commonplace. There was one on March 12 on the Intombi River and less than three weeks later on Ihlobana Mountain. After having been without her husband for four years, it seemed cruel to Gwen that she should have had him back only for a few months before losing him to a savage war in a dangerous continent. His men had looked to her like raw boys as they climbed awkwardly, bent under enormous packs, into the train.

Suddenly, as they crossed the busy station, Gwen was filled with an enormous pity for Hoey. She had long ago forgiven him for deserting her, but now it was almost as if it had never happened. There was nothing to forgive. In her love, she saw him as the one badly done by. He had been condemned, it seemed, to be forever restless—to be engaged in some endless battle with himself, the old enemy. But, despite the great burdens placed on him at birth, he'd done his best. He had come back to her a better man, purified by his experiences in the years they had lost. Their life had been better than ever before. And then, again, fate had cruelly exerted its awful influence on him. While others, men like Robert, remained safely at home, Hoey had been lured off into discomfort and danger.

'Poor Tom,' Gwen said aloud in her anguish.

'You're worrying needlessly,' Robert comforted her. 'It may even be all over before Tom arrives out there. It will be another month before he reaches Zululand. Anyway, these initial successes the Zulus have had can't go on. They're a courageous lot who naturally know their own country best and so they've been able to give our men some nasty surprises. But in the long run, assegais are useless against rifles and artillery.'

'He could have been safely at home,' Gwen sobbed. 'If you had all been nicer to him from the very start everything might have been different.'

It was the first bitter thing he had ever heard her say.

A week later Fiona left for Perth. 'Don't stay any longer than you must,' Robert said as they drove in his carriage to Queen Street Station. Then, anxious that the words might be too revealing, he added casually, 'You'll want to be settled in Glasgow or wherever you're going to live before the winter starts.'

Her heart was more open than his. 'I'll think of you all the time, Robert.'

His hold on her hand tightened. 'For me there'll be nothing but work.'

She gave him a slightly forced smile. 'Are you sure?'

'I'll have little choice. We've taken over larger premises. We'll be busier than ever moving to them.'

'That's good. You won't have time for mischief.'

'Nor inclination.'

'Then I suppose you'll have given up that place?'

'What place?'

'Your place in Garnethill.'

'What on earth has made you think of that?' He looked out of the window to hide a mixture of irritation and embarrassment.

It wasn't the time to tell him that she often thought of it. 'Well, come along. Have you?'

He couldn't decide whether her expression was teasing or accusing.

'No. I haven't actually given it up yet.'

'Really!'

'But, of course, I intend to. I've had no use for it for long enough. I'll give it up tomorrow. It's only a rented place.' He began to fumble in a pocket. 'I won't go near it again. To prove it, here's the key. Go on, take it!'

'Don't be silly, Robert. I was only teasing you. I don't want the key. It has nothing to do with me.'

Should he tell her that at that moment it had everything to do with her? Perth was only sixty miles away, but he felt she was leaving his world. He had been sincere in saying that for him now there would be nothing but work. He knew no one. He had become a machine for making money—money he never spent because he had few personal demands and no one to spend it on. Worse, he had forgotten how to relax except in her company. She was his only escape from the emptiness of the life he had created for himself. All day the air had been ominously still and he had been aware of a tension that existed only partly inside him. Now there was an unusual indigo light that could only herald evil weather. Soon the sky must burst and send down if not a thunderbolt then at least a deluge. He felt the same swelling oppression that filled the day. Part of him knew Fiona could supply the stability and tranquillity lacking in his life. She was the missing symbol in the formula. But another part shrank from the obvious step. A few simple words would commit him. Once committed, doubt would wither, but as on the afternoon by the river, caution held his tongue.

He took her arm and for the rest of the way they swayed gently together in silence.

The weeks following her departure were even more crowded than he'd expected. Apart from normal daily business he was personally supervising the conversion into a blending and bottling warehouse of a disused tobacco store they had bought in a cul-de-sac off Argyle Street. Coopers were building large blending vats on the spot while carpenters constructed a series of racks on which casks of whisky could be stored several tiers high. The activity was deafening. Next to the blending vats was the bottling hall and beyond that two long tables where girls would sit labelling bottles.

'We want one process in the operation to lead on naturally to the next,' Robert explained to Fergus as he took him around. 'Instead of things being all over the place, as they are at the moment. It's a pity we didn't have another McNair who could be put in charge here. He's doing very well down at Lochbank.'

Fergus was pleased. He felt McNair's success was somehow a credit to himself. He stood back to look up at the high warehouse walls.

'His wife and two boys must know a difference,' he said. 'That was a very good idea you had.' He stopped and looked thoughtfully around the big building. 'Why don't we take another gamble and promote Peter Ross to manage things here?'

'Oddly enough that did occur to me a few weeks ago but I couldn't make up my mind if he was ready for anything as ambitious yet.'

'You would have to keep an eye on him for a time,' Fergus said. 'But I think he's wasted just doing the blending. I think there's more in Ross than has come out yet.'

Robert laughed. 'It was certainly a stroke of genius to see the answer to inconsistent colouring in whisky in an old woman's homemade toffee.' He pointed down the long floor. 'Maw Meechan's coming with us, you know. I'm having a special little place built for her over there. She's given up making toffee apples now. She prefers working for us.'

'Excellent,' Fergus said expansively. It always pleased him to find loyalty among his employees. He regarded himself as an enlightened employer, and was. 'And give some thought to what I've suggested about Ross. If you try to do it yourself you'll find it too much for you on top of everything else.'

Something in Robert always made him combat any suggestion that he worked too hard. 'Now that the distillers' boycott has cracked wide open I'll have more time than I've had for years,' he said. 'We're suddenly getting all the whisky we need. Still, the more I think of Ross as manager the more I like the idea.'

Fergus' own recent inclination had been to shed work burdens where he could. That year he had resigned two of his charitable appointments. In his own business he had closed another of the less remunerative branches, along with the Corkcutters' Arms.

'There's more to life than work and money,' he told a surprised Rita. 'It's time I learned to take things a bit easier. Instead of chairing some boring meeting I'll be able to get to more auction sales for Gwen.'

It was while he was in this relaxed, undemanding mood that he received a letter from London. He looked at the crest embossed on the envelope in gilt—he couldn't decipher it. There was a stiff sheet of paper signed at the bottom with the name Beaconsfield. In a daze he read the Prime Minister's letter.

*'I have it in mind on the occasion of the forthcoming list of Birthday Honours to submit your name to the Queen with a recommendation that she may be graciously pleased to approve that you be raised to the baronetcy. Before doing so I would be glad to be assured that this mark of Her Majesty's favour would be agreeable to you.'*

At first Fergus felt no elation. Wonder possessed him and even some doubt. Sir Fergus King! Was he really worthy of this great honour? And after all this time, when hope had almost gone? He had prayed; even, he supposed, schemed a bit for this but was he really worthy? Of course he was! There were elaborate precautions designed to make sure the unworthy were not honoured. Years ago, when he had realized his ignorance of the Honours System, he had spent time discovering exactly what happened before the Prime Minister sent out these letters. In his mind he saw the various steps. The Prime Minister preparing an initial list of eligible individuals, perhaps in consultation with the sovereign. Then, the list being submitted to the Scrutiny Committee. Quietly, its enquiries going out all over the country, the committee would assess the candidates for moral purity. Some would be stricken from the list at this stage.

Those who survived would have their names passed to the Parliamentary Whips for assurances that they hadn't promised to pay money into Party funds for any honour received. Eventually the Prime Minister would submit to the Queen a list of nominees against whom no objections had been unearthed. It was then for the Queen to give final approval. Fergus lifted his letter and reread it. He had passed the test—and for an honour greater than he had hoped for. A knighthood, which would have died with him, was all he had wanted. Instead, he had received a hereditary baronetcy. He was the first of a line that would go on for as long as his heirs produced heirs. Sir Fergus King, 1st Baronet of ... where? A moment's thought told him there could be only one place. In his head, he sounded it out again in full. Sir Fergus King, 1st Baronet of Ardfern. It seemed that, at last, everything he had worked for had been achieved. He had been rich for years. Now his prized respectability would be raised and made safe in the ranks of chivalry. He hurried out excitedly from his study to tell Rita.

It was Rita who gave the news to Robert when he came into the house later in the morning to collect papers he had left in his room.

His slightly withdrawn expression puzzled her almost as much as his words. 'Oh, has it arrived?'

She frowned. 'What do you mean, Robert—has it arrived?'

'I've been wondering when it would.'

'I don't quite understand. You sound as if you knew it was coming.'

'I did know.'

'How could you? Your father didn't even know.'

'Well . . .' he hesitated. 'I knew because I arranged it.'

'Robert!'

He looked along the hall, then took her by the arm and led her into the drawing-room where they wouldn't be overheard.

'I hadn't meant to tell anyone, but there's no harm in you knowing, Mother. So long as you don't tell Father.'

'Tell your father what, Robert?'

'What I've just told you. That I bought him the title. We all know it's what he's always wanted and there didn't seem to be much hope, otherwise, did there?'

Rita was shocked. 'But you can't buy titles.'

Robert began to regret his rash revelation. 'Don't worry about it, Mother.'

'You couldn't possibly have had anything to do with your father getting a title.' Her voice began to trail away. 'It's for . . . for his public services.'

'Yes, that made it a lot easier. Father does have a good record of public service, but unfortunately that isn't always enough. After old Sir James Spence died Father didn't have a chance.'

Rita turned away. 'I believe you're telling me the truth, Robert. I don't like it at all. Why did you do it?'

'I owe Father a lot, though he would be surprised to hear me say it. It seemed a way of repaying him. It was a way of giving him something he would never have been able to get for himself.'

'Your father would never have given money for a title.'

'That's what I mean. And then . . . if I'm completely honest . . . I suppose I was thinking of myself to some extent. Father was angling only for a knighthood. It would have died with him. A baronetcy will pass to me . . . in time.'

Perhaps for the first time, Rita saw her son as a stranger might have. For a miserable instant she felt something as bitter as dislike.

It would pass, no doubt, but at the moment it could not be denied.

'I wish you hadn't told me this,' she said coldly.

'I didn't mean to. I should have kept my mouth shut.' He tried to drape a veil of respectability over what he had so rashly revealed. 'It's happening all the time. Father won't be the only one, by a long way.'

'It's something I'll have to keep from your father. And I do not like keeping things from him, Robert.' She went to the door. 'You must not on any account ever tell him what you've told me. It would'—she shook her head—'I don't know what it would do to him.'

One hazy morning a few weeks later Robert walked along Princes Street, Edinburgh, in the direction of the West End Station. He had spent the night in the capital after a long day with customers. He had had too much food and drink and been late getting to bed. When he wakened he felt slightly bilious. The feeling had persisted until a few moments earlier. What had distracted him from his upset was the sound of a pipe being played somewhere high on the ramparts of Edinburgh Castle. The piper was unseen, as was the castle. Only the steep wall of rock on which the castle stood was visible. The damp night mist that rolls like smoke from the River Forth and turns Edinburgh into 'Auld Reekie' was only now beginning to disperse. It had taken on a faintly golden glow as the hidden sun thinned it down, and momentarily he saw a turret, then the outline of a cannon.

Still the piper remained hidden. Only his music floated down through the mist. It was a march for the changing of the guard. Robert felt his blood responding. He wasn't musical. He couldn't have named the tune. But he felt his arms begin to swing and his stride adjust itself to the stirring rhythm. There was magic in this music to which generations of men had marched and fought. Few Scots could resist it. Even Sassenachs and downright foreigners had been known to thrill to it.

Suddenly, he knew this was what he had been looking for. This great music of Scotland could be turned to his commercial advantage. For months he had felt his advertising had become tame. To link his whisky to the barbaric splendour of the pipes would be a marvellous scheme. He would organize a piping contest. The King's Royal Pipe Band Championships.

His imagination raced on. He saw a background of sea and hills and heard the strange wail and moan of the pipes and the beat of the drums. Bands from all over Britain would enter. It would be an event he would stage every three years, each time in a different town of Scotland. He would start it off in Helensburgh. Glasgow itself was too industrialized. But Helensburgh was near enough for Glasgow people to come for the day. Fergus would no doubt condemn the idea as a stunt—but it was a stunt, Robert was certain, that the public would enjoy. And one that would sell whisky. Already he could see the pipers marching along the shores of the Clyde with the green hills beyond. The kilts would swing as the men went through the town in a broad ribbon of tartan. He would call it the March of a Thousand Pipers. The first prize would be five hundred pounds. And after every contest he'd send the winners piping round the world.

His thoughts came back to the reality of Princes Street as a girl stepped from a doorway into his path. He tried to stop, then to go sideways, but he couldn't avoid her. He threw an arm around her to stop her falling and called out a breathless apology. Then, their eyes met. The traffic noises retreated as if hands had been placed on his ears. He was aware that the mist had at last dissolved. The drab greys of the street had taken on a warm tinge of gold. Almost as if in an aureole the girl stood.

'Mary,' he said.

For a moment his heart sickened as it seemed she didn't recognize him. Then the small, sharp face opened out into a slightly be-wildered smile as he took her arm and guided her back to the doorway.

'I haven't hurt you? You're all right?'

She spoke his name with a shy breathlessness, as if in some way testing her capacity to deal with it. 'I'm suffering more from surprise than anything else.'

'I was dreaming about something,' he said. 'I didn't know where I was.' He looked at her. 'And now I know even less. What a way to meet again. I had forgotten you lived in Edinburgh now.'

'You knew?'

'Yes.'

'How did you know?'

'Someone told me. I forget who it was.' He could hardly tell her about Fergus' Maker of Confidential Enquiries.

He glanced along the street. 'Look here ... you can't be in a great rush. Could we go somewhere and sit down?'

She hesitated. 'Weren't you hurrying?'

'Only to catch a train to Glasgow. But there's a very good service. I'll get the next.'

'There's a pleasant tea room just round the corner.'

'This is a cut above Miss Frame's,' he said when they were seated.

'And the view's better.'

Their table was at a window looking across the Princes Street gardens to the castle. The long grey fortress, forbidding in mist or dullness, floated cheerfully now in sunshine as on the wrappings of so many rounds of shortbread. From one of the flagpoles the Scottish Standard stood out stiffly in the breeze. Soldiers in red tunics moved on the esplanade.

'It's supposed to be one of the great romantic views of the world,' Mary said.

He turned from the window with an exuberant smile. 'Never mind the view. What about you? Your health was fragile.'

'You knew I had been in Switzerland?'

'Yes.' He was relieved she didn't ask who his mysterious informant was.

'Edinburgh seems to agree with me. Our house stands high and the air's very clear. Glasgow has become too smoky.'

She hadn't heard of his success in business and the name King's Royal was unknown to her. 'Mother and I live very quietly,' she said, as if in apology.

He noticed that although she listened politely as he gave a brief account of his business, her smile was enigmatic and she didn't ask questions.

He wondered what she thought of him now. Had she ever regretted their decision to part? He doubted it. With her, it had not only been a matter of obeying the dictates of good sense but of observing the code of a rigorous and unbending religion. If his clear-headedness had been blessed, then hers had been twice blessed. Had she ever loved again? She wore neither a wedding nor an engagement ring, but it was impossible to think of her going through life alone. She was not yet twenty-five and was if anything more beautiful than before. Her face, although still small and thin, had acquired an intriguing and inscrutable maturity. She looked friendly, but at the same time slightly aloof, as if she had a preoccupation. She was poised, yet she was wary. Covertly, he examined this beautiful enigma more closely, remembering the open and eager girl with her *Manual of Nursing* and satchel of lecture notes. Of her illness there was no trace. Her eyes were clear and they held his with calm interest. The good bone structure of her face was prominent, but it suggested a delicate fragility rather than gauntness. Her cheeks had colour and her hair shone, the dark strands drawn back in the loose simplicity that he remembered. A memory of the soft, warm silkiness of her hair drifted to him across the years. He was not disturbed by it. Time had turned what would once have been pain into something gently pleasing.

He said, 'Of course, you won't work now as a nurse?'

'I had to give up nursing. The doctors said it was too strenuous for me.' She smiled as if in doubt. 'I suppose they were right. It seems such a long time ago.'

'I'm sure you must have missed the work. You were dedicated to it.' Her violet-silk suit and feathered hat, he saw, were expensive and stylish. 'And now? What do you do now?'

She lifted her head a little. 'I read. I walk. I am learning to play the piano.' Her expression was serene but he felt certain she was mocking herself. Had she been spoiled a little by cynicism? It would hardly be surprising. For her, too, after they parted, there would have been months of bitter heartbreak. Then her long illness. He looked again for signs of it and once more satisfied himself there were none.

'For three months every winter Mother and I go to the Mediterranean coast of France. My doctor recommends it. The fog and sleet of the Scottish winter would be bad for me.'

'I hope one day soon you'll be well enough, Mary, to face even a Scottish winter.'

'No. I will always have to be careful.' It wasn't a complaint. The prospect was one with which she had obviously come to terms. 'I must be thankful we have the means to make it easy.'

She stopped, and then added, as if in explanation of the implied affluence, 'Father died two years ago.'

'Yes. I was sorry to learn that.'

She seemed slightly amused that he should know so much about her. 'He left us comfortably provided for.' She said it as if, unquestionably, she would always have to look after herself.

'Do you ever come to Glasgow?'

'For two years I wasn't in it at all, but I've been there on the last three Thursdays. I visit someone who's ill.' She gave him a sidelong glance. 'An old acquaintance of yours. It's odd he should have enquired about you only last week.'

He was surprised. 'To my knowledge, none of my friends is ill. Who is it?'

'Father Campbell.'

It was a name he had never expected to hear again.

'You must recall him.'

'Of course. But I'm surprised he should remember me.'

'Do you think you meant so little to him?'

He was shaken by the natural and unembarrassed way she spoke of the past. He had thought it better avoided. He smiled stiffly. 'Perhaps it's true we tend to remember our failures rather than our successes.'

'I don't think that's why he remembers you.'

'No. He'll remember me through you.'

'Not just that, either.'

'Then what?'

'I think perhaps he has a guilty conscience about you. At any rate, his conscience is not quite clear.'

'He was emphatic enough at the time. I can't remember anything that looked or sounded like doubt.' He was annoyed and surprised that he couldn't keep the edge out of his voice. He hadn't realized that he still harboured a slight resentment at the part that old man had played in the formation of his hollow life.

'I think possibly that's what worries him. I know he blames himself in some way for my illness.'

'It wasn't him,' he said with a slight smile. 'Not only him. The whole structure of things was against us.' He was surprised to find he had been infected by her dispassionate manner. 'We strayed into an impossible situation and in the end we made our decision to walk out of it.'

'Yes. It is ridiculous, but I think he sometimes wonders if you, too, were marked by the experience. By illness, I mean—physical or mental. You see'—she seemed to think an explanation of the priest's aberration must be attempted—'he's very ill.'

'I'm sorry to hear it. Perhaps he's the one who was marked, but I'd have thought professionalism would have protected him from anything like that.' His sarcasm alarmed him. It shouldn't have been so near the surface after so many years.

She moved her chair a little as a band of sunshine struck the window. 'I wonder if any of them are very happy. There must be an awful lot of pretence. They mustn't ever show doubt about anything that really matters. It must lead them sometimes into decisions—about other people's lives, for example—that they later regret.'

'Your faith hasn't weakened, has it, Mary?' His tone was gently teasing, but at the same time tinged with sympathy.

For the first time her smile looked open and uncomplicated. 'Not in any basic way, but nowadays I find I'm inclined to ask questions where before I wouldn't have.'

'That can't be anything but healthy.' He looked at his watch. 'I'll have to be thinking about my train. You must tell Father Campbell you've seen me.'

'It will give me something to talk about. He's paralysed after a stroke and I have to do most of the talking. It's quite difficult sometimes.'

'It's a long journey for you every week.'

'Yes, but I feel I must make it. He was very kind to me when I was ill. Even when I was in Switzerland he wrote every week.'

Suddenly, Robert had a vision of his own selfishness. He had never seen so clearly before that his life was devoid of good deeds. It was a disconcerting realization. Almost without further thought he said, 'I wonder . . . would it mean anything to Father Campbell if I visited him and he saw for himself that I am blooming and not harbouring bitterness?'

She hesitated for only a moment. 'I'm sure it would help him.' Her eyes brightened. 'It would certainly leave him with a smaller area of his conscience to examine.'

342

'Is that what he does?'

'All the time, I think. He's preparing himself for death. He's seen so many people die that he knows the signs as well as any doctor.'

'He's dying?'

'They don't think he has very long.'

'Then I should go as soon as possible. What day is this? Tuesday? Will you be visiting him on Thursday as usual?'

'Yes.'

'Could I go along with you?'

Her gaze strayed to the window for a moment or two longer than it would have done if she was really as unaffected by their past as had until now seemed possible.

'I suppose if you turned up at the nursing home we could go in to him together. He's in a house on the south side of the river run by the Little Sisters of the Poor. I can give you the address.'

They sat for only another minute or two and as they went down the stairs to the street he sensed in her a sudden interest that hadn't been there before. They said good-bye, but just as they were about to turn away from each other she said, 'I suppose . . . I hope you don't mind me asking, Robert, but are you married now?'

He experienced an inexplicable pleasure at the sight of her composure slightly disturbed at last.

'No,' he said. 'I'm not married.'

Her smile, so controlled, came to baffle him again. What was it saying? There might have been sympathy there or the faintest, friendliest mockery. Poor boy! It all depended on the intonation.

She began to turn away, and as she did so the sunlight from above the castle caught the lustre of her dark hair, giving it a soft richness that he wanted to put out his hand and touch.

'Good-bye, then, Robert,' she said. 'I'll see you on Thursday.'

In the train, his sense of excitement subsided. He was left with uncertainty. As he looked from the window at fields scarred by mineworkings and rutted cart tracks he began to wonder if he had done something very foolish. Father Campbell's conscience was a matter for Father Campbell. If it troubled him, was it any more than he deserved? This harsh judgement annoyed Robert because he saw it at once as an evasion of the real cause of his unease. It had been pleasant to meet Mary again and to talk to her for a while.

But there, if he was wise, it should have ended. Any attempt to extend the moment could only be sterile and unsettling, perhaps even painful. Was it even honourable? Though he had so far been too unsure of his emotions to discuss marriage with Fiona, she must, by this time, feel it was his eventual intention. And it was ... it was! To have entered into a commitment that would put him in Mary's company again was hardly the way to stabilize his feelings for Fiona. And yet ... he did want to see Mary again.

As he swayed to the movement of the train he had a glimpse of swans on a small loch with wild yellow iris growing around. Sheep lay against the warm, scattered stones of some fallen fortress. Then the train took a wide sweep and clattered on to a long viaduct. He stared out at the iron supports and tried to clear both girls from his mind by thinking of the new business arrangements he had made in Edinburgh. It was useless. He kept seeing Mary. He consoled himself with the thought that Thursday would soon come and go, taking her with it. After all these years she could have no real call on his heart. His interest in her now was as a friend from the past. It was completely understandable and uncomplicated.

It was to be a day of unexpected meetings and the next one drove all thought of Mary from his mind. When he left the train in Glasgow and walked across the station he met Arthur Morrison. They stared at each other for a few moments, unable to avoid the confrontation. Then Robert smiled. The power this man had exerted over him for years had ended. He had triumphed, as he had promised he would. There was no reason why he shouldn't revel a little in the moment.

'It's not often you come to this wicked city,' he said. 'Not another vendetta, I hope?'

Morrison's expression was cold. Clearly he'd forgiven nothing. 'Not another one,' he said. 'The same one.' His voice was harsh with dislike.

Robert eyed him with sudden wariness. 'Don't tell me you still don't accept us? Most of the other distillers seem to have realized we are doing them no harm.'

'Perhaps most of the other distillers have no sense.' Morrison made no attempt to conceal his bitterness.

'Perhaps not, but fortunately it doesn't affect the quality of their

344

whisky. In any case, they've clearly become bored with your bloody boycott.'

A slightly exultant look came on to Morrison's face. 'There's more than one way of skinning a cat,' he said.

Robert shrugged. 'Have it your own way,' he said and began to walk on.

Morrison put out a hand but didn't touch him. 'Just a minute, King.'

'Well, what is it?'

Morrison looked hard at him for a moment. 'Don't gloat too soon because some misguided people have started selling whisky to you again.'

'If you were wise you would follow their lead. Despite everything we're still ready to start filling Tamnavar again.'

Morrison ignored this. 'Are you familiar with Section 6 of the Sale of Food and Drugs Act, 1875?'

Robert laughed. 'I'm afraid not. I leave the law to the lawyers.'

'Then I advise you to familiarize yourself with it. You can buy a copy of the Act from H.M. Stationery Office.'

'I prefer lighter reading.'

'Under it, it is an offence to sell anything that is not—in the words of the Act—"of the nature, substance and quality demanded".'

'And what is that supposed to mean?'

Morrison's face darkened with loathing. 'It means,' he said, 'that we are going to prosecute you, King. You may have wormed your way round us but you won't find it so easy to ignore the courts.'

Robert took out his watch. 'All that is very interesting,' he said, 'but I've other business to attend to.'

As he walked back to Washington Street his uneasiness grew.

Fergus looked alarmed when Robert told him of Morrison's threat.

'This is terrible,' he said accusingly. 'I've always conducted my business legally.'

'We are conducting our business legally.'

'How do you know? I can't imagine Morrison was talking to hear his own voice. They must have had legal advice.'

He pushed away the papers he had been working at and slumped worriedly over his desk.

'I don't think for a minute that it will ever happen,' Robert said, as much to console himself as to reassure Fergus. 'It's not for them to prosecute. Someone would have to complain to the nuisance inspectors.'

Fergus walked to the window and stared unhappily at the rain that had started to fall from a low grey sky. 'They'll soon enough find someone willing to do that.'

'The authorities would have to be convinced that we were breaking the law. Their view would not be as biased as Morrison's.'

Fergus clung to the black side. 'I know from my days in the Corporation that the nuisance inspectors love a test case. It adds zest to their lives. It's a change from weighing bags of coal or peering into milk cans. Take my word, if there's half a chance they'll prosecute once it's brought to their notice.'

'They'll still have to prove their case.'

Fergus shook his beard at the wet sky. 'Prove it or fail to prove it, there will be a scandal,' he said with quiet conviction. 'I've been forty years in business without anything like this. We'll be the talk of the country if we end up in court.'

'Blending has become big business,' Robert reminded him. 'If Morrison means what he says, we might be the people in the dock but everyone will realize that a whole industry's on trial.'

At last Fergus arrived at the heart of his worry. 'If the Queen hears about this I don't know what will happen,' he said limply. 'She won't like it. It might ruin everything for me.'

For a moment Robert was disconcerted. After his talk with Rita he had tried to forget the impending title. 'Don't worry about that,' he said turning guiltily away. 'The Queen won't know a thing about it until it's too late. Her birthday is only a couple of weeks off. The Honours List will be announced then. It will be months before any prosecution could be under way.'

Fergus brightened a little. 'Are you sure?'

'Perfectly.' He forced himself to be cheerful. 'Anyway, apart from that you're worrying unnecessarily. Morrison once called us pirates. Well, the British have always had a soft spot for pirates— and a tradition of giving them titles.'

Fergus put on his coat and went out still frowning at his son's levity. Water lay now in dirty pools in the hollows of the neglected street and down the grey tenements wet spread in dark patches. He didn't bother with an umbrella. Sometimes, when he was

346

depressed, he found a perverse pleasure in letting the rain drizzle on him. His boots were strong and his coat thick. Rita, of course, would scold him if she knew.

In Argyle Street, a man in a group talking outside a bank lifted his hat. Fergus heard one of the others say, 'Who's that?' but was too far away to catch the reply. He invented one—'Oh, that's one of the Kings.' 'The Kings?' 'Yes, you know, the whisky Kings.' 'Ah!' He was aware—not always pleasurably—that the name had now become one of the best known in Glasgow. Fame bred resentment. There would be plenty ready to glory in the spectacle of the name being dragged through the courts.

A newspaper seller called out the latest bulletins from Zululand, but Fergus hardly listened. He had no sense of being at war. It was a conflict for politicians and professional soldiers. Trade was unaffected. Possessions weren't threatened. It was too far away for anyone to care about unless they had a husband or a son fighting there. He had intended visiting his club, but passed it, suddenly remembering that he, too, was affected by the Zulu War. What touched Gwen must touch him. He walked up a steep cobbled hill to Bath Street.

His beard was straggly and dripping when he arrived at Gwen's. She was alone in the shop. 'Why didn't you take a cab, Father, or at least an umbrella?' He was reminded of Rita as he watched her fuss with his hat and coat, looking for some place to hang them.

'Put it on the floor,' he said with alarm as it looked as if she might spread the wet coat over a table he admired.

He lifted a Japanese figure carved in ivory and inlaid with mother of pearl. 'How much are you asking for this, my dear?'

'Isn't it marked?'

Fergus lifted the tag and peered at it. Then, with a low whistle, he replaced the figure on its stand. 'Not worth it,' he said, moving restlessly on to a Worcester cup and saucer. 'Not worth it at all. I've never liked that foreign stuff. Take my advice, Gwen. Stick to good English pieces. You'll be safe with them.'

Gwen let him prowl. She had her own heavy thoughts. She'd slept badly since Hoey left and today she had a headache. Hoey was rarely out of her mind. He was so far away, and news was so long in reaching home, that even when she had a letter from him it brought little comfort. Anything could have happened since he

347

had written it. She remembered Hoey's own stunned words as he read of the massacre at Isandhlwana—'They've all been dead for three weeks.' By day she imagined Hoey bitten by snakes, mauled by lions, or burning with a mortal fever. At nights she started awake, trembling, from seeing him fall under a hail of spears. She was aware that Fergus had stopped moving and was looking around the shop.

'You haven't sold that Hepplewhite wine cooler already, have you?'

'Yes. A dealer came in yesterday.'

'How much did you charge him?'

When she told him he looked disappointed in her and moved away again, muttering. 'I warned you about dealers. If you take my advice you'll keep them out.'

'*I* am a dealer, Father,' Gwen said rebelliously. Against her fears Fergus' concern about money seemed petty.

He stood with his back to her looking out of the window. 'They'll only cheat you,' he said as if she hadn't spoken. He lifted his coat from the floor and put it on. It was a long time since he had felt so restless. In the windows of several shops he passed he saw bottles of King's Royal. Was the whole damn thing going to come tumbling down around them? It was all very well for Robert to be flippant. He would have to smile on the other side of his face if the courts upheld the Pot Still Association's contention and ruled that King's Royal was not whisky. Where would they be then? In Queer Street. Down the Clyde on a banana skin. They had at least one hundred thousand pounds sunk in blended stock. And there was another fortune tied up in bottles, labels, and boxes, not to mention the vats and racks they were having installed in the new warehouse.

Fergus cursed the day Robert had tricked him into this business. Fortunes weren't made as easily as Robert had made his. His own eyes, of course, had been dazzled by the brilliance of it all. In the bright light of so much success it was difficult to think now that he had failed to see the obvious. That there must be a reckoning. That the day must come when the ledger would have to be squared.

As the rain came down on him Fergus considered his son's unconcern. There was an irresponsibility there that frightened him. He sensed something of the gambler in Robert, a streak of reckless-

348

ness that enabled him to take risks, knowing that the outcome might as easily be calamity as success. It wasn't Fergus' way of doing business. He knew now that if he had been wise, he would have set Robert up in business but taken no part in it himself. If he had done that there would not now be the awful prospect of his name being thrown about in the newspapers. Honoured by the Queen, dishonoured by his son. A cab, passing too fast, sprayed muddy water on him and in trying to avoid it he went under a leaking gutter.

He sneezed loudly several times as soon as he stepped into the warmth of the hall at Park Place. Rita took one look at his soggy boots and ordered a tub of hot water and mustard to be placed in the bedroom. Fergus sat on the bed and docilely put his feet into the tub. He felt like having a little attention. Rita could always be relied on for that.

# 20

The Little Sisters of the Poor lived behind an ivy-covered wall in Langside. Japonica, clematis, and roses climbed over the low, grey-shuttered house, and the garden ran down in a green slope to where a willow trailed over the slow water of the River Cart.

A shrine had been raised to the Virgin in à rocky outcrop on the riverbank and in this miniature grotto Mary sat. She was smiling her slight smile and did not speak when Robert approached. She wore a wide blue hat with yellow rosettes and a short veil that stopped just below the level of her eyes.

He halted some yards away, disconcerted by the devotional setting. He looked at her for a sign, but as the silence lengthened, his embarrassment deepened. Her expression was serene and he wondered if she was praying. The willow moved in a faint breeze and its long green fingers traced patterns on the river. At last, nodding towards the statue, he said, 'Is it all right to speak?'

She turned her secretive smile on him. 'Oh, yes. Quite all right.'

He sat on one of the other seats. 'I thought perhaps you were—' He shook his hands helplessly to indicate his ignorance of what might be done in such a place.

'I was just thinking how beautiful the blossom is across the river,' she said. Her expression annoyed him slightly for its quality of unfathomable placidity. 'Nothing more spiritual than that.'

There were two trees and a wide spread of trembling white through which the mellow evening sunlight filtered, dappling the river.

'It's beautiful,' he said. 'Do you know what it is?'

'I think it's gean, the wild Scottish cherry.'

'They look like very old trees. Probably they've been there for a hundred years.'

The thought seemed to please her, for she nodded brightly, then clasped her hands and turned fully in his direction. 'What time is it, Robert?'

'Almost six. Shouldn't we be going in? You have Edinburgh to go back to, tonight.'

'At six o'clock they'll ring the angelus. There's no point in moving until after that. It will be pleasant to hear it down here by the river.'

She had hardly finished speaking when a bell began to toll. The leisurely sound came from the direction of the house.

'There it is,' she said.

Even across the religious divide, the gentle melody of the bell evoked for Robert an unhurried world, a contemplative life. He asked, 'What happens now?'

She looked past him again to the blossoming cherry trees and the swaying willow. '*Angelus domini*. The nuns and the people who work about this place will be saying those words. They're the beginning of a little devotional exercise. It's a reminder to them that there's another world—that their labours here have a limited worth. The Angelus bell rings three times a day.'

'I don't think I've ever heard it before.'

'No. This is not a Catholic country now. Here, it's rung only in private places like this. In Catholic countries it rings out publicly from the churches at six o'clock in the morning, when the working day begins, halfway through at noon, and at six in the evening when work ends. In France you see the peasants stopping work in the fields to pray when the Angelus rings. To me it's a very soothing sound.'

He nodded. 'There's a peaceful ring about it.'

After a while she stood up. 'I think perhaps we should go in now.'

Father Campbell lay in a room with perhaps a dozen beds in it. The beard that had been black five years ago now was white. Where it had been shaggy it had gone wispy. He was asleep with one hand showing outside the bedclothes, a rosary entwined in his thin fingers. Robert looked at the face. The strength had gone from it. Around the temples a tracery of blue was visible and then nothing, neither life nor colour. All the other beds in the room were occupied. A few ravaged faces turned momentarily as he and Mary entered the room; thin shoulders were raised, then subsided. Not for them, this interruption. The beds, Robert noticed, were all different, some of wood, some brass, some iron. The clothes that covered the patients were patched, darned, and threadbare. The floor was bare scrubbed wood.

Mary, seeing his surprised inspection of the room, said, 'There are better places, but he especially asked to be brought here. His whole life has been spent with the poor. He wants to die with them.'

There was one chair at the bed and she sat on it. A nun opened the door and, seeing them there, came in. She smiled at Mary and said, as if wondering at the speed of time, 'Another week gone?'

She went to the head of the bed and stood looking at Father Campbell for a few moments. 'He will waken soon,' she said. 'He has little sleeps often.' She brought a chair for Robert, then left them as, further along the room, a grey figure lifted itself in a bed and began to whimper.

They sat on either side of the bed looking at the priest. His chest rose and fell almost imperceptibly and once or twice his lips moved soundlessly. Robert began to wonder at the impulse that had brought him here. It had hardly been necessary. It was true this man had spent a few brief but decisive weeks in his life, but not in a way calling for gratitude or remembrance. He'd been impelled to come here not so much for Father Campbell's benefit as for his own, moved by that sudden, depressing glance into the essential selfish hollowness of his life. Even then, he wouldn't have come if it hadn't been that Mary would be there, too. He had been reluctant, that day in Edinburgh, to feel that a reunion so unexpected should also be so brief.

'He looks very peaceful.'

To Robert, Father Campbell simply looked lifeless, but he felt he must agree.

'Very, but if I'd come alone I don't think I would have recognized him. He has lost all his authority.'

Her eyes rested on the sleeping priest. 'I think that's what saddens me most. We're all so vulnerable.'

Again Robert looked along the room. At the far end, near the bed where the nun was giving something from a medicine bottle to the man who had been whimpering, a crucifix hung. Here and there on the walls there were religious pictures—of saints, he supposed—all so healthy and seraphic compared to the people in the beds. He could hear the nun's voice but the words she used were foreign to him.

Mary smiled as if she had interpreted his expression. 'That's Gaelic,' she said. 'The old man is from somewhere in the West Highlands and she is from the Outer Hebrides—South Uist, I think. I've never seen her anything but cheerful, yet like all the nuns she works harder than a domestic servant.'

'You've done your share of this work.'

'Yes, but apart from their nursing the nuns have religious duties as well.'

'I admire that type of nun,' Robert said. 'They do good work, with people who probably wouldn't get much attention otherwise. I must say, though, I'm more doubtful about the ones who simply shut themselves away.'

'There's a place for the contemplative orders. The Church sees them as powerhouses of prayer.' She leaned forward. 'Hello, Father.' The priest's eyes had opened. Robert watched them turn with slow surprise in the direction of Mary's voice.

'My child.' His lips moved awkwardly through the paralysis but the words were distinct. 'Bless you.' His eyes stared up again at the high ceiling. 'I hadn't realized you were here. I go such long journeys.'

'You were sleeping, Father. We didn't want to waken you.'

His lips twisted, but the slight spark in his eyes told them he was smiling. 'Plenty of time for sleep.'

'I've brought someone to see you.'

'Someone. . . .' His eyes turned until he saw Robert.

'Hello, Father Campbell. Do you remember me? Robert King.'

For long moments it seemed the priest did not remember. *This poor, sick man*, Robert thought. *I shouldn't be here. I can only disturb him. I've come for myself, not for him.*

'Yes.' A shrivelled arm moved a little as if perhaps the priest wanted to shake hands.

Robert took the striving hand. It was cold. He held it between his own for a few moments, then put it back gently across the sunken chest, trying to cover it with the bedclothes.

'I met Robert by accident,' Mary said. 'When I told him I was coming here he said he would like to see you again.'

Father Campbell seemed to slip away on one of his drifting journeys. They sat at the bed in silence. Outside, the trees still had sunlight on them but Robert felt cold. It was a miserable place for a man to die. The pillowcases, he noticed, had some faint lettering on them as if words had once been stencilled there. He realized with a shock that they were flour bags, so thin and faded with age that the miller's name had almost disappeared. The luxury amidst which he lived, the riches he was amassing, even his ambitions, suddenly seemed shameful. He could not have said why. Certainly he wouldn't want to lie ill in a room like this, so comfortless and ugly. There could be no virtue in poverty. Poverty in itself could not induce worthiness in God's eyes. Robert was startled to find himself thinking of God. He was glad when Father Campbell began to speak, his lips twisting unnaturally and his tongue seeming to get in the way—and yet, the words easily understood.

'I've been ill . . . but the nuns have been very good to me.'

'Yes. Mary and I were saying how hard they work.'

'They're saints . . . some of them. Mary was a nurse until she became ill.'

Mary leaned forward. 'That was a long time ago, Father.'

The priest turned from her. It seemed to be Robert whom he wanted to speak to now. 'You are not a Catholic, Robert . . . I remember that.'

'No.'

'But you've come to see me.'

Robert felt a slight choking in his throat.

'I'm happy you came.'

The door opened and the Highland nun came in again. She stopped at the foot of the bed. 'You're a popular man, Father,' she said. 'Such lovely young visitors. They do our poor house credit.' She went to the head of the bed and rearranged his pillows, then went off again up the room.

Father Campbell's hand trembled slowly towards his head. 'It was a hemorrhage I had. Something small, I think. Unfortunately, it was of the brain—I suppose it went to the weakest place.' He smiled and his hand fell back on to his chest. He was sleeping when they left.

'You're very quiet,' Mary said as they sat in Robert's carriage on the drive back into Glasgow. 'The sight of someone so ill has depressed you. Perhaps you shouldn't have come.'

'I suppose in your years as a nurse you became accustomed to seeing people like that.'

'That sounds almost like an accusation.'

'It wasn't intended as one.'

'I don't think he's unhappy, do you?'

'No. And I think you were right. He was glad to see me.'

'Oh, he was. I'm sure of it. Something tells me he'll have one less thing to worry about now.'

'If only he was in a nicer place.'

'He doesn't mind.'

'I suppose not, but it seems a dreadful departure point even when the destination is everlasting life.'

She made no reply and he pondered his strange bitterness all the way to Queen Street Station. It had something to do, he felt, with the forceful reminder he had had that there were people whose happiness did not depend on material prosperity. He had been surrounded all his life by people with possessions and who judged other people by the possessions they had. He had never doubted the soundness of this test and he resented being betrayed into questioning its validity now—even for a few moments.

They waited for Mary's train almost in silence. It was still light and birds sang on the girders under the glass roof of the station. There was a smell of steam and smoke and a noisy bustle about the place that usually pleased Robert. Where were all these people going? What took them from home? Tonight he looked at them with disinterest. He had to force himself into cheerfulness.

'There's a quality to the countryside in the late evening that I always find attractive,' he said. 'I quite envy you the journey.'

He knew now that she was no longer the girl—or perhaps he was no longer the man—of five years ago. Yet he was reluctantly drawn by the riddle of this calm smile, by the friendliness that seemed to dissolve and recede as you tried to touch it, as if the real girl was always somewhere farther on. Why couldn't he accept his bewilderment instead of feeling he must understand her now, even if only for a moment? He was reminded of how he kept returning to some of his father's paintings, trying to fathom the quality he knew to be there but could neither grasp nor forget.

'Yes, a lovely softness comes down at the end of a day like this,' she said. 'Even the word for it has a beautiful sound. *Twilight*. Or our own Scottish word. *Gloaming*.'

He snatched clumsily at her hand. 'This won't be the last time I'll see you, Mary?'

She seemed surprised at the fierceness of his grasp. 'I think it should be,' she said.

'No.' *Why did he persist?*

A porter went past calling out that the Edinburgh train was now at the platform. There was a loud shriek of escaping steam which made her answer inaudible. She repeated it. 'There's little point in us seeing each other again, Robert.'

Her calm seemed a little shaken. Or was she only thinking of her train?

'At least give me your address.'

'Why?'

'So that I'll know where you are.'

She told him and he scribbled it down as they walked quickly towards her train. She stopped him at the barrier. 'Don't come any further.'

'I must see you get a seat.'

'There will be many seats.'

She turned and waved to him as she stepped into a carriage but although he waited until the train left she did not appear again.

There was hope the Zulu War would soon end. If the Irish Fenians could also be quelled, the Empire would be quiet again. Meantime, there was Sir Arthur Sullivan's 'The Lost Chord' for comfort. It was two years old now but still being played everywhere. It had been hailed as the song of the century.

It seemed to follow Fergus and Rita wherever they went during the two days they spent in London at the end of June. It was even played in the restaurant where they dined a few hours after the investiture by the Queen at Buckingham Palace.

Fergus was embarrassed when asked for his name whilst making the table reservation.

'Sir Fergus King.' His voice sounded strangely hollow.

Was there such a person? Until that morning, no, not officially. Only since the Queen had lightly touched his shoulder with her sword.

The man taking the reservation looked at him with interest and respect, but to Fergus it seemed suspicion. Rita laughed when, seated in a candlelit alcove, he confessed his diffidence to her.

'I'm sure I'll feel exactly the same way, my dear, the first time anybody refers to me as Lady King. I suppose it's a bit like wearing a new hat. A certain measure of self-consciousness is inevitable.'

Fergus, who had never thought to hear his baronetcy likened to a hat, marvelled at Rita's homely acceptance of their new grandeur. It was comforting. He had come out of the palace and walked across the courtyard towards the lunchtime sightseers, experiencing a lonely sense of anticlimax. Why had he wanted this distinction so much? And now that he had it why did he have such a feeling that perhaps he would have been better without it—perhaps more at ease unnoticed in the ranks? He cursed the ruinous introspection that was inseparable from his Highland nature.

'We will soon become accustomed to it,' Rita was saying. 'It's nice to have but it won't really make much difference.' She was resolutely keeping from her mind Robert's part in the affair. At times she could even convince herself that Fergus would have acquired a title by merit alone. Robert had merely hastened the day—wasted his money. If he was married he would have other things to spend it on.

'I do believe you are in danger of becoming glum, my dear.' She looked at his empty glass. 'Why don't you have a brandy?'

He swithered and then smiled. 'I'd better not. I've done very well.'

They sat for a few more minutes until Rita, sighing contentedly, said, 'Well, I suppose we had better think about getting back to the hotel. I have enjoyed the excitement of this trip but I won't be sorry to be home.'

Fergus gave her a fond look. In the kindly candleglow it might have been Gwen sitting there. She looked so young. 'You are never happy to leave home for long, Rita. You haven't changed.'

'I suppose not, dear.'

357

'I know. Home's best, but . . .' he fingered his beard thoughtfully '. . . I had been thinking we might steal another day. There's
so much we haven't seen in London. It may be years before we
come back.'

Rita opened her handbag and looked into it. 'But our arrangements are for tomorrow, Fergus . . . the hotel booking and our
reservations on the train.' It was a faint protest.

He waved negligently. 'That can all be attended to, my dear.'

'But there is another consideration, Fergus.' She closed her handbag and leaned forward. 'I was not supposed to tell you but I can
see I'm going to have to.'

His head tilted.

'There's no need to look worried. It's simply that Robert has
prepared a surprise. And here am I about to spoil it.'

'Well?' He was remembering other surprises Robert had given
him. 'Speak up, Rita.'

'Robert has planned a reception . . . a ball.'

'A ball! What for?'

'He thinks there should be a celebration.'

'What's he got to celebrate?'

'Silly! It's not for him. It's for you. He wants to celebrate your
getting the title.'

Fergus puffed. 'Is that necessary? He knows I don't like to fuss.
Everybody knows about the title now. Let's get used to it quietly.
Dear knows!'

'I'm afraid you won't be able to stop him. The invitations are out.
There will be over three hundred guests. I didn't realize we knew
so many people.'

'But neither Ardfern nor Park Place will hold all those people,
I could understand a small family party . . .' He shook his head.
'He's flying too high, as usual.'

'It's not to be at Ardfern or Park Place. Those are our houses.
Robert wants this to be his affair. He had decorators and workmen
ready to move into one of the empty warehouses at Lochbank the
day we left.'

'The distillery! What an idea! Those old warehouses are like
barns.'

'He's having a hardwood floor put in for dancing and the walls
will be draped. He says it will be very grand. He has taken profes-

358

sional advice and the catering is to be done by one of the big hotels.'

'Does he realize what that will cost?'

Rita shrugged. 'That's a matter for Robert.' She patted his arm reassuringly. 'I'm afraid you'll just have to grin and bear it, Fergus. After all, it's very kind of Robert. He was determined to do it. I think it will give him great pleasure.'

Fergus leaned back with a resigned expression. 'Well, I would hate to deny him that,' he said cryptically. He looked round the room. 'Where's our waiter? I think I'll have a brandy, after all.'

# 21

The guests were announced resoundingly by a servant in scarlet and gold livery. Sir Charles and Lady Moncreiff! Professor and Mrs. Hamilton! Provost and Mrs. Macdonald!

Robert extended a tingling hand which so far had been shaken by more than two hundred people.

In full Highland evening dress of red tartan kilt and blue tightly-buttoned tunic, the lace jabot delicate against his tanned face, he was a man transformed. The soberly-dressed and slightly stiff Glasgow businessman had become a figure of dash and splendour. His stance was strong and solid, his eyes bright as he surveyed the swirl of fashionable women and bemedalled men.

Laughter and excited voices filled the grassy stretch in front of him as guests lingered with drinks in the soft evening light. Others, having admired the view, had gone inside, for at last the long day's sun had slipped away.

In the afterglow, the mountain tops were aflame. A scented breeze spread smooth ripples of gold across the loch and swayed the wild foxgloves.

In a field set aside for carriages, horses dipped into brimming nosebags. Coachmen, bright in uniforms of red, blue, green and gold, dusted harnessing and smooth monogrammed coachwork. A marquee had been erected for them and from it laughing men emerged with tankards of foaming beer.

McNair, stiff and uncomfortable in formal dress, suddenly took his wife's arm and led her across the grass to another couple standing apart from the resplendent groups.

'This,' McNair said with a sigh of relief, 'is Peter Ross. And, no doubt, Mrs. Ross.'

The ladies bowed self-consciously, rustling in their unaccustomed finery.

'Thank God for the sight of somebody I know,' Ross said, relaxing visibly as he grasped McNair's big hand. 'And thank God for such a crowd. We can get lost in it.'

He pulled at the lapels of his tail coat. 'I don't know about you, McNair, but this is the first time I've been done up like this. We're not used to high society. I feel like a trussed turkey.'

'You've got me for company,' McNair said wryly. Then, quickly, as if guilty of disloyalty, 'But we mustna complain. Mr. King's tailor must have worked through the night making these togs for us.'

Mrs. McNair, her round, motherly face flushed with excitement, said, 'I don't know why you're so worried, Andrew. Mr. Ross and you look very distinguished.'

'Aye, so long as we keep our mouths shut I suppose we'll pass for gentlemen,' Ross said with a grin.

His wife, a tall, dark-haired woman, had gained confidence from the company. 'Well, don't let it give you a taste for the high life, Peter,' she said playfully. 'Tomorrow you'll be back to old clothes and porridge.'

Mrs. McNair, who had the same squat look as her husband, said, 'In these clothes men all look the same, but the magnificent gowns these ladies are wearing make me feel shabby.'

For a few moments the two wives stood looking about in wonder, silently comparing their own simple and inexpensive dresses with the exciting products of London and Paris. Tiaras and necklaces, diamonds and sapphires, rubies and emeralds, sparkled in the glowing air and here and there sable capes were drawn closer as the first hint of evening's chill touched the breeze.

'A hundred pounds wouldn't pay for some of those gowns,' Mrs. Ross said enviously.

Her husband's eyes twinkled as he nudged McNair. 'It would seem some of them hadn't the money left to get a proper top put on, especially at the front.'

Mrs. McNair, whose own broad bosom was well covered, hovered between a blush and a demure laugh. 'I hope they don't catch cold.'

'Ross! McNair!'

361

It was Robert hurrying towards them, silver buttons and buckles gleaming. He took Mrs. McNair's rough hand, sympathizing with her nervous smile. For them, he knew, the pleasure would be tinged with embarrassment. But only for a time. Soon there would be such a whirl of fun that their inhibitions would slip away. 'Madam, you look charming,' he said, giving her fingers a friendly squeeze of reassurance.

He turned. 'And this must be Mrs. Ross, who looks equally charming.' And, he thought, not just so overawed.

Ross nodded towards the display of wealth and elegance. 'This is a grand occasion, Mr. King. Too grand for the likes of us, but your father and mother will be pleased.'

Robert made a face. 'Father's still complaining at the fuss.' He hesitated. 'But don't think it's just for him. It's for you as well.'

'For us?'

'Well, for all of us in King & Co. After all, our luck has changed.' He turned to the women. 'Your husbands know what I mean. The company has reason to celebrate.'

The women smiled without understanding. Ross, seeing their expressions, said, 'You see, Mr. King had a long struggle.' He gave Robert a staunch look. 'But he's won his fight.'

McNair's voice rumbled impatiently into the ensuing silence. 'You're puzzling them more than ever, Ross. Can I call a spade a spade, Mr. King?'

Robert nodded. 'You usually do.'

'Well,' McNair said bluntly, 'there was a boycott against Mr. King's whisky. Some of the old distillers tried to crush the life out of him. The devils wouldn't sell him the whisky he needed. Well, their damned boycott has collapsed. Mr. King's able to buy what he wants now.'

Robert laughed at McNair's angry expression and raised voice.

'You must forgive us, ladies. It seems we men can't forget our work.'

Wisps of white cloud trailed over Ben Lomond and on the lower slopes bell heather was opening in a gentle blue haze.

'It's a beautiful place to work.' Mrs. Ross sounded enchanted. 'Peter pointed out your cottage to me,' she said to the McNairs. 'I envy you living here. Even the air seems scented.'

'That's the water lilies, Mrs. Ross.' McNair pointed to the hill behind the distillery. 'There's hundreds of them up in the dam.'

Robert signalled to a girl carrying a tray. 'Everyone's going in now,' he said, 'but you have time for another drink before joining them.'

McNair declined the punch and took a glass of King's Royal. His wife watched him savour it. 'He thinks and talks whisky, these days,' she said proudly.

'Well, before we drift on to that subject again. . . .' Robert took her dance card and then Mrs. Ross's. 'I hope I can reserve a little of your time for later in the evening.' He put his name on both cards. 'And now I'll have to get back to my post. I see there's another carriage arriving.'

'Your father's, if I'm not mistaken,' Ross said.

Rita's pale green dress was based on the crinoline, but not so voluminous. The neck was cut square, but modestly, and the tiny sleeves were puffed and embroidered. She looked eager and girlish beside Fergus's bulky, well-tailored dignity.

'I think you should go straight in,' Robert said, ushering them forward.

For a moment Fergus froze, stunned by the sight of flowers, silk drapes and chandeliers where before there had been cobwebs, dusty stone and gnarled rafters. Then, recollecting his pose of tolerant protest, he looked round with an elaborate frown. Robert winked at Rita, who had a slightly bemused smile.

Fergus drew slowly on his cigar. 'This will leave a hole in your pocket,' he said slyly.

Robert laughed. 'Let me worry about that, father. Just you concentrate on enjoying yourself, and seeing that mother does likewise.'

Suddenly Fergus smiled, his broad frame relaxing into a comfortable hunch. 'You've done a remarkable job with this place, Robert. You're to be congratulated.'

'I thought you would like it.'

'But those columns can't be real marble?'

'No, they're painted, but very cleverly.'

'There's only one thing missing—a staircase for the ladies to come down.'

'They'll just have to look beautiful without it.'

Fergus' eyes were still exploring. 'I had a look at the guest list before we left home. You don't seem to have forgotten anybody.'

'I hope not. There was only one non-acceptance.' His eyes were mischievous.

'Oh?'

'Yes. Arthur Morrison's.'

Fergus' expression became half-scandalized, half-amused. 'You didn't have the cheek to invite him?'

'I couldn't resist it.'

'No. You wouldn't. You always have believed in rubbing things in.' He raised his head slightly. 'There's rather a strange scent in here. What is it?'

'Gwen tells me it's French perfume. Very expensive stuff.'

Fergus looked suspiciously at Rita but she, bathed in the innocent fragrance of lily of the valley, shook her head to disclaim responsibility.

He waggled his beard. 'I wasn't aware that French perfume was now . . . accepted . . . in our society.'

'I like it,' Robert said in a way that invited agreement, his expression quizzical.

Fergus appeared to be seeking out the perfumed ladies. 'Yes,' he said, sounding as if he felt he should have been saying 'No.'

Rita laughed. 'Even some of the best shops in Buchanan Street now have it on the counters, Fergus. Along with face powder and rouge. I must say, I was surprised the first time I saw it. Until recently, they kept it out of sight.'

Fergus turned decisively from the glittering fashions. 'Why don't you have one of those fancy handbags, Rita?'

'Oh, vanity cases are only for very fashionable ladies, Fergus.' Her manner was airy. 'I don't need one.'

Her smile, he thought, was wistful and her answer puzzling. She was the best-dressed and most attractive woman in the place. What was she talking about?

'Then why do they need them? What do they keep in them?'

'Powder puffs and maquillage, though most of them wouldn't admit it.'

'Oh.' Before Fergus could comment further on this revelation they were surrounded by a number of laughing couples.

'Sir Fergus! Lady King! What a happy occasion!'

Another couple appeared.

'Father! Mother!' It was Gwen, flushed and breathless but sparkling from the polka she had danced with Colin Lindsay. 'What a beautiful dress. I'm sure you didn't get that one for ten shillings.'

'No, I'm afraid it was very expensive.'

Robert, who had been watching the door, straightened suddenly, squaring his shoulders. He kissed Rita quickly on the cheek. 'Father's going to love every minute of it,' he whispered. 'But I must go. Fiona has just arrived. She has travelled specially from Perth to be here.'

He walked eagerly to the door, thinking that if Fergus had been perturbed by French perfume Fiona's gown would be an even greater disturbance to him.

It was of billowing pink tulle, the satin bodice ending in a sharp point above the waist. The decolletage was startling and on anyone less exuberantly open and healthy might have looked brazen. The skirt was trimmed with a spray of artificial roses. She carried a fan and in her hair there was a small ornament of exotic feathers.

He took her hands and kissed her, his admiration warm and undisguised. 'You look radiant, Fiona. And how glad I am to see you. There are three hundred people here but I've felt rather lonely.'

The affection in her smile was lingering. 'And you are magnificent, Robert. I've never seen you wear the kilt.'

'I thought something special was called for.'

'Which tartan is it?'

'Our own. The MacGregor. The Kings are a sept of the clan.'

He gave her his arm and led her across the floor aware that, as always, she was the focus of many male eyes. The orchestra had begun to play a Viennese waltz.

'Will we dance, or would you like a glass of wine first?'

She gave him a dreamy look, leaning close. 'Fill me first with kindly wine then take me to the ball.'

'You sound like Colin Lindsay.' He clasped her hand. 'But you look as only you can.'

She laughed. 'Colin Lindsay couldn't write a line like that. It's stuck in my mind from a play I saw years ago.'

They sat for a while happy in each other's company, then rose to the tugging strains of a violin.

As he felt her closeness he was filled with unwanted thoughts.

The old Fiona had gone. But what was to be done about this new one? He cursed the faint guilt she could inspire in him now. As they moved in graceful patterns he was preoccupied. She was as enticing as ever—in fact, more than ever, since spoiled youth had gone and a share of life's burdens had settled so charmingly on her smooth shoulders. As they turned and then came towards each other he let his fingers slide over scented skin. The intimacy of her slow smile told him that she knew the caress was not accidental.

'I think you've missed me, Robert.'

She could never resist teasing him, but now it provoked more than a mere physical response. Could this melting partnership, he wondered, induced tonight by the spell of wine and music, be successfully extended to a life shared? Bafflingly, he saw another girl and felt the pull of another mysterious attraction. Resolutely he banished the distant threat, willingly surrendering in the magic of the moment to Fiona's more immediate and bountiful allure.

Colonel and Mrs. Maclean! The Hon. Simon Forbes and Mrs. Forbes! Bailie and Mrs. Paterson!

The voice at the door boomed tirelessly on.

'I didn't know the Kings moved in such exalted circles,' Colin Lindsay said as he walked Gwen to the long supper tables, laid with silver and crystal dishes.

'Neither did I.' Gwen was tired from nights of sleepless worry and she was looking forward to sitting after the strenuous dancing. 'Robert's really showing off. But shouldn't he still be at the door to meet these people?'

'I don't suppose he can be expected to stand there all night. Besides ...' Lindsay's smile was significant '... I think Fiona Fraser's taking up all his attention.'

'With that dress, I'm not surprised.' Gwen had never forgotten Fiona's youthful reputation.

Lindsay was staring at the buffet. 'Whoever arranged this is an artist,' he said. 'It seems a shame to eat it.'

There were quails stuffed with foie gras, langoustes, salmon cutlets and mousses made of chicken and ham—all beautifully embellished and displayed.

Beside them a girl squealed as a young man handed her a plate on which sat a mince pie covered with flaming brandy sauce.

'There,' said Lindsay, 'is a cunning combination of the plebeian and the exotic. Shall we have some?'

Gwen looked doubtful. 'No. I'll have something cold, Colin. I'll leave the exotic to you.' She glanced along the tables. 'What I'm really looking forward to are those sumptuous jellies and creams.'

They filled their plates then hurried across the floor as a couple vacated a luxurious settee with gilded ornamentation and pink damask upholstery. Lindsay settled his humble pie on a marble table and watched with interest as the transforming flame subsided. 'These could be dangerous for men with beards,' he remarked as he stuck a fork in it.

In a high slit window above them twilight gathered and stars appeared.

'I hope I'm not monopolizing you, Gwen,' Lindsay said after a while as if struck suddenly by the possibility.

'Of course not, Colin. I'm grateful for your company.'

Company? It saddened him that it could be no more. He looked at her closely. To say she looked tired would be tactless, but he could not resist a comment.

'It must be very worrying for you with Tom in Africa.'

'Yes.' She appreciated his sympathetic interest. 'He's always in my mind, but I try to take a little comfort from the fact that thousands of wives have the same anxiety.'

There was an unselfish understanding in the remark that he thought typical of her.

Hoey had often been in his thoughts since his sudden homecoming had nipped what Lindsay had felt to be a blossoming friendship with Gwen. He could see now that the fond feeling he had cherished for her in her loneliness, and still felt, had been foolish. But it persisted however much he tried to quell it. There could be no future for him with Gwen. She was a married woman in love with her husband. Even before Hoey's return he had been closing his mind to reality. And yet, tonight he had been irresistibly drawn to her. Not that there was anything unnatural or improper in that. She was unpartnered and she was an old friend. If he could help distract her from her anxieties for a few hours he would have performed a small service of . . . affection. It could be no more than that.

A servant removed their empty plates. With an inward sigh for his romantic and unrealizable dreams Lindsay rose.

'Now for the wicked sweet things,' he said with determined brightness. 'I see James over there tucking into them.'

As he spooned a sticky assortment on to two plates he wondered how Gwen had thought of him before Hoey's return. That he had been fond of him, and had come to rely on him a little, she didn't doubt. And being a woman, she could hardly have failed to sense the growing warmth of his attentions. If there had been no Hoey. ... What? Lindsay comforted himself with the thought that where there had been fondness love might in time have followed. He crossed the floor in a dream.

Something in his expression as he handed her a plate filled Gwen with a flash of tender understanding for which, thinking of Hoey in Africa, she at once felt guilty.

She looked at the mouth-watering jellies heaped with cream. 'Thank you, Colin,' she said, 'I don't know what I'd do without you,' and could have bitten her tongue for the look of gratitude that came on his face.

Around them, the merriment heightened. As a goblet was emptied a servant would immediately appear from the tangle of balloons and streamers to refill it.

Except on the fringes, conversation could be conducted only in competition with the music and the cannonade of champagne corks. The reels became faster and noisier and the jigs more thunderous. As one set of exhausted couples sank on to settees or chairs another surged on to the floor.

So uninhibited was the fun that McNair and Ross squared their shoulders and asked Gwen and Rita to dance. Fergus mellowed to the point where he was able to lead Fiona gallantly through the Brownie's Reel with only half his mind on the calamity he was certain must overtake her dress.

There was the Petronella and the Strip the Willow. When the first orchestra was worn out another took over.

And when the guests with furthest to travel were ready to leave Athole Brose was served to see them on their way.

Robert, watching the mixture of whisky and honey being strained through oatmeal, felt his arm grasped roughly and heard an excited voice at his ear.

'The Malt House is on fire.'

He stared into McNair's face, the words hardly registering.

'One o' the men's just been in. I had a quick look, and it's bad.'

McNair's expression had more force than his words. 'How bad?'

'The roof's ablaze.'

'Where's Ross?'

'Out there seeing what he can do.'

'Tell my father, then round up all the men you can. There's a field full of coachmen out there.'

He turned and shouldered his way unceremoniously through the dancers leaving startled faces staring after him.

As the fresh air struck him he stood for a moment breathing deeply, preparing himself for the unthinkable. Then, running, he turned a corner of the warehouse and stopped again, staring in horror. At one end of the Malt House flames had burst through the roof. In the glare he saw smoke gushing from the high ventilator that gave the distillery its distinctive pagoda top.

Figures moved in front of the burning building. He ran to join them and recognized some of the workers.

'Is there anyone in there?'

'They're a' oot,' the nearest man spluttered, choking as they were swamped by smoke.

Robert pulled the man clear. 'What happened? How did it start?'

'Ah don't know, Mr. King. We were workin' in the Still House when we smelled fire. When we rin oot this is what we saw.'

The Malt House and Still House were in fact one building with a wall separating the two sections. At one end, barley was soaked and allowed to germinate before being dried in a kiln over burning peat. The dry, friable malt went into storage bins until needed for mashing, brewing, fermenting and, finally, distilling.

The contents of the bins, Robert realized, would have gone up like straw when fire reached them.

Ross came running. 'The Still House is full of smoke but there's no fire yet.' He had thrown off his tail coat and now he tore open his collar. 'I thought I'd choke in there.'

Panic rose in Robert. 'What the Hell can we do?'

A fire in the country, he knew, was usually totally destructive. 'They've got a fire brigade in Glasgow now, maybe one in Dumbarton, but there's nothing within miles of us here.'

Ross shook his head. 'We'll get no help from the butts, Mr. King. We'll hae to fight it ourselves.'

'With what? We don't have a pump.'

They staggered back, covering their heads, as sparks from the roof showered them. The roar of the flames was loud now and slates cracked like pistol shots. One flew past Robert's head.

'Look out for those slates,' he shouted to the men.

Guests were coming from the converted warehouse. The music had stopped. Nearer, McNair and the coachmen he had collected pounded over the grass.

'Get buckets and pails, anything that'll hold water.' Robert ordered. 'We can fill them at the reservoir. The Malt House is finished but there's a chance we might save the still.'

This was the heart of the distillery. They could buy in malt, but if the still, that great copper retort shaped like an onion with the neck of a swan, was destroyed Lochbank was finished.

'God save us. This is terrible.' It was Fergus, wild-eyed and panic-stricken. Behind him came a throng of guests, their fine clothes strange in the baleful glow, jewellery reflecting the fire.

A woman screamed as a burning timber arched through the air and landed at her feet, flames scorching her dress.

'Keep those women back,' Robert shouted. 'Get them to Hell out of the way.'

The women, startled at the rudeness, began to retreat, shooed by some of the men.

McNair came out of a shed with men carrying ladders. They put them against the Still House wall and McNair led a group of them on to the roof while others scrambled towards the dam carrying buckets. Soon a chain of buckets was being passed down the hill and on to the roof. Steam hissed and rose in scalding clouds as the crouching men threw water at the advancing blaze.

Robert and Fergus led another group of guests and coachmen into the smoke-filled Still House and threw water wildly. Through the smoke they saw the partition wall glowing red. And in the centre, like some great beseiged idol the still reared, throbbing, it seemed to the roar of the fire.

Robert had thrown away his jacket and torn off his jabot. Repeatedly, his shirt torn and stained, he ran through the fumes

370

hurling water towards the wall. It was bulging now and beginning to crumble.

Once, as he came out, he saw a woman pass, tottering from the weight of a water-filled container. It was Fiona. He caught her arm. Her dress was wet, torn and blackened. Her hair hung about her shoulders in damp strands.

'Get back with the rest of the women,' he gasped. 'Leave this to us.'

Despite his hand on her arm she splashed the water she was carrying through the Still House door, then fell coughing and choking.

'I want to help, Robert.'

'It's too dangerous.' His hand tightened on her arm.

'It's just as dangerous for you.'

He dragged her away. 'I'm here because it's my distillery.'

'Part of it's mine,' she sobbed, the tears running from her stinging eyes. 'Don't forget that.'

She struggled clear and began running back to the dam.

Fergus paused long enough to splutter a bark of admiration. 'My God,' he said hoarsely, 'that girl has pluck.'

Soon the whisky casks in the Still House began bursting. The rending explosions sent burning wood flying from the gaping roof. Waves of searing air engulfed the nearest men, sending them backwards, beating their hands at the showering particles of fire. Then, from the door and from every crack at the base of the building, streams of liquid fire began to run. The burning spirit quickly formed a creeping sea of fire trickling eerily towards No. 1 warehouse. Shrubs in its path exploded into flame, driving the blackened men before it.

Robert dropped his bucket and leaped forward. 'Leave it,' he shouted. 'We've done all we can. The still's bound to go next. The whole bloody building will go up with it.'

For a moment they stood as if transfixed and then let him herd them to the sheltering walls of No. 1 warehouse.

McNair, blackened like a sweep, faced Fergus and Robert with his shoulders drooping. 'Ah'm sorry,' he said in a broken voice. 'If the still goes up we'll be out of production for at least six months.'

'It'll go up, all right,' Fergus said bitterly.

'Ah can't help thinkin' I'm responsible.'

They looked at him. 'Why?'

'I'm in charge here.'

Robert shrugged impatiently. 'It's nothing to do with you.'

'But how did it happen, Mr. King? We've got strict fire precautions.' His voice flared. 'If I find any of them were up to anythin' they shouldn't . . . ' His fists clenched.

Fergus looked at Robert with a strange expression.

Robert, sensing something in his father that had been vaguely hovering in his own mind, said, 'Are you thinking what I'm thinking, Father?'

Fergus, his eyes on the blazing mass, shuddered. 'You don't mean . . . the pot distillers?'

'Well, somebody put up to it by them.'

'My God, Robert, it's a terrible thought,'

'That day I bumped into Morrison in Glasgow I saw he hated us. Maybe a court case isn't enough for him.'

'I don't know what to think.'

'I don't suppose we'll ever know, but if it should turn out. . . .'

Before he could finish there was a blinding flash and a blast that sent them reeling. The Still House split asunder. For a moment it hung in the air, then, the masonry hurtling everywhere, it subsided in an inferno of blue and orange light. As they staggered away the high-proof liquid contents of the still came spurting out to join the river of burning whisky.

'Jesus, that's what I was afraid of.' It was Ross, pointing to the floating fire. 'It's heading for No. 1 warehouse. If we can't stop it that whisky in there will go the same way.'

Robert watched in petrified dismay. Thousands of gallons of matured whisky, the result of years of distillation, lay in racks in the warehouse. The still could be rebuilt but the old whisky was irreplaceable.

'We haven't a hope of stopping it,' Fergus said.

McNair tugged at Robert's arm. 'There might be a way.'

Robert shook his head.

'There might be a way,' McNair said again. 'If we breached the dam. . . .'

'Breached the dam?'

'Aye. There's millions of gallons of water up there. If we let it out. . . .'

For a moment Robert's heart rose, then dropped. 'Those old sluice gates are rusted solid. You told me so yourself.'

'We could blow the dam apart.'

'With what?'

McNair pointed. 'That old shed's full of paraffin.'

Fergus had heard. 'Would it work?'

Ross seized Robert's arm. 'We could try, Mr. King.'

Robert turned decisively to Fergus. 'Leave this to us. Clear everybody out of here. If we can do it there'll be a deluge.' He stopped and turned about. 'Where's Fiona? Make sure you take her with you.'

Fergus gave him a look. 'Don't worry about Fiona. I'll tie her up if necessary.' A wan smile appeared on Robert's worried face. 'You'll probably have to.'

McNair was already on his way, shouting. 'Bring as much rope as you can find, Mr. King. We'll use it to lash the drums in place, and then as a fuse.'

Ross and McNair ran to the shed, rolled out a fifty-gallon drum of paraffin and manhandled it up the rocky hillside. The dam had been formed of logs spiked together.

'The sluice gate's the weakest point,' McNair said. 'We can fix the drums to it.'

The reservoir was at its summer level and the top of the dam was above water. Carefully they rolled the drum along the top until they reached the gate. As they manoeuvred it into position Robert joined them with a coil of rope.

'I'll lash this down,' he said, 'while you two get another drum.'

By the time he had finished, slithering and slipping on the slimy logs, McNair and Ross were back. They lashed the second drum beside the first.

Below them, fire had taken hold of No. 1 warehouse. Flames from the Still House shot high and close to the loch a belt of birch trees was on fire. Robert glanced at the nightmare scene, the loch bathed in orange light and the sky blackened with smoke. No. 1 warehouse, he saw, was in a direct line from the dam.

'This might just work,' he said, gasping from exertion and the fumes in his aching lungs. He saw the flickering faces of the guests grouped round the building where so recently they had been dancing and drinking.

Ross knocked the bung out of the top drum and pushed a length of rope inside. He pulled it out dripping with paraffin.

'Keep it short,' McNair said. 'There isn't much time.'

Robert looked at the drums. They were small against the bulk of the dam. 'Will two be enough?'

Ross straightened out the fuse. 'All we want to do is blow a hole in it. Once the flood starts it'll tear the whole thing apart.'

'Then I hope to God we can get clear.'

McNair brandished a box of matches. 'Start getting clear now,' he said grimly. 'Both of you. I'll give you a minute's start.'

Robert reached for the matches. 'I'll do that.'

But McNair was quicker. 'I seem to remember you saying once you couldn't swim.'

'Can you?'

'A bit, but I hope I won't have to.'

'How long will that fuse last?'

'Ah don't know.' McNair gave a diabolical grin. 'Ah've never done this before.' He took a match from the box. 'Now run like hell for high ground.'

'For God's sake be careful.' Robert shot a last worried glance at McNair and then, with Ross behind him, slithered across the dam to the bank. They reached it in seconds and ran up the hill.

They turned and saw McNair silhouetted against the fire's glow, crouched over the paraffin drums. A match flared and then the fuse spluttered into fire. For ages, it seemed, McNair did not move. Robert rose, shouting.

'What the Hell are you waiting for?'

'He'll want to make sure it's lit,' Ross said. 'Here he comes.'

With beating hearts they watched McNair rise, fire streaking along the rope behind him. Twice he fell, once almost sliding into the water. Then he was ashore and scrambling to join them. As they pulled him, exhausted, behind sheltering boulders, the fire reached the paraffin.

A white, smoky flame shot six feet above the dam, lighting the water lilies. For seconds that was all. When the blast came it was as a surprise. Flame belched in a wide circle and as suddenly went out. A gusher of water rose white to the sky and came deluging over them. Above the rumble of the fire they heard wood creak as water surged through the gap where the sluice gates had been. As the pressure mounted the broken logs on either side shuddered and groaned and then disintegrated, releasing a tidal wave.

'We've done it,' Robert shouted.

They stood watching the frothing flood tumble down the shallow valley towards No. 1 warehouse, spreading wider the further it travelled. The foaming breaker in front was tinged with orange as it neared the fire. As fire and water met there was almost instant blackness and a volcano of hissing steam. So sudden was the transformation that they stood in dumb wonder, unable to grasp the completeness of their success.

Then, above the roar of the surging flood, they heard cheering.

Robert waved a limp acknowledgment. 'It's out,' was all he could say.

McNair, his voice a croak, said, 'At least we've saved the whisky.'

As they went wearily down the hill Robert saw a figure break away from the crowd. It was Fiona. They met by a blackened tree. For a moment they stood looking at each other and then she was in his arms.

'Your beautiful dress is ruined,' he said tenderly, stroking her hair. 'I'll have to buy you another.'

Her laugh was little more than a sob of relief.

'Is that all you can say, Robert? It was you I was afraid for. I wanted to be with you, but your father kept me back.'

His arms tightened round her. 'What a girl you are, Fiona,' he said softly.

She lifted her head from his shoulder and faced him with a hint of her impish smile. 'And what does that mean?'

'I'll tell you some other time.'

McNair and Ross, grinning sootily, left them embracing in the darkness on the edge of the thundering water.


In an engagement three weeks before the Zulu War ended on July 4, Hoey won the Queen's Medal for bravery. News of the award was published on the day Lord Beaconsfield announced the capture of King Cetewayo and the surrender of his people.

Few details were given in the short official citation. Gwen and the family had to content themselves with knowing he had twice crossed a river on the heights above which two thousand Zulus were massed for one of the last battles of the war.

Gwen's pride was exceeded by her relief that the war was over and Hoey was safe. Her happiness was only slightly dented by a footnote to a letter from him a few days later. The regiment had been ordered home, but not to Scotland. They were to take up garrison duties at Dublin Castle for a few months.

'It's almost as good as being home,' Rita said when Gwen gave her the news. 'You'll be able to visit Tom in Ireland.'

'I suppose I could.' Gwen brightened visibly.

'Of course,' Fergus said. 'It's no distance. A boat sails from the Clyde every afternoon and docks in Dublin next morning.'

Fergus, shocked though he still was by the loss of the distillery, had been impressed by Hoey's award and had steeled himself to add a congratulatory postscript to one of Gwen's letters. It was not so much that he felt Hoey's unexpected conduct had cleaned the slate. It was more basic than that—more disturbing. Perhaps the Man About Town had a strong credit side to his nature after all. When he thought about Hoey, Fergus had a sudden sense of hurrying time. He would be old. He realized with a shock that Gwen and Hoey would soon be middle-aged. He must try to ensure some stability for Gwen in the years to come. The hopeful gleam struck in far Africa must not be allowed to fade. What was good in Hoey must be encouraged. Fergus saw his duty clearly and, for the first time in years, he made an effort to speak about his son-in-law almost as he would any other member of his family.

'How does Tom think he'll like being garrisoned in Ireland?' he asked Gwen when they were seated one day on either side of the fire in her shop.

'I had a letter from him yesterday,' she said. 'His quarters at the castle are old-fashioned and uncomfortable but he finds Dublin a splendid city.'

'No word of him getting home for a few days?'

'I'm afraid not. He seems to think it will be months before he gets leave. I told him I would go over there for a week or two. He thinks it a wonderful idea but says I should wait till the regiment's properly settled in. He'll have more free time then.'

'But when will that be?'

'Oh, just a couple of weeks.'

'Good.' Fergus hunched suddenly forward. 'I've been meaning

to ask you, my dear. What exactly are Tom's plans for the future? I mean, does he regard the Army as a permanency?'

Gwen kept looking into the fire so that Fergus wouldn't see her surprise at his sudden change of tone. A moment later she became aware that his gaze was also fixed on the fire. She sensed that the question had cost him a lot in swallowed pride but was in fact only the prelude to something even more personal.

'I really don't know, Father,' she said.

'He obviously makes a good soldier,' Fergus said, 'but unless he's likely to end up a general there isn't much point in it.'

Gwen felt she must resist this dismissal of the Army. 'I wouldn't necessarily say that. I would rather have him at home but I have to admit he seems happiest in uniform. Besides, now the Zulu War is over he'll be at home quite often. And when he's not, I can go to see him. He obviously prefers the Army to a shipping office.'

Fergus found himself persisting. 'Unless there was the likelihood of promotion I would have thought it was a life only for when a man was young,' He leaned forward hesitantly. 'What I want to say, my dear, is this. I wouldn't like Tom to stay on in the Army only because he feels there's nothing else for him. We could manage something.'

They sat in silence for a few moments. The flame of the fire flitted about them on the deep polish of old furniture. Outside, horses' hooves and carriage wheels struck sharp sounds from granite cobbles. Rattling noises came from the back room where Miss Murray polished silver.

Gwen stared unseeingly into the fire. Here at last, plainly and with humility, Fergus was holding out what she had longed for all her married life: ungrudging acceptance of her husband. Strangely, her spirits didn't rise. The hope once cherished lay like a stone on her heart. She knew now that in that direction lay too much risk of upset and misery. Whatever Tom did in the future he must never work for Fergus again. She rose, shivering slightly, and stood behind her father. The warm heart of the fire cast her shadow on a wall.

'I must get Miss Murray to light the lamps,' she said at last. 'I hadn't noticed how dark it's become. I've never seen such an August afternoon. I'm sure there must be a storm coming.'

The evasive rejection of his offer did not escape Fergus. Oddly, he didn't feel rebuffed. He had thrown the lifeline. Gwen knew now it was there. He would tell Hoey himself, of course, when they next met. He sat in the strange summer darkness feeling he had just put down a heavy load. It had been an effort for him to speak, but once started the words had come sincerely. Now he felt a comfortable peace settling about him.

He looked around the shop. He always enjoyed its mellow evocation of another, more leisurely age. But the stock was getting low again! Not a bit of walnut in the place. He never let walnut pass at auctions, but Gwen put such a small profit on that the good pieces went out almost as soon as they came in. Dear knows! She would never learn. Tomorrow was viewing day at Morrison McChlery's. He hoped there would be something worthwhile. He hadn't come across any first-class pieces for ages.

'Good afternoon, Sir Fergus.' Miss Murray passed with a lighted lamp. The green beads of the shade tinkled against the bowl.

He gave her the self-conscious smile that the new style of address could still bring to his face. He tried to guard against this gaucheness but when taken by surprise he couldn't hide his pleasure. Miss Murray, he knew, relished his title, thinking, perhaps, that it made her job even more refined and ladylike.

He said, 'Where did I put my hat, Sadie?'

As he rose, looking about, a fierce flash of light illuminated the shadows of the shop. Miss Murray clutched at the lamp and turned a startled face to the window. Almost immediately a deafening drumroll of thunder crashed over the street. Huge drops of rain began pounding the cobbles. Pedestrians in summer clothes jammed into doorways and closes on the other side of the street.

'I knew something like this was coming,' Gwen said. She came out of the back room with a hand to her cheek. Her voice was a pitch higher than usual. 'Thunder always frightens me.' She gave a short, breathless almost apologetic laugh.

'Thunder can't touch you,' Fergus said with a parent's light-hearted scorn. 'It's the lightning you have to worry about.'

'Thank you, Father.'

He turned away, grinning, as he realized he hadn't helped.

'Sorry, my dear. You're like your mother. One peal of thunder and she wants to get under the table.' He crossed to the window and looked up through the rain to the black sky. 'I hope she's indoors, and has company.'

Another sheet of lightning flashed above the street and Gwen put her hands to her ears as they waited for the thunder.

'In half an hour the sun will probably be shining again,' Fergus said. 'In the meantime, I'll just sit it out here. Don't let me stop you working.' He looked about. 'I put a *Herald* down somewhere.' He took out his watch. 'Isn't it about now Miss Murray puts the kettle on?'

Hoey's letters continued to praise Dublin. The ordinary people were apathetic about Home Rule, he said, and friendly to the troops. Parnell and his kind appealed only to the intellectuals. The Fenians were simply a gang of homicidal maniacs who couldn't see that the past was the past. Two had just been hanged for murdering a land-owner for no other reason than that he was English.

Gwen, who knew little of Irish politics, preferred the passages in Hoey's letters which spoke of Dublin's elegant Georgian houses, the leafy squares, the expensive shops, the sandy strands around the bay. Best of all was his news that in Queenstown, an exclusive seaside suburb, there were houses to be rented by the month. He was in touch with an estate agent. When he found a suitable place she could join him. His duties would allow him to live out of the Castle. Summer by the sea would be pleasant, and a house, even if rented, more homely for her than a hotel. Servants were plentiful, diligent, and good-humoured.

In preparation for her trip to Ireland Gwen went happily around the shops with Rita picking out new dresses and half a dozen hats. Hoey had said the Dublin women were very fashion-conscious. She didn't want to let him down. She urged Fergus to spread his net wider at two or three forthcoming auctions. Miss Murray could be trusted to run the shop efficiently while she was away but she would have to be left with a plentiful supply of goods.

Fergus, since gaining his title, had found himself subjected to increased demands on his time for charitable works. He felt morally bound to accede to some of the requests—he had got what he wanted and he must cheerfully continue to pay the price, even when it went up. Nevertheless, he determined that nothing should inter-fere with the help Gwen had asked for. He set up a wholehearted search for antique furniture and porcelain at auctions throughout Ayrshire, Renfrewshire, and Stirlingshire. For two weeks he felt almost on holiday from business and good works. For the first time in his life he began to suspect that, managed properly, retirement could be congenial. If this was a foretaste of how a man could keep himself happily and usefully occupied, then perhaps in a year or two he might begin gradually to ease into the background. If Hoey continued to be a changed man, and had the sense to give up playing soldiers, there could be good opportunities for him. That still left the problem of James. Fergus shook his beard. Being able to paint was a fine thing, but he wished James would show some sign that he realized the importance of business. Still, that must come. It ran in the family. Even Gwen! Dear knows! James mustn't be pushed or hurried. Life had treated the boy tragically and he must be given time to arrive at things for himself. Presumably he would tire soon of the novel interest he'd found in painting. Some of his seascapes were quite good, especially since he hadn't had a single day's training. It would make a fine hobby for him.

Almost as if Fergus' mellowing must be offset, Robert's appetite for work continued to grow throughout the summer, despite the bruising and stiffness that remained from the night of the fire. The move from Washington Street to their new premises off Argyle Street had been made. Fergus had refused to face the chaos attendant on the huge transfer of stock and machinery. But, as with the Corkcutters' Arms, he appeared for a last sentimental look around. He was surprised to find Robert equally affected by memories.

As Fergus' carriage jolted them out of the broken slum street for the last time, Robert said, 'Perhaps one day they'll put a plaque up for us.'

Fergus looked out at the grey walls. 'What could they say on it?'

'Oh, I don't know. What about—"This was the birthplace of Scotch whisky as we now know it"?'

For Robert, the sentimental mood hardly lasted the drive along Argyle Street. As well as supervising the move to larger premises, taking on extra staff, and dealing with the exciting but taxing problems brought by continually expanding sales, he was deeply involved in organizing his March of a Thousand Pipers.

Fergus had listened to this idea with a bewilderment he tried hard to mask. He had come to realize that his son's mind worked on a different level from his own. Where once he would have protested he now kept quiet. Things seemed to work out. Even Robert's most improbable schemes seemed to yield a good return in terms not only of increased business but even in public goodwill and affection. Things were changing. Everybody was at this new advertising craze. At least Robert hadn't yet sunk as low as Lipton, the ham and egg man. Driving pigs through the streets of Glasgow with LIPTON stencilled on them! Fergus recalled the distasteful spectacle. His carriage had been held up by the crowd for a good fifteen minutes. Dear knows! It wasn't his way of doing business.

The response of pipe bands around Britain to Robert's tentative enquiries was overwhelming. He had contacted regimental pipe bands, police pipe bands, and the pipe bands of various Scottish works, associations, and gatherings. All were eager to compete in the championships he proposed.

Helensburgh town council promised support and some fields on the edge of the town were nominated as the site. The last Saturday in October was to be the day.

'You've been in too much of a hurry,' Fergus said when he learned the date. 'Summer's the time for an event like this.'

'It wasn't possible to have it any earlier,' Robert said. 'You've no idea the work there's been in organizing it at all.'

'Then you should have waited till next year.'

Robert knew this would have been the sensible thing to do, but his impatience had made it impossible. Realizing he had found a weak spot, Fergus persisted.

'You're taking a big risk with the weather in staging a spectacle like that practically in the middle of winter,' he said with exaggerated gloom.

'Nonsense!' Robert was stung despite himself. 'October in the west of Scotland is often one of the loveliest months of the year.'

'It can be cold.' Fergus seemed to enjoy the thought. 'And the days are short. There won't be much fun listening to bagpipes played in the dark.'

Watching the expression of lugubrious relish on his father's face, Robert began to laugh.

'What a picture of misery and disaster. We'll have to issue them all with candles and umbrellas. And if it's as bad as you make out they'll probably play nothing but laments.'

Seeing the humour in his own pessimism, Fergus cheered a little. 'I suppose you'll get away with it, as usual,' he said. 'You seem to have the luck as well as the cheek of the devil.'

An hour later, when the midday post arrived, their cheer was shattered. It contained a summons citing Robert to appear at the Sheriff Court to answer a charge of contravening Section 6 of the Sale of Food and Drugs Act, 1875. Morrison had kept his word.

As he read the summons for the third time Robert groaned. 'Have you noticed the date set for the trial?'

Fergus, sitting limply at his desk, looking sick, shook his head.

Robert threw the summons on to the desk. 'It's two days before the pipe band championships.'

To Fergus it hardly seemed to matter when shame descended on them. The possibility of a prosecution had been in his mind for months, but he had gone on hoping it would never happen. Now the scandalous reality was lying on the desk in front of him his mind had flooded with paralyzing self-pity. Out of the numbness only one thought kept coming to him: *It was all Robert's fault.* He had warned him to keep out of whisky. 'In Scotland, whisky is a sin,' he had said when they first discussed it that snowy Good Friday night at Ardfern all those years ago. Since then, he had been happy to share in the soaring profits. But now, with retribution staring him in the face, he was more certain than ever that his original advice had been right. There was money in whisky but no respectability. He hadn't even needed the money. He'd been tricked into this. And now his name would be sullied in public. All the years of care had come to this, and through no fault of his own.

He looked up bitterly. 'What will people think of us?' To his credit he hadn't yet thought of the financial implications.

Robert looked at him impatiently. 'I haven't been found guilty yet.'

'You can hardly deny you're blending malt with grain. We've made a virtue of it.'

'There will be no question of denying that. It will be a matter of proving we're justified in doing it.' He snatched the summons from the desk.

'There will be less scandal if you simply plead guilty.'

Robert looked astonished. 'And lose the business!'

Only then, it seemed, did Fergus remember it wasn't just his

382

good name that might be ruined. 'God help us,' he said. 'What a mess.'

'We're going to fight this,' Robert said. 'We have nothing to be ashamed of.' He walked to the door. 'I'll go along right away to Boyd, Paton, and Galbraith. We must engage the best possible man to put our side of the thing.'

'You had better cancel this damned piping nonsense,' Fergus called after him.

'I can't do that. Everything's too far advanced.'

Fergus tugged miserably at his beard. 'We'll be an even bigger laughingstock if all those bands turn up to pipe for a whisky that's been banned by the courts.'

Robert turned on him with a snarl. 'Can't you damned well cheer up a bit?'

But it quickly became evident that the depth of Fergus' gloom might be even more in keeping with reality than Robert's aggressive optimism. Two days after being given the bad news Mr. Hutt arrived unannounced from London—the living, agitated confirmation of the potential disaster facing King's Royal. He spelled out the seriousness of the situation in a way that drained the last dregs of buoyancy from even Robert's heart.

'I made arrangements to leave as soon as I received your letter,' he said. 'I felt it was too grave a crisis to be discussed in writing.'

His sombre expression gave Robert his worst jolt so far.

'I wanted to tell you personally,' Mr. Hutt said, 'that I've cancelled all our deliveries. I've instructed our travellers to accept no new orders till the outcome of this case is known.'

Robert struggled to look even faintly confident. 'Was that absolutely necessary, Mr. Hutt? We intend to carry on as normal.'

Mr. Hutt's expression was understanding. 'You, I suppose, must put the best face on it. My inclination is to begin disengaging now.'

Robert could not keep the shock from his voice.

'You can't mean you're going to abandon our whisky?'

'Not willingly. Of course not. But I'm afraid, until the case is settled, you'll have no more orders from us.' He leaned forward. 'This is a test case. If it goes against you it goes against all of us. Although an adverse Scottish ruling would carry no weight in England, it would be immediately followed by a similar prosecution south of the border. We'll all be out of business. I don't want to be caught with stock on hand that I cannot sell.'

'Our lawyers say that if we're going to fight we should carry on as normal.'

'I hope you're not going to let any ordinary lawyer handle this,' Mr. Hutt interrupted. 'Get the best man. They all live in Edinburgh, don't they? Whoever he is, get him, no matter what it costs. I'm quite willing to split the expense with you.'

'We have retained J. Murray Anderson. He has a whole string of murder cases to his credit. He was the junior at the Madeleine Smith trial. We're lucky to have got him.'

Mr. Hutt gave him a brooding look. 'Madeleine Smith?'

'Yes. The poisoner.'

Mr. Hutt rose with a long sigh. 'That's what I thought. Perhaps I have a nasty mind but I wouldn't remind anyone else of that particular fact if I were you.'

He left Robert squirming with embarrassment.

J. Murray Anderson was a small fat man of about sixty with a balding head and a strong red face. His first meeting with Robert was in the lounge of a Glasgow hotel to which he came in a bad temper from a long and as yet unfinished trial at the High Court.

The hotel, suggested by Robert's lawyers, had a long association with the legal profession. The walls of the room they sat in were suitably decorated with illustrations of famous trials, caricatures of celebrated counsel, including Anderson, blood-curdling photographs from old copies of the *Police Gazette*.

When Robert ordered two glasses of whisky, Anderson, with a sharp glance at the bar, said, 'Bring me a single malt.' He looked pointedly at Robert. 'I can't stand these new blended concoctions.'

After this disconcerting start Robert's dislike of his defender was irreversible.

'How long will the trial last?' he asked at the end of their talk.

The whisky had made Anderson's face even redder. 'No time at all,' he said, closing his folder of notes. 'There's damned little either side can say. You'll know one way or another by the afternoon of the second day.'

After another whisky his sour temper eased into sardonic humour. 'Don't worry, my boy. I don't like your damned whisky, but I'll make a good case for you. I'll tell your lawyer here in Glasgow what I want done. I won't let you sink without a struggle.'

The closer the trial drew, the higher Fergus' tensions ran. Mr. Hutt's ominous decision to cease distribution of King's Royal had been the final blow to what little morale he had left.

All his life he had been a worker rather than a fighter. His success had been due to physical stamina and shrewd determination. He had pushed a heavy object along an uphill road. But when the natives had been hostile he had always detoured or withdrawn to avoid trouble. He wanted money and recognition but, even more, he wanted peace to enjoy them. He had achieved riches and position in his own way and now, in his late middle-age, to see everything calamitously threatened made him desperate. He moped and fretted by day and lapsed into nightmares when he went to bed.

His frequent outbursts at Robert swung from bitter recrimination to black prognostication, depending on the degree of his distress. Endlessly he lamented the day he had been tricked into such a reckless adventure and sombrely forecast not only Robert's inevitable conviction but the extent of the financial doom to follow.

Always he had kept a protective barrier between Rita and his business worries. Now, for her, he fought to maintain an appearance of reasonable confidence, but the effort left him limp and increased his resentment of Robert, the source of his misery.

One night about three weeks before the trial he arrived home late. He refused dinner and went straight upstairs. A little later he reappeared and asked Robert to join him in the study. He had been missing from his office all day and looked tired and nervous. One of the windowframes had warped and the curtains swayed a little in a draught created by the chill wind sweeping over the city from the north.

Fergus shivered and turned his chair from the desk to face the fire. He pointed to another chair. 'Sit down, Robert. I want to talk to you.'

His manner was peculiarly hesitant and the grey that had recently grown in his beard seemed more pronounced. His shoulders were hunched and his velvet smoking jacket hung carelessly open. There was tobacco ash on it.

His wan appearance surprised Robert and made him wary. He braced himself to endure another of the long, familiar nightmares.

Could the catalogue of catastrophe be laden with some new ruin? He took out his pipe and began to fill it in silence. Fergus appeared to struggle for appropriate words. At last they came in an agitated rush.

'I don't want this trial to go on, Robert. Can you understand that?' His fingers moved nervously up and down his lapels.

Robert took the unlit pipe from his mouth. 'I can understand perfectly. I don't want it, either. Do you know some way of stopping it?'

Fergus leaned anxiously forward. 'Yes. If we swallow our pride and do what the pot distillers want we can avoid scandal and save a lot of money.'

Robert shook his head wearily. 'We've been through all this, Father. Morrison tried to get me to give in years ago. I beat his boycott. Do you think I'm going to bend the knee to him now, especially when he might have been responsible for the distillery fire?'

Fergus' attitude begged for understanding and at the same time tried to offer it.

'I know how difficult it would be for you. You've been badly done by, but it would make sense to salvage what we can rather than be ruined.'

'I don't think we will be ruined. How can they stop anything as popular as blended whisky? It's the drink of the future.'

'Someday, I suppose, blended whisky is bound to come. But you've forgotten something. You don't have any writ from heaven on it. It might be some other man who's destined to bring it. Perhaps you're too early. The way hadn't been prepared. Perhaps the established forces were bound to crush you. But, at least you know you've made the road easier for someone later on.'

While Fergus was speaking Robert had gone to the window and pulled back the curtain. The draught coming through the gap in the frame brought a smell of damp grass. He peered out. In the cold glare of the gas jet he saw dew glistening on the grassy slope across the street. The cherry trees rattled their trailing branches.

He turned and blew smoke about the room in exasperation. 'My God, Father, will you stop delivering a funeral oration over me? I'm not dead yet.'

Fergus looked shrunken in the big chair. 'You're not dead, true, but you've been badly beaten about. We've been fighting a running battle for years. There's a limit to what you should endure for money. You've made a sizeable fortune. Why risk it? To abandon King's Royal wouldn't end your business career. You have money to start something else, something less worrying. And there's still my business doing better than ever. I have a partnership waiting for you!'

'No.' Robert's face was expressionless and his voice curt.

Fergus pressed on, almost beseechingly. 'We have a fortune tied up in boxes, bottles, and blended whisky. But if you're convicted we won't be allowed to sell any more blended whisky. Everything we hold will become worthless.' He rose suddenly from his seat, his eyes pleading. 'Be sensible, Robert, and make a deal with the pot distillers. This is a far worse threat than the boycott. See Morrison. Tell him that if he drops the prosecution, we'll run the business down, closing completely in a few months when the stocks are used up.'

At last Robert's growing anger became uncontrollable. Until now, the territory had been familiar, but this was something new. He jumped to his feet, his face twisted in disbelief.

'You must be mad to make such a suggestion. I'm going to fight this case. Has it ever occurred to you we might win?'

'Win or lose,' Fergus said with a distracted tug at his beard, 'there will be scandal.'

'I don't give a damn about scandal. The *business* is what I'm concerned with.'

Fergus straightened, his lungs seeming to fill until his velvet jacket gaped. He faced Robert, his head jutting pugnaciously. 'But I care about scandal.' His voice was fierce now. 'I refuse to be dragged through the courts for you. *I* have my good name to think of . . . more than ever now.' He swallowed noisily as if his outrage was choking him.

Robert took a step forward, staring as if seeing something new. 'So that's what's worrying you? Your precious title! I might have known. Well, you might not give a damn about the business, but I don't give a damn about your title. I will not go crawling to Morrison just to keep your bloody baronetcy clean and pure.'

Fergus' aggression collapsed. He stood for a moment with his

387

hands to his temples as if in pain, then he felt behind him till he touched his chair. He sank down brokenly into it, his eyes still on Robert, his voice low.

'You're too late.'

The words were strangely ominous. Robert stiffened. 'What do you mean, too late?'

'I went to Edinburgh today and saw Morrison. I made a deal with him.'

Something sharp and icy seemed to pierce Robert's chest. 'You did what?'

'I thought I'd be able to talk sense into you.'

A jet of gas hissed in the coal fire and the burst of yellow flame that followed lit the horror on Robert's face.

'You told Morrison I'd close down King's Royal if he dropped the prosecution?'

'Yes,' Fergus said, and added pointedly: 'Our business.'

'Oh, my God, I don't believe it.' He swung away as if the sight of Fergus had become unbearable. 'You must be off your head.' He stood staring into the dark reaches of the big room, his shadow cast on the trembling curtains by the desk lamp.

A sigh heaved painfully in Fergus' chest. 'It's the best thing for both of us,' he said. 'You'll see that later.'

Robert whirled on him, his face inflamed with rage. 'I'll never see it, you senile old fool. I won't be bound by your boneless deal. You didn't consult me.'

Fergus winced at the contempt. 'It was my money that started you off. I am your father.' His voice carried little conviction.

'You are also the minority shareholder.' Robert bent furiously over him. 'You exceeded your authority. Having a title doesn't give you the power to decide my life. You can take the train back to Edinburgh tomorrow and tell your arsonist friend Morrison there's no deal. No deal at all.'

'Think about it till tomorrow,' Fergus said weakly.

'I won't think about it for a single second.' Suddenly his overriding desire was to inflict as much suffering as possible. 'And here is something else for you. The title you're so pitifully worried about was bought for you with my money. You didn't earn it. *I gave it to you as a present.*'

Fergus gaped blankly at him.

'Do you hear me? Can you take that in? I bought your baronetcy for you.'

Fergus' fingers tightened like claws on the arms of his chair. 'You didn't buy it.' His voice was shaking. 'I worked twenty years for it. It was a reward for my public services.'

'Oh, no.' Robert shook his head violently, his eyes blazing. 'It was a reward for the five thousand pounds I donated to your party funds. And what's more, I was thinking of it as a present for myself as much as for you. When they carry you away from it, it will come to me.'

Fergus struggled out of his chair. 'If this is true I'll renounce it. You'll never have it.'

'It's true and you *can't* renounce it,' Robert taunted him. 'You can revert if you like to calling yourself plain Mr. King, but the baronetcy lives on. There's nothing you can do to stop it being mine one day.'

'I don't believe it,' Fergus shouted. 'The Chief Whip would have to have told the Scrutiny Committee of any donation as large as that.' There was a demented quality in his voice now.

'Only if it came from you,' Robert said with gloating scorn. 'But you didn't have the courage to make it. *I* did it for you. The Chief Whip was able to put his hand on his heart and declare you clean.'

The blood was thundering through him. It hadn't been his intention ever to tell Fergus that his title had been conferred in return for a political gift. The cruel revelation had been torn from him by his fury. Now it began to frighten him. He remembered what Rita had warned, her expression almost scared: 'I'll have to keep this from him. I don't know what it would do to him.'

Fergus had been struck a shattering blow. His expression was stupefied, his mind staggering between disbelief and self-pity. His pride had been mauled beyond endurance but as he floundered about for words brutal enough to smash Robert the realization came to him that he was unarmed. There was no imputation massive enough. He turned shudderingly away.

'Pack your bags and get out of this house.' His voice was hoarse and gasping. That they would still have to share an office was something that could be faced later. 'You can fight this prosecution alone. Do not expect me to give evidence in your defence.'

Robert walked limply to the door. 'I don't need your evidence,' he said. 'Nor your house.' He stood for a few uncertain moments looking at Fergus crouched in front of the fire on the edge of his chair. Then, drained of everything but regret, he went out.

Robert's anger was replaced by a burning worry which he couldn't throw off. His father was a pessimist and always had been about King's Royal, especially when trouble arose. On the other hand, he was a shrewd judge of situations. Could he possibly be right on this occasion? Having survived years of storm, was the business at last heading for legal extinction?

The prospect was too frightening to be faced. And yet ... his mind went trudging on through mudbanks of depression.

If it did all collapse, somehow he would survive. But what would happen to the two men on whom he had come to rely—Ross and McNair? They were a faithful, hardworking pair. Was it fair to let them go on thinking their jobs were secure?

Next day he sent a telegram to Lochbank telling McNair to come to Glasgow. He arrived looking fitter than Robert had ever seen him. The tweed clothes he wore increased his appearance of sensible solidity. 'Rebuilding Lochbank seems to be agreeing with you,' Robert said.

McNair's reassuring face wrinkled with pleasure. 'I feel I'm on top of things at last,' he said. 'The men are working well with me. I was worried about that at first, but they're a grand lot.' He hesitated. 'I've always been used to rough-and-ready Glasgow folk, but these country people are ... they're gentlemen, Mr. King. That's what I've found.'

Robert laughed. 'Don't let them think that, McNair, or they might start getting ideas. But what about your family? How are they?'

'Getting on famously. My wife is blooming and the kids love it. They've never had such freedom.'

Robert sent for Peter Ross.

'Let's all sit down,' he said. When they were settled he sat on the edge of his desk, wondering how much he should say. 'I don't want this to go any further,' he said at last, 'but I'm afraid the company has run into trouble.'

Ross looked at him keenly, a smile hovering on the edge of his concern. 'I don't remember us ever being free of it for very long,' he said. 'What's happened now?'

The independence of his own business days still lingered in Ross. It was an attitude Robert was pleased to see surviving. McNair was the sturdy plodder, Ross the keen thinker who never hesitated to state his view or accept new responsibility.

'This could be immeasurably more serious than anything we've had to face so far,' Robert said. 'Even worse than the fire. I felt it only fair to tell you what's happening.' He walked to the window. The sun had gone and the tenement opposite looked grey, the stone old and crumbling. 'A prosecution has been brought against me. I've been charged with defrauding the public. They're trying to say that King's Royal is not whisky.'

McNair's honest face contorted with shock. 'It's the best whisky there is,' he said indignantly, turning to Ross for support. 'I've never heard anybody complain about it. And I served enough of it in the Goosedubbs.'

'Maybe not, but they're going to drag me through the courts, anyway.'

'That's terrible.' McNair fumbled for his pipe while Ross frowned.

'I'm sorry to hear this, Mr. King,' Ross said. 'It isn't right. They've got a knife in you, and always had.'

'It might not be right, but they're determined to do it.'

'I'm sure everything will turn out all right.'

'We can't assume that. That's why I've got you in here. What I wanted to tell you is this. If the case goes against me, King's Royal will be finished. We won't be allowed to sell it as whisky. The business will be ruined. Everything we've worked for will go.'

He looked at them. 'You're both family men. You have others to think of besides yourself. I felt it only right to tell you that if you want to look about for other jobs while there's time, I won't blame you. I think you should have it in mind.'

He walked away from them. There was a long silence in which he sensed the two men looking at each other. Neither spoke.

'You don't have to say anything right now,' he said. 'I just wanted to alert you. You can go away and think about it.'

McNair moved restlessly in his chair. 'If King's Royal goes out of business would it be the end of Lochbank as well, Mr. King?'

Robert shrugged helplessly. 'I haven't been able to think it all out yet myself,' he said. 'But if the worst happens, what need would we have for a new distillery?'

Ross leaned forward in his chair. 'What do you think the chances are? After all, King's Royal *is* whisky. How can anyone say it isn't?'

'They're making out that the only whisky comes out of a pot still and that by blending pot-still malt with spirit from a patent still we're changing the nature of the drink. It's the old enemy—the pot distillers—who're behind it. As for our chances'—his voice quickened—'I think we will win.' Did he really think that? He put caution into his voice. 'However, I must tell you that my father takes a less optimistic view. He thinks we're on the road to disaster.' He sighed. 'You'll have to consider it.'

He saw McNair give Ross a quick glance, then say with quiet certainty: 'I don't have to think about it, Mr. King. I'll be at Lochbank until you tell me I'll not be needed. I won't be looking for another job until I know I need one.'

Before Robert could speak, Ross rose from his chair with a dry laugh. 'I'm sorry you beat me to that, McNair. I'd like to have been the first to say it, because it's exactly what I feel myself.' He looked steadily at Robert. 'I'll go on with my work till you tell me to stop.'

The display of loyalty took Robert unawares. His smile was a mixture of gratitude, embarrassment, and warning. 'I hope you both know what you're saying.'

'If we don't at our ages, we never will,' McNair muttered with a sidelong grin at Ross.

A surge of comfort went through Robert. The warm steadfastness of the two men was a tonic after his father's gloomy defeatism.

'I don't mind telling you I was very depressed when we started this talk,' he said. 'You've cheered me immeasurably. I'm glad I can count on your loyalty. I would like you to know I appreciate it.'

McNair looked at the floor.

Ross said, 'As well as loyalty, I'm sure we'll both want to give any help we can. All you have to do is ask, Mr. King.'

'If there's anything I'll let you know,' Robert said. 'In the meantime'—he nodded to a cupboard—'I think, Ross, that you should pour each of us a glass of the fraudulent King's Royal. You know where it is.'

When they left, the room seemed very empty, but in an odd way Robert no longer felt so alone.

# 22

Hoey took Gwen shopping in Grafton Street. They went to the races in Phoenix Park and made day trips to Bray and Wicklow. On a sunny Sunday, with the church bells ringing, they drove through the Dublin mountains to Glendalough and wandered among the ruins of monastic Ireland. And, on the day before she was due to sail again for Scotland, they took a train from Amiens Street Station to the fishing village of Howth.

The sand was warm and dry. They sat on it eating bread and cheese and cream cake bought in a shop opposite the harbour. Sea-gulls sat on the masts of fishing boats as men worked with nets and rigging. A boy painted a boat drawn up on the beach.

Hoey, in civilian clothes, took off his tweed jacket and folded it into a pillow for Gwen. She lay back with her face to the sun.

'Ireland's put colour in your cheeks,' he said. 'Your mother and father will see a difference in you when you go home. You were pale and tired the day you arrived.'

She made a petted sound. 'So would you have been if you'd been on that awful crossing. I was sure the boat would sink.' She raised herself on an elbow. The blue of her blouse looked cool against the sunlit sand. 'There was more to it than that, of course. I had been worrying about you. I had nightmares all the time you were in Africa.'

Hoey made a face. 'If the truth be told, so had I.'

'Now, now, you mustn't admit that, Tom. They might take your medal away.' She lifted sand and let the fine grains trickle through her fingers on to the back of his hand. 'Heroes are supposed to have nerves of iron.'

Hoey lifted a small white shell and flicked it towards the smooth, incoming sea. 'I'm no hero,' he said decisively. 'I just didn't know what I was doing.'

She had found him reluctant to talk about his time in Zululand. She kept her voice lighthearted. 'Oh, yes, you are. A silly hero, perhaps, but the one I love.'

He put a hand on her shoulder and squeezed it gently. His voice had hoarsened a little. 'I don't think I deserve it, but I've never been happier.'

'Nor have I, Tom.' She lay back against him.

'I'm glad I rented the house at Queenstown,' he said. 'It's been fun. I've never known a month go so quickly. It was just like it was when we were first married.'

'A second honeymoon,' she murmured.

'Yes. I've always shied a bit when I've heard other people say that. Now I know what they meant.'

She smiled with her eyes closed. 'It's funny, Tom, but now I'm glad you went back to the regiment. I was disappointed and lonely at first. And all the time you were in Africa I hated your regiment. Now . . . I feel we owe it something. I don't know how to put it.'

'There's no need,' Hoey said. 'I know what you mean.'

She turned to him with a smile that was enquiring and slightly anxious. 'And there won't be any more wars, Tom. Will there?'

He shook her gently. 'I shouldn't think so. Not after the whipping we gave the Zulus.'

'And, anyway. . . .' She hesitated as she realized she was about to say something that might alter their happy mood.

'Yes?'

She shook her head to suggest it wasn't important. 'I was just going to say you would be out of the Army by then.'

'By the time there's another war? I hope so.'

'What will you do when you leave the Army?'

'Help you,' he said simply. 'I think I could become quite attached to that old junk you sell.' He said it with such certainty that there could be no doubting him.

Her heart rose with such unexpected pleasure that she could only stare.

'I mean it.' He jumped lightly to his feet. 'But we won't go into that just now. Let's walk along the habour wall. We might get a breeze up there.'

He put out his hand to her and they stood for a few moments brushing sand from their clothes. The trees on the Hill of Howth stood tall and strong against the hot sky. In hillside gardens people sat under bright sun-umbrellas gazing out over the village roofs to the sea.

'I wonder if they're having weather like this in Glasgow?' Gwen said as they scrambled up a grassy banking.

'You know, that's the first time you've mentioned Glasgow for a week. When you came here at first you kept worrying about the shop and wondering how Miss Murray was managing.'

'Ireland seems to have been good for me.'

'It's the air. There's something in it. It affects all visitors the same way.'

'It's difficult to believe there can be such unrest and violence here. The people all seem so easygoing.'

'It's these damned Fenians,' Hoey said grimly. 'They're a black-hearted lot, poisoned with bitterness. Cowardly ambushes, arson, and murder. It's all they live for. And they're as elusive as foxes. They skulk about in the woods and up in the mountains and if we get anywhere near, people hide them in barns and attics.'

'I thought you said the ordinary people had no time for politics?'

'They haven't, but they still won't betray their own kind.'

Even at the end of the long harbour wall the air was motionless. They stood for a while watching children casting lines. Gulls made lazy circles over boats and packing sheds. The smell of fish and salt was strong in the heat, but fresh. Occasionally, eddies of unbroken water lapped the harbour wall as a boat went in or out.

Perhaps a mile offshore there was an island. Its rocky sides rose from the water into long green slopes. Hoey pointed to it.

'In the old days they kept watch from there for invaders,' he said. 'They call it Ireland's Eye. It seems a great spot for lovers' picnics.'

Gwen turned to him with a challenging gleam. 'We could row out to it. Are you feeling energetic?'

Hoey flexed his muscles. 'I'm ready for anything these days. Shall we go?'

They ran, laughing, along the wall till they found a boat for hire. After some initial fumbling with the rowlocks and a few wild strokes that almost landed him on his back in the bottom of the boat, Hoey

396

did well. He pulled strongly and steadily, with Gwen telling him when to right the course.

Two or three times he stopped to rest on the oars. There was little current and the boat hardly moved. They leaned over the sides, peering for fish and clutching at passing strands of weed. As they neared the island he let Gwen take one of the oars. They completed the last few hundred yards in a series of comic circles. After an hour spent in tender lovemaking among the rocks they rowed happily back to Howth. They had tea in a seafront hotel and fell asleep on the short train run into Dublin.

McEwan could smell smoke. It came pleasantly in through the half-open window. He lay, with his eyes closed, analysing it. It wasn't difficult. The man who had taken his place was burning leaves. McEwan considered further and decided they were birch leaves. He hadn't been out of his room above the stables for three months. It was the stair. He could go down, suffering only an annoying breathlessness. To come back was a chest-burning effort that stretched him out on his bed for hours.

The maids from either the big house or Mrs. Veitch's cottage tidied the place for him and brought him meals. He couldn't get used to it. It worried him. Even when marvelling at his good fortune he felt guilty and apprehensive. How long could it go on? Surely, if he didn't die soon, they must send him away? He must be a nuisance. And an expense. The thought of what this idle luxury of his must be costing Fergus turned McEwan cold with fright.

He stirred in his bed as the scented smoke of late summer drifted past the window, beckoning him with insubstantial white fingers. How many leaves had he swept in these grounds? How many fires had he lit? He sniffed at the well-remembered perfume, sign of another season—season soon to come. They all had their characteristics. No need to leave the room to know what was going on out there. In early spring the busy birds told their hopeful story while the windows reflected the tender yellow light of opening daffodils on to his ceiling. On still summer mornings he wakened to the scent of a rose growing against the stable wall. The wasps of early September landed on his windowsill sated from their gorging of fallen fruit. And now, with autumn near, the first white signals were spiralling from the gardens of Row, misting the rocky shores of the Gareloch, rising to the hills where soon the bracken would fall over in ragged heaps of tangled gold. When winter came. . . . But McEwan did not dare think about that. By then, a year would have passed since he had last raked a path or turned a spadeful of earth, a year in which he had given the Kings no service.

Lured by smoke-borne memories, McEwan manoeuvred himself painfully from the bed and crossed stiffly to the window. The leaves of Virginia creeper were beginning to show patches of red against the grey walls of the house. McEwan, as a boy, had watched an old gardener plant that creeper. Now it had climbed as high as the turrets. He peered in both directions from the window but he couldn't see the new gardener or his fire. McEwan remembered the times he had warmed his hands at fires lit at the back-end of years gone—the soakings and the freezings he had endured in these grounds.

The floorboards creaked under his feet as he levered himself higher and strained to widen his view. It was then he saw James. He was sitting in front of an easel straddling a narrow path leading to the loch. There was a foreground of grass, then some trees with a shimmer of blue water beyond. James was hunched forward in his chair, his crutch on the ground and his hands busy with palette and brush. He seemed engrossed in his painting but to McEwan he did not look very comfortable. The times he had shouted that boy down out of trees where the branches were rotten!

McEwan heard all that was going on from the maids. This afternoon some of Mr. James' new artist friends were coming to take afternoon tea with the Kings. McEwan didn't think painting a great career, but the young rascal had always been loath to study. And now there he was with only one leg, never to climb the hills again, never sail, probably never marry.

It was the family business he should be in. There would be a nice office waiting for him. McEwan was sure of that. With a fire behind his desk, and clerks to do his bidding. McEwan couldn't think why James should want to sit out in the open, often in wind and cold, messing about with paints. He'd seen some of the paintings. They weren't what McEwan would have expected of a well-brought-up young gentleman. They weren't smooth and shiny like the ones hanging in the big house. They seemed almost unfinished, as if James had only got a brief look at his subject and had quickly put down whatever brief impression remained with him. And yet, as McEwan knew, there was nothing quick about it. Mr. James had all the time in the world to sit there and look at the trees or the waves coming up on the shores of the loch, with maybe a fishing boat passing and some children playing on the rocks. Certainly, he'd liked the colours of James' canvases. But there was more than just colour to painting.

He shook his head and returned to the pondering of his own troubles as a hot jag of pain went down one of his arms. Sometimes he lost count of time. One day was so much like another. He'd started noting down, each morning, the date and which day of the week it was. He lifted his homemade calendar from the chair by his bed. This was a Tuesday. It didn't seem to matter. There was nothing to look forward to. And yet, apart from the worry that his continuing existence was an imposition on Fergus, he was not unhappy. Since his future appeared to be short and featureless his mind tended to go back. Last night it had returned to the year of his arrival at Ardfern. He thought that had been in 1845. It was difficult to be certain. Anyway, he had been a strong, eager boy of fourteen when Colonel Armstrong had taken him on. McEwan realized with a start that if he lived through another winter to the sixteenth of March, 1880, he would be forty-nine years old.

James lifted his crutch, struggled awkwardly from his chair, and moved back from his painting. The impression he had been striving for—that of the sun dispelling mist from over the sea—had been achieved with more success than he could have expected. He found himself even daring to hope that when he showed the canvas to Mr. Guthrie and Mr. Walton, two local artists to whom he had been introduced by Colin Lindsay, they would be impressed. Once or twice recently they had taken him with them on their painting expeditions to Rosneath on the other side of the Gareloch. Guthrie was about twenty-one and Walton a little less. But James, although not much more than a year younger, felt them greatly senior to him.

While he was a fumbling beginner they seemed assured in their aims. It was their spirit of lighthearted but determined revolt that appealed to him most. Although his interest in Socialism had cooled, he still felt there was much in the world to rebel against. Guthrie and Walton, he had found as he sat on the grass with them at Rosneath while they sketched or painted, were in rebellion against the established Scottish painters. James didn't entirely understand their motives, but he was in full approval. Old men were always stuffy—always thought their way was best. James felt they should be deflated whenever possible. It didn't matter to him whether the men were physicians, engineers, or painters.

James hadn't yet realized their interest in him had arisen because they saw that his approach to his subjects was as unconventional as their own.

When he had asked Guthrie where he should go to study, the reply had been surprising. 'I don't think you should do any studying just yet, James,' Guthrie had said. 'Just go on painting a while in your own way.'

James took his new painting from the easel and began to go towards the house. His friends would be arriving soon.

'Hello, James.' It was Mrs. Veitch at the door of her cottage.

'I didn't notice you, Grandmother.'

'No. You were too engrossed.' She began to come forward, holding out her hand. 'Let me see. I hope it's nicer than the one you did of that old wreck on the beach. I could hardly make out what it was supposed to be.'

James looked anxious. 'Well, the way the light was that after-noon, Grandmother, it did seem to me that everything blended into various tones of green and blue.'

Mrs. Veitch, who had recently started to use a stick, leaned on it. She held out her other hand.

James saw he was now expected to show her the new canvas. 'Mr. Guthrie and Mr. Walton seemed to like the one of the wreck,' he said. 'They're coming to tea this afternoon,' he added quickly, hoping to distract her. 'Are you coming too?'

She paused in her study of the still wet canvas. 'Your mother invited me, James, but I declined. I've set Millie to clean the silver this afternoon and I want to see she does it properly.'

She handed back the painting without comment.

'I'm sure you would enjoy meeting Mr. Guthrie and Mr. Walton,' James said. 'Father likes their work. He's bought two of Mr. Guthrie's paintings and one of Mr. Walton's.'

Mrs. Veitch began to swivel back towards the cottage on her stick. 'He'll be needing more walls if he goes on buying paintings,' she said. Then, seeming to feel this statement should be moderated, she added: 'But I suppose somebody has to support you artists. It would be a dull world without pictures.'

'Perhaps they could call on you for five minutes before they leave, Grandmother? I'd like you to meet them.'

Mrs. Veitch pointed her stick at a rosebush below one of the cottage windows. 'Have you ever seen such heads on a rose in October?' she asked.

'Can I bring them, Grandmother?'

She touched her curls, snowy now and not quite so tidy as once. 'I suppose you can, James. So long as they clean their boots well before they come in.'

It was Fergus who'd suggested that Rita should invite James' painter friends to Ardfern.

'They seem clever young men to me,' he said. 'Their views on trends in art should be worth hearing. Besides, I want to ask if they think it worthwhile of us encouraging James to pursue this painting of his in a serious way.'

'And if they don't, Fergus, do you think it will make any difference to James? He seems more and more dedicated to whatever it is he's trying to do. I must confess I haven't appreciated anything he's done so far....'

'I don't think I know an awful lot more about it than you do, Rita, but I believe I've an inkling of what James is after. Whether it's of value or not is another matter. And you're perfectly right ... what other people think may make no difference to him.'

'Anyway, Mr. Guthrie and Mr. Walton must come to tea,' Rita said. 'That is, if they can be persuaded to desert their easels for an afternoon. They seem to spend all their time working at Rosneath.'

'I'm sure it will be helpful to have the opinions of young men talented enough to actually exhibit and sell their own work,' Fergus said. He gave her a guarded look. 'I am possibly too used to the established men, too set in my tastes, to be able to judge James fairly.'

He didn't mention that the company of Guthrie and Walton would also be a distraction. Fergus had been seeking distraction since the night Robert walked out of the house in Park Place, leaving him with all the bitter doubts about his title, still unresolved, perhaps to be with him forever.

Rita had noticed a greater readiness in him recently to entertain or be entertained and had half guessed the reason. She thought sadly of Robert living alone now somewhere in Garnethill in a tenement flat, laden with money, success, anxiety, and disappointment. As if the impending trial wasn't worry enough without this sudden, puzzling breach in the family. What had happened between her husband and her son? Neither would tell her. Rita tried not to take it too seriously. Everything passed.

She sighed and looked around the room to see that her flower arrangements were in position.

Guthrie and Walton had said they would arrive at about three, catching the ferry that left Rosneath for Row at half past two. The crossing was a short one and the walk to Ardfern from the jetty would take only ten minutes.

James remembered his grandmother's fears for the cleanliness of her cottage when he saw his two friends come up the drive. He was on the steps of Ardfern as they rounded a clump of bushes. Both were in heavy boots and had long stockings pulled up to meet their breeches at the knees. They carried rough sticks. Guthrie wore a straw boater and Walton a felt hat the shape of a kitchen bowl. It might originally have been made for a woman.

They waved cheerfully and Walton, pointing to the easel that James had recently left, said, 'I see you've been working.'

'Trying to,' James said, wondering if the opportunity would arise to show them the progress of his latest work. He was still excited at the success he seemed to have achieved with that mist slowly lifting from the sea like a thin veil of golden-white milk.

Fergus stifled a smile at Rita's expression as the two painters came into the drawing-room. Even for the country their dress was informal for men invited to take tea with a titled lady and her baronet husband. Fergus found himself watching their pockets for brushes or tubes of paint.

Walton, perhaps sensing Rita's surprise, plucked at his neat black beard and cast a glance at Guthrie. 'We've come straight from painting, Lady King,' he said. 'You must excuse our roughness.'

Rita gave him her kindest smile. He was only a boy, yet so mature, Fergus had said, in his work. 'You seem very sensibly dressed for sitting about outdoors,' she said. 'I am always urging James to wrap himself up well. He sits at that easel of his for hours. I'm quite worried about what he'll do when winter comes.'

'These artistic chaps never feel heat nor cold,' Fergus said. 'They're only half of this world, after all. Isn't that right, gentlemen?'

'Quite right, Sir Fergus,' Guthrie said with surprising seriousness. 'If we were more of this world perhaps we would have the courage to charge higher prices for our paintings.'

'Oh, the money only comes after you're dead,' Rita said, noting the assortment of paint marks round the flaps of their jacket pockets. 'We've pointed this out to James, but he seems to think money unimportant.'

'I think it very important,' Walton said. 'Very important, indeed,' he added with emphasis. He took a pipe from his pocket absent-mindedly and then, realizing where he was, hurriedly put it away.

James, who had never had to think of his painting in terms of money, found Walton's statement disturbing. Fergus, he knew, would support him while he painted—forever, if necessary. It was a shock to him now to realize that from their undisguised interest in money his two friends were not so fortunate. Clearly, they had to think of their painting in terms of earning, or at least augmenting, a living. This made all the greater their kindness in giving so much time and encouragement to his primitive efforts. It perhaps also explained the fiery zeal in both of them. The haste he had sometimes seen in them to complete a painting was no longer so puzzling. Perhaps there had been someone standing by ready to pay for it. Another disturbing thought came to James as he thought of his own painstaking labours. Perhaps the speed with which his friends sometimes worked resulted in the lack of cluttering detail that was such a hallmark of their work. Perhaps it was only out of this rush that real, spontaneous art came. Was he only—good God!—a dilettante? The thought worried him so that he interrupted Rita loudly. 'Would you like to see Father's paintings?'

He looked anxiously at Guthrie and Walton.

Fergus turned to Rita. 'Is there time before tea? I had thought of afterwards, but James seems impatient. Perhaps he's right. We'll lose the best of the light soon.'

'So long as you don't talk too much, my dear.' Rita explained

403

this admonition in an aside to the two visitors. 'You'll find my husband a very great enthusiast.'

As James went ahead with Walton, Fergus said to Guthrie, 'I want you to answer me something quite honestly. Will James ever be a real painter?'

Guthrie's face, normally raffish and slightly sardonic around a thin black moustache, became solemn.

'Come on, man,' Fergus urged him. 'All I want is your opinion, not a hundred pounds on it.'

But Guthrie was not to be hurried. When at last he answered the words came carefully. 'With hard work I think James might one day be a very good painter indeed,' he said.

Fergus' eyes lightened but after a moment he shook his head. 'I must say I can't see what he's aiming at.'

'That's what makes it so interesting. I don't think even James himself knows yet.'

'Then, damn it, surely I should be getting him some tuition, although I understand you've put him off that idea?'

'I did, Sir Fergus. It's very possible James has a natural and original talent of his own. To put him under a teacher might destroy it.'

Fergus looked doubtful. 'Or it might help bring it out.'

Guthrie shrugged as if to suggest there was a risk, but that he would be prepared to take it. 'If the teacher was a truly great man, yes, he might bring out whatever it is James is struggling with. But normally what happens is that the pupil absorbs the teacher's style. Of course, eventually his own talent, if it's a strong one, will break through anyway, but even then possibly only in a distorted or diluted form.'

Fergus gave Guthrie a friendly look. 'You can imagine Lady King and I worry about that boy,' he said. 'Fate hasn't been good to him and I don't think we're equipped to give him the encouragement he needs.' He smiled. 'We're simple business people. James is the only artistic one of us.'

Guthrie looked around him. 'But this is the most artistic house I've ever seen.' The statement was obviously sincere.

Fergus, taken aback at the compliment, waved a hand as if to minimize any credit.

'I'm just a collector,' he said. 'There's not much merit in that.

Knowing how to show the stuff once you have it is a much greater achievement. Lady King does all that.' He looked enquiringly at Guthrie. 'Would you say arrangement is a creative affair?'

'Very much so.'

'Good!' Fergus was delighted. 'Good! Then it's from his mother that James gets his artistic bent.' He opened a door. 'We'd better catch up with James and Mr. Walton.'

They had hardly entered the room which Fergus thought of as his gallery when the door opened again and a maid hurried in. She looked agitated.

'There's a Miss Murray asking to see you, sir.'

'Asking for me?'

'Well, she asked for Lady King, but milady must have slipped out into the garden. I can't find her.'

'Let this Miss Murray wait in—' Suddenly Fergus remembered. 'It's not Miss Sadie Murray who works for Miss Gwen, is it?'

The maid was clasping and unclasping her hands. 'It is, sir. And, sir . . . I'm afraid . . . Miss Gwen has sent her urgently.'

Fergus hurried from the room. Miss Murray looked frightened. Panic began to choke him.

'What's happened, Sadie! Tell me at once.'

'It's Mr. Hoey, sir. Miss Gwen has had terrible news. He's been shot by the Irish. She had a letter from his colonel in the midday post. She sent me here right away to tell you.'

Fergus turned to the maid, who had followed him from the gallery. 'Find Lady King wherever she is,' he said. 'And order Craig around with the carriage at once.'

They arrived at Gwen's flat less than three hours later. The maid who opened the door was red-eyed. They found Gwen sitting almost in darkness. The curtains were closed although it was still light. Only one lamp had been lit. It stood on a table in the centre of the room. A letter lay beside it.

Fergus lifted it although he knew what it contained. Miss Murray had given them the news exactly as Hoey's old friend and commanding officer Colonel Dryden had written it to Gwen.

Hoey had been shot in the chest two days earlier in a Fenian ambush on the Malahide road. His condition, though serious, was not giving rise to concern. He was in hospital in Dublin and the colonel would keep Gwen informed.

Gwen looked at them listlessly. 'After fighting in Africa he should have been allowed home, Mother,' she said. 'It wasn't fair to send him to Ireland.'

Rita knelt and put an arm around her. 'It's terrible, my dear, and we know how worried you are. Your father thinks you should be with Tom. He'll sail with you to Dublin tomorrow night.'

Gwen stared at her. 'I should have gone on the Dublin boat tonight.' She held out a sheaf of paper. It was a telegram. Fergus read it. LIEUTENANT HOEY'S CONDITION HAS WORSENED. SUGGEST YOU COME EARLIEST.

Gwen bowed her head and began to sob. 'I should have sailed tonight, but I was too confused. And from the letter it didn't seem so serious. I didn't know what to do. If only you had been in Glasgow, Father. By the time the telegram came the boat had gone.'

Fergus put his hand on her shoulder. 'Don't cry, my dear. We can still travel tonight. The Belfast boat doesn't leave the Clyde until nine. Tomorrow morning in Belfast we can catch a train to Dublin. It's less than a hundred miles. We'll be there by midday.'

Rita rose. 'I'll tell Isa to pack some things for you.' An hour later she saw them out on to the landing. 'I'll pray that Tom is much better by the time you arrive,' she said as they went down the stone stairs.

'I'll stay here tonight,' she told the maid when the carriage taking Fergus and Gwen to the docks had left the street. 'Just in case there's ... anything.'

At shortly after eight o'clock next morning she heard a knocking at the outside door. A few moments later the maid came into the bedroom and handed her a telegram. It contained a message of only three words: LIEUTENANT HOEY SINKING.

Gwen and Fergus arrived in Dublin at noon by train from Belfast. It had been raining and the streets which had seemed so bright when she walked them with Hoey were now drab and strange to her.

Fergus held her hand as they sat in the cab taking them to the Castle. 'We'll soon be there, my dear,' he said.

'If only they had sent him home,' Gwen said leadenly. 'They should have sent him home from Africa. It wasn't fair.'

'I'm sure Tom will be getting the best possible attention,' Fergus said comfortingly. 'There must be good doctors here. It's a capital city. They'll have called in the best help they can get.'

The cab clattered into the cobbled forecourt of the Castle.

They were taken along depressing stone corridors to Colonel Dryden's office. He was a tall, wide-shouldered man of about forty. He looked at them worriedly and gave Gwen a wan smile.

'You have my deepest sympathy, Mrs. Hoey,' he said gently. 'I have heard so much about you from Tom. I'm only sorry we should meet under such circumstances.' Then, stiffening a little: 'I promise you that we will find the villains. The country's being scoured for them now.'

The cold military room and the grave man in front of her were unreal to Gwen.

She held tightly to Fergus and said, 'Where is Tom? Take me to him, please.'

'Of course. But ... I must warn you, Mrs. Hoey. He's very low.' His voice dropped and he put his hand out to her. 'Very low, indeed.'

Gwen began to cry. 'I must see him,' she sobbed.

'The doctor will take you. I will send for him now.'

Hoey lay alone in a small room at the end of a long corridor in the hospital block. His eyes were closed and his black hair had been plastered untidily across his head.

Gwen bent over the still figure and kissed the colourless face. One of Hoey's hands lay on his bandaged chest. She took it between her own. 'He's so cold,' she said, turning to the doctor. 'Is he warm enough?'

'I'm afraid he's very ill, Mrs. Hoey,' the doctor said. 'His blood pressure keeps dropping.'

'Has he been seen by a specialist?' Fergus asked. He felt numb with pity for Gwen.

The doctor nodded. 'We called in Mr. Kevin McBride. Everything has been done that can be done.' He took Gwen by the shoulders. 'Please sit down, Mrs. Hoey. I'll leave you with him. If he stirs I won't be far away. One of the nurses will call me.'

He went out leaving them sitting on either side of the bed.

Several times Gwen took Hoey's hand and spoke his name softly. 'Can you hear me, Tom? It's Gwen. We've come to see you. Can you hear me? I have something to tell you, Tom.'

407

Hoey didn't stir and each time she sank back into her chair, her face more graven with departing hope. Through her mind travelled a procession of the years since she had met him. They had been mainly worried, unhappy, and sometimes bitter times, but her love for him had never been extinguished. It couldn't all end here in this draughty room without another word spoken. She began to pray for him, searching her heart for words vibrating enough to express her yearning.

After the first hour Fergus slipped into an exhausted trance, sitting up with a start whenever Gwen moved or spoke softly to Hoey. Sometimes the door of the room would creak open and a nurse would look briefly in, then silently withdraw. Once she shook her head slightly at Fergus in a gesture of hopelessness.

In the middle of the afternoon a maid brought them in a tray of tea. Fergus took his, but despite his coaxing Gwen refused to touch the cup he poured for her. He felt ashamed that he had been able to drink the tea and when the maid came back to remove the tray he went into the corridor after her to smoke his pipe. When he returned Gwen was sitting with her head bowed against Hoey's cold cheek. His breathing seemed to Fergus to be even less noticeable than before. Not long afterwards he died. It was the nurse bending over him and then turning with a resigned expression of sympathy that told them it had happened.

When the realization came, Gwen threw herself forward on the bed, making pitiful crying noises. 'Tom,' she sobbed casting off the arm Fergus placed on her shoulder. 'I wanted to tell you. I wanted you to know.'

'Gwen, my dear.' Fergus' hands were on her shoulders again.

Slowly Gwen turned to face him. 'If only he could have known,' she said brokenly. Her face was wet and twisted with grief.

'Known what, my dear?'

She began to shake again with uncontrollable sorrow. 'I'm going to have a baby.' Her voice choked on the flood of tears. 'Now he'll never know.'

# 23

The grey stone of Glasgow was beginning to brighten with thin autumn sunshine as Robert walked to the Sheriff Court shortly before ten on the morning of October twenty-third. The air was sharp and dry and the people around him stepped lightly as if cheered by the pleasant weather. He felt listless and heavy. He was pale from weeks of worry piled on years of nonstop work. He had a numb feeling that he might have to face the death of his dream.

He had been unable to eat breakfast and had walked all the way from his flat in Garnethill in an effort to calm the apprehension that had kept him awake most of the night.

The sickening reality of the situation had at last clouded out his determined pose of optimistic serenity. He was on his way to stand trial for an offence which he might well pay for not only with his business but with his freedom.

That King's Royal was appreciated by millions and in constant demand in an ever-growing market did not matter an iota in law. J. Murray Anderson had announced that depressing fact in an outbreak of the red-faced relish that so offended Robert. Flouting the law to popular acclaim did not diminish the breach, Anderson had boomed. Was King's Royal whisky? Nothing else mattered.

The final collapse of Robert's morale had taken place when he discovered, during his final consultation with Anderson, that he would be required to sit in the dock during the trial—and, if he was found guilty, he might be sent to prison.

Anderson had let the demoralizing facts out gradually as if nurturing them as a final blow to Robert's self-esteem.

'Sit in the dock?' Robert had been appalled. 'Like a thief or a murderer?'

'Exactly so.' Anderson had drawn the words out.

'But I thought I'd be allowed to sit with you at your table.'

'The dock's where you'll spend the trial,' Anderson said curtly, almost as if he considered that to have Robert anywhere near him in court would bring the law into disrepute. 'And you'll have a policeman on either side of you.'

'It's degrading and unnecessary,' Robert complained. 'I'm not a criminal.'

'I hope I can convince the jury of that,' Anderson said. 'I don't want to have to visit you in Duke Street.'

At this buoyant reference to the city prison Robert stared at the florid face in disbelief. 'But surely if the worst comes to the worst all I'll get is a whacking fine? The real punishment will be in the collapse of my business.'

'The Act provides for up to two years' imprisonment,' Anderson said, his voice pitched as if in court, his stance suggesting a pose for the jury.

'Why didn't you tell me this before?'

Anderson shrugged. 'You didn't ask.'

'Surely there's no danger of it coming to that?'

'If you're found guilty it could. It all depends on the Sheriff. He may be a malt man like myself.'

Robert's temper flared at the callous mockery. 'I sometimes wonder whose side you're on, Anderson,' he said bitterly. For the moment he could almost believe the man part of the pot distillers' conspiracy.

Anderson's eyes sparked with their eccentric light. 'Like all lawyers I'm on the side of the angels,' he said gleefully.

Robert's spirit had almost collapsed now that he was faced with the full gravity of his situation.

Later, when he was alone, he experienced a violent anger at Anderson for his lack of feeling. Should he dispense with this vain and boorish man? But juxtapose that to Anderson's great reputation. *This* was what he was being made to pay for, not only in hefty fees but in enduring the man's infuriating arrogance. His reward would surely come in Anderson's court performance.

By then it would have become a personal matter for Anderson. It would not be Robert King on trial. It would be J. Murray Anderson. His pride and his reputation would be involved. He

410

would strive to win with all his gifts, because if he lost it would be a blow to his vanity. And not one he would be allowed quickly to forget. A verdict of guilty would bring shattering repercussions not only for King & Co. but for the whole whisky blending industry. Millions of pounds were at stake. The whole legal profession would be watching this trial. Anderson would be on stage. He would give of his best. Meantime, he'd have to be suffered.

A picture of Anderson's rough face and menacing shoulders came now to Robert as he stopped and looked across Ingram Street to the courthouse. Two policemen stood on the steps. He realized with a shiver that once he entered that dull grey building he would regard even Anderson as a friend. There would be no one else.

Fiona, her holiday over, had said she would attend the trial. 'I promise you won't see me,' she said, 'but at least you'll know I'm there. If your father's not going to be there you must have someone.'

'I would rather you didn't,' he said, thinking of the shameful seat he would have to take in the dock, and of the policemen with truncheons on either side of him. He had forced a smile. 'But I'll take you to the March of a Thousand Pipers on Saturday. Go down and stay with Grandmother Veitch. I'll see you there.'

'But I'll be anxious to know the verdict. Will you send me a telegram?'

'There'll be no need. Anderson says the thing will be over by early afternoon of the second day. I'll see you that same evening at Ardfern.' *If they haven't locked me up by then*, he thought with a sudden surge of panic that brought a grim picture to him of Duke Street Prison's bleak bulk.

She saw his face. 'We'll all be thinking of you, Robert,' she said helplessly.

His first sight of the packed court was another shock. Every seat was taken—there were people standing and an extra table had been moved in for the press.

'All the London newspapers have sent reporters,' Anderson whispered.

The satisfaction in his voice roused Robert. 'Don't sound so damned pleased about it. *You* might relish being a national spectacle, but I don't.'

The trial opened quietly. In a droning voice the Procurator

Fiscal outlined the charge to the Sheriff—referred to by Anderson as 'Old Maxwell'. When Robert's plea of not guilty had been entered, the prosecution case opened.

Two nuisance inspectors explained how, after a complaint, they had ordered a case of whisky from King & Co. They had been supplied with King's Royal. This product was well known to be a blend of malt whisky with neutral or silent spirit made from un-malted cereals in a patent still. As a result, people attempting to buy whisky were being given something else—namely whisky adulter-ated with another substance.

Anderson ignored the first inspector but faced the second, said to be the senior. He beckoned to the court usher and said, 'Bring exhibit one and place it in front of me here.'

The usher, an elderly man, lifted a rough wooden box from a corner and, his face reddening with exertion, carried it over. The sides of the box were stencilled KING'S ROYAL. BLENDED SCOTCH WHISKY.

Anderson put his foot on the box and looked at the nuisance inspector. 'Is this what King & Co. gave you when you asked for a case of whisky?'

The inspector said it was.

'Wouldn't the burden on the ratepayers have been lighter if you had bought one bottle instead of twelve?'

The inspector looked uncomfortable but kept quiet.

Anderson, who seemed not to expect an answer, opened the lid and looked into the box. It was divided into twelve compartments. There were bottles in eight of these.

'Was the case full when you bought it?'

'It was.'

'Four bottles are now missing. What happened to them?'

The inspector looked at the floor. 'I can't say, sir.'

'Did you open a bottle when you got this case back to your office?'

'Yes, sir.'

'Did you taste the contents?'

'I felt it my duty to do so.'

Anderson's smile was friendly. 'You found it a pleasant duty, I hope?'

'Oh, no, sir.'

'No?'

'No, sir.'

'Don't you like whisky?'

'I sometimes take a refreshment, sir.'

'Well?'

'This stuff didn't taste like normal whisky.'

'And you didn't like it?'

'That's correct, sir.'

'Did you keep the case locked up for safety?'

'Oh, yes.'

'I see. You had it under lock and key. You didn't like the taste but somehow four bottles have vanished. Thank you, inspector, that will be all.'

The inspector's boots made dejected sounds on the wooden floor as he clumped to the back of the court. With a slight smile at Anderson the Fiscal called his next witness: James Galbraith, clerk, age twenty-seven.

Galbraith, prompted by the Fiscal, explained how he had called at premises owned by King & Co. and asked for a bottle of whisky. What he had been given was a bottle of King's Royal. He had felt deluded and cheated, he told the Fiscal.

Anderson, when he came to cross-examine, looked silently across the court at the witness for several seconds before approaching him with a menacing jut of his neck.

'Tell the court, Mr. Galbraith, who you work for as a clerk.'

The man looked uneasy but his voice was clear and firm. 'The Scottish Pot Still Association.'

Anderson seemed taken aback. 'And you felt deluded when you went to a place owned by King & Co. and were supplied with a bottle of King's Royal?'

'I did.'

'I suggest you were hoping you would be given a bottle of King's Royal.'

'I clearly asked for a bottle of whisky,' Galbraith said evasively.

'Are you aware that your employers, the pot distillers, abhor Mr. King's blend?'

'Yes.'

'Then I suggest that you could hardly have been deceived when you were handed a bottle of it. You knew perfectly well what it was. If you didn't want it you should have refused it.'

While the next witness was being called Anderson came over to the dock. 'I don't suppose you know what to make of it all?' From him it was as good as an expression of sympathy.

'I don't,' Robert confessed.

'In this case I intend working from the time-honoured gladiatorial concept of the law.' Anderson smirked. 'The Crown puts them up and whatever they say I knock them down with whatever bludgeon I can lay my hands on.' He was grimacing as if actually striking his victims. 'It all adds up in the minds of the jury.'

The next witness arrived as if he had been hurrying, and the court usher looked annoyed. 'Slipped out for a smoke, probably,' Anderson said with unusual understanding as he went back to his table.

'George Hunter Kyle,' the witness said when asked for his name. 'Aged fifty-three,' he added. He was a bent man with curling grey whiskers.

'What is the nature of your business?'

'I am a paint manufacturer.'

The sheriff put his pen down and leaned back in his chair looking glum. *He looks as if his mind's already made up*, Robert thought dismally, then took comfort from the fact that it was not up to the Sheriff. The jury would decide.

'Do you in your business,' the Fiscal asked, 'have occasion to use what is commonly known as neutral or silent spirit, a form of alcohol obtained from a patent still?'

'I have.'

'Will you tell the court what your workmen do with this spirit?'

'They use it to dissolve resins in the manufacture of varnish.'

'Varnish?' The Fiscal turned to the jury with a scandalized look.

'Yes, sir.'

'Would you consider drinking this spirit?'

Mr. Kyle smiled. 'I would not.'

'Why not?'

'I've seen what it does to varnish.'

The Sheriff looked sternly at the public benches as if daring anyone to laugh.

After several more questions about the disintegrating effect

414

silent spirits had on previously solid substances the Fiscal sat down. Anderson rose and walked hesitantly forward as if slightly awed by the witness.

'Are you a drinking man, Mr. Kyle?'

Mr. Kyle looked at him warily. 'I am not an abstainer.'

'As they say in Glasgow, you take a refreshment?'

'Yes.'

'But drinking is not your hobby?'

'Certainly not.'

'Nor a field of study for you?'

'No.'

'Have you ever been inside a distillery?'

'Never.'

'Do you, when you take a refreshment, prefer brandy to whisky, like most gentlemen?'

Mr. Kyle clearly wondered where he was being led, but the invitation was irresistible. 'Yes.'

'Have you ever tasted King's Royal?'

'No.'

Anderson's helpful smile had gone. 'Would it be fair to say that in fact you know practically nothing about whisky, even as a consumer?'

Mr. Kyle hesitated.

'Would it?'

'Yes.'

'In fact you are simply a paint manufacturer?' He made it sound like the last refuge of the ignorant.

The grey whiskers bristled. 'I've stated that I am a paint manufacturer.'

'A paint manufacturer with absolutely no knowledge of whisky,' Anderson elaborated with satisfaction. 'But to continue. In your evidence you seemed to imply that you regarded silent spirits as non-potable because they were used as a solvent in your factory?'

'Yes.'

'That is all you have against them?'

'It seems sufficient to me.'

'Do you use any other solvents in your factory? I'm thinking particularly of water. Do you dissolve any of your paint pigments in water?'

'We do.' Robert thought Mr. Kyle sounded slightly reluctant to admit this, and with reason, since it was obvious that soon Anderson would pounce again.

'Would you be prepared to accept from me that the most widely used industrial solvent of all is ordinary water.'

'I suppose so.'

'Don't suppose. Do you accept it or not? I am not forcing anything on you.'

'Yes.'

Anderson was suddenly scornful. 'And can we take it, Mr.'—he rummaged in his notes—'Kyle, that you have no objections to drinking water?'

He sat down without bothering to hear the reply that was almost inaudible.

From the start, Robert had stared fixedly ahead, looking at the witnesses only occasionally. His headache had worsened. Outside the air had been fresh. In here it was heavy and lifeless. The high windows looked as if it was years since they had been opened. He heard the Fiscal say, 'Call Arthur Morrison.'

A desire rose in him to leap from the box and run. It would be a triumph for Morrison to see him arraigned here.

He realized that Anderson had risen and was speaking to the Sheriff. 'I would like to ask, milord, if the prosecution intend to produce any specialist witnesses.'

The Sheriff looked enquiringly at the Fiscal, who said, 'May I enquire what type of specialist witnesses Mr. Anderson has in mind?'

'Do you have a chemist or analyst to testify that the case of whisky purchased by the nuisance inspectors was not what it purported to be?'

The Fiscal looked slightly taken aback. 'In the interests of brevity, milord, we did not think that necessary. It's a well-known fact. A whole industry has grown up around this blended product. The accused can hardly seek to deny what he's doing when in his advertising he makes a virtue of it.'

Anderson, looking astonished, said, 'In that case, milord, I ask that the charge be dismissed. In my submission, without testimony there can be no case to answer.' He flounced to his seat and sat down.

416

The Sheriff didn't hesitate. 'I will hear the remainder of the evidence.'

The Fiscal said, 'You are chairman of the Scottish Pot Still Association and proprietor of Tamnavar–Glenlivet Distillery, Mr. Morrison?'

'Yes.'

'Have men been distilling whisky in the glens of Scotland for a long time?'

'For hundreds of years.'

'It is one of our most ancient and honourable crafts?'

'One of our most ancient and honourable arts,' Morrison corrected him with a smile.

The Fiscal bowed. 'I quite understand your pride, Mr. Morrison, and agree with it. When did it first come to the notice of your association that an attempt was being made to launch on a large scale as whisky a drink that was not whisky as you or any other malt distiller would recognize it?'

'About four or five years ago.'

'Did you regard this as a serious threat?'

'A grave one.'

'Why did you consider this threat as particularly serious? Surely people have adulterated whisky before.'

'They have, but all previous culprits were aware of the heinous nature of their act. They carried it out in secrecy and on a small scale. Until Mr. King arrived no one had ever blatantly proclaimed their adulteration or set out bare-faced to convince the public that the adulterated article was preferable to the original.'

'You've no doubt that to add silent spirit to malt whisky is an act of adulteration?'

'None at all. The operators of these patent stills have only recently struck on the idea of calling their product grain whisky. They've been encouraged by Mr. King's success. They see a huge new outlet for their product. But what kind of spirit is it which, if it goes into a cask marked for Mr. King, is known as grain whisky but if it goes into a cask destined for an explosives factory is known as plain spirit?'

Morrison, as he spoke, kept looking angrily across the court at Robert.

'It was never thought of as whisky previously and it is not

whisky now. It has none of the recognizable characteristics. It's a neutral alcohol.'

He stopped, noticing at last that the Fiscal had been holding up his hand as if trying to stem the torrent.

'Before we go too far I want to take you up on something you just said, Mr. Morrison. You said casks of this silent spirit were sent to explosive factories if I heard you right?'

'I did.'

'For what purpose?'

'To be used in the manufacture of explosives,' Morrison said with satisfaction.

'Fascinating. A previous witness told us it was used in the making of varnish. Do you know if it has any other similarly intriguing uses?'

'Yes.' Robert's dejection grew as he watched Morrison's eager expression. 'They use it to make chloroform.'

The Fiscal nodded happily. 'That is a thought-provoking list. Will you now tell the court what this versatile spirit does to malt whisky when it's mixed with it?'

'It takes away much of the taste and character. The resulting mixture bears a closer resemblance to French brandy than to pure malt whisky. To call it whisky is deception of the public and a threat to a traditional industry.'

Half an hour later Morrison was still in the witness box. The Fiscal had led him gently through his evidence, listening to every answer with a congratulatory expression. Now, under cross-examination, Morrison had lost some of his composure. He had become wary of Anderson's red smile of encouragement.

'I wonder, Mr. Morrison'—Anderson fumbled through some pages of notes as if he had lost the place—'I wonder if you would agree there is a demand for a well-balanced blend of malt whisky and grain whisky?' He corrected himself cheerfully. 'I forgot. You prefer to call it silent spirit.'

'We do not dispute the demand.'

'Thank you. Do you agree that there is no legal definition of whisky?'

Morrison hesitated. 'There's no *legal* definition, but—'

Anderson interrupted. 'So your answer is that you agree?'

'It is, but I would like to add that—'

'I did not ask for an addition.'

The Sheriff coughed, then addressed Morrison directly. 'What do you wish to add?'

'Only, milord, that though there is no legal definition of whisky, everyone knows whisky with paraffin added would no longer be whisky.'

The Sheriff nodded and sat back with a faint smile. 'I think Mr. Anderson would accept that.'

Anderson nodded amiably and said, 'Do you object, Mr. Morrison, to water being added to whisky?'

'Not at all.' And then, with a quick glance at the Sheriff, he added: 'Although for some there's too much water in it already.'

Anderson did not join in the laughter. He stood fanning himself thoughtfully with his notes. Robert had to admire the quick way he was able to turn Morrison's joke to advantage.

'I think a great many whisky drinkers would agree with you there. Many people would say that water injudiciously added would change the nature of their drink.'

Morrison saw the danger. 'No. The adding of water is merely dilution.'

Anderson put down his notes. 'Let us examine *that* a little more closely. Are you saying that no matter how much water is added to whisky it remains whisky?'

Morrison looked uneasy. 'Yes.'

'You're telling the court that if you had a glass of whisky and I poured a half-pint of water into it you wouldn't feel some drastic change had taken place?'

'The adding of water is merely dilution,' Morrison persisted.

Anderson leaned forward with a brutal glare on his face.

'I suggest that is a view you must hold to because, like all distillers, you yourself add water to your whisky before you sell it.'

'Certainly not.' Morrison gave his tormentor a stubborn pout.

'You see, Mr. King says he's merely diluting the strong taste of your malt by adding grain.'

Morrison was not to be shaken. 'We say he's *adulterating*, not diluting.'

Anderson walked thoughtfully to his table and put his notes on it. Then, very deliberately, his face solemn, he returned to his position in front of Morrison. His voice when it came was harsh and his face bleak.

'Did you for several years wage a merciless vendetta against the accused, attempting to crush him out of business by conspiring with other distillers to starve him of supplies of whisky?'

Morrison's shock was plain. He stumbled slightly over his answer. 'I did not.'

'Were you inspired to this wicked act by a fear that his success would mean a drop in your own profits?'

'That is not true.'

'And when the accused, by his youthful energy and ingenuity beat your base boycott did you then, maliciously, engineer this action?'

'No, not maliciously.'

Anderson sat down.

When he was told that Morrison was the last prosecution witness the Sheriff adjourned the court for lunch.

Robert accepted Anderson's invitation to accompany him to a nearby restaurant. A ragged vendor at the corner was brandishing a newspaper and calling out his version of the news. 'Great Whisky Trial Disclosures,' the boy shouted. 'Latest! Latest!'

Robert was certain every eye in the street was on him. What would tomorrow's headline be? TWO YEARS FOR BARONET'S SON?

He left most of his lunch untouched and saw with dismay that Anderson, subdued and preoccupied, had little appetite, either.

'It's disgraceful to have me sitting there with a policeman on either side when I'm allowed out for lunch,' Robert said.

Anderson looked at him, frowning as if his thoughts had been disturbed. He ignored the complaint. 'When we go back I'll call you first,' he said. He glanced at Robert, assessing him, then shook his head as if to say he was being unfairly burdened.

'Your appearance is against us,' he said.

'I can hardly be blamed for my face,' Robert said indignantly.

'It's not just your face, although that needs some hair on it. You look like a dandy. I would prefer you looking older and more solid, less the overambitious young man that you are. It's a pity it wasn't your father in the dock. That jury would never convict a baronet on a trumped-up charge like this.'

Robert groaned. 'I take it all this means things aren't going very well?'

'In pure law right's on our side. They're a long way from proving you've changed the nature of whisky. If it was the Sheriff on his own I'd be happier. But we have to contend with a jury of ignorant laymen. Every true Scotsman has a mystic vision of whisky. If they take the view that the national dram has been tampered with. . . . Bah!'

He raised his hand and called bad-temperedly for the bill, which he handed to Robert to pay.

'We'll have to get all this stuff about varnish, explosives, and chloroform out of their heads,' he fretted.

When they came on to the street he suddenly ran out and stopped a cab. 'There's something I must do,' he said, jumping into it.

Robert walked back to the courthouse alone. As he passed the vendor on the corner a delivery van reined up to drop another supply of newspapers. *Scandal always sells well*, Robert thought, then realized that was what Fergus might have said.

An hour later he nervously climbed the steps of the witness box with some other words of Fergus' sounding doomfully in his memory. 'Some day blended whisky's bound to come, but it might be some other man who's destined to bring it. Perhaps you're too early. Perhaps you were born before your time.'

He stood stiffly waiting for Anderson's first question.

'Has your company ever had a single complaint—a single legitimate, disinterested complaint—about King's Royal?'

'The only complaints we've ever had have all come from the Scottish Pot Still Association.'

'Do you consider that you are deceiving and deluding the public?'

'Certainly not. From the start we've made it clear what King's Royal is. Everyone who buys it knows it's a blend. They buy it *because* it's a blend.'

'Once your King's Royal showed signs of becoming established, did something happen?'

'Yes. Mr. Morrison, chairman of the Scottish Pot Still Association, asked us either to stop selling it or stop calling it whisky.'

'Did you refuse?'

'I did.'

'What was his attitude then?'

'He was very angry.'

'And then what happened?'

'Suddenly every distillery stopped supplying us.'

'You were made the victim of a boycott?'

'Yes.'

'Did you, as a consequence of this boycott, have to ceaselessly travel the country buying supplies wherever you could charm or coax them out of people by paying exorbitant prices?'

'Yes.'

'And did this go on for years?'

'It did. It was only recently that the boycott began crumbling. We thought we had finally been accepted.'

'And shortly after this vendetta began to fail you found yourself facing this charge?'

'Yes.'

'For years the pot distillers have made you suffer?'

'Yes.'

'I have one final question for you, Mr. King, and I refer not to the case of King's Royal purchased by the nuisance inspector, because for all the evidence we've had here to the contrary, the bottles might contain milk, but to the central issue. Why do you blend malt whisky with the product of the patent still?'

'Because the result is more in keeping with public taste.'

Anderson promptly sat down as if, among intelligent people, no more need be said.

The Fiscal stood examining Robert for some seconds as if seeing him for the first time.

'Would you like to be a millionaire, Mr. King?' he asked at last.

Robert smiled. 'I've never met anyone who wouldn't.'

'I asked about you. Would you like to be a millionaire?'

'Certainly.'

'Did you seize on the adulteration of traditional malt whisky as a means to this end?'

'I seized on it as a legitimate form of business.'

'Would you rank silent spirits in any way with any of the malt whiskies you're charged with adulterating, say a fine Glenlivet such as Macallan or Mortlach?'

'Of course not.'

'These great whiskies are produced in small, almost precious quantities whereas your so-called grain whisky is a characterless spirit produced in great volume?'

'Yes.'

'Like a chemical?'

'I know nothing of chemical manufacture.'

'But you did hear earlier of its industrial uses. Does it sound the sort of spirit people would want to drink?'

'Not on its own.'

'What is the proportion of malt whisky to silent spirit in your King's Royal?'

'Seventy-five per cent malt to twenty-five per cent grain.'

The Fiscal seemed to digest these figures, though Robert knew that Morrison would long ago have supplied him with them.

'Now, Mr. King, I want you to think very carefully. Could this proportion of silent spirit be extended indefinitely in your opinion without the genuine whisky character being lost, or would a point be reached where in your judgement the public would be deluded if this point was passed?'

'Perhaps.'

'Where would this point occur?'

'I don't know. I've never exceeded twenty-five per cent grain and never will.'

'But in your judgement, as an expert blender, where would this critical point occur?'

Robert knew this was dangerous territory but he felt that to answer truthfully would do him less harm than to appear stubbornly unco-operative. 'I wouldn't like to see the percentage of grain exceed the percentage of pot still,' he said quietly.

'So you think anything in excess of fifty per cent grain would be a fraud on the public?'

'I did not say that.'

'Did your answer mean that more than fifty per cent grain would be going too far, that you wouldn't go to that point yourself because the change from pure pot still would have then become too marked?'

Robert felt hesitation would only make the Fiscal's point more dangerous. 'Yes,' he said boldly, 'I do.'

The Fiscal pounced. 'For you, Mr. King, fifty per cent silent spirit would be too much. Can you not see that for others your twenty-five per cent might be too much?'

Without waiting for an answer he adopted Anderson's tactic, turned his back on Robert and sat down.

Anderson next put a Mr. James Whyte, public analyst, in the witness box. Then, turning to the Sheriff, he said, 'Milord, a significant lack in the prosecution case was analytical evidence to show that the King's Royal purchased by the nuisance inspectors was not in fact what it purported to be. The defence has been more thorough.'

He turned to the analyst. 'Will you explain to the court the commission you were asked to carry out?'

'Certainly. Twelve marked bottles were delivered to my laboratory. I was asked to examine them with a view to stating in how many cases the contents consisted of pure pot still malt whisky and how many of pot still blended with grain whisky or silent spirit.'

Anderson turned to the Sheriff. 'In the interests of saving the court's time, milord, perhaps I might be allowed to state the result of this analysis in very simple terms, with Mr. Whyte here to verify my statement.'

The Sheriff looked at the Procurator Fiscal, who shook his head gloomily. 'Proceed, Mr. Anderson.'

'Thank you, milord. The analyst has been totally unable to say which bottles contained pure malt whisky and which contained malt blended with some other substance—a question, I would remind the court, which the Scottish Pot Still Association has the boldness to suggest is a very simple one, indeed.'

He turned to Mr. Whyte. 'Do you verify that that was your finding?'

'I do.'

'To elaborate just a little, please tell the court in simple terms why you could come to no conclusion.'

'In any analytical examination of pot still malt whisky one would look for certain characteristic impurities. In this case all the bottles contained the expected impurities, though all in different degrees.'

'And what did you conclude?'

'That all the bottles might contain pure pot still malt or they

424

might all be pot still malt combined with a quantity of patent still spirit. A third possibility of course was that there might be some permutation of the two.'

'In short, you were baffled. Even after careful chemical analysis it is impossible for you to be more precise.'

'Yes.'

'Was there no level you could draw and say that the bottles with characteristic impurities above were pure malt and those below blended?'

'No, sir.'

'Why not?'

'Because no distillery produces a whisky exactly like the whisky of any other distillery. Consequently, pot still malt whiskies from twelve different distilleries would in any event vary in the amount of impurities they contained whether they had patent still spirit added or not.'

'Does the level of characteristic impurities go from very high to very low?'

'Yes. A Lowland whisky, for example, being light in character, would contain a very much lower percentage of impurities than a pungent Glenlivet.'

'Is it the case, then, that Scotch whisky owes its famous taste to the impurities it contains?'

The analyst smiled. 'I am afraid it does. Malt whisky is a very inefficient distillation.'

'Which is the purer, malt whisky or the so-called silent spirit?'

'Silent spirit by far.'

Mr. Whyte left the witness box to a rustle of interest in the public benches and a few quiet exclamations of what Robert thought might have been shock or disagreement. Despite himself he had to admire the energy and skill with which Anderson was pleading his case. His reading of the man's character had been correct. For all his sarcasm in private his courtroom advocacy was wholehearted.

The Sheriff showed an unusual energy as he consulted his papers. 'I see, Mr. Anderson, that we have now reached the end of the evidence for the defence.'

Anderson rose hesitantly as if apologizing for interrupting.

'Yes, Mr. Anderson?'

'It is true that there are no other names on the list, milord, but if it pleases you I would like to recall Mr. King.' A deprecating smile. 'There's something I forgot to ask him.'

The Sheriff's expression suggested he didn't believe Anderson would ever forget anything. 'Is it relevant?' he asked sceptically.

'In my fallible judgement it is relevant,' Anderson said humbly.

The Sheriff leaned back with a sigh. 'Very well,' he said resignedly. 'Recall Robert King.'

Anderson hadn't prepared Robert for this and the latter walked to the witness box feeling surprised and apprehensive.

Anderson seemed to choose his first words with special care. 'It has been an implicit part of the prosecution case that you've been duping an ignorant and gullible public, Mr. King. I want you to say if your trade lies mainly with working people or with the middle-class professional and business type of person.'

'With the latter.'

'In other words, with the more educated and presumably less gullible?'

'Yes.'

Anderson went to his table and lifted a parcel. He handed it to Robert and said, 'Please open this, Mr. King.'

Anderson watched with satisfaction as the Sheriff and everyone else in court leaned forward slightly as Robert fumbled with the string and brown paper wrapping.

A chair screeched on the floor as the Fiscal rose angrily. 'Milord, I protest at this blatant suspense. I doubt the relevance of my learned friend's line of questioning but I've no doubt at all the court's time would have been saved if this parcel had been opened in Mr. Anderson's own time.'

The Sheriff cleared his throat. 'Yes. Please be as quick as you can, Mr. King.'

Anderson, trying to look as reasonable as the formation of his face would allow, helpfully produced a knife. When the brown paper at last fell away Robert was holding a bottle of King's Royal.

'There's an emblem at the top of the label,' Anderson said, walking with it to where the jury could see. 'Will you tell the gentlemen what it signifies?'

'It is the Royal Warrant,' Robert said.

'And that means?'

'It means we've been appointed suppliers of whisky to the Queen.'

'That is a high honour?'

'A very high honour. We're very proud of it.'

'Not the sort of honour that is handed out indiscriminately?'

'No.'

'For example, does the whisky produced by Mr. Morrison, who came here to testify against you, hold this particular honour?'

'No.'

The Fiscal's voice was querulous. 'Milord! Really—'

'I am almost finished, milord,' Anderson said quickly. He turned again to Robert. 'So Her Majesty the Queen is graciously pleased to buy your King's Royal? Has she ever complained about it?'

'Never.'

As Anderson stood the bottle of King's Royal prominently on the table the Sheriff looked at the Fiscal. 'Have you any questions?'

The Fiscal gritted his teeth. 'No, milord, I think by now the jury will be familiar with my learned friend's methods.'

'In that case the court is adjourned until ten tomorrow morning.'


All day Fergus had sat by the fire in Gwen's shop, hidden from the customers by a silk embroidered screen, his ears closed to the cries of passing news vendors. Miss Murray had thoughtfully kept her own newspaper out of his sight.

It was enough, Fergus felt, to know that throughout the city there would be men delighting in his son's dishonour.

With Hoey only ten days dead he was, with Rita, now devoting all his time to Gwen. The depth of her grief had alarmed her doctor. The conventions of widowhood, he said, were less important than the urgent task of dispelling her despair. Could she be taken somewhere on holiday?

Gwen had refused.

The doctor had been insistent. Some attempt must be made to turn her from her loss—towards a brighter and more hopeful future in which she would have her child to care for. Perhaps she could be persuaded to leave her own flat and stay with her mother and father?

Gwen had refused.

The doctor had looked grave and said that if there wasn't to be a risk of Gwen's mind being permanently marked, she must have constant company, even though she might appear indifferent to it. Rita was now living with Gwen at her flat. Fergus had taken over the supervision of the shop.

All the endless day he'd sat brooding. Whatever the outcome of Robert's trial he felt that soon he would withdraw from business. He had given enough of his life to that.

One or two more birthdays and he would be sixty years old. Some men went on far too long. He wouldn't make that mistake. He had his other interests. He would keep on some of his charities and he would give more time to his paintings. Park Place could be sold. Rita and he would move to Ardfern. With only one house, of course, it would be difficult to accommodate all their things. The furniture wouldn't be such a problem. They would keep only the very best pieces, and Gwen, if she kept on her shop, could have the rest for selling.

The paintings would not be so simply dealt with. He had become more involved with them. His interest quickened a little despite his worries. Perhaps they could build on a gallery at Ardfern. There was plenty of room and it was something he had often thought about. The place they referred to as 'the gallery' was simply another room of the house. The light, coming from a single window, was inadequate. The paintings suffered for it. In a proper gallery the lighting should come from above. What was wanted was a long narrow room with a flat glass roof. . .

His mind wandered on. He heard the door open. It was Rita. Every day she came to collect the mail in an attempt to raise some interest in Gwen.

'Nothing but a few invoices,' he said, rising to give her his chair. 'How is Gwen today?'

Rita held her hands to the fire. 'It's difficult to know, but for the first time, this morning, I felt I saw a spark of interest in her.'

Fergus brightened. 'That's what we've been waiting for, my dear.'

'Oh, but it was so little, Fergus. She still spent most of the day staring into the fire or sitting by the window looking down into the street as if hoping she might see—'

'Rita!'

They had made a pact that they wouldn't become morbid. If they did, they'd be unable to help Gwen.

'I'm sorry, Fergus. I was going to tell you . . . Gwen made some remark about wondering how she'd manage her business here when the baby comes. But when I tried to draw her out, she seemed to lose interest.'

'It's a step,' Fergus said gently. 'A small step, but until now there hasn't even been that.'

They sat for a while in silence. Behind them a long case clock chimed. To Fergus it was a comforting sound. He recalled something Gwen had said about the clock during one of their discussions. 'Remember,' she told him, 'that clock has ticked at least a hundred years away.'

*Time*, Fergus thought. *Time! Time! Perhaps time is all Gwen needs.* He clung to the hopeful idea. Behind them the clock ticked away a few more minutes. His eye caught the warm reflection of the fire on the faded mahogany of a sofa table. Despite his cares he was able to admire it. Gwen loved all these things. Surely, so long as they were here, she wouldn't give up—above all, not with the baby, the baby Hoey had not lived to know about, to love in his place? She had fought back before. Surely, this time, life hadn't piled too great a weight on her? His poor Gwen! Tears that weren't altogether empty of hope began to form in his eyes. He felt Rita's hand clasp his.

'I think,' Rita said, 'it may be more important than we imagine that Gwen has at last spoken of the baby. Soon, we must hope, she'll want to live for it. Meantime we must keep her from her memories. In a week or two we must try to persuade her to come down here, even if only for an hour or two each day. People would talk, of course.' She paused as if knowing that here Fergus would wish to speak.

'Let them,' he said quietly. 'Let them damn well talk.'

'After all,' Rita said, 'this shop was important to Gwen once before. Perhaps it could help her again. We must help her to see she still has much to live for. In another month or two she will become more aware of her baby. Life will take Gwen over again, I'm sure, if we can just help her till then.'

Suddenly, for the first time in many visits, her eye was distracted by an ornament. She rose, almost absentmindedly, and moved it a little to the right.

Fergus, watching her, said: 'Colin Lindsay looked in. He's a hesitant sort of chap but I think genuine. He wanted to enquire after Gwen.'

'That was thoughtful of him.'

'And he offered any help we might need with lifting and moving things. Even with deliveries.' He stared into the fire. 'People rally round in time of trouble.'

Rita nodded. 'I've always liked Colin. I think Gwen does, too, though she always laughed at his separatist notions. He's been a kind friend to her.'

There was a cough and Miss Murray's head came around the screen.

'Excuse me, Sir Fergus, but there's a gentleman here asking to speak to you.'

'Who is he, Sadie?'

'He didn't give his name but he said to tell you it was very important.'


As he walked to court next morning Robert's mood alternated between optimism and despair. The oppression of the court was even more intense than previously, the dusty green walls felt more suffocatingly close and the windows smaller and higher. It had rained during the night and the sky was lined and grey.

This morning, he knew, Anderson and the Fiscal would make their final submissions, the Sheriff would direct the jury, and then would come the last dragging wait for the verdict.

Anderson seemed preoccupied. He even bade Robert a polite good morning, as if feeling he owed him at least that. To Robert's alarm Anderson became visibly nervous as the Sheriff entered. He bowed distractedly, as if suffering some private ordeal.

First the Sheriff arranged his papers. Then he had a whispered conversation with his clerk. It was not until he indicated the defence submission could begin that the reason for Anderson's fidgeting was revealed.

'Milord,' he said, 'before we reach the speeches I must humbly crave the indulgence of the court.' His attitude was indeed craven, Robert noted.

The Fiscal looked up sharply. The Sheriff's expression went wary.

'I would beg your lordship's permission to call one additional witness.' Anderson's voice had gained slightly in confidence as if now that he was on his feet he was finding it easier than he had expected to risk the Sheriff's anger.

The Fiscal clattered to his feet. 'Milord, I protest. Yesterday my learned friend forgot some of his questions and had to recall a witness.' His voice was sneering. 'Today he's found an absolutely new one. This is totally irregular. The Crown is entitled to have a summary in advance of all evidence. I'm quite unprepared for anything any additional witness might say.'

For a moment the Sheriff looked undecided, then he said: 'I concur absolutely, Mr. Fiscal, with the basis of your objection. Nevertheless'—he hesitated—'wouldn't you agree that in the interests of justice. . . .' He left the sentence unfinished.

The Fiscal's face was grim. 'If that is your lorship's ruling.' He sat down, shaking his head.

The Sheriff turned to Anderson. 'You may proceed,' he said.

'Thank you, milord.' Anderson could not hide his smile. He signalled to the court usher and said loudly, 'Call Sir Fergus King.'

The words rang round the court, but nowhere more loudly than in Robert's head. He watched in astonishment as his father came through the swing doors and walked with bowed head to the witness box. He listened dazedly to him take the oath in a low voice, looking at no one.

It was only when Anderson spoke that Fergus looked up, steeled to face another eye. He straightened his shoulders, remembering Anderson's instructions. He was dressed in his most impressive clothes, every article speaking of dignified expense. His beard had been carefully brushed and trimmed.

Even in the state of numb uncertainty to which he had sunk, Robert could not help admiring his father's patriarchal appearance. Before it had always struck him as being old-fashioned and stuffy. In these solemn surroundings it had an undoubted nobility. There, Robert suddenly realized, stood the man Anderson would have preferred to defend. He had said so yesterday at lunch. By what manipulation had he managed it? For that this weighty titled citizen should become in the jury's mind Robert's co-accused was soon revealed as Anderson's devious intent.

'The accused is your son?'

Fergus had never found it more difficult to find his voice and his reply was almost inaudible.

'You are his partner in business?'

'Yes.'

'Do you have commitments other than business ones?' Under his insistent questioning Fergus recited the whole list of charitable institutions on which he served.

'For many years you were Glasgow's Senior Magistrate?'

'Yes.'

'You acted as a police judge?'

'Yes.'

'For your years of selfless public service Her Majesty the Queen recently conferred a baronetcy upon you?'

'Yes.'

'Have you felt at any time that your King's Royal was a fraud on the public, a negation of all your other good work?'

To this Fergus had no difficulty in giving a decisive reply.

'At no time,' he said clearly.

'Will you tell the court why you didn't previously appear?'

Fergus swallowed, convinced despite the attentive attitude of the jury that all must see through Anderson's crude sham. With an effort he spoke the rehearsed words: 'My son forbade it.'

Robert closed his eyes in an agony of sympathy for Fergus.

'Why, Sir Fergus?'

'He wished to protect me from the unpleasantness of publicity.'

'But your sense of duty, your sense of loyalty, has brought you here today to stand, so to speak, at his side.'

'Yes.'

'Thank you, Sir Fergus.'

Anderson turned to the Sheriff. 'I have no further questions, milord.'

The Sheriff looked at him coldly. 'That is the extent of your examination of this witness?'

'It is, milord.'

'Very well. Mr. Fiscal?'

The Fiscal rose, angrily throwing his pencil on to the table. 'All I ask,' he said bitterly, 'is that my earlier objection to the admission of this witness be recorded.'

Anderson, his purpose accomplished, sat down with a shameless leer.

His speech to the jury was brief.

'My submission to you, gentlemen, is a simple one,' he said. 'Despite the wider implications of this trial, despite the financial disasters that a verdict of guilty could bring to many people, despite the many workingmen who could find themselves without jobs, the case against Robert King hinges in my submission on the sale of just one case of King's Royal, and one case only. The charge in my view can only be considered proven if the prosecution has shown beyond reasonable doubt that the twelve bottles of King's Royal purchased by the nuisance inspector did not contain what any reasonable person would consider to be whisky—whisky with its taste made more acceptable, perhaps, but nevertheless still, in its essential nature, whisky. I heard no evidence to this, but it is the one simple question I wish you to consider. If it has not been proved to you that these particular bottles held adulterated malt, then you can only acquit Robert King.'

Anderson had spoken from his table, standing with his hands on the back of his chair. The Fiscal addressed the jury at close range, pacing slowly the length of their enclosure and then back again.

'Gentlemen,' he said, 'my learned friend has tried to tell you that this prosecution must fail because the Crown did not produce an analyst to testify as to the contents of the twelve bottles of King's Royal purchased by the nuisance inspectors. His own analyst's sworn evidence that no helpful analysis is humanly possible is, I submit, sufficient answer to that point. The Crown did not come here to attempt to prove the impossible. Legal gymnastics such as that we have been content to leave to the defence. The accused does not deny that his King's Royal is a mixture of pure pot still malt whisky and silent spirit. It is only necessary, therefore, for the Crown to satisfy you that by adding silent spirit he is adulterating the malt to the extent of changing its nature. If we have succeeded in doing this then we've shown the accused to be guilty as charged. I am not going to go over the evidence again. All I wish to do is remind you of some of the testimony with regard to silent spirit. Only in recent years have its producers sought to divert some of it from its true outlet—namely, industry—and to promote it as a potable spirit under the name of grain whisky. Grain whisky! It is a contradiction in terms. Scotland's whisky is a malted liquor. I ask you to reject the term "grain whisky". *There is no such thing.* Simply remember a torrent of fluid going for the manufacture of explosives and varnish—and then try to imagine yourselves knowingly drinking some of it. If you would shrink, as I am sure you would, from drinking a glass of that fluid in a paint factory, then I submit that you have no alternative but to regard its addition to malt as an adulteration and find the charge against the accused proven.'

The various points scored by either advocate had long since stopped registering with Robert. For two days hope and despair had chased through his mind until it sagged. When Anderson spoke he felt hopeful. Now, after the Fiscal's submissions, he was convinced ruin and imprisonment sat beside him.

He realized that the Sheriff had turned to the jury with a sympathetic smile. 'It is now my duty, gentlemen of the jury, to give you what help I can in reaching your verdict. You have been treated to a great deal of skilful advocacy, and considerations have been put before you which you may well decide are quite unconnected with the issue you've been called on to decide. A lack in this case, as the defence has been at pains to point out, has been the prosecution's failure to show—indeed, they have not even attempted to show—that what the nuisance inspectors were given was other than what they asked for. As a result of this you may feel that it has not been proven that the bottles of King's Royal purchased contained, as alleged, malt whisky blended with grain spirit, or, indeed, with any other substance. You may feel, to the contrary, that the defence analyst's evidence forces you to the conclusion that this could only be proven if the blending had actually been carried out in front of witnesses. Further, you may ask yourselves, even had blending been proven, if this would not still have left the vital question: *Has the nature been changed?* Only if you feel that this question has been answered in the affirmative could a prosecution succeed under Section 6 of the Act. On the other hand, you may feel that no analytical testimony was necessary. You may agree with the prosecution submission that the presence of grain spirit in King's Royal has not been denied by the defence—that, indeed, they have publicly proclaimed it. This still leaves the question of whether or not it has been proven that the addition of grain spirit to malt whisky sufficiently changes the nature of the drink for it to become a fraud on the public.

'You have heard a great deal in the last two days about explosives, varnish, chloroform, favours bestowed by Her Majesty the Queen, and even'—here he allowed himself a glance at Anderson—'the charitable works of one of the witnesses. You must give to these matters the weight that you feel they are due. You may well feel on consideration that they have no weight at all. It is for you to decide. You may find it helpful in arriving at your verdict to purge from your minds all questions relating to the popularity of King's Royal. You must also put from your minds any concern for the consequences that would flow from a verdict of guilty. These consequences, you've been told, could be extremely grave for a great many people other than the accused. That is a serious matter but not one you can properly concern yourself with here. I now direct you to withdraw to consider your verdict.'

As the court cleared to wait for the jury's return Robert looked anxiously about. He stopped Anderson. 'Have you seen my father? I must speak to him.'

'He left as soon as he'd given his evidence.'

'How did you manage to talk him into it?'

Anderson looked bland. 'I simply reminded him that you were his son and that you needed his help. He reacted as any father would.'

Robert turned from Anderson's watching eye. 'I must thank him. He is haunted by the thought of scandal. It must have been a terrible ordeal for him. Was it necessary to inflict it on him? Nothing he said amounted to very much.'

Anderson looked at him sharply. 'You don't know juries like I do. Your father provided the aura of solidity and worth that you so sadly lack.'

Robert accepted the rebuff silently. Fifteen minutes later the court usher went along the corridor ringing a bell to signal the return of the jury.

For Robert the next five minutes were to be locked forever in a haze. Anderson was hustling him back into court. He heard the iron gate of the dock clang and felt the bulk of the two policemen settle beside him.

'Court stand,' he heard the usher call.

The Sheriff entered and his clerk turned to the jury. 'Have you reached a verdict?'

'We have,' the tall thin man at the nearest end of the bottom row of jurors said.

'What is that verdict?'

'Not guilty.'

A gasping sound filled the court as if many breaths had been suddenly released. Robert's heart was thumping and sounds travelled to him from a great distance.

The Sheriff was speaking to him.

'Robert King, you have been found not guilty of the offence as charged. You are free to leave the dock.'

An immediate hubbub started in the public benches but the Sheriff quelled it with a few loud raps of his gavel.

'Before the court rises I want to add this. As a result of this case it might well be desirable for Parliament to consider framing a definition of what whisky is. This, however, is a matter purely for the Legislature.'

There was no sense of elation in Robert. He felt only gratitude that the long suspense was over. Anderson, his face moist and suddenly tired, shook his hand in silence.

The Fiscal leaned across the table with a rueful smile and, ignoring Robert, said to Anderson: 'Well, James, you succeeded in turning that into a pretty circus.'

Anderson rallied. He slapped the Fiscal on the shoulder. 'I hope you managed to pick up a few tips, Charlie boy,' he said. 'Old Maxwell must be slipping. A year ago he would never have let me away with half of that.'

He noticed Robert's subdued expression.

'You are taking it soberly,' he said. 'Just as well. Don't get too cock-a-hoop. Nothing final's been settled here. They can keep on raising actions like this against you or any other blender, whenever they get the notion. Old Maxwell had the right way of it. One day, Parliament will have to sort the whole whisky mess out.'

Robert turned away. A few spectators still lingering in the public benches stared at him curiously. He went through the swing doors and into a corridor dreary with institutional green and brown paintwork. He put on his hat and hurried along the corridor, his footsteps echoing on the worn stone. Suddenly, as he came to the main hall, he was surrounded by reporters.

What were his plans now? Was he going to have a celebration? Was it true that soon he would have made a million out of King's Royal?

The questions came to him in a confusion of sound. He held up his hands. 'Gentlemen, if you have any serious questions I will try to answer them, but I can only manage one at a time.'

A man with a grey beard standing next to him said, 'What exactly does this judgement mean for your company, Mr. King?'

Robert took off his hat and looked thoughtfully into it. 'It means that the pot distillers will have to learn to live with us,' he said. 'And I hope they will. Blended whisky isn't a threat to their malt. The heart of every worthwhile blend will always be one of the fine whiskies from Speyside. There's more than enough room for all of us. We're a very small country and we have the whole world as our market.'

It was an olive branch that he hoped now, at last, Morrison would accept.

'You don't regret the trial, then?'

'Of course I regret it. It's been a strain on our family for months. But I've just told you one good outcome. Another bonus to us is that I don't think the pot distillers will ever dare mount another boycott against us.'

'But won't this case have harmed the sales of King's Royal?'

Robert smiled. 'On the contrary. Thanks to your newspapers we have had many thousands of pounds of free advertising all over the British Isles and probably in foreign countries as well. Our name has been taken to places where it was previously unknown. I am confident our business will continue to grow.'

'You see no end, then, to the demand for this new blended whisky?' The man who asked sounded doubtful—perhaps he was a malt drinker.

Robert smiled. 'I'm delighted to say I do not. After all, it's no longer a novelty. It's proved itself. My eventual aim is to sell King's Royal in every country of the world that will take it. I think it's a drink Scotland can be proud of. It originated here in Scotland. It can only be produced in Scotland. Only Scotsmen can make it. I wish I had the men here today who help me. I would have liked you to meet them, two of them in particular. They are fine men— Scotsmen like myself—born and bred in Glasgow. With these men working beside me I have no fears for the future.'

He began to edge away but another question came at him.

'Now that you've won this case, Mr. King, what will your next step be?'

'Well, our first step will be to release supplies held back pending the outcome of the trial. Next month, for example, a few cases of King's Royal will sail for New York. The United States is a market we are very anxious to test. But now'—he put on his hat and began moving towards the door—'if you'll excuse me, there's some business of pressing urgency I must attend to immediately.'

*There is so much of pressing urgency*, he thought, as he came out on to an Ingram Street no longer as grey and depressing as when he had come along it the previous morning. ... To see and thank his father and hope for some sensible reconciliation. To go to Fiona at Ardfern as he had promised. But first ... a stray thought that had come to him as he sat in the dock had slowly expanded until it now preoccupied him. This was a Thursday afternoon. If Father Campbell was still alive Mary would be arriving soon in Glasgow to visit him. He knew from their last meeting when her train would reach Queen Street.

From a corner of the station he watched her come through the ticket barrier and walk towards a line of cabs. She wore a coat of some shiny blue material and she carried a small travelling bag.

What did he think he was doing? There was another girl waiting for him at Row. He should be at the ticket office paying his fare to Helensburgh.

As Mary stepped into a cab he hurried to the street, pulled the door open, and got in beside her.

'What luck,' he said. 'I have an hour or so to spare before my train. You won't mind if I drive to Langside with you?'

She began to protest and for a moment he thought she was going to pull open the hatch and speak to the driver. Then she laughed. 'If you like. But it's silly.'

'How is Father Campbell?'

'He's gone on longer than anyone thought possible.' She nodded towards her bag. 'I stay overnight at the convent now. It's better than travelling home late at night.'

He remembered the bare floors, the worn bedsheets, and the pillowcases made from old flour bags. 'It can't be very comfortable.'

They were on Albert Bridge. Sea-gulls circled the river. A ship with tall masts and a maze of rigging was manoeuvring out from the quay wall. A beggar leaned against the parapet of the bridge squeezing a mournful tune from an accordion.

'If it's good enough for the nuns,' Mary said, 'I can put up with it for a night. Besides I like the atmosphere of the convent.'

He sensed something in her words beyond the surface meaning. 'I thought you said you had started to ask questions?'

'Oh yes.' She smiled and her voice was matter-of-fact. 'But that doesn't stop me seeing that the nuns have a peace that doesn't exist out here.'

She stopped the cab in the road outside the convent. 'There's a little side gate you can walk me to,' she said. 'It's quicker to the room they've given me than by the main drive.'

He wondered if this was true or if she simply didn't want to be seen with him. 'If you wait you can take me back to Queen Street Station,' he told the cabbie.

A hedge of shiny leaves and small pink flowers hung about the grey wall. It was faintly scented. The gate was iron with chipped green paint and it creaked when Mary pushed it open. 'I'll manage from here,' she said.

'Yes. I won't come in.' He stood, still holding her bag, even less sure now why he'd come, or what he wanted from her. This girl represented another dragging part of his life, living on despite everything in a troubled corner of his heart. Was he still trying to justify that hardheaded parting all those years ago? Was it forgiveness, absolution, some sort of final peace, that he really wanted from her?

In the trees beyond the wall birds sang among the fluttering leaves.

She was watching him closely. 'Don't you have anyone, Robert? I can't believe there isn't a girl somewhere.'

He wondered for a moment if she was mocking him, but her expression was open—even, perhaps, concerned.

'There is a girl,' he said. 'I've known her for years. She's a friend of the family.' *Something*, he realized with a stab, *Mary has never been.* He wondered if the same painful thought had come to her. Momentarily, her eyes closed but when they opened the unfathomable smile was still there, held as if by some inner view of the world that he now knew he would not only never understand but never even be able to ask about.

'Well?' she prompted gently. 'You must have some intentions towards this girl. You wouldn't have mentioned her otherwise.'

'Yes. I sometimes feel I'm not being fair to her.' He hesitated. 'I don't know whether I love her or not. I can't be sure.'

Behind her, at one side of the path leading from the gate, there was a tangle of jagged shrubbery thick with brambles. Wasps moved heavily among the fat black berries.

'I wonder,' she said softly, 'if you've ever really loved anyone, Robert?'

'Yes.' The answer came as if torn from him. 'I loved you, Mary.'

She might not have heard him, and when she spoke it was like the last word on everything. 'People who do not love each other can sometimes marry happily,' she said. 'Just as people who are in love must sometimes part.'

She turned and closed the gate. She went past the busy wasps and walked towards the shadow of the tall trees where birds still sang. She stopped at a bend in the path and waved to him. Her face—was it only the distance and the shade of the trees?—looked extraordinarily happy. He wondered if he knew now the secret of her smile. The last he saw of her was a flash of pale blue shimmering through the leaves.

Along the road, harnessing jangled as the waiting cab horse moved. For a few more moments he stood by the gate. There were open fields behind him and the sun stretched his shadow along the wall. He heard a door shut. He thought of another door that had closed five years ago and would have been better never reopened. Well, that door, too, he knew, had closed again tonight.

The pink flowers shone delicately against the dark-green hedge. The road as he went down it was filled with their scent.

A piper on the platform began to play as the train came to a halt at Helensburgh. Robert recognized the tune—'*Dumbarton's Drums*'. Farther up the train, men in Highland dress were jumping from the carriages. Bagpipes and drums were being pushed out of windows and through doors. He recognized the uniform. This was the band of the Royal Scots being welcomed to the sound of the regimental march past.

Two or three months earlier he would not have been able to name either the tune or the regiment. Now he knew a bass drum from a tenor drum and could tell 'Caberfeidh' from 'Peace and War'. He could differentiate between two-four and six-eight time and had learned that the only drummers who wore trews were those of the Royal Scots and the Scots Guards.

Helensburgh was almost as busy as on a summer afternoon. Many of the bands and their supporters had already arrived. Tomorrow, when all these pipers and drummers started practising, there wouldn't be an empty field or a quiet street in the town.

He had to wait for a cab but when at last he got one the horse moved off at a trot. Clearly, the driver was anxious to get back as quickly as possible to where the business was. The streets were filled with kilts and Glengarries and it was only as they neared Row that the road took on the peaceful look proper to an October evening.

The air was still. Leaves detached themselves from trees and fell to the ground in a slow swirl. The hills were russet or golden where the bracken had died. From the train, he had watched the sun sinking behind the peaks of Arran. Now, the ridge of the Rosneath peninsula was pink in the afterglow. The trial and its worries seemed much more than only a few hours behind him. The peaceful beauty of the loch completed his sense of detachment from the past.

There was someone on the shore. As they drew nearer he recognized Fiona. He stopped the cab. She waved when she saw him coming down over the rocks.

'What happened?' she called.

'Not guilty,' he shouted with a sudden sense of freedom surging inside him. He took her hand and pulled her, running and stumbling, along the shingle. 'Not bloody guilty.'

They sank, laughing and gasping, on to the rough grass.

'How wonderful, Robert!' she said when she had breath enough. 'But I knew.'

'Oh, yes. Now that it's over it will turn out that *everyone* knew.'

He lifted a stone and skimmed it out into the loch.

The day had almost gone and the water, although flat, had turned a cold grey. It looked as if it would be very deep even a few yards out. The hulk along the shore was silhouetted against the last of the light.

He said, 'What are you thinking about, Fiona?'

She continued to look across the loch to the dark outline of the hills on the other side. 'That I am always happiest by the sea.'

'I'm glad you are back now,' he said.

'Yes. Perthshire's a lovely countryside but I missed the west coast.' She began to rise. 'It's getting dark. We'd better go. Your grandmother might be worried about me. It's good of her to put me up.'

He helped her to her feet, then stood very straight in front of her, his heart pounding. The words he'd once stifled in doubt came quite easily now.

'Will you marry me, Fiona?'

She looked at him without answering. Her expression was impossible to analyse.

Panic began to rise in him. Had he left it too late—taken her too much for granted? He was overwhelmed by a stabbing realization of his need for her. He could see now with a luminous clarity what he had dimly sensed for so long. Mary was an enigma, and always had been, a pale, shadowy dream of his youth. Fiona was real. She would fit in. She was strong and healthy. Her nature was impulsive and warmly assured, a balance to his own tendency to cold introspection. That she had so successfully assumed so many of her father's business responsibilities had revealed another dimension—one in keeping with his own sense of destiny. Fiona was one of them, really. A fighter. A King in all but name. She would be able to share his problems and understand his ambitions. Fiona, the wild girl of the years that he was now, at last, ready to shake off, could be his partner not only in love but in his life's dream.

As he looked at her almost beseechingly he saw her expression warm and soften. A look of wonder spread slowly across her face. 'Oh, I will, Robert, I will. I will be proud and happy to marry you.'

He took her carefully into his arms as if it had never happened before and when they kissed it seemed to be the first time.

Behind them, small waves rippled over the pebbles. Night rose from the loch and came out of the woods across the road. The hulk was black now and indistinct. A smell of dampness came from the hills. The sky was clear and soon there would be frost. Tomorrow the garden of Ardfern would be beautiful with dew.

We hope you have enjoyed reading this book
– now try KING'S ROYAL whisky,
bottled by Clyde Distillers, Glasgow
and available at most retail outlets

CLYDE DISTILLERS LIMITED
81 MURANO STREET GLASGOW G20 7RF
041–204 2633